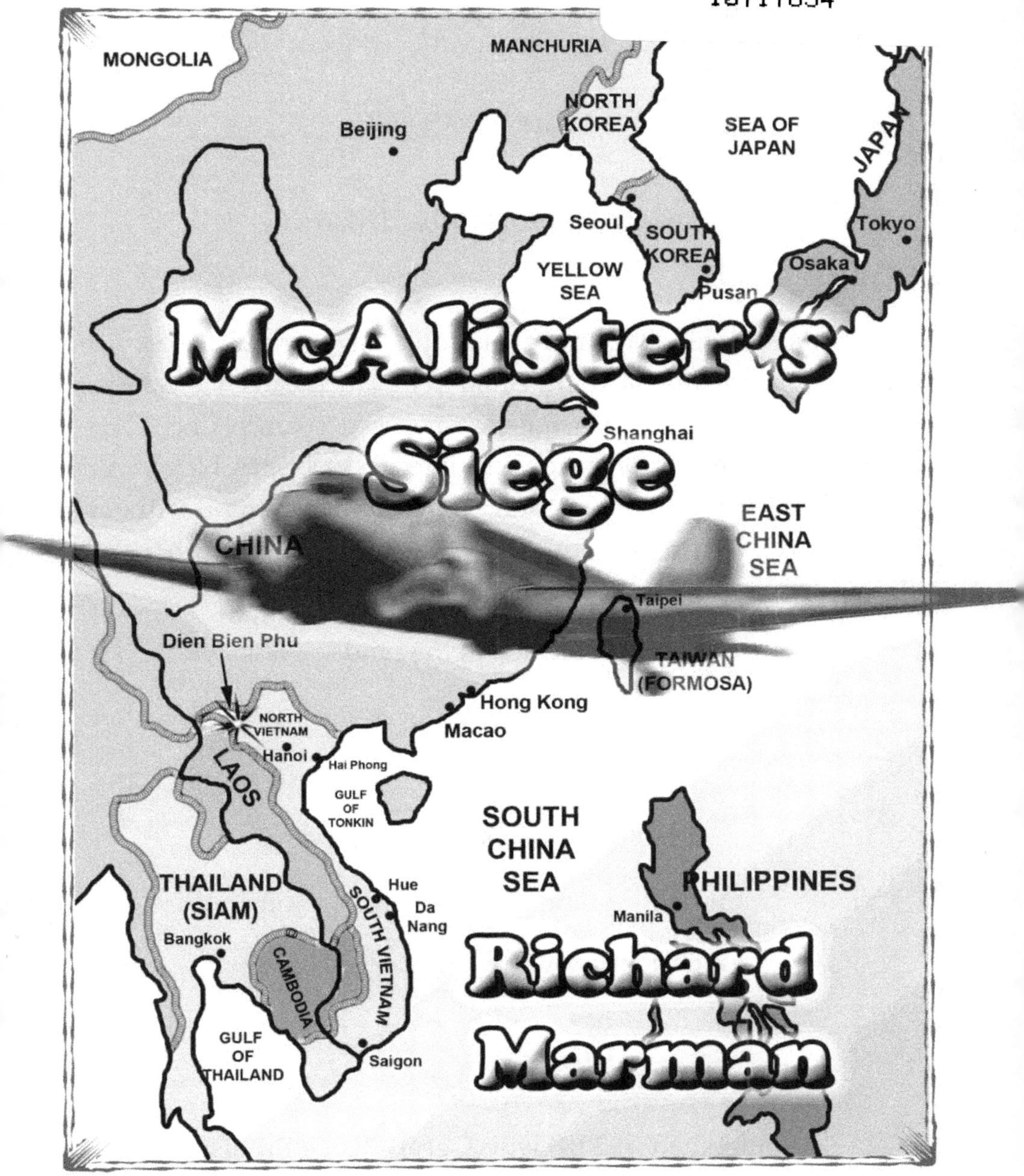

McAlister's Siege

Richard Marman

COVER ART AND DESIGN, ILLUSTRATIONS AND GRAPHICS

BY RICHARD MARMAN

Published in England

by

Abela Publishing

Sandhurst, Berkshire, England

Email: Author@RichardMarman.com

Website: www.RichardMarman.com

ISBN 13: 978-1-92568-0-942

Republished in 2018 with Ocean Reeve Publishing

First Edition, 2014

Books by Richard Marman
Available from Abela Publishing

<u>The McAlister Line</u>
(In historical order)
McAlister' Trail
McAlister and the Great war
McAlister's Way
McAlister's Hoard
McAlister's Siege
McAlister's Spark

<u>Web and Wave Illustrated Adventures</u>
(For children of all ages)

A Tale of Two Turtles
A Whale's Tale

Acknowledgments

I'd like to especially thank my wife Judy and my daughter Sally for their help in following the progress of this manuscript. Thanks to Sheila Yong and Wendy Kleine for their feedback and initial proof reading and Judy Bandidt for the final, goal-keeping edit. Thank you to Wing Commander John 'Trackless' Millsom for DC-3 aircraft technical support. Finally cheers to John Halsted for being so enthusiastic about this series.

This book is dedicated

to my wife Judy

and my daughters

Sally and Elizabeth

Glossary

Ack-Ack	Anti-aircraft guns
ADG	Aerodrome guard
AFB	Air force base – refers to USAF establishments
ASAP	As soon as possible
ASI	Airspeed indicator
ATC	Air traffic control
Autorotation	Landing a helicopter after an engine failure
AUW	All up weight – a plane's weight including fuel and payload
AVGAS	Aviation gasoline – high octane petrol for piston-engine aircraft
AWOL	Absent without leave
B-47	Six-engine jet heavy bomber fore-runner of the ubiquitous B-52 that led to the development of modern civilian jet airliners
Bo Doi	Viet Minh soldier singularly or as a unit
Blue Lanterns	Bottom rung of the triad hierarchy
Boggy	Short for *bog-rat* a term for RAAF pilot officers
Casevac	Casualty evacuation (medivac – medical evacuation is the term used today)
CAT	China Air Transport – Air Charter Company operating in the Far East founded by General Claire Chennault – one of CAT's major clients was the CIA
CAT	Clear air turbulence
C-46	Curtiss Commando twin engine cargo plane

C-47	Douglas Dakota twin-engine workhorse cargo plane also known as a DC-3, *Gooney-Bird* or Skytrain – ten thousand were built
CIA	Central Intelligence Agency – US spy guys
C-in-C	Commander in Chief
C-of-G	Centre of gravity
C-119	Fairchild twin-engine, twin-tail boom transport plane also called the 'Flying Boxcar'
Customers	CIA operatives who flew on CAT flights
Dak	Abbreviation for the Douglas DC-3 Dakota
DCA	Department of Civil Aviation – today's CASA – Australia's aviation regulatory body
Dead Stick Landing	Landing with no engine power
Diggers	Australian soldiers
Doodle-Bug	German V-1 rocket launched from sites in Northern Europe targeting British cities, especially London
Dry Lease	Leasing a plane, but supplying your own crew
DZ	Drop zone – pronounced dee-zed – landing area for parachutes
EXO	Executive officer – American military unit second in command
FAA	Federal Aviation Authority – the US aviation regulating organisation
FAC	Forward air controller
Fat Man	Atomic bomb dropped on Nagasaki
FOD	Foreign object damage – an aviation term referring to debris that interferes with aircraft engines or flight controls.

Foot	Imperial linear measurement equivalent to 30 centimetres — Danny told his story using imperial measurements that were the Australian standard until decimalisation on 14th February 1966. Zach didn't convert any units from the imperial system
Formosa	Present day Taiwan
49-ers	Second tier of triad hierarchy
Gallon	Imperial liquid volume measurement equal to approximately four litres
Gloster Meteor	British built twin-engine jet fighter
GONO	*Groupement Opérationnel Nord-Ouest* — Group of Operational Forces North-West i.e. the French Union Force at Dien Bien Phu
HE	High explosive
HF Radio	High frequency radio used for long-distance communications
IAS	Indicated airspeed — the reading on the ASI, but only the plane's actual speed at sea-level
ICAO	International Civil Aviation Authority, established in 1947 with headquarters based at Montreal
IJA	Imperial Japanese Army
ILS	Instrument landing system — a lateral and vertical radio signal displayed on a plane's instrument panel allowing pilots to approach a runway in bad weather
Imperial Ton	Weight measurement equalling 2240 pounds
Junkers JU-52	Obsolete pre-WWII three-engine transport plane still in service with the French Air Force in the 1950s

Knot	Nautical mile per hour — approximately two kilometres an hour
Knucklehead	Fighter pilot
Lighty	Light aircraft
Little Boy	Atomic bomb dropped on Hiroshima
LZ	Landing zone — pronounced 'ell-zee'
Mae West	Military flotation jacket
MASH	Mobile Army Surgical Hospital
Mayday	Radio transmissions prefix pilots use when declaring an emergency
Mig-15	Advanced Soviet single-engine Jet fighter in North Korean service
NCOs	Non-commissioned officers — corporals, sergeants, warrant-officers
NDB	Non directional radio beacon - used to guide pilots to a station in cloudy weather
Pak's Palace	North Korean interrogation centre run by the infamous Colonel Pak
PAN	Radio prefix used by pilots when they are declaring serious situation aboard
Pilot Officer	Lowest commissioned officer rank in the RAAF and RAF equivalent to a second lieutenant
Pound	Imperial weight unit — approximately 450 grams
POW	Prisoner of War
PSP	Pierced steel planking - interlocking metal plates that can be laid quickly to construct runways and roads. Also known as Marsden Matting
Quid	One pound — Australian currency unit until decimalisation on 14th February 1966
RAF	Royal Air Force

RAR	Royal Australian Regiment
Red Cap	Military policeman
Red Pole Enforcer	Triad middle-management heavy
REM	Rapid eye movement – the last part of your sleep pattern which regenerates your brain
REX	Region Express — Australian airline serving country centres
RN	Royal Navy — its air branch is the Fleet Air Arm
ROK	Republic of Korea (South Korea)
RPT	Regular Public Transport — a term used for scheduled airline services
Runway Threshold	The start of the runway
Runway Under-run	A cleared area before the threshold that is not suitable for aircraft use
SAR	Search and Rescue
Seabees	US Navy Construction Battalion
Sitrep	Situation report
SOPs	Standard operating procedures
Short Ton	Weight equalling 2000 pounds
Spooks	CIA agents
STOL	Short take-off and landing — refers to planes that operate from small areas
The Hump	Air routes over the Himalayas from India to China used to resupply troops and partisans fighting the Japanese during WWII
Tok Pisin	'Talk Pidgin' — patois used universally in New Guinea

USAF	United States Air Force — formed as a separate military branch in 1947
VB	Victoria Bitter — Popular Australian lager
Vinogel	Wine dehydrated to a third of its volume drinkable when rehydrated
VHF Radio	Very High Frequency radio used for short range 'line of sight' communications
V1	The maximum speed a plane can reject its take-off and stop in the runway distance remaining
Wet Lease	Leasing a plane including its crew
Yard	Imperial linear measurement slightly less than a metre

Phonetic Alphabet

ICAO established this system in the 1950s to clarify airborne radio conversations. There were still discrepancies for a while, i.e. A for Able, B for Baker and G for George sprang to Danny's mind, but although he had a vivid memory of most events, he couldn't remember them all so Zach has cited modern usage to avoid confusion.

A	Alpha
B	Bravo
C	Charlie
D	Delta
E	Echo
F	Foxtrot
G	Golf
H	Hotel
I	India
J	Juliette
K	Kilo
L	Lima
M	Mike
N	November
O	Oscar
P	Papa
Q	Quebec
R	Romeo
S	Sierra
T	Tango
U	Uniform
V	Victor
W	Whiskey
X	X-ray
Y	Yankee
Z	Zulu

Prologue	Merimbula, New South Wales
Part 1	China
Chapter 1	The Flying Whale
Chapter 2	A Step Towards the Orient
Chapter 3	Getaway Trail
Chapter 4	The First Leg
Chapter 5	Flight Plan North
Chapter 6	Chequerboard Approach
Chapter 7	Earthquake
Chapter 8	Freedom Trail
Chapter 9	A Little Bit of Piracy
Part 2	Korea
Chapter 10	The Proposal
Chapter 11	Danny's Bride
Chapter 12	Danny Goes to War
Chapter 13	Casevac
Chapter 14	Forward Air Controller
Chapter 15	Aviation of the Future
Chapter 16	Search and Rescue
Chapter 17	The Customer is Always Right
Chapter 18	Covert Ops
Part 3	French Indochina (Vietnam)
Chapter 19	Cease Fire
Chapter 20	Paris of the Orient
Chapter 21	Angela
Chapter 22	Beatrice
Chapter 23	Gabrielle
Chapter 24	Trapped
Chapter 25	Para Patrol
Chapter 26	Rats and Angels
Chapter 27	Earthquake's Last Ride
Epilogue	Merimbula Airport

Prologue — Merimbula, New South Wales

'Do you have a passport, Zach?' Grandpa Danny asked me once when I was staying with him during school holidays.

My name is Zach McAlister and I'd started visiting my grandpa back in 2010 when my mum was sick. She's fine now, but I'd really come to like the old dude and kept travelling down from Sydney to see him. Merimbula is a seaside town on the southern NSW coast. Grandpa lives on a property about half-an-hour out of town. He said he enjoys my visits especially since my Nan died in 2008.

We get along great and he's taught me a load of neat stuff like surfing, horse riding, how to cook and run the farm. He also plays a mean guitar and we jam together whenever we get the chance. One of the times I like best is before dinner when the chores are done. We sit on Grandpa's verandah and play Scrabble. Grandpa has a couple of cans of VB and I have a coke. Like my dad I don't drink, but while I think it's a moral issue for him, I just don't like the taste.

One of the reasons I like hanging out with Grandpa isn't just that I'm starting to beat him at Scrabble, but it is the time when he tells me about his life as a teenager and young man. He has a neat three-bay shed where he keeps his guitars, amps and a whole bunch of other cool junk he's collected during his travels. He keeps a lot of it, including photo albums, in a metal chest. He calls his stuff 'artefacts'. Among other things, he showed me a Chinese dragon statuette that he claimed to be solid gold. If that was right, it must be worth a fortune.

Grandpa often tells me about some specific item from the chest and the adventures associated with it. I used to write his stories down in notebooks, but I'd fill them so quickly, I use my laptop now to record everything Grandpa tells me. He used a lot of jargon and abbreviations so I've written a glossary for you. If I've missed any you'll have to *Google* them for yourselves.

'No, I don't have a passport,' I replied, laying out all seven of my tiles, squeezing between the 's' and a 'd' of two other words. 'That's "shredhead" and I get a triple letter score on the "h" and a double word score and a fifty point bonus ...'

'"Shredhead" isn't a word,' he protested, flipping through his *Macquarie*.

'Wanna bet?' I said punching the spelling app on my iPhone.

'Well ... dammit ...' he said shaking his head.

I told you I was getting good at this game. I've learnt a bucket-load of new words and don't say 'like' all the time any more. It used to drive Grandpa crazy.

'Why do I need a passport?' I asked as I totted up my mega-score.

'It might come in handy. You should get one.'

'I'm on Dad's I think, but I haven't had any need to use it. We never go anywhere. Not like you when you were a kid.'

'Yeah, your dad is a bit of a stay-at-home. He was always a serious kind of bloke, even when he was a kid. We probably shouldn't have called him Julian. I reckon that is bound to affect a fella. All he ever wanted to do was settle down in a steady job and marry a nice girl. I guess he achieved his goals. Nevertheless I should have put my foot down about calling him Julian, but your Nan was dead set on the name. She was a big John Lennon fan, you know.'

I must admit, I hadn't thought about a passport and certainly not about overseas travel until I finished school.

'You never know when you might travel. I was like you and hadn't given it much thought until Mad Monty mentioned it.'

'Mad Monty' was an eccentric Afro-American pilot who'd taught Grandpa to fly way back in 1951. Grandpa had run away from boarding school to look for his dad who'd gone missing in New Guinea during WWII. With Monty's help Grandpa finally found his dad who was living on an island in the Bismarck Sea. Grandpa also met a mega-babe called Angela and they had an on-off relationship for a while, but it didn't seem to work out. Surprisingly, one of Grandpa's most treasured artefacts was a 1953 Queen Elizabeth II coronation mug.

'Angela sent that to me from England. It sat proudly on the shelf of my dad's pub for years,' Grandpa said with a smile. He was really sentimental when it came to Angela who'd made such a big impact on his teenage life.

I got in contact with Angela who is now a hot-shot doctor in London. I told her about Grandpa and where he was living and she decided to fly out for a visit. She was due to arrive at Sydney the following day. Mum and Dad would see she transferred to the regional flight and we'd meet her at Merimbula Airport. Grandpa was pretty excited about seeing her again. He and Nan were happily married for ages, but I think he's always secretly held a bit of a torch for Ange.

'New Guinea was still an Australian administered territory back then,' Grandpa said. 'So I thought a passport didn't matter much either, but Monty had other ideas. As it turned out it was a good thing he did, although there were a couple of hoops we had to jump through.'

'How come?'

'It was a matter of identity and legal status. My dad was still officially AWOL from the army and *still* married to my mum although she'd shacked up with a bloke called Stanley Hallet. Luckily I was in thick with Andrew Tynan who was Bishop of Rockhampton at the time. He pulled a few strings and had the marriage annulled on grounds of desertion, which was a pretty big stretch back in those days when Catholics took a very dim view of divorce and separation.'

'That didn't reflect very well on your dad either,' I ventured.

'He didn't care. He never planned on returning to Australia and of course he'd set up house with Mayu by then.'

Mayu was an ex-comfort woman who'd been abandoned by the Imperial Japanese Army when its troops were beaten out of New Guinea. She'd stayed on *Kago Ailan* where Grandpa's dad, George, ran a pub. Mayu retired from life as a working girl and settled down with George. However, George's AWOL position (some might even have said he was a deserter) was also unresolved. Fortunately Grandpa had met two senior Australian Army officers, Lieutenant Colonel Ted Serong and Brigadier

Charles Spry who'd helped him in a tussle with a gang of Filipino pirates led by a psychopath called Frenchy Duval.

Brigadier Spry became head of ASIO, while Ted Serong was not without influence. Dr Holyman, Angela's dad, had also sent a medical assessment to the Australian Department of Defence, stating that George was not in a mental state to be responsible for his actions. That seemed to finally satisfy the Army to let George go without feeling it'd lost any face. Between them 'Silent Charles' Spry, Ted Serong, Dr Holyman and the Defence Department smoothed over George's past misdemeanours and had his honourable discharge formally ratified. Six years after the war, nobody was particularly interested anyway, but it meant George could drink at an RSL club if he felt like it.

'I was supposed to fly co-pilot for Monty in the Dak when we took Frenchy Duval back to the Legion, but I only got as far as Singapore because I didn't have a passport.'

Frenchy Duval was a quintessential bad-arse who'd deserted from the French Foreign Legion and caused Danny and Angela all sorts of grief for several months. They'd bested him in the end and Ted Serong had agreed to take him back to French Indochina to face whatever justice the Legion meted out. Unfortunately Danny and Monty had to return to New Guinea, but Ted Serong was as good as his word and organised a French Air Force Junkers-52 tri-motor to fly Frenchy to Hanoi.

So with that lesson learned, Danny applied for his own passport. With references from two war heroes and the Bishop of Rockhampton, other than 'jumping through a couple of hoops', Danny had no difficulty obtaining one. As he said, it came at a very appropriate time ...

Part 1 — China

Tokyo
China
Pacific
Ocean
Hong
Kong
Clark
AFB
Indo
China
Guam
Palau
Borneo
Kago
Ailan
Lae
Indian
Ocean

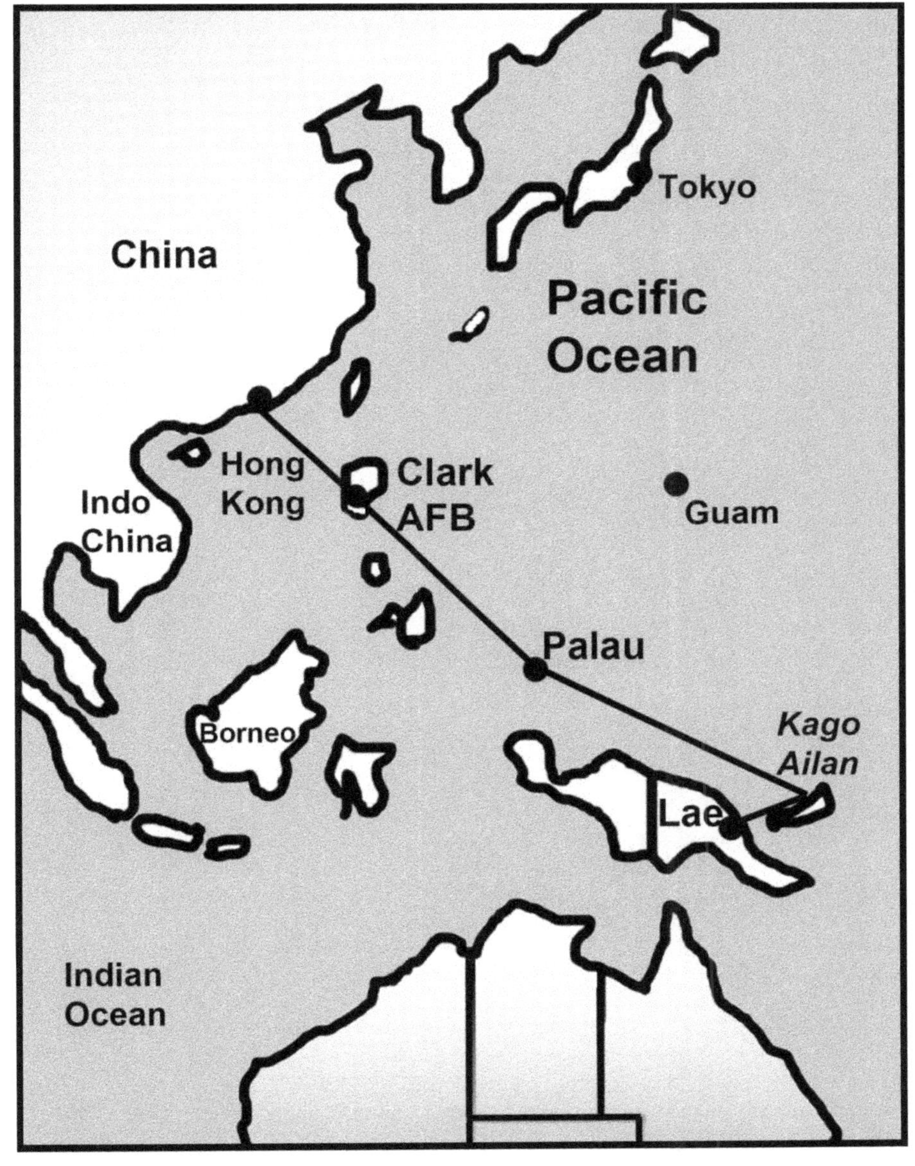

Chapter 1 — The Flying Whale

'Victor-Hotel-Alpha-Bravo-Delta, clear to land runway one-one,' the controller's voice rattled through the headset into Danny's ears. He banked the Noorduyn Norseman high-winged, single-engine plane over the Huon Gulf onto final approach. He was returning from a milk-run to Goroka, Mt Hagen and Madang so the plane's floats had been removed and refitted with a conventional undercarriage.

He was seventeen now and Angela had been gone for nearly a year. He missed her and had written some soppy letters over the months. At first she'd replied, affirming that she loved him, but her letters grew less frequent and certainly less intimate. She was busy studying medicine at Guy's Hospital in London and her interests appeared to be moving on from a teenage romance in a tropical paradise.

Danny may not have been over Angela, but he was too busy to dwell on heartache. Through Monty's astute tuition, Danny now held his commercial pilot's licence and command instrument rating. He'd also passed all his theory subjects for his senior commercial subjects, which would qualify him for an airline transport pilot's licence when he'd accrued sufficient flying hours. They were building up rapidly as Monty kept Danny airborne most of the time.

Danny had spent the night with Jim Taylor who had been a great adventurer in the past. Now he ran a burgeoning coffee plantation at Goroka where he and his wife Yerima had started their family. Along with his regular freight and mail, Danny carried a twenty-five pound sack of coffee beans for Monty who loved the beverage. Danny was developing a taste for it too.

Danny loved flying in the morning when the weather was fine and conditions calm. He never tired of the majestic scenery that reared on either side of his flight path. It was almost noon when the Norseman approached Lae. Danny had landed at Mt Hagen and Madang to pick up and off-load routine cargo on schedule. In fact Danny was so enjoying the flight he forgot all about Angela and turned his mind to a spot of spear-fishing later that day, but that changed in an instant.

As Danny lined up the Norseman on the runway, five hundred feet below a seemingly harmless incident was unfolding on the Huon Gulf.

A lone pelican, while shovelling its beak through the surface, had struck it lucky. It scooped up a shoal of bait fish and was ready to gulp the lot when a flock of scavenging gulls swooped in. Normally they wouldn't bother a pelican. It was quite capable of seeing them off and even swallowing one, but a full bill-bladder pulsating with tasty tit-bits was overwhelmingly tempting.

The pelican's best option was to get airborne. It could fly higher and faster than the idle gulls. So it lumbered into the air with the flapping rabble in hot pursuit. The pelican was weighed down by its load of fish, but it wasn't giving up lunch to a pack of indolent, delinquent gulls that should have been quite capable of fishing for themselves.

Danny spotted the pelican just as it climbed into his approach path. Hitting such a large bird could spell disaster, especially in a small plane like the Norseman. Danny wrenched the control column to the right. Instinctively he knew to bank sharply and turn the plane behind the pelican. Trying to get ahead of it would simply mean he'd fly into the bird due to its forward speed.

He dodged the pelican by inches and ran smack into the flock of gulls. They splattered into the Norseman's wings and several were shredded to bloody feather-clouds. The noise was deafening above the engine's roar. Danny wrestled with the controls as the plane rocked and buffeted with each sickening impact. Those birds that survived peeled away, diving for the safety of the gulf in a cacophony of squawks and screeches.

The prop vibration increased to a bone-jarring shudder. Every time Danny advanced the throttle the shaking grew more severe until the plane rattled so alarmingly, Danny wondered if it would rip apart.

Shit!

He could either risk keeping the power on and hope the Norseman held together, or cut the engine and pray he had enough altitude to glide to the airfield. The idea of ditching a high winged plane didn't appeal to him – pity the floats weren't still attached.

Bugger it! I'll try for the strip.

'Romeo-Alpha-Papa, confirm operations normal,' the tower control's voice crackled uncertainly in Danny's headphones.

No, they're not bloody well normal!

'Pan! Pan! Pan! I've just experienced multiple bird-strikes,' Danny replied as calmly as he could. 'I'll try to make the field. Require emergency services standing by.'

Danny could almost hear the Claxton wailing as the controller phoned Lae hospital and the fire station for support. The airfield was due to be equipped with its dedicated fire truck, but red-tape and lack of resources had delayed its arrival.

Maybe the five-hundred foot descent to the runway wasn't far, but it was the longest two minutes in Danny's life. The ground seemed to be rushing up to him with appalling speed. He used the engine in short bursts — just as long as his nerves could stand the engine vibration — to reduce his descent-rate.

As soon as he was certain he would at least make the grass under-run, he cut the motor and glided for the last few feet. The vibrations stopped immediately and the instant hush was reassuring. With no power the rate of descent increased, but Danny had practised dead-stick landings so often he easily adjusted.

At the last minute he flared the plane. It bounced slightly before settling onto the grass and coasting onto the sealed runway. Danny switched off the fuel supply and battery and engaged the park-brake. He clambered from the pilot's seat, opened the side door and scrambled down the entry steps.

The plane looked a wreck. Red gouts of gull-mush covered the engine cowl and wing leading edges. Gross smelling plumage and bird-gore stuck to the airframe. Danny wrinkled his nose and gagged, but he was down safely — alive.

He heard the fire-truck and ambulance sirens as Monty raced across the strip from the *Alabama Aviation* hangar. He was followed by Dave Bradley, their mechanic and a tall stranger wearing what looked like an airline uniform including a peaked cap. The ambulance overtook the running men before screeching to a halt only inches from the propeller. The fire-truck had correctly assessed there was no danger of combustion and approached more cautiously.

Dr Stephen Graham leapt from the ambulance tail gate and strode towards the Norseman.

'Are you okay, Danny?' Dr Graham asked. He knew Danny well after he'd operated on Angela's father who'd been accidently wounded by feuding tribesmen. Danny and Angela had both helped Dr Graham save Dr Holyman by donating blood during the procedure.

'Yeah I'm fine, thanks doctor. Just shaken up. I hit a bloody great flock of seagulls.'

'Can't say the same for the plane,' Dr Graham observed.

'Jeeze, Danny,' Monty gasped as he fought for breath after racing half way across the airport. 'I don't know why I let you near my planes — you're jinxed.'

But Danny saw the relief in Monty's eyes while Dave made a cursory inspection around the plane.

'Looks worse than it is,' the engineer surmised. 'I'll clean up the wings and machine out that dent in the prop. It'll need a full inspection and engine run, but I'll have her up and running in no time. Come on, let's push her back to the hangar.'

'Just a moment,' Dr Graham said. He gave Danny a quick, on-the-spot examination to check for concussion and whiplash. Danny assured him the landing had been smooth and quite unremarkable so there was nothing to worry about.

The good doctor appeared satisfied, but admonished Danny to call into his surgery if he felt dizzy or experienced any other side-effects. Danny thanked him, the ambulance team and the firemen who seemed a little disappointed they didn't have an actual blaze to conquer. When the ambulance and fire engine raced away Danny released the Norseman's parking brake then he, Dave, Monty and the mysterious stranger pushed the plane back to Monty's *Alabama Aviation* hangar.

'Hey Danny, this is Felix Smith,' Monty said as they approached the hangar.

'Pleased to meet you, Danny,' Felix greeted cordially.

Thirty-four year old Felix Smith was a cheerful, handsome fellow in a square-jawed, all-American boy sort of way.

'G'day, Captain Smith,' Danny replied cheerfully.

'Call me Felix. We're kinda on a first name basis in CAT. You did a good job getting your crate down, Danny. You kept a cool head,' Felix said. 'You seem very young, if you don't mind me saying so.'

'Not at all, you're only stating a fact. I'm seventeen.'

'I remember I wasn't much older than Danny when I was chasing Kraut fighters all over Northern Italy during the war. Same goes for you flying Goonies over the Hump, eh Felix?' Monty said and both men chuckled.

'It was a matter of ditching and losing the whole plane or just risking a bit of engine damage, I guess,' Danny said.

'Not to mention my coffee,' Monty said. 'I don't reckon sea water would do it any good at all.'

'It's safe in the back,' Danny reassured him.

Everyone nodded sagely as they pushed the Norseman into *Alabama Aviation's* hangar. An aircraft was parked beside Monty's DC-3 and it was huge. The fuselage and wingspan dwarfed the *Gooney-Bird* by at least ten feet in every dimension. The plane was unpainted raw metal bearing no markings other than its registration. The fuselage looked like a bloated cucumber with a cockpit dome that may have been streamlined, but gave the plane the appearance of a metallic blimp.

'Holy smoke, that has to be the ugliest plane I've ever seen. It looks like a ruddy great whale,' Danny declared.

Monty glared at him while Felix looked just a little pained.

'I dunno ...' the stranger drawled.

Danny looked at Monty uncomfortably.

'It's *his* plane, isn't it?' Danny whispered.

Monty nodded.

'Sorry, Felix,' Danny mumbled. 'I wasn't thinking.'

That was true. Pilots were generally fiercely defensive about the planes they flew, even if they were right horrors to manage. It was a matter of pride that they could master the beast, which made them protective of their machines. Felix Smith was no exception.

'It may be slow and clunky-lookin',' he observed, 'but it'll go twice as far as your Dak and carry twice the payload.'

While Dave fussed over the Norseman, Felix joined Danny and Monty in the hangar office for coffee. It turned out that Felix Smith was a senior pilot for China Air Transport who'd flown for Chiang Kai-shek's nationalists against Mao's Communists during the Chinese Civil War that broke out right after WWII. The Communists won in 1949, so CAT withdrew its operations just in time to make itself useful in the Korean conflict that erupted a year later. Many of their aircraft were based in Tachikawa airfield near Tokyo.

'You're a long way off course, Captain,' Danny observed as he pulled some forms from Monty's filing cabinet. He'd have to fill out an air incident report for the bird-strike. He made a note to phone the tower for the exact time and their account of the incident.

'I'm ferryin' a bunch of military heavies down to Australia and New Zealand. Your Mr Bob Menzies and Sid Holland want the lowdown on how the war's going. I guess they get plenty of wires and diplomatic reports, but General Van Fleet's sendin' down a couple of generals to sweet-talk 'em anyway.'

'A lot of plane for a couple of guys,' Danny said.

'Generals like it that way, but they don't travel alone,' Felix replied with a shrug.

About then a truck rolled up and parked next to the C-46. Felix's co-pilot, engineer and crew-chief jumped down and started loading the supplies for the trip. The passengers piled out of the truck after the aircrew. It appeared the generals travelled in style, but they saw that their entourage, including several senior officers, pitched in to help pack the rations aboard the plane.

'Time to go,' Felix said with a grin. 'Can't keep the brass waiting, can I? We're fuelled up for Sydney. It was nice meeting you, Danny.'

He shook hands all round.

'Remember to think about my offer, Monty,' Felix said with a wink as he left the office.

Danny and Monty followed Felix. He waved a cheerful farewell to Dave and quickly checked his plane. His crew were ready for start-up and all the passengers were aboard. Felix climbed the ladder and took his place in the captain's seat. He unlatched the flight-deck side window that looked enormous compared with the *Gooney-Bird*'s tiny portal.

Felix's crew-chief, or loadmaster as they were becoming known, stood twenty yards in front of the plane's nose. Any closer and Felix would have been unable to see him. A portable fire extinguisher cradled in a dolly stood beside the loadmaster. The loadmaster held up two fingers to indicate the starboard propeller was clear. After a great deal of growling and belching blue smoke, the starboard Pratt-&-Whitney R-2800 radial engine rattled into life. The chief held up one finger and the port engine clattered alive. There seemed to be a massive amount of noise and smoke to Danny, but everyone else looked unconcerned. The loadmaster gathered the wheel chocks then pushed the fire extinguisher to the fuselage door where the generals' aides helped him load the gear before he too clambered aboard and closed the door.

Felix waved from the cockpit as the plane rolled away. Danny watched the great, lumbering aircraft line up, take-off and climb along the Markham Valley before gaining enough altitude for Felix to bank left and pick his way through the mountain passes to the south.

'He seemed like a nice guy,' Monty commented as they returned to the office.

'Yeah, I hope I didn't hurt his feelings about his plane,' Danny sighed, 'but it *is* soooo ugly.'

'Beauty is in the eye of the beholder, I guess. I know what you mean though I've heard the poor old Commando described as the *Curtiss Calamity* and, as you so astutely observed, *The Whale*, which is a bit harsh. It's hard to think that the same company built the P-40. Now that plane was a right looker.'

'Hang on,' Danny said, 'what was all that about an *offer*?'

'Well, I was gonna talk to you about that.'

'Oh ..?'

'Yeah.'

'Right now is good.'

'Okay. I'm thinking of selling *Alabama Aviation*.'

Chapter 2 — A Step Towards the Orient

'I thought you loved flying here?' Danny said, staring at Monty in amazement.

'Yeah, but ...'

'But what?'

'Ain't we kinda gettin' in a rut?'

'I'd hardly call flying in New Guinea routine,' Danny reminded him. 'Just look what happened this morning.'

'Sure, but you can have a bird-strike anywhere — except maybe Antarctica. Penguins can't fly.'

'I'm sure they have other flying birds like albatrosses and stuff, but don't get off the subject. Why do you want to sell up? The business is going well.'

'Well, enough, but we ain't gonna become millionaires.'

'Money isn't everything and that cash we got from that gold bullion really put *Alabama Aviation* on an even keel.'

'Yeah, only there's always something ... another bill ... another DCA check ... more air-route charges and airport fees goin' up all the time. Not to mention we work seven days a week. We can't afford to knock back any charters. When did you last have a day off?'

Monty seemed a bit edgy to Danny who couldn't determine why.

'We hang out down at the shack all the time,' Danny insisted. 'I really like it here.'

Monty owned a two-bedroom beach hut fronting onto a coral lagoon and Danny had moved in after he started working for *Alabama Aviation. Shack* was a pretty inadequate and unflattering description of Monty's place. It was very comfortable, even boasting electric power to run Monty's fridge and electric guitar amplifier. They spent what little spare time they had jamming with the guitars, spear-fishing on the reef or lounging in hammocks under the palms. Monty had two casual girlfriends called Koina and Jara who, among other benefits, tidied up after him on an equally casual basis. Once during an overnight stay Jara had become friendly with Danny to try and ease the pain of Angela. Although Danny was appreciative, his response was lukewarm at best, so she didn't bother with him after that.

'Yeah we hang out for an afternoon, or a couple of hours. Otherwise we're just eating and sleeping ... well mostly,' Monty added slyly. 'When was the last time you saw your dad at *Kagotaun?*'

Kagotaun was a rough-and-tumble island settlement situated on the eastern side of the Vitu Archipelago in the Bismarck Sea. It could be best described as a Wild-West frontier town populated by the human flotsam washed up after WWII. Danny's father, George McAlister not only ran the pub, but also had built a beach-house on the northeast tip of *Kago Ailan* where he and Danny went snorkelling and long-board surfing.

'I see Dad whenever we fly over to *Kago Ailan*,' Danny said defensively.

'Yeah, but when have you really spent time with him? When was the last time you went surfing? Remember, he was the reason you came to New Guinea in the first place.'

That was true. Danny had endured some hair-raising adventures to find his father who'd been reported missing while fighting the IJA along the Kokoda Track.

'Okay, what's the deal?' Danny sighed.

'CAT wants to wet-lease the *Gooney-Bird*. The company is flat out resupplying UN units all over Korea. I'll need a co-pilot.'

'Me?'

'Precisely.'

'It sounds dangerous.'

'What we need is a bit of excitement.'

'You keep forgetting flying in New Guinea is exciting.'

'You can always come back here if you don't like it. The pay's six-hundred a month.'

Danny's jaw dropped.

'Six hundred American dollars?'

'Sure thing kid, you'll be rich in no time. You'd be lucky to make that much in a year hanging around here. And it'll stop you moping over Angela.'

Whether Danny was convinced or not didn't seem to bother Monty. He *assumed* Danny would go along with it after he'd mentioned the pay-cheque. Monty rambled on about what a great opportunity it would be for Danny to gain some operational experience in the big bad world outside New Guinea. Danny had to agree it did sound exciting.

'Also it's not quite as simple as that,' Monty said enigmatically.

'Sounds pretty simple to me.'

'Yeah ... well ... I kinda owe someone a bit of cash ...'

'Oh?' Danny eyed Monty with a frown. 'And who might that "someone" be?'

'Crazy Al Chong. Last week I got into a game of Armstrong's hold'em in his down-town bar.'

'You played poker with Crazy Al Chong? You've gotta be stark raving bonkers!'

'I'd had a coupla drinks.'

'I'd need to drink a pub dry before I'd gamble with Crazy Al.'

Those were wise word from the teenager. Crazy Al Chong was an ethnic Chinese Indonesian bad boy who'd skipped Jakarta in 1946 one step ahead of the Dutch authorities for double-dealing with the Japanese. He saw no reason to return home after independence in 1948 so now he was a local Lae identity with fingers in every money-making pie around town. You want a girl ... you go to Al. You want cash ... you go to Al, although you'll pay usury rates. You want someone to disappear ... you go to Al, although it'll cost you. He owned a sleazy, smoke-filled bar in town where the liquor and girls were cheap although of dubious provenance. Al retained a gang of street heavies to keep order and ensure you fulfilled your obligations.

'How much do you owe him?' Danny asked.

'*Five hundred quid,*' Monty mumbled under his breath.

'How much?'

'Five hundred quid,' Monty finally admitted.

'Jeez Monty, what were you thinking ... no don't answer ... you weren't thinking. Do you have that kind of cash?'

'Well no, we used the last of the gold bullion to buy the *Gooney-Bird* outright, remember.'

Danny sighed.

Blimey I sound like Angela.

He had no reservations about helping Monty out, but his bank account had dwindled when he became a partner in *Alabama Aviation* and had invested the bulk of his savings in the company. Right now he was asset-rich although cash-challenged.

'I've probably got a hundred quid left,' Danny said. 'Will that help?'

'No, Al wants payment in full. Anyway it's Friday, the bank won't open until Monday and Al wants his dough tomorrow.'

'So you're saying we need to get out of town before Al's boys come around.'

'You've got the picture in one,' Monty beamed. 'I knew you were a bright boy. We won't need much cash anyway. CAT will foot the fuel bills and maintenance costs from now on.'

'You'd already agreed to take the job?'

Monty shrugged.

'Captain Smith only asked you to *think* about his offer.'

'He was just messing with me. He knew I had to smooth it over with you first.'

'The sneaky bugger. "Call me Felix", yeah, right.'

'So you're in?' Monty said.

'I don't really have any choice, do I? *You* certainly can't hang around and it looks like my job has just been pulled out from under me.'

'One door closes — another opens. Come on let's get our gear from the shack. I'm not leaving my guitars behind.'

'What about a loadmaster?' Danny asked. That was an important crew member on a cargo plane. You needed someone to supervise loading, unloading and calculating the plane's weight and balance. The pilots could do the job, but it would seriously slow down their turn-around time. A dedicated specialist was a far better option.

'We might have to find someone from the CAT outfit,' Monty said. He'd already asked around, but got no takers.

'What about the shack?' Danny asked.

'Jara and Koina will take care of it,' Monty assured him glibly.

'They're hardly going to wait indefinitely for you to come back.'

'No, I don't suppose they will. I'll cross that bridge when I come to it.'

This was pretty much Monty's life philosophy anyway.

They jumped into his Morgan three-wheeler and roared away to the beach hut.

'What about *Alabama Aviation*?' Danny asked.

'Dave said he'll hold the fort until we decide what to do with it. A couple of charter companies have been sniffing around with an eye to buy the competition. We'll see what offers they come up with.'

Monty pulled up beside the shack and they piled out. They quickly packed a grip each and stashed them onto the front seat. They secured Monty's Fender Broadcaster and tweed-amp along with the Gibson ES-150 acoustic guitar to the luggage rack bolted to the car's rear. Danny was used to travelling light, but made sure he stuffed his passport into his shirt breast pocket. He also packed his Kodak 135mm Pony camera, several rolls of film, his sketch pad and drawing material. Drawing and photography were his hobbies, both of which he'd become quite good at.

'I'll miss the place,' Danny admitted as he gazed across the lagoon to the Huon Gulf.

'You'll be back with your pockets bulging with money in no time,' Monty assured him. 'You wanna last beer before we go?'

'Shouldn't we file a flight plan?'

'Okay. I figure we'll go via Clark Air Force Base in the Philippines. We won't have trouble finding the place, I've been there plenty of times before ...'

'You're considering leaving town, are you, Monty?' a voice hissed behind them.

Danny and Monty spun around to see Crazy Al Chong standing on the veranda framed by a couple of gargantuan, head-shaven minders. Al was a short, stocky fellow who liked to wear Hawaiian floral shirts and cargo shorts and smoke Filipino cigars. To Danny's relief, none of the trio appeared to be armed. They didn't need to be.

'Well howdy there, Al. Now what gave you that idea?'

'Let's just say a little bird told me,' Al replied evenly. 'I keep an eye on my business interests – which includes you, Monty. Nothing happens in this town that I don't know about. So I thought I'd better follow you down here and protect my investment, so to speak.'

'Al ... Al ... old buddy, you know I'm good for the cash. I just need a little more time. Why me and Danny here are just working on pulling it all together.'

'In the Philippines?'

'Oh you heard that bit?'

'Fortunately for me, yes, but unfortunately for you.'

'Now Al let's not do anything we'll regret. We don't want your boys there to do anything dumb.'

'There's no "we" about it, Monty. I have a position to maintain in town, you see. I'll have to make an example or I'll have bad-debts up to my eyeballs.'

Crazy Al nodded almost imperceptibly, but it was all that was needed to unleash his thugs.

'Where's your ruddy gun?' Danny hissed. 'This would be a good time to use it.'

'It's in my bag.'

And that was lying in the Morgan three-wheeler.

There was no more time for discussion. Al's heavies, who were appropriately named 'Ramrod' and 'Crowbar', now moved to either side to tackle Danny and Monty individually. The henchmen were great lumbering brutes who used one tactic only – bludgeoning muscle-power. Their sheer mass was enough to roll over any opposition, but Danny and Monty had both seen their share of bar fights and had their own brand of street cunning.

Monty grabbed a cane chair and smashed it across Crowbar's face. Cane splinters sprayed across the veranda, but made little impression on the oncoming attacker. Danny darted backwards through the open doorway and shoved one of Monty's lounge chairs across the breach. Ramrod grunted as he barged through, slinging the furniture aside.

Mad Al's goons were slow and lumbering while Danny and Monty, although boxing well above their weight, had agility on their side. Danny dodged Ramrod's flaying fists, but he was confined inside the hut. Ramrod caught him, nearly shaking him into oblivion. Meanwhile outside Monty tripped on one of the veranda boards that had never been particularly even. Crowbar seized his chance and grabbed Monty, heaving him head-high before hurling him through the window into the hut.

Monty smashed through the window frame. Luckily there was no glass pane or he'd have been shredded. Monty slammed into Ramrod who grunted and dropped Danny who thumped to the floor.

Al hadn't moved. He retrieved a Filipino cigar from his shirt pocket and a matchbox from his pants. He lit the cigar, dragging down a couple of puffs before casually reaching through the window and lighting one of the curtains with the flaming match. The cotton fabric blazed alight in seconds. The flames instantly spread to the coconut fibre walls that were ideal fuel for a fireball.

Totally disregarding the flames, Crowbar stormed through the door. Amid the choking smoke Monty was pummelling Ramrod's head while Danny recovered and landed a couple of solid kicks to the giant's midriff. Crowbar had difficulty making out anything much. Flames now erupted with alarming speed and smoke swirled everywhere within seconds.

Ramrod recovered after a thrashing that would have put a normal person down for hours. Monty and Danny beat a hasty retreat into the kitchen, but Al's gorillas were right on their heels. Crowbar wrenched Monty's prized fridge from its spot, ripping the plug from its socket. More sparks flew, igniting another fireball right in the centre of the shack. Effortlessly, Crowbar flung the fridge at Danny and Monty who dived either side as it smashed to the floor. The fridge door burst open cascading beer cans and bottles across the floorboards.

Danny and Monty grabbed the cans and bottles, hurling them at Crowbar and Ramrod. Glass smashed and amber liquid sprayed across the room leaving a fizzing residue of froth. Both Danny and

Monty scored plenty of direct hits. A can slammed into Crowbar's face, breaking his nose – not for the first time either. That may have slowed him up, but didn't stop him. He merely advanced more cautiously as blood streamed from his nostrils.

Once all the cans and bottles within reach were exhausted, Danny and Monty chucked whatever else was close at hand – fruit from the bowl, bric-a-brac, a flour sack, Monty's precious coffee and tea canisters, *anything* – but the missiles either bounced off Al's heavies or were merely brushed aside.

By then the smoke filled everyone's eyes which streamed with tears. Even Ramrod and Crowbar's strength was nullified by visibility that was now close to zero. Smoke was not the only danger. Flames crackled on all sides and now flared into the roof which was made of tinder-dry palm thatch. The ceiling exploded raining down fiery chunks of timber and dried fronds. A beam crashed down between Danny and Monty and their assailants, driving both sides apart.

'Time to go,' Monty yelled, grabbing Danny's arm.

Danny was becoming disorientated at this stage and smoke inhalation was taking effect. Choking and dizzy, he let Monty lead him to the bedroom. They dived through the back window, taking the frame with them. Just at that moment the shack roof gave way and crashed down, destroying anything below.

Danny and Monty somersaulted as they hit the sand. They picked themselves up and dashed for the Morgan three-wheeler. Monty leapt into the driver's seat – never mind the door – while Danny scrambled on top of their travel bags. Monty gunned the accelerator and they sped away.

Chapter 3 — Getaway Trail

'At least the bastards didn't get my guitars. Those two goons are probably toast by now,' Monty yelled over the Morgan's engine that he revved well beyond its specifications. He seemed far too cheerful in Danny's view, but they'd made it clear away ... or had they?

Crazy Al had shown scant concern for his henchmen when he set Monty's shack alight. In fact he'd probably made matters worse. Ramrod and Crowbar were more than capable of dealing with Danny and Monty even if they took their own sweet time about it. The smoke and flames had only hampered them, enabling their victims to escape. But Crazy Al wasn't called *Crazy* for nothing.

As the roof crashed down, Al's two heavies raced from the shed, beating out the flames that flared on their clothing. They both dashed down the beach and dived into the lagoon. Fortunately the flames hadn't taken hold and neither man was badly burnt. Al employed tough guys anyway and a spot of minor singeing shouldn't slow them down in his opinion. Al considered his goons were simply 'human resources', not people.

Smoke screened Monty and Danny as they bolted for their car. At first Al wasn't sure whether they'd been consumed in the fire and neither Crowbar nor Ramrod could confirm that important detail one way or the other. Al ranted for his men to stop being sissies and get out of the water.

He chivvied them back to his car parked a hundred yards from the hut. He'd ordered Ramrod, who was his driver, to stop far enough away from the hut so Danny and Monty wouldn't hear them arrive. As they lumbered towards their vehicle, Al noticed Monty's three-wheeler was gone. He put two-and-two together in no time.

Although he'd never learnt to drive, Al owned an open-top 1938 French Delage Tourer. He loved his car and kept it in pristine condition, which was not an easy task in New Guinea's humid tropical climate.

'Get after them!' Al screamed.

'Where, boss?' Ramrod asked.

'The airport, you fool. They'll make for their plane.'

Ramrod swung the driver's door open and leapt behind the wheel. Crowbar dashed around to the passenger side and he too piled in. The engine roared into life and Ramrod drove away until he realised they'd left Crazy Al behind.

Ramrod dough-nutted the car in a screech of tortured brakes and burning rubber, before returning to where Crazy Al stood in a fury.

'You idiots,' Al roared as Crowbar bounded out of the car and opened the door for his boss who climbed into the back seat.   Al never opened doors for himself, and this was no exception. You didn't keep minders and do your own menial tasks – no sir!

Al's own brand of protocol would never have allowed his goons to sit on the red-leather seats in their ragged, sea-drenched clothing, but in this case he had to prioritise.

The Tourer sped after Danny and Monty who were now tearing through Lae town centre towards the airport just as Al had rightly deduced. Monty and Danny were frustrated by the hundreds of pedestrians and cyclists who cluttered the streets without any consideration for motor traffic. There were plenty of beast-of-burden powered carts and small trucks whose mechanical condition limited their maximum speed restricting the way as well. In other words, it was hardly an ideal getaway route. Al's Tourer fared no better although he was less concerned about hitting innocent townsfolk than Monty or Danny. Ramrod and Monty blasted their car-horns, but neither was able to make a lot of difference.

As the Morgan flashed past the police station, several patrolmen poured out of its door into the panic-stricken streets. It only took seconds for them to realise that their town was being thrown into chaos by a rampant motorcar. Two officers raced for their vehicle and careered out of the parking lot just as Al's Tourer charged into view.

The two cars would have collided at right angles if Ramrod hadn't swerved to the right while the police driver pulled to the left. As it was the cars slammed into each other side-on in a grinding, sickening impact. The side panels of both cars were gouged and distorted so badly that the doors were rendered useless. Al bounced so high he nearly fell from the open-topped car. He grabbed Crowbar's collar and hung on tight with one foot dangling over the automobile's side.

Crowbar was half-throttled, but he managed to manoeuvre Al into the back seat. Ramrod gunned the Tourer and they sped after the Morgan. The police car fared less well. It swerved after the crash and slammed into the street boardwalk, smashing down awning posts, veranda roofing and scattering vendors' displays in all directions. The car stalled as steam gushed from its split radiator. The two officers struggled from the wreckage, stunned but not seriously hurt.

The car was immobilised, but other quick-witted policemen including an inspector and a sergeant, boarded a truck and were soon in hot pursuit with the siren blaring.

Meanwhile Ramrod had regained full control of Al's Tourer and they were gaining on the Morgan three-wheeler, which wasn't really built for phenomenal performance. To make matters worse, Crowbar pulled a Smith & Wesson .38 revolver and fired the entire chamber at the Morgan. Two of the bullets slammed into the roadway only inches from the Morgan's rear tyre. Another two just flew wide while the last two shots slammed into the Morgan's boot. The crack of lead puncturing the car's metal body was enough to make both Monty and Danny jump in their seats.

'Bloody hell, Monty, these bastards really mean business. You sure have pissed Al off,' Danny yelled.

'Well, don't just sit there perched on those bags. Get my gun and fire back. There are spare magazines in there somewhere.'

Danny unzipped Monty's grip and scrambled around for his 1911 Colt automatic. He found the gun and three magazines. He jammed the two spares into his pocket and slammed the other mag into the pistol butt. He cocked the weapon and blasted off a salvo.

One bullet drove through the Tourer's windscreen, leaving a neat puncture hole. The slug ended up burning a hole in the front seat upholstery.

About then Al realised that his beautiful automobile was rapidly turning to junk. He flew into an even bigger rage and urged Ramrod to speed up with a tirade of expletives. The Tourer bounced erratically so Crowbar was having difficulty reloading his revolver. He fumbled for bullets in his pockets, but dropped half of them and they clattered under the seats. Eventually he loaded half the chambers.

The Morgan roared through the airport entrance. The tyres screeched as Monty spun the steering wheel and raced straight for *Alabama Aviation's* hangar. The car thudded to a halt beside the *Gooney-Bird.* Fortunately the cargo door was open. Monty leapt out of the car and grabbed their bags while Danny turned to see the Tourer bearing down on them with Al still standing between the two front seats, waving his fist and roaring insanely. With surprising calmness Danny levelled the Colt and carefully aimed at Ramrod.

Danny squeezed the trigger. The bullet planted another neat hole in the windshield, but this time the whole glass pane glazed into a million tiny cracked segments. Ramrod's forward vision was completely lost until Crowbar's fist smashed the glass into shards. He wasn't quite quick enough and the Tourer temporarily flew out of control, swerved and slammed into three 44-gallon drums standing beside the *Alabama Aviation* hangar. One drum tumbled over spilling AVGAS across the tarmac.

The Tourer's motor stalled while Al tumbled forward, landing on top of Ramrod. Crowbar was the first to recover from the jolt and manhandled Al off Ramrod who frantically struggled to restart the car. Although the headlights were shattered, the Tourer was a tough automobile and the radiator remained intact.

Meanwhile Danny heard a roar behind him and a blast of air as Monty fired up the *Gooney-Bird's* starboard engine. Danny tossed the chocks aside then clambered into the plane just as Ramrod reversed the Tourer away from the fuel tanks. They were just in time. Danny reloaded the pistol and emptied the magazine in Al's direction. He figured if the boss was put out of action, then the goons would give up the chase. Danny didn't hit Al, but several bullets hit the fuel drums. Red hot slugs ripped through the metal tanks which were safe enough, but the super-heated bullets zinged through vaporising fumes from the spilt AVGAS.

There was a whoosh as the fuel flared into a giant fireball. That was enough to turn the punctured tanks into 44-gallon bombs.

Once again the Claxton wailed while the dismayed tower controller phoned the fire brigade.

Monty was already taxiing using only one engine as Danny slammed the cargo door shut. He felt the plane shudder from the explosions, but Monty kept going. Danny clambered into the co-pilot's seat.

'Start the port engine while I keep her on the taxiway!' Monty yelled.

Taxiing a twin-engine, tail-wheel aircraft with only a single motor running was tricky and would have been impossible in Felix Smith's C-46.

The Tourer was lifted off its back wheels by the blast, but slammed back onto the ground and the car kept going. Dave Bradley, who'd wasted no time getting to work on the Norseman, heard the uproar and was about to investigate when the hangar window panes shattered inwards. He dived for cover, but the greater danger was fire spreading into the hangar. He grabbed a fire extinguisher, towed it outside and sprayed foam over the blaze. His quick action certainly saved the hangar and the Norseman plane he was working on. A stack of cargo pallets helped to shield the hangar as well. There was another foam fire-extinguisher along with a couple of CO_2 units. Dave sprayed the lot into the flames which held the fire at bay until the fire truck arrived from town.

Then the constabulary lorry barrelled into the confusion. They'd forgotten they were initially after the Morgan – indeed the two officers most focused on that particular task were still sitting dazed beside their car outside the police station. The truck contingent had their sites firmly set on the Tourer.

Crazy Al urged Ramrod to speed after the *Gooney-Bird* although Crowbar had used his remaining ammunition to no effect. He scrambled around the car floor looking for more shells, but it was useless. They'd all rolled into inaccessible crevices. He sat back in the front passenger seat and, glancing rearwards saw the police truck.

'The coppers are right on our heels, boss!' he cried.

Al wasn't interested. He wanted to get his hands – or rather Ramrod and Crowbar's – on Monty and beat him to pulp. He didn't mind giving the kid a good hiding while he was at it. Al already blamed Monty for the damage to his car which was getting close to a write-off.

'Cut them off!' Al screamed. 'They can't take off if we block the runway.'

So while Monty steered the *Gooney-Bird* for take-off on the southeast runway, Ramrod swerved onto the taxiway that ran parallel to the take-off run. Crowbar looked doubtful, but there was no arguing with Al in his present frame of mind.

The tower controller who'd been busy calling for fire brigade assistance now realised that Monty wasn't simply taxiing the plane clear of the fire, but intended to take off.

'Alpha-Bravo-Alpha,' he radioed, 'vacate the active runway, you do not have clearance to line up.'

'Sorry, tower,' Monty replied, 'we've got business out of town.'

'You don't have an airways clearance ...'

'No time now, we're rolling.'

And he pushed the throttle to set take-off power. The *Gooney-Bird* inched forward as the props cut into the air. As it gained speed Monty pushed the control column forward, lifting the tail so the plane fuselage was now parallel with the runway and running on its main wheels only.

'Alpha-Bravo-Alpha, there is an obstruction on the runway,' the controller's voice warned. He sounded nervous. Not only was there an inferno beside one of the aerodrome hangars, but now it looked like there'd be a runway collision as well. He didn't need that amount of paperwork.

'You should abort your take-off.'

'Not your call,' Monty replied, which was true enough. Only the pilot-in-command can ever make that decision, although the fact that Monty was taking off without clearance might have made the point less certain.

Ramrod had turned the Tourer onto the far end of the runway and was now accelerating northeast directly towards the *Gooney-Bird.* To make matters worse the police vehicle was only yards behind the Tourer. Al screamed and waved his fists like a berserker. Ramrod had to decide what he feared most – the oncoming plane or his boss's wrath – no contest, he drove on.

'Monty. It's ruddy Al. He's blocking the runway,' Danny said.

'So he wants to play chicken, does he?' Monty replied, relishing the situation rather more than necessary in Danny's opinion.

Danny had never thought about a plane's take-off run time. Normally it didn't seem to take that long, but now time dragged endlessly as the ASI needle crawled around the instrument face. The tower controller's continual warnings over the radio only added to Danny's discomfort.

Just as it seemed impossible to avoid colliding with the Tourer, Monty hauled the *Gooney-Bird* into the sky. At 60 knots the plane was only a couple of knots above its stalling speed and barely fast enough to keep airborne and certainly below the minimum controllability speed should an engine fail. Pilots never took off below that speed. They needed enough airflow to apply a rudder force to counter the asymmetric yaw of a single engine at full power, but Monty had to compromise.

Instinctively Crowbar and Ramrod ducked as the props sliced the air just inches above them. Al was still standing, seemingly oblivious to the peril facing him. The prop missed him too as Monty gained another foot of altitude. Unfortunately the *Gooney-Bird's* landing gear was still extended, hanging below the prop disks. The port wheel thumped into Al's face, ripping his head from his shoulders, flinging it back along the runway. Al's skull bounced onto the police truck bonnet and slammed into the windscreen. The driver instinctively ducked, pulling the steering wheel savagely to the right.

As the *Gooney-Bird* flashed overhead the truck pitched onto two wheels balancing precariously for a second before slamming onto its side and crunching to a stop on the grass beside the strip. The constables tumbled out with only minor cuts and bruises. They rushed to the front cabin and helped the inspector and driver out. Both men dusted themselves down, shaking their heads in bewilderment.

Crazy Al Chong's head lay in the grass close by. His decapitated torso slumped forward, flopping over the front seats, drenching Ramrod and Crowbar with arterial blood until Al's heart sensed there was no longer a brain to control it so it stopped beating. Crowbar scrambled into the back seat and pitched Al out of the Tourer while Ramrod drove out of the airfield at full speed.

The Tourer was discovered abandoned some hours later, but Ramrod and Crowbar were nowhere to be found.

Meanwhile Dave watched the fire crew fight the blaze to a standstill. While they doused the remaining smouldering flame pockets, he drove the Morgan into *Alabama Aviation's* hangar and parked it behind the Norseman. He reverently placed the guitars and amplifier in the office then draped a tarp over the car. He figured Monty would come back for his property when he was good and ready. If the police impounded the car, Monty would undoubtedly have a lot of awkward questions to answer.

Meanwhile the *Gooney-Bird* gained altitude and set a north-eastern course.

'That was interesting,' Monty said with a grin.

'Don't you ever do a normal take-off?' Danny demanded.

'Yeah, lots of times, you only remember the motivating ones.'

'Well that's all well and good, Monty,' Danny said tapping the fuel gauges. 'But how much fuel do you think we have on board?'

'Ah ... with all that excitement, I hadn't kinda gotten around to thinking that bit through.'

Chapter 4 — The First Leg

'We didn't actually have time to refuel, did we?' Monty reminded Danny who was looking doubtfully at the fuel gauges.

'There's enough to make it to Finschhafen easy, I reckon. Maybe Madang at a stretch,' Danny said with justifiable confidence. Aviation regulations required pilots to carry enough fuel in their planes to last at least half-an-hour when they arrived at their destination – even more if there was bad weather forecast there. Monty's policy was to carry fuel to an alternate airport if the payload allowed.

'Gotta go further than that,' Monty replied, levelling the *Gooney-Bird* at six thousand feet and setting the throttles for thirty-five inches of boost and leaning the mixture lever as much as he dare without overheating the cylinder-heads or causing the engines to back-fire.

'We're using the aux-tanks already, what's wrong with Finschhafen? The strip's long enough.'

'Too close to Lae. The cops will have notified anywhere nearby is my guess. We've gotta get off the main island.'

'Where do you suggest?'

'*Kago Ailan*. No cops there and plenty of fuel drums.'

'That's a hundred-and-fifty miles away!'

It was actually even further than that from Lae, but Monty had been steering a north-easterly course since take-off.

'We'll never make it.'

'Yes we will. We've got nearly a hundred gallons left. Flying time's an hour-and-a-half from here. No sweat.'

It was closer to eighty gallons and Monty had a habit of saying 'no sweat', when there was every reason to sweat. That was all Danny needed. He'd already experienced a *Gooney-Bird* ditching when flying to New Guinea from Queensland. The pilot in that case was a ne'er-do-well ex-RAAF renegade who had taken a few maintenance short cuts that led to the crash. Fortunately no one had been lost on that occasion, but it didn't make Danny feel any easier about Monty's 'press-on' decision. At least the weather was fine with unlimited visibility, so they wouldn't have to divert around any storms on the way.

The Lae tower controller spent ten minutes demanding they return to the field, but Monty didn't reply and eventually switched the radio off.

The trouble with their route was that there was nowhere to land in an emergency. Umboi Island was just a jungle-covered volcanic relic while Cape Gloucester was a maze of mangroves that, along with the IJA, had made the Maine Corp landings so hazardous during WWII.

Another factor that Monty hadn't had time to consider was wind direction. Head-winds slowed the plane down, while tailwinds helped it along. Danny opened the Lambert Conformal map from the *Gooney-Bird's* navigation bag which held plotting equipment and instrument let-down charts. The route between Lae and *Kago Ailan* was well marked as it had been on *Alabama Aviation's* schedule when Monty and Danny flew Dr Holyman on his medical rounds.

Fixing their position as they crossed the New Guinea course was easy. Danny readily identified Umboi Island. Working on distance gone against time he was able to calculate their ground speed. He also worked out the *Gooney-Bird's* speed through the air, which varied with altitude because the atmosphere became less dense with height, thus causing less air-resistance. Theoretically they could simply climb to cruise faster, unfortunately engine performance dropped off as the air thinned, so they were forced into an altitude/engine power trade-off.

'So what do we do now?' Danny asked, but unable to keep his eyes off the fuel gauges. 'I suspect we're wanted men back at Lae. I think we broke just about every aviation and traffic regulation in the book.'

'We were running for our lives,' Monty replied. 'We were justified, but it'll take a lot of explaining and you don't think Crazy Al will forget all about the money I owe him.'

'According to you, we'll make so much money flying for CAT you'll come back with your pockets bulging. Five hundred quid will be nothing.'

'He'll probably want 100% interest, especially since we scared the pants off him during that take-off.'

Monty and Danny of course had no idea they'd done far more than *scare-the-pants-off* Crazy Al.

'Our ground-speed is one-hundred-and-thirty knots,' Danny said after fiddling with his aviation computer that was no more than a circular slide-rule. ETA *Kago Ailan* one hour: fuel remaining one hour if the wind doesn't change.'

'That's okay,' Monty beamed. 'We'll get lighter as the fuel burns off then we'll use less. We'll have plenty on arrival. Now stop watching the quantity gauge. It'll make you nervous and that makes me nervous.'

'I don't think seventy-five gallons is going to make much difference weight-wise, Monty.'

'What made you such a *glass-half-empty* guy all of a sudden?'

'A short life expectancy, I'd say.'

There is a term aviators use called *specific ground range* which just means how many miles the plane will fly per gallon of fuel burnt off. Danny spun his calculator – known in aviation circles as a prayer-wheel — and discovered the *Gooney-Bird* was making two-and-a-half miles to the gallon. Seventy-five gallons equated to one hundred and eighty-seven miles.

'See,' Monty said in an *I-told-you-so* sort of tone. 'We've got twenty miles to spare.'

Of course that depended on the gauge accuracy and calibrations.

There was about a thousand pounds of miscellaneous freight in the cargo compartment, including tea chests, sugar bags, cartons filled with cans and kitchen hardware that were all destined for various locations on *Alabama Air's* usual supply circuit.

'If it makes you happy Danny, go pitch out as much of that crap as you can. It'll keep your mind off the fuel and we might get an extra mile or two when we lighten up.'

Fortunately paratrooping was one of the *Gooney-Bird's* wartime roles. A plug panel had been fitted to the cargo door. Without it Danny would have been unable to open the door against the plane's slipstream. He slid the panel open to be greeted by the blast of air rushing past the fuselage. He spent the next half-an-hour untying the payload, hauling it piece-meal to the door and pitching it out. Whether it made a significant difference was problematic. Those customers to whom the cargo was consigned would be livid, but Monty had never planned on delivering the cargo anyway. He'd made a mental calculation of how much to reimburse them when he made his fortune with CAT.

By the time Danny returned to the cockpit he was drenched with sweat, but relieved to see the Vita Islands in view. He relaxed and finally thought they'd make it. Shortly they saw the three islands at the far eastern side of the archipelago which interested them most and had been the location of their previous adventures.

Kago Island was the largest. There was a single settlement called *Kagotaun* in *Tok Pisin* where Danny's father lived with Mayu. *Daiman Ailan* was a smaller island to the south east. It was a leper colony run by a former Catholic priest and nun. Michael Kennedy had married Marion-Celeste and while they planned to start their family, they still cared for their patients on the island. They hadn't renounced their faith so much as reduced the time they spent practising it. Danny was very fond of Michael and Marion-Celeste. He bore a scar on his left cheek from a sword wound. Marion-Celeste had stitched it up, saving Danny's face from serious disfigurement.

The last and smallest island was unnamed and known by the locals logically as *Nogat Nem Ailan.* Until recently it had been a Filipino pirate hide-out, but Danny, Angela and Monty with a lot of help from their friends drove the pirates out and so far they hadn't returned. The fact that their leader, Aleron 'Frenchy' Duval, a Foreign Legion deserter had been captured and returned to his regiment in Indochina probably had a lot to do with it.

The indigenous people were all to a greater or lesser extent *Cargo-Cult* devotees. The island and town was named because of the masses of Japanese and allied military hardware, or cargo as it was known, left behind after WWII. The islanders had salvaged as much as they needed, but you could still find pretty much anything mechanical you needed if you hunted around the rainforest long enough.

Kago Ailan morphed from a hazy blur on the horizon to a clear outline. The volcano on the north-eastern tip of the island simmered sinisterly and was probably due for another eruption at any time now. In living memory, no casualties had ever been suffered from the volcano's magma-laden flatulence, so the locals simply accepted the mountain's tantrums as part of their lives.

With ten miles to go and the airstrip in sight the port engine coughed and spluttered with shudders that rattled the airframe alarmingly. Monty instinctively identified the wayward engine from the erratic instruments on the central panel.

'Feather number one,' he ordered.

Danny looked at him doubtfully.

'We're well within range of the strip. We can shoe it in on one engine.'

Danny selected the prop-lever to feather and the fuel-mixture switch to cut-off. The engine vibration stopped instantly.

Danny and Monty exchanged glances. They were both pretty sure what the problem was.

'Water?' Danny said.

'Most likely. We didn't have time to drain the tanks did we?'

There is always the likelihood of fuel drums containing some water due to condensation. Some water simply stays emulsified in the AVGAS and evaporates in the engine as the fuel burns off, but some sinks to the bottom of the tank. After a plane has been parked for a day pilots and engineers always drain the bottom of the fuel tank to check for any gathered water. Normally a few pints clears the water contamination, but right now that water was diluting the *Gooney-Bird's* meagre fuel reserves to a critical extent, causing the engines to falter.

Monty had no other choice. If he allowed the engine to run roughly for any time it could seriously damage the cylinders. Only moments later the starboard engine cylinders misfired.

'Feather number two, Danny. We'll glide from here.'

There was no choice. It was either glide or risk the remaining engine disintegrating before they landed. Then they were going nowhere.

Danny closed down the remaining engine. You'd expect silence once the engine roar had ceased, but that was not actually the case. Wind noise made up for much of the din inside a plane's cockpit while the fuselage and wings creaked and groaned as they were buffeted by the airstream.

Danny pulled out the aircraft flight manual and flipped to the performance section. He briefly checked the chart.

'Best lift-drag ratio IAS for our weight is eight-five knots.'

Best lift-drag speed would give them the longest glide distance. That distance was always the same, but the speed needed to achieve it varied with aircraft weight. Monty eased back on the control column to reduce the plane's speed. As the gauge settled precisely onto the correct speed both Danny and Monty knew the glide ratio was 14:1. That meant they'd go fourteen feet forward for every foot downwards.

Danny made a quick mental calculation. The maths was not hard. They were at six thousand feet and a nautical mile equalled six thousand and eighty feet. Close enough to be the same. Their gliding range was just less than fourteen miles, which didn't include the turn to line up on the runway. All turns reduced lift and increased their glide angle.

Another phenomenon pilots use for judging where their plane will wind up is the target's position in the windscreen. If it remains stationary, you'll hit it: if it moves you won't. It's very handy for avoiding other planes and bird flocks. *Kago Ailan* was now close enough for them to see it was indeed rock steady in the windscreen and they'd make it – except they had to lower the landing-gear at some stage which increased wind drag and would dramatically steepen their glide path.

Danny was growing even more nervous if that was possible. At altitude nothing appears to move very fast, but now they were so close to the sea surface the sensation of water flashing past was plainly evident. Danny's hand hovered above the landing-gear selector.

'Wait for it … wait for it,' Monty said calmly.

It seemed too late. They'd almost reached the runway and even then it looked as if they'd only just make the under-run.

'Gear down,' Monty finally said calmly.

Danny selected the lever down, instantly feeling the drag affect as the wheels dangled into the slipstream. With no engines to supply hydraulic power to drive the gear down, they had to rely on gravity and a cockpit hydraulic hand-pump that Danny started pumping for all he was worth. Three lights flashed red on the instrument panel indicating the undercarriage was moving, but not fully down. The normal transit time was about twelve seconds, but with only hand-power available that could take longer, but at least gravity helped.

'Oh shit,' Monty muttered.

'What?'

'Two things. We ain't gonna make the runway and there's a plane taking off and heading straight for us.'

'The gear isn't down yet, either!'

There wasn't time for Monty to say more. He had only one chance to force the gear down and maybe reach the under-run.

He pulled sharply on the control column. The Gooney-Bird's nose jerked upwards while both pilots felt the G-force through their bodies. Monty's action affected the plane in three different ways. Two were good while one was bad:

- The extra G effectively increased the landing gear weight driving it down more quickly.
- The extra lift caused the aircraft to soar a few feet over the beach towards the under-run, but
- The IAS needle swept anti-clockwise as the airspeed dropped towards 60 knots. The airframe buffeted as airflow tumbled away from the wing surfaces. The *Gooney-Bird* approached stalling speed when the wings no longer provided sufficient lift to keep the plane airborne.

With no slipstream to maintain the balance of high and low air pressure above and below the wings, the plane dropped like a stone. Danny had no time to worry. His eyes were firmly glued on the three red instrument lights. A second before the plane bounced to the ground, the lights flashed green and Danny snapped the lever on the cockpit floor to lock, ensuring the undercarriage was held down by a locking pin.

Fortunately the *Gooney-Bird* had so little altitude to lose and with the wheels fully extended and locked into the place, it bumped onto the ground just inches beyond the beach and then ploughed into the grass-covered under-run. After a couple more bounces, the plane settled onto the ground. From the air that grass looked benign enough and should have posed no problem. The plane could simply roll onto the runway. In fact the dense grass was over ten feet high.

From the cockpit Monty and Danny could see above the grass as the *Gooney-Bird* swathed a path through. It was a rough ride until they burst onto the runway scattering a herd of wild pigs in front of them.

Still the light plane, a single-engine Cessna 140 rushed towards them. The pilot reefed his plane into the air, skimming over the top of the *Gooney-Bird*. The Cessna's shadow flashed across the *Gooney-Bird's* flight deck. The Cessna pilot's comments remain unknown since Monty had switched off his radio just after leaving Lae. The right-of-way issue was ambiguous. Normally landing aircraft have priority, but Monty had failed to broadcast his arrival. Undoubtedly the Cessna pilot hadn't noticed the *Gooney-Bird* until he was on his take-off run. His decision to continue the take-off proved wise. Had he braked to a stop, the *Gooney-Bird* would have slammed right into his Cessna.

Danny once again pumped the hydraulic lever to supply brake pressure as the *Gooney-Bird* lumbered to a halt. He only stopped pumping after Monty applied the park brake.

'Struth, Monty,' he said. 'Do you ever do a *normal* landing?'

'Told ya'll – no sweat,' Monty said, although even he sounded relieved.

'Yeah Monty, you had the situation under your usual control. We'd better have a look at the engine cowls and flight controls. There'll probably be some grass to clean out.'

Then Danny noticed a lone figure standing beside the strip, eyeing the *Gooney's* arrival with interest. A single suitcase was on the ground beside him. As Danny attached the boarding steps to the door and clambered down, the solitary figure rushed across the strip to meet him.

'Danny, Monty, you bad-bum bastards,' a voice called.

'Long Li!' Danny jumped down to meet his Chinese friend.

Sim Long Li was a legend who'd helped Angela and Danny through many of their adventures. Danny embraced him warmly while Monty shook his hand vigorously.

'I thought you were in Australia working for Colonel Serong,' Danny said.

'Got sick of it, didn't I? Taught 'em all I know anyway. Ted Serong's got a number-one bad-bum team there. They don't need me anymore. I just flew in via Rabaul and Hoskins on that *lighty* you tried to wipe out.'

They chatted on. Long Li, along with his Coastwatcher friend and colleague, Wally Trinder, had been hired as consultants on jungle combat by Colonel Serong who'd set up a training camp at Canungra in the south Queensland hinterland. Long Li had been there the best part of a year and felt it was time to come home. He lived on *Kago Ailan* too where he ran a one-man rickshaw business as well as turning his hand to pretty well anything.

'Hey you sound different,' Danny observed.

True enough. Long Li came from Singapore. Although English was used universally in the colony, Long Li's family were fishing folk who had little use for it. Their native dialect was Mandarin, which they used most of the time. Long Li's English had been decidedly broken, often mixing his *rs* and *ls*. Yet now he spoke with a broad Australian accent and used many Aussie colloquialisms he'd picked up while in Queensland.

'What the blazes are you doing here?' Long Li asked. 'Other than trying to kill anyone in the immediate vicinity.'

Danny explained how they were flying north to join CAT with the prospect of full-time, lucrative, long-term employment.

'You know, you turning up here gives me a grand idea,' Monty beamed. 'Have I got a deal for you, Long Li?'

The Chinese fellow eyed Monty suspiciously.

'What deal? I don't trust you. I know you're a bad-bum spiv.'

Long Li still hadn't learnt to say *bad-arse*.

'How can you say that, buddy? I can make you rich,' Monty gave him one of the engaging smiles he used when he was trying to get around Angela.

'Who needs rich? I got all the share of that gold bullion I need. Ted Serong paid me good too.'

'Am I thinking what you're thinking?' Danny asked doubtfully.

'Yep, sure thing. Long Li we need a loadmaster and we think you're just the man for the job ... and you speak the lingo.'

Monty grinned with satisfaction, although he wasn't accurately stating the case. Long Li certainly knew Mandarin and a smattering of Japanese, but no one had mentioned anything about Korea yet. However the idea of another adventure appealed to Long Li. He stuck out his hand and shook Monty's vigorously.

'Okay, I'm in,' Long Li said simply.

'Excellent! Let's head for George's pub and have a drink on it. We'd better get a truck and tow the *Gooney* clear of the strip and arrange some gas too.'

Chapter 5 — Flight Plan North

No one was there to meet them. As the *Gooney-Bird* had made no engine noise during its approach, no one in Kagotaun heard its arrival. So they walked into town. It was only a mile or so and they didn't rush in the tropical heat. It took about twenty minutes.

'First time we came here you met us with your rickshaw,' Danny reminded Long Li. 'You took us into town for a bob.'

'It should have been half-a-crown, but bad-bum bastard Monty stick gun in my face.'

'Oh, you're not still whingeing about that, are you?' Monty said. 'We were in a hurry.'

'You're always in a hurry,' Danny reminded him.

'Only when I'm forced into it by petty-crims and the cops.'

As they walked, they reminisced about the day they met, recalling some of their adventures. When they reached Main Street they went straight to George's pub. He and Mayu were of course delighted to see their friends. It had been a long time and it was a case of hand-shakes all round with hugs and kisses from Mayu.

While she poured beers, Monty explained what he'd need to get the *Gooney-Bird* airborne again.

'Earl Branigan will have everything you need in his lockup and there is plenty of petrol.'

Long Li finished his drink and volunteered to fetch Earl from his shed. Earl was an ex-Marine who'd gravitated to *Kagotaun* after the war when his marriage and life in general had fallen apart back in the States. He was tough, resourceful and the best, although not necessarily the cleanest guy to have on your side in a tight spot. When he returned Danny was surprised to see he was clean-shaven and had generally cleaned up his act. His shirt and shorts were neatly pressed and his work boots in good shape. Beside Earl was nineteen-year-old Kwok Mei-Hua who clung to his arm. The last time they'd met, she'd flirted shamelessly with Danny much to Angela's vexation. Now she gave him the sisterliest of sisterly pecks on the cheek with eyes only for Earl.

More reminiscing followed and it took time for Monty to bring the conversation back to their current crisis. To confirm the point, George's HF radio crackled behind the bar. Dave Bradley was on the other end. He gave George a brief summary of what had happened at Lae, thinking Monty and Danny might be heading to *Kago Ailan*.

'We're here okay, thanks Dave,' Monty said taking the microphone from George.

'I gather you've taken up Felix Smith's offer,' Dave replied. 'Just as well, it's a wasps' nest back here right now especially after knocking Crazy Al's block off.'

'What?'

'According the police inspector you took his head clean off with the Dak's undercarriage. He's talking murder or manslaughter at least.'

'C'mon, Al was going to kill us – well me anyway.'

'Everyone told you not to gamble with him ...'

'Yeah, yeah whatever. Do the cops know where we are?'

'Not yet, I don't think so, but it won't take them long when they come up blank everywhere else.'

'We'll be outta here first thing tomorrow.'

'No sweat. I'll look after your car and guitars until you sort things out. You still wanna sell the business?'

'If the price is right. Liaise with the lawyers in town. Tell 'em to put a clause appointing you chief mechanic, if you want to.'

'Will do. We'll hold the money in a trust account until we hear from you.'

'You're a legend, Dave thanks. Take out a handling fee for yourself, okay?'

'Already thought of that. Cheers and good luck.'

'Well that kinda burnt all your bridges with one match,' Earl observed. 'We'd better go and take a look at your plane.'

Danny exchanged glances with Mei-Hua who just shrugged, winked and gave him a *so-he's-my-guy-now* look.

The *Gooney-Bird* was in pretty good shape considering the abuse it had endured. Monty, Danny and Earl carefully inspected every nook and cranny of the machine. Other than clearing out grass stems there was no evidence of damage. Danny thought he noticed a dark stain on the port tyre that was possibly some of Crazy Al's DNA, but the tyre looked none the worse for wear.

'Good thing you had the props feathered,' Earl observed. 'Otherwise you'd have shredded that grass into confetti and your Dak would be joining the *Goose* yonder for major overhaul.'

Monty's Grumman *Goose* seaplane was parked at the side of the strip. It had been there for over a year now after it had been almost destroyed by gunfire while Danny and Monty and George rescued Angela from Filipino pirates. Monty flew across to *Kago Ailan* whenever he could to make repairs which were almost complete now Earl was helping him and doing most of the work.

Monty and Danny loved the *Goose* and looked forward to the day they could fly it again, which would have to be deferred for now.

'Let's get the *Gooney-Bird* refuelled,' Monty said. 'I want max range. We can leave straight after breakfast.'

Monty had his priorities, but as it turned out, they left even earlier than that.

The task of refuelling the plane was soon over. Earl was the fuel contractor for the island so providing sufficient aviation gasoline was no problem. He was doing quite well from the trade as planes from Rabaul and Hoskins regularly flew in supplies for *Kagotaun*. Monty gave both engines a thorough run and magneto check. He was pleased to report both worked perfectly. He also checked the flight controls to ensure no debris was caught in the cables. He was happy to report there were no signs of FOD.

They'd already worked out their route and this is where Monty's Pacific island-hopping experience proved invaluable. *Kago Alain* to Manila in one stage would stretch the *Gooney* to its full range, so they decided to refuel and overnight at the American Pacific trust territory of Palau. The territory was about fourteen hundred miles away. It was then another thousand miles to the

Philippines. As co-pilot, it was Danny's job to plot the course on the map and work out the fixes along the way.

Of course Monty and Earl couldn't resist a catch-up celebration, although Danny was a little more restrained. He wanted a clear head in the morning. Danny had nothing against a night's festivity provided he had sufficient sleep. So he turned in early while Monty partied on.

Danny was pleased he'd stayed sober because George woke him at about four in the morning. Monty remained comatose and snoring with relish.

'What is it?' Danny asked groggily.

'Dave just radioed in.'

'Blimey, doesn't he sleep?'

'He does, but apparently the police don't.'

'So?'

George repeated what Dave had told him. Dave was sleeping over at *Alabama Aviation* so he could start work on the Norseman at first light. Suddenly cops were crawling all over the airport. The irate inspector burst into the hangar asking where Danny and Monty had taken the *Gooney-Bird*. Dave stalled as long as he could, but the inspector already had a pretty shrewd idea where they'd gone. Monty and Danny's previous brushes with Frenchy's pirates were now legend and the inspector knew that *Kagotaun* was one of Monty and Danny's favourite bolt-holes. The police had checked everywhere else within flying range anyway.

The upshot was that the inspector commandeered a twin engine de Havilland 104 Dove and planned to fly to *Kago Ailan*. The island runway had no lights, but the plane could still leave Lae at night, planning to arrive at *Kagotaun* first light. Luckily once the policemen had finished interviewing Dave, they rather lost interest in him, so he was able to get to the radio set after they left *Alabaman Aviation's* hangar.

'It's about two hours to sun-up,' George said after consulting his luminous watch. 'They'll already be airborne.'

'We can take off using the plane's landing lights,' Danny said confidently.

Legally of course they too should wait for daylight before taking off from an unlit strip, but as they were already on the run from the law, bending a few more rules could hardly make any difference.

'Earl and I can mark the strip. We'll stand both sides of the runway with a torch each. That'll help you keep on the centre-line.'

'No problems.'

Well there was one problem actually. Monty was unconscious and no amount of shaking could wake him. Finally George lost patience, filled a pale of water and tossed the lot into Monty's face. The effect was instantaneous and lethal. Monty came to, swinging punches in all directions. He felt as if a knife had been plunged into his skull which was about to explode.

'Monty, we've gotta get out of here,' Danny insisted.

'No we don't,' Monty growled, 'we got plenty of time.'

He flopped back onto the bed and was asleep again in seconds.

'Crikey, Monty, wake up you dope,' Danny urged, trying to rouse him once more.

'I'll make coffee,' Mayu said. She'd been woken by the commotion.

'Thanks, love,' George replied. 'I'll get Earl and Mei-Hua. We'll need all the help we can get.'

'Do you think Earl will be in any better shape?' Mayu asked.

'The difference between Monty and Earl is how they hold their liquor,' George said.

That was a bit harsh. Although Monty enjoyed having a good time he was usually responsible when it came to flying and booze. But this time he'd partied way past ten then crashed. Although he'd told Dave Bradley he was leaving first thing in the morning, Monty actually planned to have eight hours sleep, wake up to a hearty breakfast and get airborne in plenty of time to arrive at Palau around late afternoon. He'd been awakened just as he transitioned from deep sleep to REM and his metabolism was quite rightly rejecting the idea.

'You'd better rouse Long Li too,' Danny reminded George as he left.

An hour later they'd gathered Long Li, filled Monty with black coffee and all bundled into Earl's truck. Mei-Hua sat next to Earl who was behind the wheel. Danny squeezed in next to her. He smiled thinly as she gave him a *you-had-your-chance-buster* look. That was true. During their last adventure together, Mei-Hua had flirted outrageously with Danny, but he only had eyes for Angela who'd promptly left to study medicine in London.

When they reached the airstrip Monty's head still throbbed abysmally.

'You drive,' he said to Danny.

'Long Li can act as co-pilot,' Danny replied. 'You'll be fine in an hour or so.'

As it turned out Danny didn't need Earl and George to mark the runway. The first streaks of dawn flashed over the horizon giving just enough daylight to make out the strip.

Mayu had prepared a box full of sandwiches, fruit, chocolate bars, coffee thermos and water canteens which Danny stowed at the rear of the cargo compartment. Long Li pulled down several of the fuselage wall-mounted seats, which Monty was more than happy to lie on and nurse his aching head. Danny shook hands with George and Earl, hugged Mayu and received yet another chaste air-kiss from Mei-Hua. He made a thorough pre-flight inspection of the plane, taking particular care to drain several pints of aviation gasoline from the tanks to ensure it was clear of water. He climbed aboard, strapped into the pilot's seat and applied the park-brake. Long Li removed chocks and secured the cargo door before clambering into the co-pilot's right-hand seat. Danny briefed him how to raise the landing gear and flaps when he was told to.

The first beams of sunlight burst into the cockpit as Danny started the engines. He quickly completed the after-start and pre-take-off checklists and back-tracked along the runway to take advantage of the maximum take-off distance. Although the *Gooney-Bird* carried no freight, it was still heavy enough with its maximum fuel load aboard.

He turned the plane, set the mixture and propeller levers and advanced the throttles to take-off boost. The *Gooney-Bird* responded beautifully and soon flashed past the small group waving farewell at the side of the runway. Danny waved back taking his eyes off the runway for a second. He was half way through his take-off run when he looked ahead and saw another plane on its landing approach straight ahead.

Blimey, not again. All this ruddy sky and I keep bumping into other planes.

The police had already arrived.

What would Monty do? That was Danny's first thought and of course the answer was obvious – press on and the devil take the hind-most. He didn't have any choice as he accelerated past V1, his rejected take-off speed. He shrugged.

Press on it is then.

The Dove pilot first saw the *Gooney-Bird* surging from the shadow of *Kago Ailan* volcano when he was descending through five-hundred feet. At first he couldn't believe he'd heard no radio call or that a plane would wait for him to land – he had priority, dammit! How could the fool in the Dak not have seen his Dove? Then he knew the 'fool in the Dak' had seen him. As soon as the plane became airborne it banked sharply to the right in accordance with the ICAO standard collision-avoidance protocol.

The Dove pilot did the same and both planes peeled away from each other just in time. The Dove completed its right-hand orbit and landed safely on the strip. A very shaken but relieved pilot, police inspector and two patrolmen stepped from their plane to a vacant aerodrome. As soon as the *Gooney-Bird* had streaked past, Earl, George, Mei-Hua and Mayu quickly piled into the truck and sped back to town. When the police finally arrived at George's pub all the accessaries-after-the-fact were tucked up in their beds and knew nothing about a wayward DC-3 or its miscreant crew.

Meanwhile the *Gooney-Bird* set a north-westerly course and cruised peacefully on. Next stop — Palau.

Chapter 6 — Chequerboard Approach

Monty recovered after another two hours sleep and several cups of coffee. He came forward and stood between the pilots' seats. Long Li handed him the en route chart and showed their latest plotted position. He checked the radio beacons from Wewak and Manus Island and peered through the cockpit windscreen. He grunted, which Danny and Long Li took as an indication of satisfaction.

Once they crossed Admiralty Island there was a great slab of Pacific Ocean ahead with precious few landmarks to guide them. However the weather was fair with no land masses for afternoon thunderstorms to form over. The cyclone season had ended as the Northern Hemisphere moved into winter, so with the auto pilot paying meticulous attention to heading and altitude, the three adventurers were able to enjoy the remainder of the flight. The engines ran smoothly and their fuel reserves were plentiful.

Monty brought Danny and Long Li a sandwich and coffee before taking over the co-pilot's seat.

'There's one hell of a bunch of ocean down there,' he observed casually.

'Nearly three-quarters of the world is covered by it,' Danny replied to show that some of his education, however harrowing, hadn't been wasted.

'How many square miles do you reckon we can see?'

'I dunno, tens of thousands maybe.'

'Okay, how many sharks do you reckon there are to a square mile?'

'How should I know?'

'Even if there're only a few, it still makes a parcel of sharks don't it?

'Shut up, Monty. It's best not to think about it and just be thankful we're up here.'

Danny'd had his share of brushes with sharks and would be happy never to repeat the experience.

'It's like flying on a clear night,' Monty continued.

'I don't see how it's the same.'

'If you look up, ain't no way you're gonna count all those stars – and that's just the ones we can see.'

'So?'

'Well they just go on and on and never stop.'

'I don't suppose they do.'

'Say you came to the end of space and it's like a great black brick wall.'

'Yeah?'

'There's gotta be something on the other side of the wall, you see. It just goes on forever.'

'Bit like the beginning of time, I guess?'

'How's that?'

'The day time began, there still had to be a yesterday, didn't there?'

'That's the trouble with long-haul flights,' Monty surmised.

'How come?'

'Too much time to think.'

After lunch they picked up a weak, flickering signal from Angaur Field. Two airfields had been established during the war and were used by both the Americans and Japanese during hostilities. After the war the largest airport, Peleliu, was abandoned, but American units still remained at Angaur since Palau had been established as a US protectorate.

They landed and followed the tower controller's directions to a parking spot. To Monty, Danny and Long Li's surprise, the Marine Corp major who met them knew who they were. At first Monty was alarmed that the long arm of Papuan law had stretched across the Pacific into American territory. However it wasn't a New Guinea inspector who had notified the US authorities, but none other than Felix Smith.

Felix knew Monty's options were limited when travelling north. He left messages at Angaur, Guam (if he chose to take the direct route to Japan), knowing he'd intercept Monty somewhere along those routes.

'Good thing you came this way,' the major drawled. 'We got a message from CAT that says General Chennault wants to meet you in Hong Kong.'

'What's he doing there? He's supposed to be in Japan or Formosa,' Monty wondered.

'He was. This is the third message we've received. He's moving around, but I dunno what he's up to,' the major replied. 'He don't confide in me, but my guess is he's wheelin' and dealin' with the Limey's for air-route franchises outa Hong Kong. Them Brit bureaucrats can make paperwork thicker than molasses.'

'It beats me how the general seems to know where we're heading all the same,' Danny said.

'They get the information from one of their major customers so it don't seem so strange to me, kid,' the major replied.

'Customer?'

'Sure. The CIA, only they don't like folks calling 'em that. CAT carried spooks all over, especially during the Chinese Civil War. Didn't do much good, the Commies won in the end. Chiang Kai-Shek's Nationalists still hold Formosa, but that's about all.'

The major invited Danny and Monty to stay overnight at the officers' club, although Long Li was relegated to the NCOs quarters. Monty was about to object, but Long Li was sanguine as he was escorted away by a burly marine sergeant. Although President Harry Truman's Executive Order 9981 had been evoked for all branches of the US armed services in 1948, declaring *'equality with regard to race, colour, religion or national origin,'* it was taking its own sweet time filtering down through the military units. You'll notice there was no mention of gender. In all fairness, as a loadmaster, Long Li merited NCO status anyway.

The following morning Long Li reported the food had been good, he was assigned a comfortable bed and the company friendly and interested in his exploits during the war. He probably had a better time than Danny or Monty. The officers tended to be either boring drunks or Ivy-League snobs who spent the entire time moaning about their isolated posting. They were also worried about the Communist threat spreading throughout Southeast Asia.

'The bastards are everywhere,' the major complained. 'First China, now Korea, Malaya and French Indochina. It's like a line of dominoes. You push the first one over and the rest tumble along after it. Burma, Indonesia and even India could be next.'

The domino analogy was nothing new. It had been concerning Western superpowers since 1945 although it wasn't until 1954 when President Dwight D Eisenhower actually coined the phrase, 'domino theory'. The South-East Asians had a valid point. European powers had lost all right to sovereignty after they failed to protect their colonies from the Japanese. Local populations wanted independence. The trouble was they always turned to Red China or Russia for the logistic help they needed and that help always came at a price.

In the presence of such uninspiring company, Danny and Monty turned in early. They arranged for the *Gooney-Bird* to be refuelled and lodged a flight plan for Clark Air Force Base. There was a certain security about being in the hands of American controllers from then on. It was something the Yanks were really good at.

The *Gooney-Bird* took off with a full fuel load and a generous supply of tasty American rations. To make matters even better, CAT management had left instructions to send the bill to the company.

'I could get used to this,' Monty said once they'd reached their cruise altitude. He'd resumed the captain's seat and munched on a *Hershey* bar with relish.

'Surely you had good rations in the Army Air Corps?' Danny said.

'You gotta be kiddin'. We were a black outfit in a white man's army so we got last pick at everything. We had a pretty good supply master-sergeant though. That guy turned into an A-grade scrounger.'

After a while Long Li replaced Danny in the co-pilot's seat and Monty gave him some flying instructions. Danny remembered how Lou Brennan, a shady ex-RAAF pilot had given him his first flight lesson en route from Townsville to Port Moresby. Long Li was getting the hang of it so Danny lay on the side-wall seats and fell asleep to the gently oscillating fuselage. Long Li woke him a couple of hours out from Clark. Monty and Danny studied the let down plates in preparation for landing. As it turned out the weather remained fine and they were guided by radar to the active runway.

What struck Danny was the size of the place. It was simply vast. So far Changi was the largest airport he'd seen and it was downright pokey by comparison. Danny was intrigued when they'd taxied across a road from the runway to the RAF parking area. A hoard of bicycles and rickshaws lined up behind a gate as the plane passed. They surged across the taxiway the instant the barrier was raised, often getting blasted by the plane's prop-wash. Danny's first impression of the Far East was that everyone was in such a rush.

Clark Field was altogether different with wide taxiways that led to parking tarmacs lined with every type of military hardware. A squadron of massive four-engine Boeing B-29 Superfortress bombers seemed to stretch for miles. They were held at Clark for maintenance servicing because of overcrowding at Japanese airfields, but would soon be bound for Okinawa and destined to bomb the wits out of Chinese and North Korean soldiers north of the 38th Parallel. No less impressive was a flight of C-97 Stratofreighters developed from the B-29. C-46s and 47s were everywhere.

The tower controller guided Monty to the CAT parking area. They were greeted by the station manager and his attractive secretary who carried a note book and recorded everything in shorthand. He confirmed that General Chennault was indeed still in Hong Kong and they were to fly there in the morning for an interview with the great man himself. The station manager's secretary, who was introduced as Valerie, observed that there were three crewmembers and not two as they'd expected. While he went back to his duties, Monty, Danny and Long Li piled into a jeep. Valerie drove them to their hotel.

'When you get to Hong Kong tomorrow, the general is staying at the Peninsula. I'm afraid we've had to find something more modest for our aircrews,' she explained with genuine regret. 'We have charts for you including the runway 13 *checkerboard approach*. It's a good idea to know what to expect.'

That evening they studied the charts during cocktail *happy-hour*.

'Interesting,' Monty opined.

'And the forecast is for a south-east wind, rain showers and overcast down to a thousand feet,' Danny said.

'Looks like we'll find out just how interesting it is then,' Monty smiled.

After supper Monty spent most of the night trying to charm Valerie, but wasn't very successful. On a base where men outnumbered women a-hundred-to-one, she could be choosey. She had her eyes firmly set on a chisel-jaw USAF lieutenant colonel so she left early, saying she'd pick them up at zero-six-hundred hours.

So chaste and sober, the *Gooney-Bird* crew were airborne at first light and set course for Kai Tak airport. Approaching late autumn the weather was indeed cloudy, consisting of flat, stratus layers. The flight was smooth with no embedded thunderstorms now the temperature had cooled. But it did mean they were directed to the *checkerboard* approach which at first was no big deal. They tracked towards the Cheung Chau NDB radio beacon which Danny tuned in and listened to its Morse code identifier – *dash-dot-dash-dash* – *dot-dot-dot-dot*. The needle pointed straight ahead posing no navigational problems. As the gauge indicator fluctuated and spun towards the rear Monty banked left onto a westerly heading. Danny then tuned the Sha Lo Wan beacon and identified its signal – *dot-dot-dot-dot* – *dot-dash-dot-dot*. The instrument pointer swung to the right. As the plane passed abeam the station Monty banked to starboard while Danny tuned in the ILS frequency and once again identified its Morse code signal – *dash-dot-dash-dash-dash* – *dot-dash-dot-dot*.

Two bars, one horizontal and one vertical, appeared on Monty's ILS indicator. Now all he had to do was keep those bars central on the gauge and he would fly along the correct course and down the glide-slope. Danny had one more NDB to tune in which was sighted at the airport. It was a busy time for the co-pilot who not only tuned the navigation aids and changed to the tower frequency, but also read the before-landing checklist as well as lowering the flaps and undercarriage when Monty required them. There were two marker beacons on track (an outer and inner that set off a flashing light and audio tone as the plane passed over them. Danny checked that the plane was at the correct height and there were no errors in the ILS.

'Six hundred feet — visual,' Danny called as they broke out below the cloud cover.

Monty looked up and there right before his eyes was the orange-and-white checkerboard. To Danny's amazement there was also a mass of buildings only feet below them. Lines of laundry were strung from one balcony to another. He was also aware of a seething throng of humanity in the Kowloon streets below.

Monty banked the *Gooney-Bird* fifty degrees to the right and to Danny's relief the runway appeared ahead just as the tower controller cleared them to land. The plane's wing-tips almost brushed the buildings as they descended the last five-hundred feet to land. A stiff southerly cross-wind sprang up that wasn't unusual for Kai Tak. Gusty cross-winds cause some pilot's trouble, but others handle them with ease. Monty was one of the latter and gently touched the starboard wheel first then the port.

'Welcome to Kai Tak,' the controller greeted with a plummy English accent. 'First time here?'

'Affirmative,' Danny replied.

'Nice job, the approach is tricky, but our pilots get used to it,' the controller remarked with an air of superiority.

Danny guessed he was referring to Cathay Pacific which had operated for six years, employing Commonwealth expatriates to fly its fleet of DC-3s. The controller guided them to the CAT parking area in a tone relegating them to a *poor-relation* status. CAT's headquarters had moved from Hong Kong to Taipei after the Chinese Civil War. Since then the company had lost its aviation dominance in the crown colony.

'Snotty Pommy bastard,' Danny muttered under his breath.

'Don't fret, Danny boy,' Monty said. 'Their Empire's crumbling around them, but they still like to keep up appearances.'

Once again they were greeted by a contingent of efficient and friendly CAT staff. Engineers swarmed over the plane and checked Monty's maintenance log. They were taken to their hotel called the *Sunlight Palace*. It was only a block from the prestigious Peninsula that still bore the bullet scars from Colonel Lee Scott Jr's WWII P-40 attack. It may not have inflicted any casualties, but scared the living b'Jesus out of senior Japanese officers billeted there at the time.

Danny was amazed at the hustle and bustle. Kowloon was just so crowded. Carts, rickshaws and honking taxis crushed through the streets amid a sea of humanity. The noise was incredible in the narrow streets framed between endless rows of terrace buildings adorned with laundry lines draped like bunting on every balcony and even across the alleyways. How anyone could find their way around was a complete mystery to Danny. The multitudes of signs were all displayed in Chinese characters. Thank heavens for Long Li.

The hotel was basic, but comfortable and clean while the staff members were scrupulously polite accompanied by the usual flurry of bowing and nodding. Porters rushed to take the crew's meagre luggage and squirrel it away in their rooms while they took advantage of *happy-hour*. Predatory hookers prowled the lounge, pestering the crew until Monty drew his Army pistol. The girls (and boys) melted away.

'Don't flash that bloody thing around,' Danny warned. 'This is still a Pommy colony, not the Wild West.'

The driver who'd chauffeured the *Gooney-Bird* crew to the *Sunlight Palace* left saying he'd check with General Chennault about an appointment. So Danny, Monty and Long Li cooled their heels waiting to be summoned by the great man.

'What sort of name is Claire for a bloke anyway?' Danny said.

'I wouldn't mention that to him if I were you,' Monty admonished. 'He ran a pretty hot-shot fighter operation during the war and from what Felix Smith tells me, he runs a tight airline too.'

After an hour they were surprised when the general walked into the lounge and introduced himself. He was about medium height, around sixty, fit looking with a ramrod military bearing and a face with more cracks than a rock face. He was accompanied by a stern looking, but impossibly handsome thirty-year-old man.

'Hi, I'm Bob Rousselot, CAT's chief pilot,' the stranger greeted with just the hint of smile as he shook hands all round.

Claire Chennault and Bob Rousselot were all business. They refused a drink and the chief pilot produced a wad of paperwork from his attaché case.

'These are your contracts, gentlemen,' General Chennault announced. 'I'd like you to study them tonight and sign them. I'll have one of my staff collect them in the morning. Meanwhile take a couple of days off. Enjoy Hong Kong's sites while we check out your bird. We'll ship you out to Takhikawa by the weekend.'

Monty gave him a *there's-nothing-wrong-with-my-plane* glare.

'Take it easy, hot-shot,' Rousselot said. He knew how to read people's faces. 'CAT mechanics will handle all your servicing needs from now on. The plane is wet-leased, but we'll do it for free just to show what good guys we are.'

Actually it was a pretty good deal and Monty knew it.

'Thanks Captain — General, we appreciate it.'

Claire Chennault and Bob Rousselot just didn't seem like guys you'd be on a first-name, buddy basis with whatever Felix Smith might have said. The two CAT executives explained that the

Gooney-Bird would operate with CAT's fleet of C-46s and 47s attached to the 315ᵗʰ Combat Cargo Squadron based in Japan.

Their task was simple: take what you're told to where you're told when you're told – period.

'We like to keep it simple,' Bob Rousselot said with another hint of a smile. 'Welcome to CAT.'

'We're fast-tracking your FAA and Chinese licence requirements, Danny,' General Chennault explained. 'You'll have to sit an FAA air law test. You'll have exemptions for everything else like our other Commonwealth pilots. There's a syllabus and past exam-papers with your contract. I expect you to complete it by the time you reach Takhikawa.'

'No sweat, sir,' Danny replied. As he was not yet twenty-one, Danny wasn't sure where he stood signing a legal document, but no one else seemed bothered.

'I understand Captain Montgomery wants you as his loadmaster, Mr Sim,' Bob Rousselot said. 'Welcome aboard, we're pleased to have you join us.'

'How do you feel about going to Japan, Mr Sim?' General Chennault asked Long Li who stared at him blankly.

'I believe the Japanese aren't your favourite bed-fellows,' the general continued.

'You are well informed,' Long Li replied.

'We have high-priced help, remember. The CIA finds out about people.'

'I'm surprised I'm on your — or their — radar, General.'

'No secret this time. We hooked up a radio link with ex-Gunnery Sergeant Earl Branigan in New Guinea. He gave you fellows a glowing reference.'

Danny was pleased to hear there was no mention of the Lae police force.

'I'm over it,' Long Li said after a pause. 'There're plenty of other wars to get on with.'

'Precisely,' Chennault nodded.

The meeting was over. The two senior pilots stood and turned to leave just as a huge, lumbering figure burst past the reception desk and into the bar. He had a face that only his mother could love and sported a shaggy beard cut Van Dyke style. With a scowl he confronted Chennault and Rousselot, but before he could speak the general raised his hand.

'*No*, Captain McGovern,' he said firmly and without raising his voice. 'For the last time — no! And this is the *last time* I want to hear about it.'

'But we can't just abandon them, General,' the big stranger pleaded. 'We never leave anyone behind.'

'We don't like it any better than you, but times change and we can't risk CAT's future operations out of Hong Kong for anything or anyone.'

As the General and Captain Rousselot turned and left, the shaggy man's shoulders dropped. He turned to the bar and ordered a triple scotch with a beer chaser. Danny was sure he saw a tear glisten in the corner of the big guy's eyes.

Chapter 7 — Earthquake

Danny, Monty and Long Li exchanged glances then turned their attention to the giant on the stool hunched over the bar. He'd already skolled the triple shot and ordered another. His face showed a mixed gamut of emotions – anger, frustration and genuine sadness. He obviously knew Chennault and Rousselot, so in a way Danny, Monty and Long Li were now his colleagues as well.

'I wonder what that's all about,' Long Li said.

'One way to find out,' Monty replied. 'The poor guy sure looks like he needs cheering up.'

'What if he wants us to mind our own business?' Danny said cautiously. The man at the bar was a big fellow with the appearance of someone who knew how to handle himself.

'Like I said – there's only one way to find out.'

So the three friends crossed to the bar and took up the remaining stools. Monty ordered more beers including one for the forlorn stranger.

'Howdy, pard,' Monty said, proffering his hand.

'Howdy pard' — *Monty you've gotta be kidding* — *puleease.*

The big man looked up.

'I'm Monty Montgomery. This is Danny McAlister and Sim Long Li. We're the new C-47 crew.'

'Jim McGovern,' the fellow replied. 'C-46 skipper. Most folks call me Earthquake Magoon.'

'Li'l Abner?' Monty ventured.

'Yeah.'

Earthquake's nickname came from a popular comic strip character. He was a big, blustering, larger than life and very destructive fellow, much like the man sitting beside Monty although he looked very subdued right then.

'If you don't mind me asking, what was all that about with the General and Captain Rousselot?' Monty ventured.

'It's that asshole, Rousselot's doin'. I know the General would go for it. He don't leave folk in the lurch, but Rousselot walking around like he's got a broomstick up his ass since he made chief pilot.'

'Go for what?' Danny asked. 'You don't look the sort of bloke who'd stop easily, if you don't mind me saying so.'

'Not at all, kid,' Earthquake smiled for the first time.

'So what was it all about?'

Thirty-year-old James McGovern was a bit of a legend in his own time. He'd been an ace serving with the 14th Air Force's *Tiger Shark* squadron who'd been credited with several kills. After the war he decided to stay in South-East Asia and joined CAT. He found his feet after a shaky start as a co-pilot. Fighters and transport aircraft were quite different flying disciplines and it took Earthquake a while to settle into the latter.

There was no love lost between Earthquake and Rousselot. The chief pilot considered him to be lazy and sloppy while the big man thought his boss was a stuffy prig. Neither was there any love lost between CAT and the Hong Kong authorities. Three years earlier Great Britain recognised Red China. In another limp-wristed appeasement deal, they agreed to hand over seventy-odd CAT planes to the Communists that were owned by the Nationalists. A lengthy court battle ensued along with some dodgy fund-raising on CAT's behalf to buy the planes before they could be delivered to the Reds.

The CIA undoubtedly had something to do with the negotiations and putting up the cash too, but no one's telling. The upshot was that although the planes were grounded in Hong Kong for a while, most of their spare parts were smuggled into Communist territory anyway. It pretty well finished CAT's Hong Kong headquarters which then moved to Taipei. It seemed that General Chennault and Bob Rousselot were trying to rebuild some bridges. Earthquake flying renegade planes into forbidden Chinese airspace would not help at all.

During the Civil War when CAT aircrews worked tirelessly to resupply the Nationalist forces, Earthquake's plane had crash-landed in enemy territory and he was taken prisoner by the Communists. After lengthy negotiations, his guards agreed to release him, but were overruled from somewhere up their chain-of-command. Earthquake finally talked his way out of captivity by accusing his guards of lying about letting him go. That appeared to have been a catastrophic loss-of-face for the guards so they eventually set him free. Six months after the crash Earthquake turned up in Hong Kong, a much leaner, meaner aviator.

'Trouble is,' Earthquake explained, 'a lotta folk helped me — including those guards in the end. Now after all this time it seems the Commie authorities have taken a renewed interest in the whole business and have arrested everyone they think was involved. They'll be tried and sent to labour camps or maybe executed.'

'How do you know this?' Monty asked warily.

'I talked to one of the guys who helped me escape. He's in gaol downtown right now awaiting trial for smuggling. I also hang out at Gingle's Cafe on the waterfront. Every smuggler, river rat and pirate passes through there. They get word from up country.'

By up country, Earthquake meant Mainland China.

'Do you think anyone has been arrested yet?' Danny asked.

'I know so. About twenty-five folk have been taken to Han Chow, a small town close to Sanshui. That includes the Zhang Wei family.'

'Zhang Wei ..?'

'Ex-land-owners and mission educated,' Earthquake continued. 'That family smuggled me extra food and medicine which damn well got me through. The Commies already confiscated all their property and parcelled it out to a bunch of incompetent lackeys. I can't just abandon them when they risked everything for me.'

'So what can you do anyway?' Long Li asked.

'There's an airstrip about a mile from where they're being held. I want to fly in, grab anyone I can and get out quick. We did that sort of thing all the time during the Civil War.'

'You're kidding, right? You plan to hop over the border and land pretty as you please?'

Earthquake nodded and even Monty was shocked.

'The place will be crawling with Commies.'

'Maybe not,' Earthquake replied. 'The Red Army has been bled white sendin' troops to Korea. There's no one left but militia. They're mostly trumped up peasants with an axe to grind against former land-owners. Some of 'em don't even have rifles. All I need is a plane. Like I said, I know the general wouldn't leave friends behind, but Rousselot's like a flea in his ear. He's so worried about offending the bloody Limeys just to get the rights to a couple of lousy air routes. It's only fifty miles over the border and we've gotta full moon for Crissake.'

'But you don't have a plane,' Monty surmised.

'Nope.'

'We do,' Danny said slyly. 'Technically we haven't signed it over to CAT yet.'

'And someone who speaks the lingo,' Monty added eyeing Long Li who grinned.

They just couldn't resist the temptation, could they? Angela would have been appalled.

*

They filed a flight plan for a training sortie. Once out of Kai Tak radar range they'd change course and head for China. Monty occupied the captain's position while Earthquake squeezed into the co-pilot's seat. Because of his two hundred pound bulk he'd installed a special canvas chair in the C-46 CAT had assigned him. Earthquake acted as navigator while Danny sat in the reclinable 'jump seat' between the two pilot stations. Long Li busied himself lowering the side wall seating.

There were fourteen seats along each fuselage wall. It would be a squash, but they should have room for everyone. To reduce the take-off weight, Monty ensured the *Gooney-Bird* carried just enough fuel for the return trip. One thing Danny noticed was how cold the weather was here late in the year. Earthquake considerately commandeered fleecy-lined leather flying jackets for each of them. The great advantage of cool temperatures was that it made the engines operate more efficiently, producing extra take-off power.

Monty nominated a SAR watch with the Hong Kong HF radio. This meant he would give regular 'operations-normal' calls every half hour. As long as the radio operator received these reports, he wouldn't worry about the plane or its crew.

There was no danger of being intercepted. Although ground units patrolled to prevent the exodus of refugees, Red China had committed all its sophisticated Russian-built planes (along with dozens of Russian pilots) to Mig-Alley along the North/South Korean border. Fortunately there were no RAF or Fleet Air Arm planes airborne that night either.

Earthquake readily picked up landmarks in the moonlight. Only occasional clouds scudded past. Waterways and tiered rice paddies reflected brightly and hill tops were easy to identify. Monty followed the Pearl River valley north west at low level. Nevertheless that sort of flying wasn't for the faint-hearted. Earthquake revelled in the experience while Monty couldn't see how it was much different to New Guinea aviation.

They found the strip close to an oxbow river bend. It was an easily recognisable feature. The town – no more than a village stockade really – stood to the east. Unlike western settlements, no lights shone from the narrow, muddy streets. Earthquake told Monty to divert well past the town before returning to land.

Whereas planes occasionally overflew the area, he didn't want to alert the residents with excessive engine noise.

Monty manoeuvred around the hill tops and made his final approach down a valley aligned with the strip. He touched down safely enough right at the very beginning of the gravel layer. It was a bumpy deceleration. Goodness only knew when the surface had last been graded. With skill and a good deal of luck, other than some uncomfortable lurching, Monty managed to dodge the worst potholes. He braked to a halt at the far end of the strip, turned the plane and cut the engines. He planned to take off in the direction he'd come to keep any noise to an absolute minimum.

Monty remained with the plane ready for a quick getaway while Earthquake led Danny and Long Li towards the village. The three men were armed with pistols from Earthquake's small arms arsenal. Of course he wasn't the kind of guy to venture through the Far East without adequate fire-power – very sensible in Danny's opinion.

As they approached they were relieved to discover no signs of alarm or soldiers mustering. What struck Danny at first was the pure medieval character of the place. The town was surrounded by a stone wall with timber panels filling any breaks. The main entrance was a system of twin gates. If the portal was guarded, it appeared that all the sentries were asleep. What did they have to stay awake for anyway? Earthquake tested the gates. They were locked and rattled as Earthquake wrenched at the timber handle.

'Ssh!' Long Li hissed.

'What now?' Danny whispered.

'There's a postern gate at the far side of town,' Earthquake explained, 'but hell, we'll just climb the wall. It ain't that high.'

He was right, the stones were loosely piled together providing plenty of purchase and foot-holes. They scrambled over the top and dropped into a laneway that ran between a line of shacks and the wall. The layout was simple enough. The main building stood in the centre of the stockade with several smaller structures closer to the walls. The whole area was so small that Danny could pretty well work out the town geography at a single glance. A bamboo barracoon had been constructed at the far end of the settlement to accommodate the prisoners. Several canvas tents stood within the enclosure.

As they crouch-ran past the main building they heard the first sounds of life. Long Li stopped abruptly and signalled the other to do the same. Slivers of light sliced through the wooden window slats. Laughter and raucous conversation came from within the doorway. There was quite a party going on so it was unlikely the merry-makers had heard the *Gooney-Bird* approach above the din they were making.

Long Li peeked through one of the larger cracks in the window. He estimated a platoon sized group of militia was inside tucking into supper with copious amounts of rice wine. Cigarettes dangled from every soldier's lips and the room's atmosphere was rank with stale tobacco smoke. About half the men were playing mah-jong and cards while a couple of bored looking whores waited to see who came up trumps and won enough for their services.

'Okay, they look like they're there for the long haul,' Earthquake estimated. 'No prizes for guessing where the prisoners are.'

They crept towards the barracoon.

The enclosure was merely secured by a padlocked slide bolt that Earthquake broke with ease and very little sound. The prisoners could have probably done the same, but they seemed resigned to their fate. Where were they going to run to anyway? Earthquake roused the sleepy, shivering occupants while Long Li urged everyone to stay calm. There were some dialect issues, but he managed to convey the general message. Many of the startled men, woman and children spoke some English thanks to an Anglican missionary who had been summarily deported after Mao's Communists took control.

Sure enough Earthquake recognised many of the people who'd helped him through his captivity. A few others had simply been scooped up in the net. But there was no sign of the Zhang Wei clan.

In a mixture of broken English and Long Li's interpretation, they discovered the family was still in their property home overlooking their confiscated terraced rice paddies and orchards on a hill along the track half way between the town and the airstrip. The militia planned to arrest the family in the morning. The barracoon was overcrowded as it was. The captives said there was supposed to be a guard on the Zhang Wei villa all night. However the militia was poorly disciplined and badly trained, while lust and the lure of rice wine were far more attractive alternatives to a cold, boring night's guard duty.

Earthquake thought the best plan was to use the postern and sneak around town towards the plane. The refugees grabbed what little they could carry and followed him while Danny and Long Li acted as rear-guard, ensuring there were no stragglers. The back gate posed little resistance to Earthquake's size-fourteen boot and the escapees surged to freedom.

The Zhang Wei house was easy enough to spot silhouetted against the moonlit sky.

'You take these people to the plane, Earthquake,' Danny said. 'You're so tall they won't lose sight of you. Get 'em all aboard while Long Li and I'll rouse the others. We'll be right behind you.'

Earthquake looked uncertain for a second, then nodded and led his fugitive delegation to the *Gooney-Bird*.

Danny and Long Li made the short climb to the Zhang Wei villa. It certainly looked a cut above the neighbouring accommodation. The house was large surrounded by a six-foot wall. The front gate lay ajar and they could see right through to the villa's front door. As the liberated captives had predicted, there was no sign of guards.

'What if there're sentries inside?' Danny asked.

'You lie low,' Long Li replied. 'Stay out of sight. I'll do the talking. I'll tell 'em they're wanted in town. Try not to shoot anyone.'

'That's not like you.'

'They're not Japs and it'll make too much noise.'

Danny kept guard outside the main garden gate while Long Li walked through the now frost covered courtyard and hammered on the front entrance. He called out something that Danny couldn't understand. After some further banging and what Danny interpreted as pleading and reassurance from Long Li, the door squeaked ajar. An elderly man stood in the light of a single flickering candle.

After more furtive discussion, Long Li called to Danny again.

'It's okay, I've explained the situation. This is Zhang Wei Peng. He's head of the household. We've got to wake everyone up now.'

'Everyone?' Danny queried as he approached kowtowing to Peng's bobbing. It was kind of infectious.

'There's only him, his wife and daughter left. His two sons were conscripted into the People's Volunteer Army. They're somewhere in Korea between the Yalu River and the 38th Parallel right now.'

'Conscripted into a *volunteer* army ..?'

'Welcome to Red China, Danny.'

'It'll still be a squeeze on the plane. Thank heavens there're no servants.'

'They all took off pretending to be good little Commies when the troops showed up.'

'Probably wise,' Danny conceded pragmatically.

It took some moments to wake the family, who considering they expected to be arrested in the morning, were sleeping soundly. It was as if they'd already accepted their destiny and were prepared for the worst which they'd endure with Oriental stoicism.

'There won't be room for any possessions,' Danny warned Zhang Wei who understood English pretty well. 'Just bring all the warm clothing you can put on.'

Soon Peng's family were assembled by the front door. They'd layered up with padded clothing and fur caps. Peng's wife, Daiyu was quite young, maybe in her late thirties indicating she'd married in her teens, which wasn't unusual. Their eighteen-year-old daughter was named Jiao. Her moon-shaped face stared at Danny framed by her fleecy hood. Even so Danny saw that she was a flawless beauty.

Why are they always so damned drop-dead gorgeous?

But there was no time to reflect on that now.

'Let's go,' was all he said as he led the way to the airstrip.

They reached the gates when the still night air was shattered by the rattle of gunfire. Rifle shots popped in the distance and

Danny saw muzzle flashes coming from the track leading to the strip. The militia platoon was dimly visible racing along the track firing indiscriminately as they went. They were only two hundred yards from the *Gooney-Bird* when Danny was sure he heard pistol shots coming from the plane. Not that either Monty or Earthquake was likely to hit much from that range at night.

One of the soldiers must have decided to do his duty and check on the prisoners, or had simply stepped outside to relieve himself and discovered they were gone. Whatever the reason the breakout had been discovered and the militia was in hot pursuit. They were pretty eager to get it done, because they knew they were in big trouble if their captives got away.

The militia surged onwards and it seemed they would over-run the plane in minutes. Monty had no choice. There were twenty-five genuine refugees on board. He couldn't allow them to be recaptured. Having tried to escape proved them guilty of treason in Communist eyes.

Then to Danny's horror, he heard the *Gooney-Bird's* engines splutter into life. Monty poured on the power with no thought of a checklist, while Earthquake emptied his pistol's magazine in a volley of parting shots from the paratrooper exit door. When the gun was empty Earthquake slammed the door shut.

The plane staggered airborne at the very limit of the strip. Monty climbed the machine ahead before making a lazy turn to fly back down the Pearl River. Soon the engines droned into silence as the plane slipped from sight. The militia fired several random shots until a sharp command from their officer silenced them.

'Oh, shit,' Danny hissed through clenched teeth as the platoon reformed and turned its attention to the Zhang Wei Villa.

Chapter 8 — Freedom Trail

'We're so out of here,' Danny whispered under his breath, turning to Long Li. 'Quick, round the back before they see us. If we can hide out they might think we got on the plane with the others.'

They hustled the Zhang Wei family back through their courtyard. Peng and Daiyu started protesting earnestly as they rushed past the house.

'What are they saying?' Danny asked.

'There's no back gate,' Long Li replied. 'Only one way in or out.'

'Bugger.'

There were two small garden sheds in the court yard, but they were far too small to conceal five people. They were also full of garden tools and several bicycles.

'We hide in house,' Jiao suggested softly in English without the slightest trace of an accent although her grammar was a little abrupt.

'It's the first place they'll look.'

'We have cellar and loft. Only chance anyway.'

She had a point. They crept back to the front entrance and sneaked inside, bolting the door behind them. The villa wasn't particularly impressive once inside. It consisted of one large central chamber along with two bedrooms and a store cupboard. The kitchen and privy looked as if they were separate, add-on buildings joined by doorways to the main house. Both were too small to act as hiding places anyway. A trap-door led from the storage area to the cellar which wasn't big enough to accommodate the family as well as Danny and Long Li.

'You all hide down there,' Danny said. 'Bolt the door and we'll pile stuff on top. Long Li and I'll take our chances in the loft.'

Peng was about to protest, but Danny hushed him.

'It's the only chance and we're the ones with the guns if it comes to a shoot-out. You don't want to get in the way of any stray bullets.'

The Chinese family descended the steps obediently. It was pitch black down there and posed a terrifying prospect. After they heard a slide bolt click into place, Danny and Long Li piled brooms, jars and several small crates over the hatchway. A wooden ladder led to the loft. Danny and Long Li clambered up to find the bamboo slats were uneven, riddled with gaps although covered with straw and sacking. A dozen chickens roosted there.

'What the blazes ..?' Danny sighed.

'They come for the night to keep warm and stay safe from wildcats and foxes,' Long Li whispered as he dragged the ladder into the loft to discourage any inquisitive militiamen.

'That's gross. They'll crap everywhere,' Danny whispered. 'I thought these people were well off.'

'It's relative, Danny — now stop being so judgemental and shut up.'

They were just in time. Seconds later the guards banged at the door, yelling for the occupants to show themselves. When there was no response the soldiers tried pounding the door down. It didn't budge until several rifle shots blasted the latch and bolt to pieces. The door smashed open and a dozen grey-clad figures burst into the villa with their rifles at the ready.

An officer strode in behind his men. He wore a peaked cap sporting a red star emblem that typified Communist Chinese troops. He drew his pistol and waved it around vaguely indicating that his men should search the building. It only took seconds for them to discover all the rooms were empty. They poked around the store cupboard, but failed to notice the trap-door. Then the officer turned his attention to the loft. With the ladder hidden above, there was no way for the soldiers to immediately climb to investigate.

Suddenly the officer babbled orders in a staccato voice. Long Li looked decidedly uncomfortable. Two soldiers drew long bayonets from their belts and clipped them to their rifle barrels. They jabbed the points between the bamboo slats on the loft floor. The troops had to stretch, but the blades still penetrated about six inches through the poles. Then one fellow had the bright idea to stand on a stool and was about to make some serious inroads into the loft when Long Li silently rolled towards the chickens. He grabbed the first roosting bird and hurled into the air. It cackled and flapped to the floor in a cloud of ruffled feathers.

Long Li shooed the other birds after it. A dozen birds filled the room in frenzied, squawking pandemonium.

The diversion worked. The peasant militiamen were neither the brightest nor most dedicated unit. They were poorly provisioned and the thought of a dozen fowls in the cooking pot overcame any sense of duty. Discipline dissolved as they scrambled after the chickens. The officer yelled to try and restore order, but his men ignored him until he fired a shot through the roof, bringing down dust, shattered tiles and a cloud of plaster. The gunshot only panicked the chickens further. Some tried to regain the loft, but Danny and Long Li shooed them away.

Finally the birds calmed down and clucked around the villa floor. The officer ordered his men to round up the chickens, which they did quite expertly. He seemed satisfied and with one final glance, he ordered his squad back to the stockade. They might be in trouble for losing the prisoners, but at least they'd have full bellies. Danny felt a little sorry for them. They were just ignorant, simple people who were being pushed around by a political behemoth they neither wanted nor understood.

Danny waited for the chatter of voices and clatter of equipment to melt away to silence before he dared lower the step-ladder. He checked beyond the villa walls to see that the soldiers had indeed gone while Long Li cleared the trap-door and called for the Zhang Wei family to come out.

'Okay,' Danny said. 'We've got two choices. Hide out until tonight and see if Monty and Earthquake come back for us. I know they'll try, but General Chennault and Bob Rousselot are more likely to ground them until they ship out for Japan. So we can't count on that. Also chances are the militia will be waiting for Monty to try again and maybe bag him before they have to tell their bosses they've lost their prisoners. Our best bet is to head for the border. The quicker we get out of here the better before those guards start to think a little harder and maybe do a more thorough search. Just bring the clothes you wear, any food you have and don't forget your identity papers. You'll need 'em when we get to Hong Kong.'

That's it Danny — nice and confident — not 'if' — 'when'.

'We've got to get down-river past Han Chow before daybreak. The river is our best bet. Travel at night, hide out by day. What we need is transport.'

'I show you,' Jiao said.

After scrounging as much rice as they could, the five fugitives went outside. Jiao led them to where the bicycles were stacked. The bikes were well maintained and the tyres pumped up. They pulled the bikes from the shed and wheeled them to the front gate before mounting up.

'Our servants took theirs, but Father forbade them taking the boys' bicycles. They'll need them when they come home from war,' Jiao explained, rather optimistically in Danny's opinion.

It had been years since Danny had ridden a bike and he was pretty shaky to start with. The condition of the track didn't help either especially as the bike he rode was a couple of sizes smaller than he'd have liked. They headed down the terraced paddy field embankments, keeping the villa between them and town. When they reached the riverside track they turned east. That was the riskiest part of the route, because it passed right beside the stockade.

At first everything went smoothly. The militia was once again preoccupied with carousing and seemed to have forgotten they were in deep trouble. Maybe they thought they might as well enjoy themselves while they could.

Peng led the way followed by his wife and Jiao while Danny and Long Li brought up the rear. They were just passed the stone wall when a lone figure stepped onto the track ahead of them. He carried a revolver and there was no mistaking him. He was the officer commanding the militia detachment. He didn't say a word, but simply raised his hand commanding the escapees to stop.

As he approached, Danny reached for his pistol, but Long Li rested his arm across Danny's and shook his head.

'No shots or they'll all be out here,' Long Li urged.

'What're we gonna do?'

'Dunno, but he hasn't called out the guard yet. Pity the Commies confiscated most of the Zhang Wei's stuff. I don't reckon they're flush with bribe money anymore. Maybe he wants to parley.'

Indeed the Chinese officer started a solemn conversation with Peng in an intense whisper. Even in the moonlit dimness, Danny saw the officer was just a kid, barely older than himself.

By this time all five cyclists stood in a line in front of the soldier who spoke in quite acceptable English when he identified Danny as a *foreign devil*.

'I have bike too,' he said.

'Seems everyone in China does,' Danny replied curtly.

'No. I mean I come.'

'With us?'

'Yes. I come. I university student, not soldier. I study in Canton, but government send me here. Go to Korea soon. They make me militia officer because I only one who can read and write. In regular army I probably am a private. They maybe shoot me for letting prisoners escape. Who know? I come with you.'

'What about the others?'

'They simple men. They don't think about tomorrow. Too many anyway.'

Danny and Long Li exchanged glances and shrugged.

'Okay. Grab your bike and let's get going. What's your name?'

'Chan James Weo,' the student-soldier replied.

I can't believe I'm saying this, but hooray for tertiary education and dedicated missionaries. At least I can communicate with these beggars.

They made good time, but as dawn approached they knew they'd have to find somewhere to hide. Long Li would go unnoticed except he wore the bomber jacket Earthquake had provided. Danny's size and appearance on the other hand just stood out. Having a militia officer along had advantages. They could pretend Danny was a prisoner under guard, but thought they'd leave that ploy until absolutely necessary. It would only draw attention to the group. They were better off staying out of sight.

Luckily the woods grew thickly along the riverbank and they hid among the trees at dawn. The night had been bitterly cold and a mist shrouded the river, but as the sun eased above the horizon, it provided some warmth. They lay low all day with only cold rice, mandarins, salted fish and river water to sustain them.

Their other problem was that China got so downright busy as the day progressed. Many people lived along the river bank as it was the life-blood of the area both as a mode of transport and food provider.

'We'll never get to the border by road, even if we had a truck,' Danny conceded.

'What do you suggest?' James Weo asked, so Danny explained and told everyone to relax because they'd been awake all the previous night and they were going to be up the entire following one.

They dozed for the rest of the day staying well hidden in the forest. Jiao crept beside Danny and sat beside him.

'Thank you,' she whispered. 'You brave man. My father say he owe you great debt.'

'He doesn't owe me anything. We aren't out of the woods yet.'

'Yes, we still in woods,' she said with a puzzled look.

'No I mean ... never mind.'

Danny'd learnt how literal oriental people could be when it came to expressions English speakers took for granted.

She removed her hat revealing her shoulder length straight jet black hair and when she smiled Danny thought she was simply stunning. She had a calm and innocent charm that Danny found beguiling. After a while she dozed off and Danny went to relieve himself. When he returned he found James Weo was in the mood for conversation.

'You know that girl is thinking of you,' James said.

'She's asleep.'

'Then she's dreaming of you.'

'How do you know that?'

'It's written in her eyes.'

'You fancy her too – it's written in yours,' Danny smiled.

Jiao certainly was a corker, but Danny wasn't sure how he felt about that. Crikey, he'd only just met the girl, so he changed the subject.

'No offence, but you don't seem to have taken to soldiering very much?' he remarked.

'None taken at all. I'm a Buddhist by birth, education and faith actually. War and violence don't come to me naturally like you.'

'It took a bit of getting used to. Don't you feel you're running out on your country, though?'

'Red China won't miss me. It's been a big mess for centuries. Civil war, bandits, warlords, epidemics, flood, famine, injustice and incompetent government – you name it, we've had it. Many people think Communism is good for China. Maybe, but they still make a mess of running the show. Millions killed in opium wars, with Japanese and civil war. Now we fight in Korea. It never ends.'

'Human nature, I'm afraid. Whatever the UN say, they can't stop wars. We're just like every other species on earth. We fight for supremacy and survival.'

'You very philosophical. You have good education.'

'Self taught,' Danny said with a grin. 'Get some rest. We've got a big night.'

The hustle and bustle along the riverbank died almost immediately after nightfall. Steady boat traffic had cruised up and down the river all day, but now the sampans and junks moored for the night. Lanterns glittered from the larger vessels while the smaller craft were secured to the bank. The road and river became silent and deserted as the local people closed the shutters and doors for protection against the oncoming chilliness.

The six fugitives finally felt safe enough to venture to the riverbank. They selected two sampans from the dozen along the shore. Danny had no qualms about pinching them. He wondered if anyone really owned anything in Red China any more anyway. Danny, Jiao and James manned the first while Peng, Daiyu and Long Li paddled behind. No one stopped them or noticed the stolen boats as the current swiftly carried them downstream. They travelled half the night with ease. The moon was only one night on the wane and gave plenty of monochrome illumination. Sometime after midnight Danny dipped his fingers into the river and licked the icy water from his fingers. He smiled when he tasted its brackishness. The water was now tidal and they were approaching the sea.

The border was close, but so were Communist and RN patrol boats which could both be dangerous. If they were spotted there was no way they'd escape in the sampans. Initially Danny thought of heading for shore and running the gauntlet with border guard patrols, but there were still lookout towers and barbwire barricades to cross. So it was time for plan B.

Chapter 9 — A Little Bit of Piracy

They had to choose their target carefully. They needed an easy enough mark, but big enough for them to get away with it. What they wanted was a motorised fishing junk, large and with sufficient speed to run the Communist border blockade yet small enough to go unnoticed and for Danny and Long Li to handle. The Zhang Wei family were not sailors and neither was James Weo.

There was also the matter of a crew to deal with. Under cover of darkness they set off to hunt out their prey. The further down river they drifted the better and more varied their prospects were, but also posed another dilemma. Grab the first boat you see and risk discovery as you make your run for it or wait for the last moment and less chance of detection and maybe less choice. It was a balance of risks.

Finally Danny saw what he was looking for. He stopped paddling, allowing the second sampan to draw alongside. Long Li nodded in agreement. The vessel they'd spotted wasn't a junk at all, but a 25 foot, single cabin ketch with an auxiliary diesel motor that had been converted into a fishing boat. Although not the most common type of craft on the Pearl River – junks held that position – this ancient vessel wasn't unique and probably a relic from bygone opium trading days. The ketch was similar to *Rocky Road* and *Lucky Lady*, two of Danny's father's boats that he'd sailed in New Guinea.

A line of great cormorants was perched along the gunwales. Their legs were tethered to the hull for the night although their neck-snares had been removed for comfort. The birds would sleep on deck ready for tomorrow's diving when the chokers would be replaced to prevent the bird swallowing the larger fish, but allowing small fry into their stomachs. Danny estimated there could be no more than two or three fishermen on board. It was too cold for them to stay on deck all night with very limited space below for any more than that to fit.

The sampans glided under the ketch's bow. Danny and Long Li secured both boats before scrambling onto the larger vessel's deck. James Weo followed. All three men drew their pistols.

There were two crew members huddled in the cabin. They slept beside a tiny, portable oil stove that provide scant warmth, but would be ready to boil tea and heat rice when they awoke. Except they were awoken early.

While Danny stood guard and scanned the deck for any unexpected arrivals, Long Li and James Weo crept close to the snoring fishermen. Long Li tapped the nearest man on the shoulder. He started, sat bolt upright and gazed in horror down the business end of Long Li's gun. The second man jerked awake with a similar reaction. James Weo simply placed his finger to his lips.

No harm will come to you. Just do exactly what we say. Now put on your warm clothes and come with us. No fuss, no noise and no one gets hurt.

Danny and James Weo herded the terrified men to their boat's side as Peng, Daiyu and Jiao clambered aboard. James spoke softly to the fishermen, bowing respectfully with every word.

A thousand pardons, esteemed comrades, but it's a change of craft for you two. Gather your birds and belongings. Put them in the sampans. Good. Now in you get and cast off. We are truly sorry for this inconvenience, comrades, but we are desperate and have great need.

James Weo pulled the last of his Yuan Renminbi Bank of China notes from his pocket and handed them over to the fishermen.

My apologies, it is all I have.

The fishermen didn't know what to make of that. They exchanged puzzled stares, but took the money eagerly. They could understand being robbed, but someone paying for the privilege was confusing. Still they paddled away thankful to be alive. River pirates weren't always so considerate, but then again there were far better soft targets approaching the river estuary. So why they'd been singled out was baffling.

Danny was pretty sure the first thing they'd do when they reached shore was find the nearest police station. He was momentarily distracted as he heard the growl of aero-engines overhead. The droning faded westward along the Pearl River. Danny shook his head. He'd made his decision and he'd have to stick with it.

He started the motor without difficulty and they cruised towards Hong Kong. Now they entered one of the most densely populated areas of Southern China with a myriad of river traffic and buildings crowding every inch of the foreshore. Their chances of going unnoticed were good amongst so much other shipping including giant ocean-going vessels. They were just a tiny speck in a huge delta with many tributaries, inlets and mud banks.

Suddenly there was an enormous risk of becoming lost, but Long Li seemed to have a natural empathy for the river's geography.

Unfortunately, navigationally it meant they were safest keeping to the centre of the main watercourse. The down-side to that strategy was that it was precisely where they were most conspicuous and ran the greatest risk of colliding with large steamers. They decided to chance it anyway and stayed in midstream.

Then Long Li spied open water and they knew they'd made it to the coast. Macau lay off the starboard bow while Hong Kong and Kowloon were to port. There was no fuel gauge aboard the launch. In fact there were no instruments at all, so Danny prayed they'd have enough diesel to at least reach neutral waters.

The ketch was rigged with fore and aft masts and a bowsprit.

'Keep her steady,' Danny said to Jiao. 'I'll see if there are any sails stowed somewhere.'

He scrounged around and found a shabby mainsail and spanker.

'Let's get 'em aloft,' he called to Long Li.

There was little wind, but the sails finally filled and the launch increased speed by a knot or two. Long Li's main task was staring into the night to ensure they avoided other craft. There were some near misses, and once they scraped the side of a motor junk, but they cruised on.

However there were alert eyes on the Pearl River Delta that night. A small Red Chinese patrol boat prowled the disputed watery boundary between Communist China and the New Territories. The craft was one of a number of such boats that cruised back and forth hunting for smugglers and refugees. Considering how overcrowded the mainland was, you'd think the

Red government wouldn't miss a few escapees and be pleased to see them go. But as in Russia, totalitarian states seemed to want to hang onto their reluctant citizens.

This particular patrol boat wasn't much larger than the ketch Danny and his companions now occupied, but it was manned by a crew of four sailors augmented by a squad of marines. Each marine carried a rifle while a light machine gun was mounted on the bow.

It appeared that the marine sergeant wasn't particularly concerned about Danny's vessel other than it differed from the surrounding junks. It was simply time for a routine check as his men were growing bored and careless after a long stretch of duty.

With all eyes looking ahead on the kidnapped vessel, no one noticed the patrol boat surging up from astern. Long Li was uncertain where the border actually lay, but James Weo was convinced they were very close.

'Looks like we made it after all,' Danny said, patting Long Li on the back and was pleasantly surprised when Jiao embraced him warmly even if it was through several layers of padded clothing.

That was when they heard the loud hailer bellowing orders. Danny couldn't understand of course, but there was no doubting the intent. He turned in dismay to see the gunboat powering forward. It would overtake them in minutes.

'What do we do?' Peng asked.

'Skedaddle,' Danny replied, gritting his teeth in determination. 'We haven't come this far just to be recaptured.'

Meanwhile Long Li was assessing the opposition. The gunboat deck was now awash with lights. He made out half a dozen marines standing on the deck and assumed that was the entire complement. A spotlight beam sliced across the surface like a tentacle searching to expose Danny and his companions.

'Get down, Danny,' Long Li warned. 'Stay in the wheelhouse. They won't be expecting a Caucasian.'

Danny obeyed while James Weo took over the helm just as the searchlight blazed onto the ketch's deck, dazzling all aboard. The light beam bounced erratically when the gunboat oscillated in the fishing boat's wake. The gunboat slowed as the helmsman tried to steady his vessel. The loud hailer rattled again unintelligibly.

'What's he saying?' Danny asked as he crouched beside James Weo.

'What do you think?' the student soldier replied. 'They want us to pull over.'

'No bloody way!'

Danny shoved the throttle fully forward, which made little difference – maybe a knot or two, but the growling engine made him feel better. More howls came from the loud-hailer although the ketch's engine almost drowned them out. What it didn't drown out was the chatter of machine gun fire as the patrol boat fore-gun opened up. A line of fountains sprayed just ahead of the fleeing boat.

Danny pressed on.

A second burst splattered closer right along the ketch's starboard bow.

Still Danny maintained his course.

The next salvo tore into the transom, spraying timber shards across the deck and shattering the rudder connections. The ketch was now uncontrollable other than manipulating the sails. Danny raced for the main sheet cleat, released the line and pulled for all he was worth to drag the sail as close to the wind as possible.

'Long Li lend a hand. Hold her tight to the wind. I can feel it biting!'

Sure enough a morning adiabatic onshore breeze filled the sails, surging the ketch's hull through the water. The marines levelled their rifles and a volley of rifle fire exploded from the gunboat. Bullets slashed through the mainsail, tearing the ancient canvas to flapping rags. In any event sail-power alone would have proved useless against the gunboat's speed. Yet the ketch's engine drove on maintaining a straight course. Danny knew they were just lucky and the smallest change in current would send the ketch in any direction.

A second rifle volley was aimed lower. Sharp cracks split the air as bullets slammed into the hull.

Jiao screamed.

'It's no good,' James Weo wailed. 'They'll kill us if we don't stop.'

'No way,' Danny yelled. 'You up for a fight, Long Li?'

'No choice,' Long Li grinned wickedly, drawing his pistol. 'They won't expect resistance.'

'James,' Danny said. 'This'll test your commitment. You've got a gun, are you ready to use it?'

James Weo nodded uncertainly. Danny was unconvinced, but it would have to do.

'Peng, get your family to the bow. Be ready to jump for it if bullets start flying. Try and grab something that'll float. Those fish boxes should do the trick.'

The gunboat's steering console was situated at the hull centre. Three marines stood in the stern while the remaining three were at the bow. Danny ducked along the gunwales making sure he stayed out of sight.

'We stay down until they get close,' he instructed Long Li. 'You take the three blokes in the front — I'll take the back. They won't expect that. Maybe we can catch 'em napping. James, you take out the helmsman.'

James Weo stared at him blankly.

'The bloke who's steering. Shoot him when we get close enough.'

James Weo looked appalled and simply stared at his gun barrel. He'd only fired it once and that was into the Zhang Wei Villa roof.

'Check you have a full clip. Make every shot count,' Danny said.

Long Li nodded grimly. Two — maybe — three pistols against half-a-dozen rifles and — maybe — a machinegun — long odds. Surprise was all Danny and Long Li had in their favour.

One source of comfort was the gunboat marines had ceased firing. Possibly they were conserving ammunition or simply knew they were gaining on the ketch and could bide their time. In less than five minutes the gunboat drew alongside the ketch, nudging its side.

As the vessels' gunwales ground together, Danny and Long Li sprang from hiding. Both loosed off a couple of rounds straight away. What happened next wasn't quite what Danny was expecting. It was really hopelessly unrealistic of him to think he could take out six armed men with one burst from a pistol on a pitching deck.

No one was hit, but the marines all ducked for cover. There was enough hardware for them to hide behind, so Danny and Long Li no longer had a clear shot. What James Weo was up to was anyone's guess. Danny dodged instinctively as a stray shot came from the gunboat. Fortunately the machinegun was too far forward to come to bear on the ketch's deck so that particular item of fire-power was pretty well out of the combat picture.

Pity we're out of cash. Now might be a good time to consider a spot of bribery.

Suddenly James Weo stepped up and stood on the ketch's gunwale, seemingly oblivious of the peril he faced. He'd discarded his overcoat, revealing his militia lieutenant's uniform. Identifying himself as a Red Army officer, James Weo screamed at the marine sergeant to stand his men down and show himself. Yelling seemed to be a good oriental military approach when dealing with underlings – probably universal military behaviour.

The sergeant wasn't to be cowed quite as easily though. Although he was uncertain, a shouting match developed between the two men. As far as Danny could work out, it went something like this:

James: How dare you attack a military officer?
Sergeant: How do I know who you are?
James: Can't you see this uniform, fool?
Sergeant: What are you doing here?
James: I have my orders. This is a secret mission.
Sergeant: Show me your orders.
James: Don't be a fool. I don't carry papers that can be captured by our capitalist enemies.

It was pretty thin stuff on James Weo's part, but considering the stress he was under, it was probably the best anyone could do. Unfortunately the sergeant had his doubts that grew every second. By then the gunboat and ketch were pretty well wedged together. Danny and the gunboat steersman both had to throttle back to idle to prevent their engines from overheating and seizing.

Seeing a great foreign devil lurking around on deck was enough to convince the sergeant that he smelt a sizeable rat. Danny and his crew no longer had the advantage of surprise and the sergeant seized his opportunity.

He spat a quick order. He men jerked up right and levelled their rifles.

'Down!' Danny yield.

He dived across the deck and rugby-tackled James Weo from the gunwales just as a fusillade of shots whistled overhead. They crashed to the deck, winded, but otherwise unhurt. Long Li fired back, but only drew return shots in his direction. The marine rifles were bolt action weapons, so the rounds came several seconds apart. Danny then heard the sergeant shout another command which he knew meant the marines were about to board the ketch. Peng and Daiyu hadn't abandoned ship, but were trapped crouched behind the ketch's bowsprit. Jiao stood defiantly protecting them, although what she thought she could do against hot lead was unclear.

Cheers, Long Li. It's been nice knowing you.

Danny was about to face the oncoming attack and make damned sure he took a couple of the red bastards with him.

Then his whole world turned brilliant red. A blinding flash filled the entire night sky. The marines were now black silhouettes framed against a scarlet backdrop. Danny heard the rattle of what could only be more machinegun fire, but was unaware where the shots fell or at whom they were aimed. Whatever else had happened, the marines stopped in their tracks. They froze just as they were about to board the ketch. Then Danny saw a parachute flare floating downwards, illuminating the night sky.

Seconds later, the ketch was overshadowed by a giant metal form that loomed across its bow and drew alongside. The ketch was now squashed between the gunboat and another mysterious vessel. Suddenly there was the clatter of confusion when armed men leapt aboard the ketch. They dashed across its deck to confront the Communist marines. Outnumbered and out-gunned the marines had no choice. They dropped their weapons and raised their hands.

Danny recognised the new-comers immediately. They were members of the Hong Kong Water Police. The craft was an ex-WW II sixty-foot motor torpedo boat – fast manoeuvrable and well armed. A tall, rangy fellow in an RN uniform strode confidently across the ketch's bow. He spoke sharply in Cantonese to the marine sergeant with such an air of confidence and control, the communist NCO simply nodded in agreement.

'What's he saying?' Danny asked Long Li.

'It's a bit out of my dialect range, but as far as I can tell he's more or less informing the Commies they're violated British Sovereign Territory and he'd very much appreciate it if they'd bugger off.'

The Hong Kong water police helped the gunboat crew disentangle the wedged vessels. Oddly, the two crews worked cheerfully together and soon the gunboat drifted away and set course back upstream.

Danny and Long Li got to their feet to be greeted by the RN officer whose sleeves bore the two-and-half bars of a lieutenant-commander.

'Now just what do we have here?' he asked in a plummy voice that smacked of wealth and privilege. But Danny noticed his left chest bore WWII ribbons from the icy North Atlantic and European campaigns as well as the purple and white stripes of the Distinguished Service Cross. He may have been some lord's toffee-nosed son and heir, but he was a gutsy toffee-nosed son and heir.

'Blimey,' Danny replied. 'I never thought I'd be so pleased to see a Pom.'

'Ah, a kinsman of Bold Jack Donahue, I presume,' the naval officer smiled urbanely.

'G'day, Danny McAlister, lately from Queensland and New Guinea. Pleased to meet you.'

'Jeremy Fuller St Chalfont-Smyth. The pleasure is all mine, I'm sure.'

'Crikey that's mouthful. You sure there isn't an honourable in there somewhere?''

'Second son of the earl actually, but Jeremy will suffice, thank you. It looks as if you need a tow, old boy. Now be a good fellow and introduce me to your companions while my chaps get us under way.'

Part 2 — Korea

MANCHURIA
NORTH KOREA
SEA OF JAPAN
Beijing
Pyongyang
38th Parallel
JAPAN
Seoul
SOUTH KOREA
Tokyo
YELLOW SEA
Osaka
Pusan
Shanghai
EAST CHINA SEA
Taipei
TAIWAN (FORMOSA)
Hong Kong
Macao
Hai Phong
GULF OF TONKIN
South China Sea

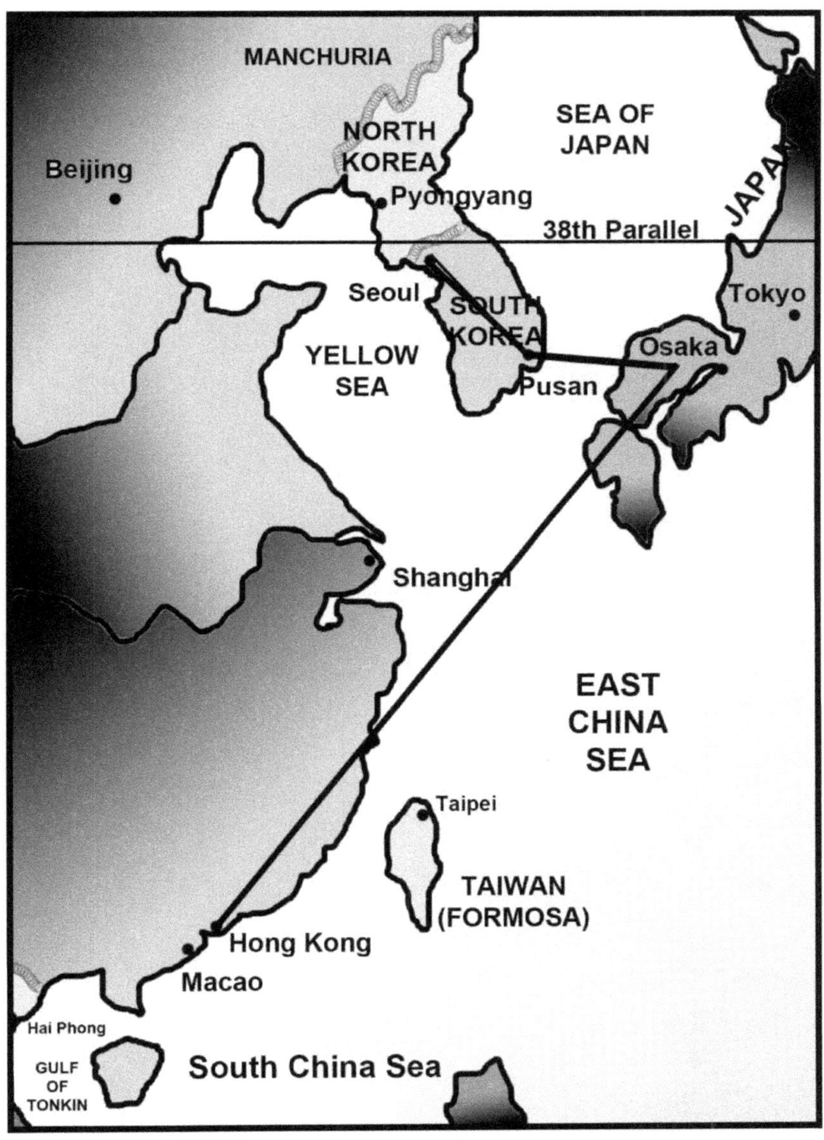

Chapter 10 – The Proposal

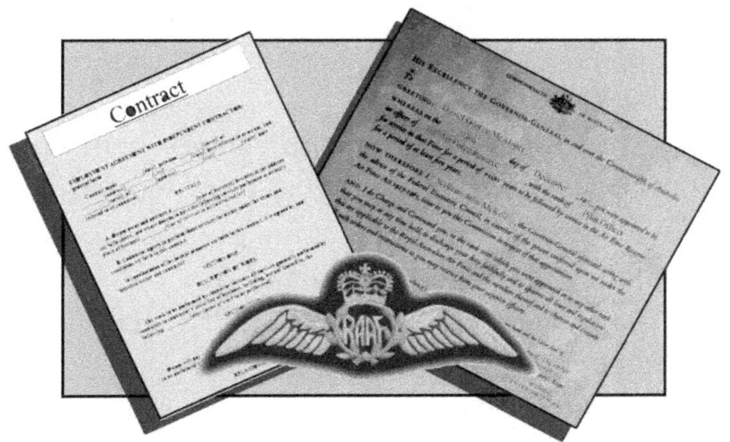

'That was handy you turning up when you did,' Danny said. 'Thanks for wading in. You really saved our bacon.'

'I would say you were infernally hard to miss,' Jeremy replied. 'You could hear the gunfire right across the estuary. We always keep close tabs on Commie patrols if we know they're around, so we were in the neighbourhood. Now just what am I going to do with you lot? I'm not entirely sure we haven't just witnessed an act of war.'

'So what? The UN is at war with China already.'

'I'm afraid it's a bit more complicated than that, old boy. We're actually at war with North Korea, not China. Even that's not entirely clear. The fact that Russian pilots fly around Mig-Alley and Chinese troops are on the ground along the peninsula doesn't necessarily signify anything. It's why I'm seconded from the RN to the Hong Kong water police — to lift the tone of the whole show and tighten up security, what? It's really a pretty grey area.'

'I won't tell if you don't,' Danny grinned.

'You'll have to answer some questions I'm sure, but you're probably okay as an Australian citizen although a civilian. Mr Sim is a Singaporean, so still comes under British jurisdiction. Mr Zhang Wei, do you have relations living in Hong Kong?'

'Hong Kong, New Territory, Macau,' Peng replied cheerfully. 'We have family all over.'

'In that case, might I suggest you contact them? You will be detained of course, but I'm sure they'll assist you in establishing your residency status. The precedents are pretty well established in your favour. You on the other hand are a different story, Lieutenant Chan,' Jeremy said. 'I am afraid I shall have to hand you over to military intelligence for questioning.'

'Will they send me back?' James Weo asked nervously.

'That's not up to me, old boy. It would be handy if you can claim some family connection in Hong Kong though.'

Unfortunately James Weo was unable to do so.

'We'll just have to wait and see then,' Jeremy concluded as they approached Victoria Harbour. The ketch was impounded while the water police searched for contraband. Of course they found nothing and cleared the vessel to be reclaimed by its owners, which was pretty unlikely under the circumstances.

Jeremy escorted the fugitives to an office at the customs building and made several phone calls. There were units from all branches of the British forces stationed in Hong Kong at the time including battalions from the Wiltshire Regiment, Argyll and Sutherland Highlanders, 25th Field Artillery, a RN frigate squadron and RAF 205 Maritime Reconnaissance Squadron. And they all wanted to have a chat with James Weo.

He was whisked away by a squad of Red Caps for interrogation to determine if he was indeed a freedom-seeker or a dastardly Commie fifth-columnist. Around midday, Peng was permitted to make a phone call of his own and within an hour a family delegation, duly armed with a notable solicitor, arrived at the lockup. Paperwork flashed back and forth, signatures were exchanged and the entire family was allowed to leave in short order.

Danny and Long Li sat glumly in the corridor awaiting their fate as Peng, Daiyu and Jiao walked past with their entourage. Peng and Daiyu stopped and kowtowed.

'Thank you both,' Peng said. 'I am in you debt. I will not forget.'

'It's my pleasure, Mr Zhang Wei. I know Earthquake will be pleased to see you're free.'

'Yes, I am indebted to Mr Earthquake too.'

'A debt repaid I would have thought,' Danny said. 'I believe you helped save his life when he was a prisoner.'

Jiao approached Danny.

'Will I see you again?' she whispered.

'Yes ... I guess ... If you'd like to. We're staying at the Sunlight Palace on Mody Road, just around the corner from the Peninsula. Or we'll be at Gingle's Bar near the Star Ferry terminal. That's if we ever get out of here.'

'I will find you,' she assured him earnestly before she left.

Danny and Long Li spent the rest of the day at the Customs House. It was a rather bleak building that Danny later only vaguely recalled as a drab, grey, green amorphous blur. There was nothing of interest to distinguish the place, although the staff members were courteously efficient. Long Li suggested they just walk out, but they were watched by a police guard who was rotated every hour. They were even escorted to the toilet. Just as they were feeling hungry a canteen staffer arrived with a food tray that included corned beef sandwiches, ginger biscuits, cocoa and considerately, a newspaper. Danny and Long Li tucked right in.

By mid-afternoon they'd read every line and even had a fair shot at the crossword. Finally Jeremy marched briskly along the corridor towards them.

'Thanks, old chap,' he dismissed the police guard. 'We won't need you now. Well done.'

The guard saluted stiffly and marched away while Jeremy turned to Danny and Long Li.

'Ah, still here, I see,' he said cheerfully as if he was expecting them to have absconded by then. 'Good show. There are some chaps who'd like a word. Old chums of yours I believe. Do come this way please.'

Jeremy led them to a small office. It contained a desk and half a dozen chairs. Standing beside the desk were General Chennault and Bob Rousselot, but most astonishing of all, seated at the desk with an open attaché case before him was Lieutenant Colonel Ted Serong.

Bugger, are we in trouble now!

The colonel rose and extended his hand.

'Hello Danny — Long Li. How nice to see you again — in one piece.'

'Thank you, sir,' Danny stammered, eyeing Chennault and Rousselot uneasily. 'We can explain.'

'Oh, I'm sure you can,' Rousselot growled with his usual implacable expression.

'Sit down everyone, please,' Serong offered.

'If you don't need me, sir, I'll be off,' Jeremy said to Serong.

'Yes, thanks for rescuing these two reprobates, Jeremy.'

'Any time. Always happy to lend you chaps a hand, even if we have to deal with that wretched Bradman fellow at every Test.'

'I'll be at the Cricket Club for dinner later if you'd care to join me and we can discuss the matter,' Serong smiled.

'I'd be delighted, old boy. Around six then,' Jeremy replied cheerfully. 'Nice meeting you Danny, Mr Sim. Ciao for now and do try to keep out of trouble in future,' he added as he left.

'Hmm, fat chance,' Serong mumbled.

After Jeremy closed the door, Colonel Serong turned his attention to the rather sheepish couple across the table.

'You caused quite a stir back in Lae,' Serong commented.

'That wasn't our fault, honestly, sir,' Danny protested. 'Crazy Al was going to kill Monty — and me into the bargain by the looks of things.'

'Yes. I'm sure he was. It's okay. Brigadier Spry has soothed all the ruffled feathers and brushed the whole thing under the carpet. Crazy Al was no great loss, from what I gather. I came straight up here when I got word. I hitched a lift with Felix Smith after he'd dropped those generals off in Sydney.'

That was high-priced help indeed. 'Silent' Charles Spry was the newly appointed head of ASIO. He and Ted Serong had helped Danny against Frenchy Duval's gang and were handy guys to have on your side.

'Thanks, Colonel,' Danny said. 'You're a brick.'

'Forget it, but that brings me to the point. There is something you can do for me in return.'

Yeah, there would be, wouldn't there? There's always a catch with these blokes.

Danny and Long Li looked at Serong suspiciously.

'This only applies to Danny, Long Li,' Serong continued. 'General Chennault has reassigned you as Monty's C-47 loadmaster. You're off to Tachikawa tomorrow. So you can shove off if you like. I think you'll find Monty and Earthquake at Gingle's.'

'Thank you, Colonel,' Long Li said with relief, wasting no time in making himself scarce.

As he headed for the door, Bob Rousselot stood and offered his hand.

'Thanks, Mr Sim. You did a good job.'

Long Li pumped the chief pilot's hand and then left with a puzzled expression.

'I don't like leaving folk behind either,' Rousselot said to Danny. 'Sometimes the big picture is harder to deal with than the details.'

'Talking of the big picture,' Serong continued, 'General Chennault and I have been discussing a project we would like to investigate.'

Danny gave him a *what-has-that-to-do-with-me* look.

'What do you know about helicopters, Danny?' Chennault asked quietly.

'Nothing, General,' Danny said after a moment's consideration.

'That pretty well puts you in the same position as everyone else,' Serong concluded. 'The RAAF has hardly put its toe into the water when it comes to rotary-wing aircraft.'

'They're new, I know that,' Danny said trying to accrue some brownie-points.

'One of the biggest problems I face with brass at the Defence Department is they're all living in the past. Policy is all based on large scale open WWII battlefields. Some of those blokes are still fighting the Great War.

'As you know I'm developing a new form of jungle combat that your mates Wally Trinder and Long Li have so ably assisted me with. It's an uphill battle to convince the generals they've got to adapt. We can't afford to let the Commies dominate the jungles of South-East Asia — especially French Indochina and Malaya.'

'What do helicopters have to do with it?'

'Do you know the RAAF has just three Sikorsky H0-3 choppers and their role hasn't really been defined?'

'Choppers are showing promise in Korea,' General Chennault added. 'Our *Customers* are starting to take an interest.'

Chennault went on to explain that Sikorsky utility choppers were proving surprisingly versatile. They were used to evacuate wounded troops from the battle field to MASH units and rescue downed pilots behind enemy lines. The *Customers,* aka CIA agents, were thinking helicopters might have a role to play in their future clandestine ops.

'But what does this have to do with me?' Danny asked.

'We'd like you to familiarise yourself with chopper operations for CAT and the Australian Defence Forces, reporting back directly to General Chennault and me,' Serong said. 'You'll be attached to the 1st Maritime Aircraft Wing and be working with the US Marines Corp.'

'Hang on. Don't test pilots normally do this sort of stuff? I'm just a kid.'

'That's precisely the point, Danny,' Serong said. 'It has been my experience that men grow more cautious with experience. Not that it's a bad thing, but who do you think will be flying these planes if they go to war in numbers? Kids like you. I want to know how *you* react to chopper flying. I want a young man's perspective. Also the RAAF isn't prepared to spend money or release experienced officers for the project. Right now they have tunnel vision with 77 Squadron Meteor operations in Korea.'

'We have assigned Monty a new co-pilot,' Rousselot said. 'We think you'll fit the bill.'

Meaning I'm the most expendable more like.

'But I'm a civilian. I won't have any authority.'

'I've thought of that,' Serong said — *he would, wouldn't he?* 'I have a commission here that enlists you in the RAAF Reserve with the rank of pilot officer.'

Serong passed a rather impressive sheet of quality paper across the table. The sheet bore the Commonwealth of Australia's coat-of-arms. The text was prefixed:

His Excellency the Governor-General in and over the Commonwealth of Australia

To Daniel George McAlister

Greetings:

Whereas *on the* first *day of* December 1952 *you were appointed to be an officer of the* Air Force Reserve, *with the rank of* pilot officer, *for service in that Force for a period of* at least five years.

NOW THEREFORE *I, William John McKell, the Governor-General aforesaid, acting with the advice of the Federal Executive Council, in exercise of the power conferred upon me under the Air Force Act 1923, issue to you this commission in respect to that appointment*

AND *I do Charge and Command you, in the rank with which you were appointed or in any other rank that you may at any time hold, to discharge your duty faithfully and to observe all laws and regulations that are applicable to the Royal Australian Air Force and members thereof to observe and execute all such orders and instructions as you may receive from your superior officers.*

The document now legitimised Danny's status in a military unit signed by the Minister for Air and the Governor-General.
Hon Philip McBride
The Right Honourable Sir William John McKell, GCMC
'That last sentence is a bit of a mouthful I know,' Serong apologised, 'but he simply means you do what you're told by your senior officers ... and that's me!'

Serong gave Danny one of his rare smiles.

'As I said, you'll report directly to me,' General Chennault added. 'I shall forward all data to Colonel Serong. Our customers are very interested in this technology. They believe there is great potential for covert operations. In the last war we had to rely on STOL planes like the Westland Lysander and Fiesler Storch. Sure they didn't need much strip, but can you imagine the advantage of no runway at all? We'll need you to pay particular attention to all aspects of helo-ops.'

'Hang on,' Danny said. 'I don't remember anyone actually *asking* me if I'm prepared to do this. I was hoping to make a career as a commercial transport pilot. All I've ever heard about choppers is they crash a lot.'

'Exaggeration, I'm sure,' Rousselot replied blandly.

'You're right, Danny,' Serong said in a tone that told Danny no one was going to ask him either. 'But think of this as a golden opportunity ... and ... it's either this deal or go back to Lae and face the music.'

'That's blackmail! Crazy Al was going to kill us. It wasn't me anyway. It was Monty!'

'We know that, but he is of use elsewhere, as I'm sure you will be.'

If Serong knew Crazy Al's fate, he didn't mention it.

Danny knew when he was beaten.

'When do I start?'

'That's the spirit. And just think you'll be paid by the Australian Government *and* CAT — talk about win-win.'

'But?'

Serong glared at him.

'There is something I'd like you do for me, if you can, Colonel.'

'I'm listening although remember your commission. I don't do deals to get my men to follow orders.'

'The Poms are holding a Commie militia lieutenant who helped us get out of China. His name is Chan James Weo. I don't think he's a threat, just a scared kid. Can you help him? I'm sure the Zhang Wei family will take him in.'

'No promises, but I'll put in a word,' Serong said and Danny knew the colonel would do all he could. Chennault, Rousselot and Serong all beamed and shook Danny's hand.

'You're booked for Seoul on Friday,' Serong added. 'Make the most of your time off. Here's a chit for a uniform, flying gear and winter clothing. That's the name of a local tailor. He'll have all the stuff made up in twenty-four hours. Good Luck. Oh, one last thing.'

Serong handed Danny a stainless steel chain with two metal dog-tags attached to it. One was circular and the other octagonal. They both bore the same information: Nationality, service number, name, religious belief and blood group.

AUST
O317367
MCALISTER D G
NONE
O-NEG

Colonel Serong had certainly done his homework. He must have checked with Dr Graham in Lae to obtain Danny's blood group. Fortunately Danny's dog-tags didn't include his date of birth. At seventeen his eligibility for combat flying was problematic. Officially the RAAF accepted sixteen-year-olds as apprentices, but they would be over eighteen before they graduated.

Colonel Serong side-stepped the issue because Danny was already a qualified pilot and he might just have added a year or two onto Danny's age when processing his commission. He wasn't the kind of man to let such a small detail stand in his way.

'Now hop it,' Serong said. 'I bet Monty and Earthquake are waiting for you.'

Chapter 11 — Danny's Bride

Earthquake McGoon and Monty were pretty well stewed by the time Danny arrived. Long Li was there too, but only drank tea while he observed the two Americans with tolerant, amused resignation. They greeted Danny raucously, but with genuine relief. Both men were embarrassed about abandoning Danny and Long Li, but no one could claim they had any other choice.

'We went back,' Monty said.

'I know, I heard the plane,' Danny replied.

'They were waiting for us. We couldn't land. The mechanics are patching up the bullet-holes right now.'

'Forget it. You came back, we made it. That's all that matters. It's a top result all round. If you feel that bad, you can buy all the beer.'

So they partied on. Earthquake explained he'd paid his smuggling informant's fine. The pirate had been released from gaol with a stern warning. After a few more Hong Kong dollars changed hands, he agreed to take the fishing ketch back along the Pearl River and reunite it with its rightful owners if he managed to sneak past the border patrols. Danny had his doubts, but Earthquake was sanguine.

'They may be rascals,' he said, 'but I ain't ever had one of these guys break their word to me yet.'

Earthquake ordered a banquet which included over a dozen courses that were placed on a lazy-Susan and shared around. Danny was famished, but had to be quick with the big guy sitting opposite him. Earthquake's appetite was legendary. Danny soon felt quite mellow and generally pretty pleased with himself. Even Long Li had abandoned his green tea for the more uplifting prospect of rice-wine. For Danny it was fatigue rather than alcohol that eventually took its toll. He'd barely slept for three days and he was exhausted.

'Time to get this young fellow to bed,' Earthquake announced. 'C'mon tough-guy, let's get outta here before you fall into your soup.'

Monty and Earthquake settled the bill that they called a 'tab' and followed Danny and Long Li into the street. They were surprised to run into Jiao and James Weo who waited for them outside Gingle's. James Weo now wore a dark business suit while Jiao's transformation was nothing short of stunning. Gone were the drab padded pants and coat. She was now dressed in a figure-hugging, elaborately patterned satin cheongsam and red stilettos. Her hair was combed to a shimmering lustre reflected against the street lighting. A fox stole covered her shoulders against the cold. No effort had been spared in her appearance – Danny was awestruck.

'Struth,' Danny said. 'How long have you been here?'

'You look simply amazing,' might have been a better opening gambit, Danny. You idiot.

Earthquake and Monty at least showed their appreciation with a couple of wolf-whistles.

'We just arrive. Mother and Father are waiting at Sunlight Palace to pay respects to Mister Earthquake,' Jiao said, pirouetting to reveal every sensuous curve of her body. She winked coquettishly and gave him a *you-like-what-you-see* glance.

'They let James Weo go after you leave Customs House,' she explained. 'I go with lawyer and Father, but number-one, big-shot colonel say they do not need him anymore. He says if we sponsor James Weo they won't send him back. Come, we go see Mother and Father now.'

Blimey that was quick, but Colonel Serong was always a man as good as his word.

Although the night's chill had descended, they chose to walk to the Sunlight Palace. It wasn't far.

'I didn't know anything that interested them,' James Weo explained as they set out. 'They pretty sharp cookies. Ask plenty questions, but I know nothing.'

'Well that's great,' Danny said clapping James Weo on the shoulder. 'I'm sure you'll take good care of him now, Jiao. I'll leave him in your capable hands.'

'No, you do not understand ...' she insisted.

'Sure I do. I told Colonel Serong you'd take responsibility for James Weo if he released him.'

'Yes. That true. That okay, but I come with you now.'

'With me?'

'Yes, my father say he owe you big favour. I am repayment. He talk to you back at Sunlight Palace.'

'You're kidding, right? Look, Jiao that's crazy.'

'Not crazy ... honour,' she said, lowering he eyes and looking totally miserable and dejected.

'But he can't just give you away like a reward.'

'He has to give me to someone. I am daughter. He needs to make good marriage. You healthy man, fill me with babies. I give you many fine sons.'

'Marriage? I'm too young for a wife!'

'That not matter, I be your number one, very fine concubine.'

The prospect didn't seem to worry her. In fact number one concubine was probably a better option than number two or three wife. Not that Danny had any other wives, but it seemed to him that Chinese menfolk had quite a lot of control when it came to dealing with females. Angela would have been appalled.

'Don't you like me? You think I'm ugly?' Jiao asked.

'No, no. You're a right little corker and no doubt, but I'm off to ... '

He bit his lip. He knew he was forbidden to reveal what plans the military had in store for him.

' ... I'm going away and it could be for a long time.'

'I come with you.'

'No girls allowed.'

This was getting awkward.

They walked along the waterfront as they talked. Danny and Jiao were slightly ahead while their companions, realising there was some sensitive negotiation in progress, kept a discreet distance behind. Earthquake was actually enjoying Danny's discomfort, but then his humour generally tended towards slapstick. Danny and Jiao's conversation was so intense they failed to notice that they were being followed by vague figures flitting among the shadows cast by the godowns on either side.

Parts of the dock were well lit, especially if any loading was in progress, but other sections were cloaked in darkness. Essentially Hong Kong wasn't any more dangerous than any other large city — safer than most in fact with its hard working, commerce-driven citizens, sound government and honest police force. Five men accompanying a lone woman should have been deterrent enough for any would-be assailants. The trouble was that Danny habitually found himself in the wrong place at the wrong time – and this was no exception.

A gang of K14 triad 'blue lanterns,' including some 49-ers, were on the prowl, looking to score brownie-points with their 'Red Pole' Enforcer by rolling a few easy marks. The K14 lads were bad-boys even by triad standards. Drugs, prostitution, murder, extortion, kidnapping, smuggling were all included in their portfolio. A pretty girl dressed to impress was worthy of their attention while five chaps, two of whom were obviously well into their cups, shouldn't pose too much trouble.

The gang would probably be able to relieve them of their wallets after dishing out a sound thrashing. There were about twenty youths in the gang that had loitered outside Gingle's bar when Danny and his friends left. Although they were firmly at the bottom of the triad food-chain, the boys were all frisky and eager to make a reputation for themselves, so they tagged along in the shadows waiting for an opportunity.

When they thought the time was right, the gang surged ahead and confronted Danny and his friends. They were a conceited bunch either standing haughtily or strutting arrogantly to reinforce their dominance before edging closer with menace.

Danny's weariness vanished as a lifetime's dose of adrenaline pulsed through his bloodstream.

'We should have caught a cab,' Earthquake murmured, gritting his teeth.

'Now's a good time to flash your hardware, guys,' Danny suggested, but neither Earthquake nor Monty was armed. They'd left their pistols at the hotel. Hong Kong was a law-abiding city, wasn't it?

And what followed was over in a flash.

James Weo strode forward and stood before the gangland thugs. His feet were firmly planted and spread apart to steady him. He raised his fists ready for action. More surprisingly Jiao shed her fur stole, letting it drop to the oily concrete. Effortlessly she ripped the seam of her cheongsam so it split to her waist before removing her stilettos. She held a shoe in each hand pointing the heels with malicious intent. James Weo and Jiao stood back-to-back, crouching and braced for the attack.

The gang surged in.

Danny realised he'd simply stood dumbly in amazement.

Pull yourself together, you drongo!

Before he could act and wade into the fray, James Weo and Jiao's arms and feet appeared to be everywhere at once. An attacker struck at Jiao, she parried like lightning and drove a stiletto into his eye. James Weo was engaged in an arm-hammering match with another triad soldier, who slumped to the ground after James struck a viscous blow straight into his nose, shattering bone in a scarlet mist.

Meanwhile Jiao allowed her next assailant to draw her closely to him before slamming her knee into his groin. It's an age-old tried and tested technique that works every time. Knowing her victim was out of the fight, Jiao didn't wait to see him drop. Spinning on her toes, she faced another on-comer and high-kicked at his face. Her heel smashed into his forehead, rupturing so many blood vessels, his brain haemorrhaged causing instant blindness and a swift death. Still she continued moving with fluid malice, taking out two more triad thugs. One went down with a crushing neck wound that ruptured arteries and his jugular – his brain's blood-supply stopped immediately and he died in seconds. Jiao raked her stiletto heel across another mugger's cheek, tearing part of his nose and left ear to shreds.

Meanwhile James Weo had paralysed a gangster with a boot to his spine and snapped another's shin bone. He then whipped a fellow's arm behind his back. Even above the screams and grunts of battle, everyone heard the cracking of broken bones.

In seconds half the gangsters had been neutralised and still Jiao and James Weo were disinclined to show mercy. The other gang members backed away and intended to escape by scurrying past their would-be victims. The space between the godowns was narrow and Earthquake hammered two more villains into unconsciousness as they tried to slip by. With amazing strength, Long Li had ripped a plank from a nearby pallet and smashed it into the back of a retreating man's head.

The survivors melted into the night. They were just small-time bullies who'd been shown no mercy, but probably didn't have the brains to learn their lesson. All at once silence fell except for the distant clank of loading gantries further along the wharf.

Jiao and James Weo were still back-to-back, yet only panting slightly after their aggressive exertion. Danny and Monty simply stood dumbfounded. They had taken no part in the struggle at all. Then James Weo and Jiao turned to face each other. They both smiled and bowed deeply acknowledging their mutual respect.

Jiao replaced her shoes and examined the slit in her cheongsam revealing her shapely thighs of golden, silky-smooth flesh. To Danny she looked like a goddess.

'Look at those ladders in my hose and I've ruined my dress,' she sighed. 'It was so pretty too.'

'Don't worry,' Monty assured her. 'We'll buy you a new dress and a pair of pure silk stockings. You've earned them.'

'How ..? What was that?' Danny stammered.

'Chinese martial art disciple,' James Weo explained. 'There are many branches, many different skills. Mostly you call Kung Fu I believe. I am black belt grade from the Jing Wu Academy. Jiao is the same, I judge.'

She simply bowed slightly indicating he was correct.

'I start when I am four years old,' she said. 'Maybe I will become Grand Master in time.'

'Well you certainly saw that lot off,' Danny said, patting James Weo's back. 'Not bad for a bloke who's rubbish with a hand-gun.'

'They scum,' Jiao sneered. 'Just novices, not worthy opponents.'

'Well now I reckon I've seen everything, Monty said. 'I notice Long Li fights more like our style. Clobbering 'em with a blunt instrument seems to work too.'

'Yeah, but you can't beat bullets,' Earthquake added.

'Bullets aren't any good if you leave your stupid gun at home,' Danny grinned.

'Let's get outta here before the cops show up,' Earthquake suggested.

They picked their way over the crippled and dead gang members and were far away before the first police whistles wailed in the distance.

Peng and Daiyu waited patiently in the Sunlight Palace lounge. Their lawyer and family members had all gone home while the couple sat contentedly drinking tea. They both rose and bowed as Danny and the others entered. Danny bowed in return. It was becoming something of a reflex. Daiyu looked suspiciously at Jiao's appearance, but said nothing.

'We ran into a bit of street trouble,' Danny explained. 'It seems that Jiao is full of surprises.'

'We taught our daughter to be prepared for life's harshness,' Daiyu said.

Meanwhile Monty and Long Li had drawn up chairs for everyone while Earthquake ordered a round of drinks. He and the Zhang Wei family were soon reacquainted and reminiscing about the time when Earthquake had been a prisoner. Jiao sat as demurely as she could, but the silken fabric of her dress continually slipped aside, exposing her legs — not that Danny minded at all.

Of course, he couldn't postpone the inevitable forever. Eventually the conversation turned to the fact that Jiao had been gifted to Danny who was by no means certain what the actual protocol was or what his negotiating position might be. At first it seemed Peng had been a bit off-hand in parcelling his daughter around, but he'd actually given the matter a lot of thought. Sure he was grateful to Danny, but he was a wily old cove as well.

Danny possibly represented Jiao's future security. Sure, Peng's family was now safe enough in Hong Kong and he'd already started proceedings to gain British citizenship, but that was a lengthy course of action that didn't necessarily guarantee a successful outcome. Hong Kong may have been part of the British Empire, but the New Territories were only leased until 1997 — certainly within Jiao's lifetime when China would reclaim its real estate. Hong Kong, Macau and Taiwan only hung by a thread should mainland China decide to swallow them up. Perhaps Peng was farsighted enough to be concerned that Jiao might once again become entrapped behind the Communist blockade. Her 'betrothal' to Danny was an added safety measure and a step up the rung of the British citizenship ladder, and a passport out of the colony should the Reds become too pushy.

Reluctantly Danny was forced to face the inevitable discussion regarding his intentions and Jiao's future. Danny knew he was on very thin ice. Zhang Wei Peng obviously had plenty of friends and allies in high places whose influence might cause Danny trouble. Although that begged the question of why did Peng need Danny at all? Surely he was quite capable of looking after his family on his own. Or did it mean that he really saw it as his duty to repay Danny for his help and Jiao was the best way to do so? It was all so inscrutably oriental.

Peng sensed Danny's reluctance and questioned him about the suitability of his daughter. Danny reassured him she was simply gorgeous and any young man's dream, which really didn't get him off the hook at all. Peng was in turn puzzled. Culturally it was not uncommon for marriages to be arranged for girls who had yet to reach puberty. Childhood was something of a luxury in drought-suffering, war-torn, famine-ravaged, over-crowded, poverty-stricken and disease-ridden China. So with life-expectancy tenuous, matches were made young to hopefully ensure future generations.

Monty, in one of his rare insightful moments, understood Danny's anguish. Danny had goals and aspirations for his own destiny which did not include a wife. Not even the exasperating Angela fell into that category.

'Excuse me Mr Zhang,' Monty said. 'May I have a word with Danny in private? We shan't be long.'

He'd become remarkably clear-headed considering he and Earthquake had been celebrating pretty well all day. Monty led Danny to the bar where they both sat on stools while Monty ordered another round.

'Looks like you're between a rock and a hard place there, buddy,' Monty declared, rather too cheerfully in Danny's opinion.

'What am I supposed to do, Monty?'

'Wed and bed the girl and live happily ever after? She's a real little honey and that's a fact. Right up there with Angela and not nearly such a pain in the ass ...'

'Be serious. I'm in a real jam. This is all so ... so ...'

'Feudal?'

'Yeah, ruddy feudal. Nobody arranges marriages anymore.'

'Wanna bet?'

'Is that what Jiao wants?'

'She seems happy enough with the deal to me.'

'I dunno. Did you see the way she and James Weo handled those triad louts? Now there's a good team for you.'

'Yeah, you wouldn't want to piss her off or she'd take your top teeth out with one kick. But, we might be able to exploit that team thing with James Weo. Now how about this for an idea ..?'

Chapter 12 — Danny Goes to War

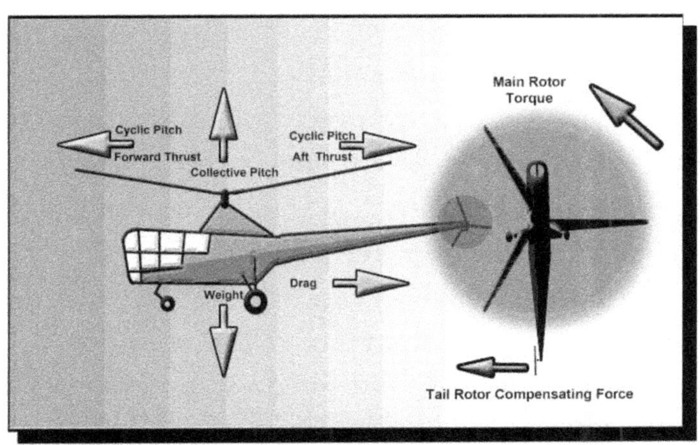

Danny and Monty rejoined the others who were being entertained by Earthquake in his usual boisterous style. Danny had been told that Chinese people were generally quiet and reserved, but the Zhang Wei family and James Weo all laughed and joked without restraint. Earthquake had that affect on people. Now it was time for Danny to employ some tact and diplomacy, which weren't really his strong points, but he went ahead anyway.

'Mr Zhang,' he began, 'your offer does me great honour. Jiao is a beautiful, gracious, intelligent, wonderful girl.'

That's it, Danny. Pile it on thick although every word you've said is nothing but the truth so far.

'I can't think of any other woman in the world I'd rather be with.'

Now that's a downright lie Danny and you know it.

'However we may have to postpone our arrangement for now.'

Peng and Daiyu frowned while Jiao looked concerned, but a smile flashed across James Weo's lips.

'As you know, Monty, Long Li and I have contracts with CAT that we must honour. We have been called away for what may be a lengthy tour of duty.'

No more than the truth there either.

'So what I propose is we prepare Jiao for my return. Monty and I own property in New Guinea. In the town of Lae on the north-east coast. That property has been severely damaged and we need someone to oversee its reconstruction. It would please me greatly if you could see your way clear to arrange for Jiao and James Weo to travel to Lae and manage that project.'

Danny saw Peng was interested. Talk of property, projects and business was his kind of language.

'We have a contact, Dave Bradley in Lae who is up to speed with our affairs. He'll liaise with Jiao and James Weo.'

'And you would trust my daughter with such a vital task?'

'I would trust her with my life, Mr Zhang,' Danny replied sincerely.

'I'm sure there will be a mountain of paperwork involved. Monty and I won't be here, so I'll have to leave that up to you, sir. We'll supply any statements and guarantors of course. We'll be moving around, but you can mail us at CAT headquarters Taipei.'

In essence it was pretty thin stuff, but Peng considered it and after a pause seemed satisfied. He didn't appear too bothered that it'd be up to him to negotiate the bureaucratic minefields. Maybe he just relished the challenge or was he clutching at straws?

'Okay. You got a deal,' he finally agreed.

Monty and Danny's plan was plainly naive and fundamentally flawed, but dog-tired while thinking on their feet it was the best they could come up with. Some factors they'd failed to consider were:

- Danny was not yet twenty-one and couldn't really speak for anyone – not even himself.

- Monty was a US citizen and only resident in New Guinea by default. The ethnic potpourri deposited in the country after WWII was left pretty much as it was. Those displaced persons, who wanted to, had returned to wherever they came from. While those who chose to stay were left to it as long as they got along with their neighbours.

- Australia still administered New Guinea. So, other than the indigenous population, the 'White Australia Policy' officially applied in the territory. True there were Chinese enclaves living in Australia — many of whom were descendants of immigrants to the goldfields a century before, but Australia of those days rarely accepted non-European immigrants.

- James Weo was an ex-Red soldier in a time when a vehemently anti-Communist sentiment pervaded Australia. That was probably justified at the time, but was hardly going to help his chances of being granted residency. What Brigadier Spry and ASIO would make of him was anyone's guess.

The list could have gone on and on, but Peng bought it. The plan was most likely doomed to failure and eventually didn't work out how anyone expected, but right then Danny was off the hook and heading for Korea.

Jiao bid him a, if not tearful, solemn farewell, promising to look after his interests diligently. James Weo shook hands all round accompanied by the usual round of bobs and bows. Earthquake wisely called a taxi to take them home before everyone turned in for the night.

Monty, Long Li and Earthquake flew to Japan the following morning.

Danny was relieved after reading the morning paper. The police attributed the triad corpses lying on the quayside to a gangster turf-war gone sour. He spent the day at Colonel Serong's tailor where he was fitted for a smart navy-blue uniform. He was supplied with two battle-dress jackets and pants and an A1 dress uniform along with an overcoat, boots, cap and badge, tie, shirts, belts, braces, socks and winter underwear. He was also supplied with a pair of smart leather parade gloves and another fur-lined pair to wear while flying in cold conditions. The tailor provided a draw-string rucksack with Danny's name and serial number stencilled onto it. Danny was especially proud of the wing insignia stitched above the left breast pocket of his uniform jackets. The single, pitifully thin epaulette and sleeve stripes denoting his pilot-officer rank was less impressive. Danny wondered if three bold sergeant's stripes would have pleased him more.

'No, no, officer number one – NCO number ten,' the tailor assured him. 'Much better you be shit of the kings than king of the shits.'

He hung onto the CAT bomber jacket Earthquake had given him. He was going to need it.

The concierge handed Danny a message when he returned to the Sunlight Palace. It was from Bob Rousselot informing Danny he was booked on a comfortable DC-4 flight to Osaka then a CAT sector to Pusan where a Marine Corps representative would meet him.

Flying on an RPT airliner was a wonderful new experience for Danny. The nose-wheel enabled the fuselage to remain level while the plane was on the ground. It was so much more comfortable than the sloping fuselage of a tail-wheel plane. He relaxed on the comfortable padded seat along with sixty other passengers in the huge pressurised cabin. A pretty hostess served beverages and a meal while Danny scanned complimentary magazines in comfortable, air-conditioned luxury as the plane soared smoothly above the turbulent cloud layers.

Yeah, I could get used to this.

Yet the DC-4 was already obsolete and destined to be replaced within a year by more reliable, even higher performance turbo-prop planes.

After landing at Osaka, Danny was transferred to a CAT C-47 for the short hop across the Sea of Japan to Pusan. Shortly after take-off the loadmaster nudged Danny saying the captain wanted to show him something.

The skipper was a CAT stalwart called Paul Holden. His co-pilot on that flight was another CAT veteran, Erik Shilling. The two cheerful, confident and supremely competent aviators welcomed Danny to the company. They knew his assignment and both agreed they didn't envy him although Holden assured Danny it was a 'golden opportunity'.

'Take a look out the port side, Danny,' Holden invited. 'What do you see?'

A vast expanse of buildings stretched away to the south. Every inch of terrain was covered with structures of all sizes. That was Japan for you. Buildings crushed together and spreading completely around the Honshu coastline and over much of the interior.

'Looks like a ruddy great slum if you ask me,' Danny replied.

'That's Hiroshima,' Holden replied. 'Didn't take long to rebuild, did it?'

Of course Danny knew of the first atomic bomb strike when over a hundred thousand people were killed and a city obliterated in an eye-blink. It wasn't so much the casualties – Japan knew all about that as similar numbers had died in the fire-bombing of Tokyo and Toyama. It was the instant finality of *Little Boy's* devastation that shocked the world. Three days later a second B-29 dropped *Fat Man* on Nagasaki and that was that. The Japanese finally understood they'd be annihilated in a week if they failed to surrender.

The controversy raged even seven years later, but Holden and Shilling were adamant that they'd prefer to sacrifice any number of Japanese dead rather than hundreds of thousands of American and allied soldiers in a bitter, protracted ground war on the Japanese mainland.

'They shouldn't have bombed Pearl Harbour in the first place,' Holden declared. 'We'd have left 'em alone if they hadn't done that.'

Would they? Who knew?

'You can just about see Kyushu Island on the horizon,' Holden continued. 'Nagasaki's on the west coast. They've done a good job rebuilding there too. Uncle Sam poured a billion dollars into the restoration.'

Soon they left the mountainous terrain of Honshu in their wake and flew over the Korean Strait before starting their descent into Pusan. Danny's first impression was of endless tracts of snow. The entire Korean Peninsula was covered with layers ranging from a few inches thick to twenty foot drifts.

His next impression as he climbed down the C-47's boarding ladder was how appallingly cold the temperature was. It hovered around freezing all day and plunged at night. Ground and flight crews huddled around 44-gallon drums of burning debris, oblivious of the fact that open-flames and aviation gasoline made a dangerous combination. Others shivered close to engine exhaust pipes, prepared to ingest a near-lethal dose of aviation gasoline fumes rather than freeze to death. It seemed to Danny that nothing short of a volcanic lava flow could raise the mercury.

It's hard to imagine the apparent pandemonium of a wartime military airfield unless you've seen one. The sheer number and variety of planes in a small area was staggering. Giant bombers, strike fighters, transports and light reconnaissance planes were parked wing-tip to wing-tip while refuelling. Maintenance trucks wove between their undercarriages while engineers swarmed over the airframes. Engines roared and rattled twenty four hours a day as squadrons struggled airborne, often returning suffering serious damage inflicted by flak and Mig fighter jets. The sheer anthill bedlam of the place was staggering.

It was a sight Danny was to become used to, not the plush comfort of modern airliners.

He was pleased to find a Jeep awaited his arrival. He proudly wore his new RAAF uniform, but quickly donned his greatcoat and gloves. He saluted the major behind the wheel. He'd practised saluting – longest way up, shortest way down – and knew it was correct protocol for officers above the rank of captain. He had no idea if his effort would pass a drill-sergeant's scrutiny, but the major simply returned the salutation casually. Danny made a mental note to brush up on military etiquette. There had to be a manual somewhere. It seemed to him there was a manual for everything in the armed forces.

The character facing Danny was handsome in that American, chisel-jawed, straight white teeth way.

'Howdy,' he greeted. 'You gotta be Lieutenant McAlister?'

'Yessir. Danny McAlister. G'day.'

'Pleased to know ya'll kid. I'm Vic Armstrong. I understand I'm gonna show you how to fly a whirlybird.'

'That's what I was told to come here to do, sir,' Danny replied.

Danny knew you *'sirred'* majors, squadron leaders and lieutenant commanders and all the exalted ranks above that. The more the better, it seemed.

'Well, you're sure gonna learn on the job. Hop in, let's get started. You're kinda big for a whirlybird jockey, ain't ya?'

Danny looked puzzled.

'It's a weight thing, you see. Choppers are always weight critical. It's a pain in the ass.'

'I don't think anyone thought about that when they assigned me. It's the sort of thing I'm supposed to report back to my bosses about.'

'Bosses? I thought I was your boss?'

'It's complicated. Most people say I'm kind of young too. Here are my transfer papers and orders, sir.'

Danny handed Major Armstrong a sealed foolscap envelope containing the relevant information outlining his mission. Armstrong briefly scanned the documents and nodded.

'That might well be an advantage,' he said enigmatically.

Danny stashed his kitbag in the rear seat and climbed into the jeep beside Armstrong. They drove to a hangar where three Sikorsky H0-3 utility helicopters were parked. Danny was initially struck by their size and fragility while no one could claim they were handsome machines. The forward glass cockpit reminded Danny of an illustration of a sperm whale he'd seen in Herman

Melville's novel *Moby Dick*. In Danny's experience, if a plane looked good, it flew well. If it looked ugly, it was a dog to handle. The H0-3 just didn't seem to fit in anywhere.

Blimey, those bastards have really stuck it to me this time. What am I letting myself in for?

Victor Armstrong sensed Danny's uneasiness.

'Sure they ain't no oil paintings,' he conceded, 'but these are the first whirlybirds that really work. We got two single seaters here with room for three passengers and then there's the dual control crate. That's the one we're taking up country. I'll teach y'all how to handle the beast and show you the geography at the same time.'

So Danny's rotary-winged aircraft conversion began in what was to become his flying classroom. He loaded his kitbag into the back seat where Armstrong had already stowed his own travelling bag. A flight manual that Danny would have to study in detail lay on the passenger seat. Armstrong explained how the rotors provided lift, talked about collective and cyclic pitch, autorotation, torque and translational lift. He showed Danny the engine, gearbox, main and tail rotor hubs and blades, winch operation, fuel, electrical, flight instrument and ancillary systems. There appeared to be an unnecessary amount of moving parts for such a simple aircraft.

'Most folk say it's made up of ten thousand components trying to tear each other apart,' Armstrong grinned.

'Thanks, that makes me feel so much better.'

'Wait till you try hoverin' the beast. You'll need a baseball park to start with.'

Armstrong's orders were to transport Danny to the 1st Marine Aircraft Wing Observation Squadron's HQ near Seoul. He was to familiarise Danny with any base the choppers might be called upon to operate from. They flew for three weeks while Danny studied at night in the freezing quarters of the support bases and MASH units they stopped at. Armstrong's estimation was correct. Actual chopper flying wasn't much different from a fixed-wing plane other than the continual vibration caused by the turbulence stirred up by the main rotor and the aircraft's inherent instability. Danny had to concentrate continually.

'You can't let go of the controls for a second,' Armstrong admonished, 'or she'll flip on her back and that's that.'

The collective pitch produced vertical movement while the cyclic pitch controlled the aircraft horizontally. Danny found throttle handling was tricky at first. Each time he moved the collective pitch he had to adjust the throttle to compensate for rotor drag to prevent the engine and gearbox over- or under-speeding. The rudder pedals that controlled the tail-rotor were critical, needing slight adjustments left or right with the change of engine torque.

'Ya'll gotta be able to pat your head and rub your gut at the same time,' Armstrong explained. His attitude to aviation reflected the Marine Corps and Army's basic approach. They thought of helicopters much the same as jeeps and landing craft. They were simply transportation, meriting no special attention just because they were airborne.

As Armstrong predicted, Danny drastically over-controlled the chopper on his first hovering attempts. The airframe gyrated madly, much to Armstrong's amusement. In time the oscillations lessened as Danny mastered the skill of keeping the fuselage steady, moving back and forth and sideways. Then one morning, just like riding a bike, he controlled the helicopter perfectly.

Autorotations were fast and furious affairs. Gliding a fixed wing aircraft was a relatively gentle manoeuvre. Practising engine failures in a chopper was quite a different experience. The plane sank like a stone. Danny had to plunge the collective pitch lever to the floor to control the rotor RPM, simultaneously stopping the fuselage spinning using the tail-rotor pedals. As the ground rushed towards them he had to raise the chopper's nose, lift the collective pitch and settle to the ground before drag slowed the rotors where they failed to create any lift.

Once again after a few practice-sessions, Danny could perform an autorotation with ease. Flaring too early or too late could result in a collapsed undercarriage or even shattered rotor blades. Pioneer chopper flying wasn't for the faint-hearted.

For the first three weeks Armstrong was content to stay in the reserve areas as Danny became a proficient chopper pilot. He learnt the geography up to the 38th parallel, but had only sensed hints of the front line. Often he and Armstrong were guided around or under New Zealand artillery batteries that blasted enemy targets. They'd spot the B-29 squadrons heading north and the swirling contrail of dog-fighting jets over Mig-Alley. Danny learnt all the radio frequencies of the dozens of units and control agencies along the battle-line.

By Christmas Eve 1952, Armstrong was satisfied that Danny met the Marine Corps flying standards, declaring him ready for combat. They were based with a detachment from the Marine Transport Squadron unit close to Inchon. The marines dubbed the base *Whirlybird Central* although the chopper detachment was only a small part of the aviation units stationed there. US Naval Seabees had bulldozed a runway long enough for most transport aircraft to operate from.

Danny shared a tent with three other chopper pilots who spent most of their time cursing the cold, Joseph Stalin, Chairman Mao Tse-tung, the UN, the American Congress, President Harry S Truman and especially the North and South Koreans for their inability to sort the whole mess out by themselves. With only a meagre stove and bottles of Kentucky bourbon for warmth, the pilots huddled under their blankets and shivered. Danny didn't care much for the taste of bourbon, but it warmed him from the inside.

Danny was learning that much of war was extremely uncomfortable and boring.

'You're a quick learner and a natural pilot, kid,' Armstrong extolled. 'I cain't teach y'all about combat. That just happens and you'll have to cope as best you can, but you're good to go. And, as a reward Santa's dropping off a present for you, kid,' Armstrong said. 'We got word it'll arrive tomorrow.'

'He can't have come far. It's ruddy well cold enough to be the North Pole right here.'

Chapter 13 — Casevac

Christmas Day 1952 dawned bleakly with little Yuletide cheer. Someone said there was a truce, but the distant thump of artillery suggested otherwise. More alarmingly, small arms fire rattled at much closer range. Chinese and North Korean patrols still infiltrated weak points along the allied line where spiteful, person skirmishes erupted.

Danny slept badly and was reluctant to rouse himself until hunger got the better of him. He trudged bleary-eyed to the mess-tent for a breakfast of salty bacon, powdered eggs, brittle toast, pinto beans and coffee. The coffee was bitter, the food tasteless, but at least most of it was hot. Vic Armstrong arrived shortly afterwards.

'They landed your stuff at Inchon last night,' Armstrong announced.

Inchon was where General McArthur's invasion force had invaded back in 1950 in an attempt to reclaim the peninsula. The move was successful although by no means decisive. The ROK army and its allies were in dire straits at the time. The Communists had pushed them into a small perimeter around Pusan. Just when it looked as if there could be an ignominious Korean 'Dunkirk', McArthur's bold initiative saved the day. The UN forces pushed as far north as the Yalu River right on the Manchurian border, but Chinese forces stopped them. Since then the war had ground into a vicious stalemate with both sides pushing and shoving anywhere from the Yalu River to south of the 38th Parallel.

A truck waited outside the mess tent. Armstrong and Danny climbed into the cabin beside the driver while a team of enlisted men filled the back.

Danny looked puzzled.

'Who're these guys?'

'You'll see,' Armstrong said as the truck rattled along a mud track towards the city.

The dockside was frenetic. Stores, munitions, reinforcements and heavy equipment all arrived there to be processed and shipped to their destinations. Armstrong asked around for a while and was finally pointed to a wharf with a cargo ship tied up. Derricks were hard at work. There was no Christmas break for the military stevedores whose job was to supply the front with its needs. It was hard to believe that elite Chinese units still attacked the city.

Several large containers now stood some distance from the unloading area while a team of engineers unpacked the contents. Standing to the side next to a 44-gallon drum a small figure gathered broken and waste packing that littered the wharf. He'd started a fire in the drum, fuelling it with whatever combustibles he found. Even rugged in military cold weather gear with a fur hat pulled over his ears, Danny recognised Long Li.

'What the blue-blazes are you doing here?' Danny cried, overjoyed to see his old friend.

'Danny. You're crazy. This bad-bum country sucks. I'm so cold my balls are up around my kidneys.'

'Howdy,' Armstrong said, 'you're the new crewman, I guess?'

Danny introduced Long Li to Armstrong. Both men nodded, but no one was going to remove their gloves to shake hands.

'Crewman ..?' Danny looked even more confused.

'That's right, mate,' Long Li said. 'General Chennault changed his mind about me being Monty's loadmaster and suggested that I might be useful here with you.'

'Thanks for saying "yes".'

'Who says I did? Have you forgotten, General Chennault doesn't actually ask, does he?'

'Oh, sorry.'

Long Li grinned and slapped Danny on the back although he didn't feel anything through his layers of clothing.

'I'm just messing with you. Nothing to be sorry about,' Long Li said. 'It's nice to have the old team back together.'

'Great,' Danny said, turning to Armstrong, 'but Long Li shares my quarters. He's a civilian really and I don't want any military class-structure bullshit. We're a team.'

'Suit yourselves, but it mightn't always be the most comfortable,' Armstrong replied evenly. 'It ain't gonna be an issue when you move up country anyway. Now let's take a look at your Christmas present.'

Armstrong's mechanics piled out of the truck. They ripped the crates open revealing the components of a Sikorsky H0-3. The parts appeared to be straight off the production-line although the company had ceased manufacturing that particular model the previous year. The fuselage was by far the largest item, but the rotors, engine, undercarriage and fixtures all had to be unpacked. The engineers worked quickly and efficiently, but it still took most of the day to assemble the helicopter, refuel and replenish the oil and hydraulic fluid.

The highlight of the whole procedure was when an airframe fitter produced a decal depicting a bird-of-paradise logo with *'Danny-Boy'* inscribed across it. The artwork was beautifully rendered in a simple, stylised design. Danny would have preferred the Alberto Vargas and Gil Elvgren style pin-ups that were painted on many of the American warplanes with names like *Tempting Tess, Devil's Darlin', Upstairs Maid* or *Shady Lady*, but he appreciated the gesture nevertheless.

'Nice touch. It was Bob Rousselot's idea,' Long Li observed.

'No girls in sexy underwear, then?'

'In your dreams, bad-bum. We couldn't make up our minds whether we should have made it a kangaroo, but Monty thought you'd prefer a New Guinea emblem.'

'Too right. Does this mean I have my own personal whirlybird?'

'Sure does. That's your call-sign by the way,' Armstrong said. 'Seems you ain't quite a marine and, from what your orders say, you've got a foot in both RAAF and CAT camps. You're kinda Mister In-Between. And to mix it up just a mite more, this here chopper belongs to the CIA spooks, so you kinda have your own jurisdiction.'

'Don't I follow your orders?'

'Yeah, but I've been told to be flexible. You're an independent command now. You'll have to make yourself useful where you can. Much of *what* you do, and *how* you do it, will be up to *you*. I guess this should answer your questions,' Armstrong added, handing Danny a manila folder containing charts and command authorities legitimising his position in the war zone.

'Don't worry, buddy. You'll get plenty of work to keep y'all busy. You're a good pilot, one of the best I've seen. You'll do just fine.'

Danny opened a sealed envelope that contained written orders from a Marine Corps general. The instructions included map co-ordinates, radio frequencies, but very little else other than he was to be utilised ad hoc or on his own initiative. Danny also noted there were no RAAF roundels or US military insignia painted onto the fuselage or any identifying number along the tail-rotor boom. It seemed the CIA didn't worry about aircraft registration.

While the marine engineers assembled the chopper components, a tanker-truck arrived and filled the aircraft fuel tank.

By early afternoon, the crew chief declared the chopper was ready for its test flight. He handed Danny a clip board with a list of functional tests he would have to perform as he flew to his destination. Danny had never performed a test-flight before, but saw it mostly required him to simply operate all the aircraft systems and tick them off as working correctly.

'Normally I'd do the test-flight,' Armstrong said, 'but if you're going to be an independent unit, you might as well start acting like one. Bring her back to base and we'll start assigning your tasks first thing tomorrow. Merry Christmas.'

Armstrong and the engineers loaded their gear into the truck and clambered aboard. As soon as they left, Long Li tossed his grip into the back seat and strapped in beside it. The engine soon fired and they were airborne. Initially Long Li looked apprehensive, but soon got used to the chopper's motion.

How cool is this? My own whirlybird.

It did seem as if CAT and, therefore by default the CIA, had been extremely generous, but they weren't philanthropic organisations. Even though helicopter technology was still in its infancy, the Sikorsky H0-3 was already past its prime. The Bell-47 bubble dome choppers had replaced it in many sectors. The Bell was a superior Casevac platform as two stretchers could be carried in pods fixed over the helicopter's skids. Indeed the skids innovation made landing easier and more stable. Now the challenge for the rival manufacturers was to produce choppers that carried a decent payload over a reasonable range.

The larger Sikorsky H-19 was already in service with the US Army and would become a reliable workhorse for the next decade.

Nevertheless Danny was feeling pleased as punch when he settled his whirlybird between the sandbag revetments at *Whirlybird Central*. A contingent of mechanics greeted him to refuel the bird and carry out its overnight service. Danny found a bunk and bedding for Long Li and they were already in the chow-line when Armstrong's truck arrived.

'How'd it go?' the major asked.

'Like clockwork, sir. Long Li and I are all ready for action.'

That was just what they got on Boxing Day.

*

Korean winter nights are long and the days short, but it hardly seemed as if Danny had put his head down when he was unceremoniously awoken by a marine captain.

'Up and at 'em, fly boy. Get over to the briefing tent. You've just found gainful employment.'

Danny and Long Li scrambled into their flying gear and grabbed a coffee from the mess-tent before finding themselves at their first operational briefing. The tent space was sparsely furnished with a table and director's chairs placed in several lines. A blackboard stood in a corner and a wall-sized map hung in front of the chairs. Three other helicopter pilots attended the briefing including Major Armstrong who stood beside the map with a pointer.

'Okay, we'll keep this short,' he said. 'The gooks (no allowance for Long Li, you'll notice) have infiltrated the Commonwealth Brigade's line here and here (he jabbed the map with his pointer). There's a fire-fight going down right now. We think the Commies are in battalion strength. You'll see our units are isolated on five peaks. The Reds are swarming around the strongholds, which are only at platoon or half-company strength. They're holding right now, they've taken hits and called for Casevac airlift and resupply.'

Armstrong went on to explain the first sortie would take ammo in and wounded out.

'What are the casualty numbers?' Danny asked.

'No idea,' Armstrong replied. 'We'll have to wait and see. The nearest MASH unit is situated here.'

He slapped his pointer onto the map once more and read the co-ordinates. There were four choppers and five hills. The commanders on the ground would have to prioritise.

Soon the choppers rattled into life and lifted skywards. They were all at maximum AUW. The ammunition boxes looked pitifully small, but weighed as much as the choppers could carry.

The flight was in echelon formation. Armstrong led while Danny fitted in as tail-end-Charlie.

The morning was perfectly clear. A white panorama spread before them which was confusing as the snow tended to mask any ground features. All the crews wore sunglasses to avoid snow-blindness. There was no doubting the battleground when they arrived though.

For one thing the radios burst into life as troop commanders told the chopper pilots the ground situation – and it wasn't good. Flashes and gouts of black smoke erupted like dirty smears against the pristine white backdrop. Tracer rounds sliced skywards, looking deceptively in idle slow-motion. Yet a single well-placed incendiary shell could bring a chopper down in a second.

'You take Hill 303, Danny. They're Aussies. You'll be able to speak the language. We'll try the Canadians,' Armstrong ordered before assigning the other choppers their landing sites.

Oh very droll, Major and how appropriate is Hill 303.

But it was reassuring to hear a familiar accent when he selected the 3RAR frequency and made contact with the surrounded platoon. Danny was aiming for a hill about a mile ahead. The area was unremarkable, just one rocky peak amongst many.

'Three-Zero-Three, this is Casevac call-sign *Danny-Boy*. I'm one minute south of your position. Throw smoke.'

'Nice to see you,' a voice replied. He sounded calm, but Danny could hear the crackle of gunfire in the background. 'Stand by.'

Danny scanned the terrain. A puff of pink smoke swelled into a cloud that hovered over the hill.

'I see pink,' Danny said.

'Pink smoke thrown,' the radio operator confirmed. 'I have you sighted. Continue on your present course. It looks safest. Put down as close to the flare as possible. We'll lay down covering fire. Enemy positions are left, right and forward. Your flight path looks clearest for now.'

'Roger. I have cases of rifle ammo for you.'

'Much appreciated – we can use it. We have two casualties.'

Although he heard a continual babble in his ears, Danny stopped talking from then on. It was concentration time. Long Li stood at the chopper door, pistol in hand in case the enemy came too close. As Danny closed in on the ridge line, tracer bullets flashed only yards ahead of the chopper. Danny became aware of heavy gunfire from his left. The 3RAR troops were pouring covering fire downhill to a massing company of Chinese soldiers.

The ground troops formed a perimeter on the hill-top. They kept up steady rifle fire into the ravines all round augmented by a Bren gun and frequent grenades. Here the Australians held a singular advantage. They could lob a Mills Bomb a lot further downhill than the Communists could throw upwards.

A dozen Communists fell under the withering fire, but they kept coming. Long Li emptied his pistol magazine at the advancing menace. He was good shot and took out two more enemy soldiers.

Danny hovered the chopper beside the smoke grenade. The rotor swirled the pink cloud into faint mist that faded in seconds. He touched down on the uneven surface. A steam of tracer rounds flashed only feet from the chopper's front windshield, but came no closer. The chopper wobbled alarmingly when one of the main wheels fell into a pothole.

'Take her two yards right, Danny,' Long Li called over the intercom. 'It looks flatter there.'

Danny lifted the chopper a foot above the surface and nudged the fuselage to the right before nestling it onto level ground. Long Li leapt from the cabin as two infantrymen approached. They kept their heads low, not only to avoid enemy bullets and shrapnel, but also the chopper's main rotor. Long Li dragged the first ammunition canister from the cabin floor so it teetered on the door sill. The soldiers grabbed a case each and dashed away. A relay of soldiers returned to carry off the remaining ammo boxes.

Once the canisters were clear, Long Li scrambled to where two men lay on stretchers. Both men looked in bad shape and neither could sit or stand. This is where the Bell-47 chopper was far superior to the H0-3. There was only room to lay one stretcher on the H0-3 floor. The other casualty lay on the cabin seat, while Long Li squeezed in where he could. Both wounded soldiers were covered with field dressings and tourniquets were applied to their arms and legs. Blood stained their entire uniforms while their faces were ashen.

'No time to lose,' Long Li said. 'Get 'em aboard.'

If the Diggers were surprised to see a Chinese crewman, they gave no indication. They couldn't tell Long Li from a South Korean anyway. Once aboard, Long Li slammed another clip into his pistol butt. He literally hung out of the chopper door as Danny lifted the collective lever bringing the aircraft to a hover.

Even in cold weather, the H0-3's power was critical. The hill's elevation didn't help either. What Danny needed was the magical freebie of translational-lift. As the chopper accelerated, translating from stationary to moving flight, airflow was forced through the rotor vastly improving its efficiency and lifting capability. It only needed fifteen or twenty knots to make a staggering change in aircraft performance.

The other effect was head wind. Right then Danny was pointing into wind, stabilising the fuselage as it naturally weather-cocked. But if he took off straight ahead, he'd pass right over the strongest concentration of enemy troops. This meant he would lose the extra airflow of a headwind which was also of great assistance to all aircraft types.

'I'm going to slide off to the right side,' Danny called to Long Li. 'Keep their heads down if you see any Commies.'

Long Li acknowledged with a 'thumbs-up'.

Using the tail-rotor pedals, Danny manoeuvred his chopper to the right when the hill fell away to a valley, now thick with Communist troops. Danny heard the plop of a mortar shell being lobbed amongst the Reds. It was followed by two more bombs and Danny seized his opportunity.

Using the cyclic stick he banked the chopper right and plunged into the ravine. Long Li held on with all his might while hanging halfway out of the fuselage door, blasting away with his pistol. Ejected shells clattered into the cabin. A couple flew right over Danny's seat and landed in his lap.

Crikey, they're hot!

Danny brushed them onto the floor, making a mental note to make sure he found them before they disappeared somewhere they might jam the flight controls. As the chopper slipped down the slope, translational lift cut in and they surged away.

'Thanks,' the 3RAR radio operator called.

'I'll be back,' Danny promised.

Chapter 14 — Forward Air Controller

Danny and Long Li ferried the wounded soldiers to a MASH unit barely twenty miles from the front line. The hospital team had cleared an area and painted a large 'H' within a circle. Danny radioed ahead so a small reception committee awaited the chopper's arrival. A triage medical team assessed the wounded men and immediately whisked them away.

'Will they make it?' Danny asked a harassed looking nurse. He could barely hear over the rotor noise.

She stared at him through weary, resigned eyes.

'You're new here, aren't you?' she yelled back.

He nodded to which she smiled thinly and turned away. She was needed urgently.

'What was that all about?' Danny asked Long Li.

'After a while I think they're afraid to answer. Maybe too many don't make it. We'd better get off the pad. The other choppers will be bringing in more casualties.'

'Yeah, let's get cracking. Those blokes'll need more ammo.'

They flew back to *Whirlybird Central* for fuel and to load up. Major Armstrong arrived shortly followed by the remaining two whirlybirds. The crews immediately prepared their aircraft for the next sortie. They were flat out which gave no one time to think about the cold.

'Load twenty two hundred round ammo boxes,' Danny instructed the marine armourers who brought the .303 bullet boxes to the chopper. The chopper's payload was only about five-hundred pounds with a full fuel load and two crew members. A two-hundred round ammo box weighted about thirty-five pounds which put the chopper around two-hundred pounds overweight.

'We won't get off the ground, Danny,' Long Li protested.

'Sure we will.'

Danny was well aware that he had insufficient engine power to hover, but he also knew a meagre load of ammunition wouldn't go far at the rate the hill defenders were using it.

The problem seemed easily resolved to Danny. *Whirlybird Central's* runway was right there, and for a chopper it was immense. Another phenomenon that assisted helicopters was ground effect. The rotor's downdraft acted as an air cushion that allowed the chopper to bounce along if it stayed close to the ground. The H0-3 had enough power to hover a few inches above ground-level, but precious little else.

So Danny eased the plane sideways until he reached the runway. Now all he had to do was push the cyclic pitch lever gently forwards. The chopper's nose wheel bumped against the runway surface. The plane bobbed into the air then settled once more, but gathered a few precious knots of speed.

Bump ... bump ... bump ... five knots ... ten knots ... fifteen knots ...twenty knots ... then translational lift kicked in. Suddenly the chopper gained a new lease of life and could lift the extra weight. The rotors sliced into the air and the H0-3 surged away.

When Danny returned to Hill 303, 3RAR's position hadn't improved. Chinese infantry were dug in at the base of the slope. They also controlled the valleys surrounding the other four hills. Detachments of the Commonwealth Brigade may have secured the high ground, but right then they were marooned and isolated without sufficient strength to either break out or advance and take the fight to the enemy.

The Commonwealth Brigade consisted of Australians, Canadian, Scottish Highlanders, and paradoxically, a detachment of Turks. With Gallipoli as their common bond, the Australians and Turks fought well together despite the language barrier. Although they'd been enemies in the Great War, ANZACs and Johnny Turk respected each other as warriors and worthy opponents. Now as allies they were troops to be reckoned with.

Fortunately the hilltop defenders were well dug in with a series of trenches spanning the summits. So although outnumbered, they could fend off an onslaught of superior strength. New Zealand artillery was making life uncomfortable for the Chinese forces with a steady HE barrage into the valleys.

Danny had marked the heavy guns' lines of fire on his map. He had to fly right into their path, but the shells soared up to twenty-thousand feet before plunging onto their targets, so Danny simply flew under their trajectory.

As he approached Hill 303 for the second time it was shrouded with black smoke from the last barrage.

'Three-O-Three, this is *Danny Boy*,' he announced once he came within radio range. 'Five minutes out. Do you have wounded?'

'Negative, but we can use an ammo resupply.'

'I thought you might. I have twenty boxes on board. I'm too heavy to hover, so I'll make a slow pass. We'll toss out the first five boxes. Where do you want 'em?'

'Slap bang in the centre of our position. Don't worry, we'll duck.'

'You get all that, Long Li?' Danny asked.

'I'm on it – no sweat.'

Danny decelerated to 20 knots which was as slow as he dared fly without losing translational lift. The chopper's rotor brushed the artillery smoke aside carving a clear tunnel through the murk. At such low speed and so close to the rocky surface, there would be very little forward travel during the drop.

'Now, Long Li!' Danny called as he approached 3RAR's position.

He felt the airframe buck as the ammunition box tumbled from the door, scraping the main wheel strut on its way out. Danny also had to compensate for the chopper's shifting C-of-G. It wasn't an exact science as Danny had thought the idea up on the spot. The metal boxes were durable and the one Long Li dropped stayed intact, but somersaulted alarmingly after hitting the hilltop. There was a real risk of the containers either splitting open or, worse still, tumbling down to the Communists below.

Once Danny made his pass, he faced a bigger danger. He flew straight towards the Communist position at a perilously low speed. The only solution was to dive down the hillside once more, picking up speed as he went. The chopper was a sitting duck. Muzzle flashes erupted from the valley as bullets sizzled past.

Danny banked sharply pulling the chopper around. Bushes and treetops flashed by with the rotor-blades only inches from the hill's rock face. Danny felt the main wheels brush against foliage as the chopper rotor sliced into the air to gain altitude. Snow tumbled from the leaves and branches, either blasted by the chopper's downwash or knocked down by the undercarriage.

'We still have four more crates to drop before we get to landing weight,' Danny said. 'We'll be lucky to get away with that many passes.'

'Just one,' Long Li replied. 'We make one more. The Reds won't expect us to come back.'

'What about the ammo?'

'You'll see. It'll be fine.'

So, with his heart in his mouth, Danny flew around to the protection of the hillside. At thirty-five pounds the ammo boxes weren't particularly heavy, but Long Li could still only manage to eject one at a time from the bucking helicopter.

'I'll turn as soon as you drop the ammo. You'll have to hang on,' Danny explained.

'No worries. Stay as low as you can.'

Danny manoeuvred for the final run in. The undercarriage barely cleared the ground as he approached the 3RAR position.

'Now!' he cried, glancing behind.

He was horrified to see that Long Li and the ammunition box he carried were no long aboard. The chopper responded instantly to the reduced weight. Danny banked steeply, circling back to the hilltop.

What he hadn't seen was Long Li pitch the ammo box out of the chopper door then leap after it. Twenty knots doesn't look fast when you're safely aboard a chopper, but Long Li was knocked breathless when he hit the ground. He rolled several times, stopping a few yards ahead of the ammunition box. He lay dazed for a second, but came to his senses, spitting out a mouthful of snow.

Two incoming mortar shells crumped close by, peppering Long Li with rocks and debris. He'd hardly regained his wits when three burly Diggers scrambled towards him. While one soldier retrieved the ammo, the other two hauled Long Li to his feet, slung his arms over each of their shoulders and dragged him to the nearest fox-hole. A stream of machinegun fire slithered in their wake. .30 calibre rounds zinged inches above them as they crouched in the trench.

'Thanks,' Long Li gasped once he'd found his breath.

'No worries, mate. You okay?'

'Yeah, just winded. The chopper will be back any minute now. There're eighteen more cases on board.'

'Beauty, you little ripper. We'd better lay down some covering fire for your whirlybird.'

With that the Diggers ran to their positions on the perimeter where they could best sight the enemy.

Now that the chopper had been lightened by the weight of one crewman and an ammo box, Danny knew he had enough power in reserve to hover. He returned in moments. Danny hadn't time to fret over Long Li. It required all his skill to hover the chopper at maximum weight on the hilltop. To make matters worse the wind was picking up, causing turbulence as it swirled through the valleys and over the high ground. Finally he touched down safely. To his great relief he spotted Long Li scramble from what looked like an inadequately shallow pit. He limped slightly, but was otherwise unhurt.

'You idiot!' Danny yelled. 'What were you thinking?'

'You sound just like Miss Angela,' Long Li grinned as he clambered into the chopper. He began hauling ammunition boxes to the side where enthusiastic hands grabbed them and whisked them away to where they were needed.

A lanky captain clambered into the cabin and stood behind Danny. He introduced himself as 'Stretch' Watson.

'Probably best not to try that again, sport,' he admonished.

'Yeah. It sounded like a good idea at the time. It'll be a regular load next time – fifteen cases.'

'Fair enough. Keep the ammo coming at that rate and we'll be fine. This extra load will keep us going. Dunno how we're going to gouge those buggers out of the valleys though.'

'What about the Kiwi artillery?'

'It's a bit random, I'm afraid. We're having trouble identifying specific targets from here. What we need is a spotter.'

'No time like the present. Take a seat if you're game,' Danny grinned.

'I'll just be a second.'

Captain Watson raced back along his defences and explained to his platoon commanders that he'd be going with the chopper. He gathered one of his radio operators and a spare radio. Both men clambered into the chopper beside Long Li. Danny had been at the LZ longer than he liked. The chopper was once again drawing enemy fire. Tracer rounds streaked a few yards ahead of the windscreen.

'Lucky they're crap shots,' Danny observed.

'I think someone has told them to shoot just ahead of aircraft so it'll fly into the gunfire.'

'Yeah, but hasn't it occurred to them that we're not moving forwards.'

'Apparently not.'

'In that case we'll go out the way we came in.'

Danny pirouetted the chopper through one hundred and eighty degrees and took off to the rear. He climbed to two thousand feet which was beyond accurate small arms fire. They flew back over Commonwealth Brigade's position.

What they saw filled them with dread. Contrasted against the whiteness, long lines of antlike figures snaked towards the south through undulating country. The enemy reinforcements were still several miles from the battle front and moving at a creep. Lines of tracer-bullets arched up deceptively slowly to meet them, but none came close.

'Struth, there must be several flaming regiments down there,' Watson said.

'That's not all. Look right smack in the middle of the infantry.'

'Tanks — Soviet T-34s. Shit, half a dozen of the bloody things. Our Intel claims they'd all been knocked out ages ago. Bloody 'I' Corps Intel didn't say anything about the Reds in any strength around here.'

'Someone forgot to tell the Reds,' Danny observed.

As they spoke the leading tank turret rotated and elevated its gun towards the chopper. Danny saw a cloud of white smoke spew from the gun barrel. A 76.2 mm shell roared past them. The rushing slipstream tossed the chopper sideways while Danny wrestled to regain control. He knew if he kept on the move erratically, it was unlikely the tanks would hit them. Another unknown factor was how much ammunition the tanks actually had.

Meanwhile Watson was relaying urgent instructions to his radio operator. He called in the Kiwi artillery and Danny knew he had to make himself scarce. At two thousand feet and just ahead of the Communist brigade, the H0-3 was right in the line of fire.

He had two choices:

- Descend and risk receiving small arms fire, or
- Retreat back towards the hills and lose accurate visual contact with the enemy positions.

Stretch Watson, gutsman that he was, wanted to stay. So Danny headed the chopper downwards just as the first Kiwi salvo streaked overhead. A dozen shells exploded amongst the tanks in great fireballs and clouds of acrid black smoke. The shock waves buffeted the chopper as if it was a cork on the ocean.

When the smoke cleared, craters surrounded the tanks, but they kept coming. The captain gave his radio operator instructions to adjust the artillery aiming points. More shells plunged into the Chinese brigade. Danny could see men were dying down there. Explosions poured into the infantry vaporising entire units and blasting troops to scarlet mush and cascading body parts.

Still the enemy advanced.

Danny was flying right along the enemy front now. Some Chinese troops fired at the chopper, but most were ducking for cover. They realised the 'flying curse' was directing incoming artillery. Although they desperately wanted to shoot down the chopper, they knew another salvo was on the way. Good sense suggested they should keep their heads down.

The tanks were still a problem. They moved fast and it was harder for the Kiwi guns to hit such small targets than blast large concentrations of troops to smithereens. Tanks of course needed infantry support, yet despite their losses, there were still vast numbers of advancing troops.

Then to Danny's horror, he saw the tanks move into line abreast, spread out to a distance where they were still difficult individual targets. The tank gunners hadn't tried to hit the chopper again. They had other prey in their sights. Their guns blazed into action, slamming rounds into the five hills.

The Commonwealth Brigade was now in dire trouble. The tanks braved the Kiwi barrage, but set about pulverising the hilltop defences. The 3RAR detachment and the other units had no response to the tank attack. Watson called for the artillery to adjust their aim and shots landed tantalisingly close to the tanks, but failed to destroy even one.

'Those hills are going to need reinforcements and they're going to need them right now.'

'There's no time for UN units to move up today.'

'Those blokes'll be massacred,' Danny observed in dismay.

'You're right, we do need some help right now,' Watson said calmly and issued more orders to his radio operator.

Chapter 15 — Aviation of the Future

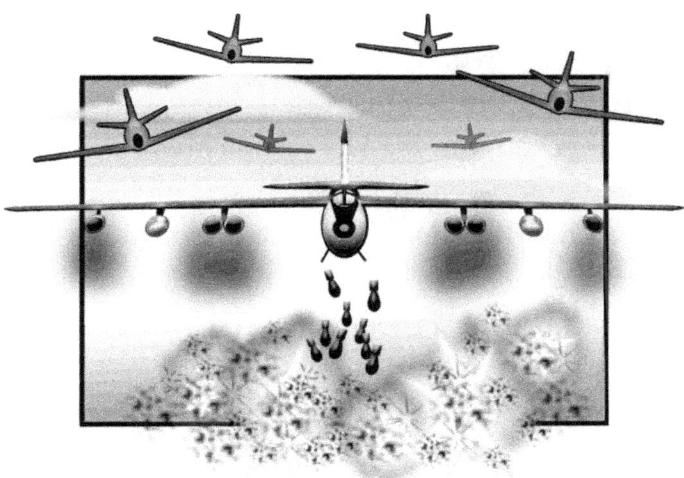

Communication has always been a lynch-pin of successful military combat, and nowhere was it more vital than during joint air-ground operations. Danny's chopper was fitted with a radio with twelve preset frequencies. They were all assigned to various units. The channels were designated 'A' to 'L'. Danny's instruction papers included an index of who used each channel. 3RAR HQ of course used one frequency, as did *Whirlybird Central*, the artillery co-ordinator, flight following and ATC, marine and naval units. Danny kept the frequency index handy, but had memorised those he thought he'd use most.

It often meant a lot of channel changing when he needed to know about artillery trajectories, other air traffic and the location of friendly forces. In this case having the extra radio set aboard was a huge advantage. Captain Watson could talk directly with his HQ and tell them the exact situation.

Right now he needed the Commonwealth Brigade's command centre. Watson's current unit call-sign was *Bravo-One-Three* indicating he was from B Company, 1st Battalion of the 3rd

Royal Australian Regiment. Danny knew that platoons were further sub-divided when operating independently. For example *One-Bravo-One-Three* would identify the first platoon of B Company. However, call-signs often changed to confuse any Chinese who'd hacked into the UN radio network.

The RAAF's 77 Squadron was based at Kimpo, near Seoul which was very handy indeed. Information rattled back and forth across the VHF airwaves as a flight of four Meteor jets scrambled into action within minutes. Meanwhile the T-34 tanks continued to pound the Commonwealth Brigade's positions.

It was common knowledge in Korea that replacing 77 Squadron's Mustang fighters with Gloster Meteors was not a popular decision. The Meteor was the first jet aircraft to fly combat missions in WWII, although the Luftwaffe quickly matched it with the Messerschmitt 262. Despite its wartime success, the Meteor was already obsolete when it entered service in Korea and no match for the Russian built swept-wing Mig-15 fighters. The USAF met the challenge with F-86 Sabre Jets, relegating the Meteor from Mig Alley to ground attack and reconnaissance duty.

And that's precisely what the men on the hills needed.

Danny relayed the tank positions to the flight leader.

'They're lined east-west over a two mile front,' Danny explained. 'They have infantry in division strength. Maybe three regiments and support vehicles in convoy along a road running north-south. Only small arms fire incoming so far. '

'Roger. Tally-ho the target. Running in now,' the flight leader said urbanely. He sounded almost bored.

Four specks appeared around fifteen thousand feet and swooped at close to four hundred knots. Danny's chopper was about a mile from the Chinese position, so he was well placed for a ring-side view. The Meteors flew in pairs. The leading jet rolled onto its back and dropped like a rocket-propelled stone. The pilot levelled at tree-top height, flying along the Chinese line. The Meteor's wings suddenly erupted in a cascade of flames and smoke as two rockets streaked towards the tanks.

The missiles slammed into the nearest tank, exploding on impact and blasting it yards into the air. The Meteor shot back into the atmosphere as the second jet launched two more rockets into the Chinese line. Both planes made four passes, knocking out half the tanks in minutes. Frenetic infantry raced everywhere, but there was nowhere to hide against the bare snow. Once the leading jets had exhausted their rockets the remaining two planes dived in for the kill. They flew impossibly close to ground level and drew considerable enemy fire, but the pilots held their nerve.

At the last moment two canisters tumbled from below the wings of both planes. As they pulled away the canisters slammed into the ground, erupting into four giant fireballs that spread in a devastating quarter-mile long blaze of pure destruction.

'Struth,' Danny whispered through clenched teeth.

'First time you've seen napalm, I guess?' Captain Watson said.

He explained napalm was petrol mixed in a jelly acid compound. It sprayed white-hot balls of flaming goop over a vast area. It was like a gigantic flame-thrower tossing solid clumps of fire that stuck to anything they hit.

'It's infantry's worst nightmare,' the captain added.

The flames died shortly, leaving a black scar through the snow. Half the tanks had been reduced to blazing wrecks with the crews incinerated in their fiery tombs. Corpses were scattered in the napalm's ragged wake, but the Meteors weren't finished with the Chinese troops yet.

The formation dived once more and strafed the infantry, raking their ranks with 20mm cannon fire until their ammunition was exhausted. The Meteors had gouged great swathes through the Chinese lines, but a division is a lot of men and many survived along with their supply convoy. Danny saw the units reforming with extraordinary discipline, courage and tenacity considering the pounding 77 Squadron's pilots had meted out.

Maybe half the tanks had been eliminated, but the Red regiments were supported by an artillery battalion equipped with 105mm field howitzers, rocket launchers and 120mm mortars.

'The buggers are reforming,' Danny muttered into the intercom while he selected *Whirlybird Central's* radio frequency.

'*Whirly Centre* this is *Danny Boy*,'

'Read you five-by-five, *Danny Boy*,' a cheerful American replied.

'We have a situation here at the Commonwealth Brigade's location,' Danny said giving controller his map co-ordinates. 'Are there any airborne units close enough to carry out a strike?'

'Sorry, we got nothing.'

The controller reported that the closest airborne bombers were a B-29 squadron. Unfortunately, they were returning to Japan, having completed their mission after dropping their bombs.

'I can get B-26s and Hellcats to you in thirty minutes maybe,' he added hopefully.

'They'll need to be quicker than that,' Danny said. 'Those boys are getting pounded down there, and I can only stay on station another twenty minutes. I'm getting low on fuel.'

Indeed the surviving tanks had resumed their barrage and were soon joined by the howitzers. Danny heard the booming impacts even above the noise of his chopper rotor. Explosions burst over the Commonwealth Brigade's defences. To make matters worse, the Chinese troops at the foot of the hills were advancing again.

'Hell, we can take on a bit of that action,' a voice drawled over the airwaves.

'Station calling, identify yourself,' the controller demanded.

'*Rattler-zero-one*, were five minutes out.'

'Negative, *zero-one*,' the controller's voice suddenly lost its casualness and sounded decidedly uneasy. 'You're on a demonstration flight. You're not cleared to combat status.'

'Then it high time we showed y'all what we can do.'

'It's not authorised.'

'Hell, boy, this is Colonel John J Savage speaking. This is *my* B-47 from *my* squadron and I'm gonna show *you* fellas a thing or two. We've got a war goin' here, boy. Our job is to kill Commies not put on shows for the brass.'

B-47?

'You still there, *Danny Boy?*'

'Yessir, the enemy position is two miles from the ridge, lying parallel to our positions.'

Danny quickly relayed the map co-ordinates.

'Roger that,' Colonel John J Savage acknowledged. 'Make yourself scarce, we've got the target in sight. We're coming in at four thousand feet. They sure won't be expecting that.'

Blimey, that was quick — how fast are they going?

Danny banked his chopper and headed back towards Hill 303. The sight before him was astounding. A monstrous plane with three jet engines hanging in pods under each wing streaked towards him. Black smoke trailed from the exhaust. The aerial juggernaut was escorted by a flight of F-86 Sabre Jets. As it banked to position for a run-in along the Chinese lines, its bomb-bay doors ponderously opened. The plane now seemed unwieldy as the Sabres streaked ahead, laying down suppression fire, ensuring the enemy troops kept their heads down.

Then a seemingly unending stream of bombs tumbled from the giant plane's belly. The entire Chinese line was engulfed in a wall of flame and clouds of black smoke. Great chunks of terrain, military debris and human scraps spewed from the blasts. Shock waves compressed the surrounding air, surging outwards. The H0-3 bucked and almost flipped over as the atmospheric tsunami swept past.

Danny steadied his chopper before returning to assess the damage. It was all over in minutes, but took some time for the smoke to clear. Once the dust settled, all Danny saw were two neat rows of black bomb-craters within a dull brown rectangle. Every scrap of snow had been melted or blown to mist. There was no sign of life in that holocaust. The Chinese force had been annihilated in a single pass. The sheer scope of carnage and destruction was overwhelming. How could just one bomber carry so much ordnance?

'What y'all see down there, *Danny Boy*?' Colonel John J Savage asked nonchalantly with more than a hint of smugness.

'You flattened them, sir. I can't see any guns or tanks and the troops have been vaporised.'

'Roger that, son. Like the man said, this is just a demo flight out to impress the generals, so we'll be heading back to Japan now.'

'I've never seen anything like that,' Danny replied.

'You're looking at aviation of the future, son. Glad to be of help. You boys have a nice day and y'all take care now.'

With that Colonel John J Savage switched to another radio frequency, set course for Tokyo followed by his faithful Sabre Jet escort, leaving all aboard the H0-3 and the Commonwealth Brigade to shake their heads in wonder. What they'd witnessed was extraordinary, yet something of an anomaly. The B-47 was the showcase equipment of USAF's newly formed *Strategic Air Command*. Normally its role was high level, long range operations, but Colonel Savage was more than happy to show off his awesome fire-power at low level.

There were of course Communist survivors on the ground, but they were in bad shape. Many were seriously wounded. Their comrades began to gather their casualties, abandoning the dead (which was unusual) as they started an agonising retreat. The Communist troops around the hills now realised reinforcements weren't coming. They were in danger of being cut off by advancing UN forces or suffering the same fate as their comrades should 77 Squadron, or worse still the giant bomber, launch another attack. Wisely they decided to withdraw before the Meteors had time to return to Kimpo, refuel, re-arm and return for more slaughter.

'Impressive,' Watson said. 'Just drop us off on your way home, thanks.'

Danny was still a little stunned at the absolute annihilation below, but his fuel was dwindling and it was time to return to *Whirlybird Central*. Captain Watson patted him on the back before jumping from the chopper door as they hovered a few inches above Hill 303.

'Thanks Danny,' he said. 'That was a bloody good show.'

'Yeah, but those poor buggers didn't stand a chance.'

'Then they shouldn't have started it in the first place, should they? Remember they'll be itching to do the same to you if they get the chance.'

And then he was gone.

That seems to be the general consensus, Danny thought, recalling his conversation with CAT pilots Paul Holden and Erik Shilling.

As he flew back to *Whirlybird Central,* Danny saw columns of UN infantry with armour support winding their way towards the five hills.

'Looks like they're getting the reinforcements they need after all,' he observed.

'Maybe they won't need us for a while, but I'm not betting a ball on it,' Long Li replied.

When they landed they discovered four bullet holes in their fuselage although no flight systems were damaged. The mechanics said they'd have no trouble riveting metal patches over the gaps. Major Armstrong met them in the briefing tent to analyse the day's work. The other pilots had continued to resupply the hilltops while Danny was on FAC duty.

All three marine crews had also come under heavy enemy fire, but had completed their missions without suffering any casualties. They discussed the day's events although nothing particularly new resulted. Danny mentioned his rolling take-off and landing. The other pilots listened with interest then argued the merits of the technique.

As no other tasks were assigned, Danny decided to catch a nap. He awoke close to dark. Long Li had gone to town to try some local cuisine, so Danny headed for the mess tent. Major Armstrong sat alone at a table nursing a beer. He looked particularly weary and jaded. Danny bought a *Coke* and joined him.

'Mind if I sit down, Major?'

'Sure, knock yourself out kid. You did good work today, well done. What's on your mind?'

'Nothing specific, I just thought you might like some company ... Well yes, something specific.'

'Something bothering you?'

'I'm trying to understand the point of it all.'

'The war, you mean?'

'This part of it. Take those five hills the Commonwealth Brigade is holding. They're of no particular tactical value. What's the point of being there at all? They're right in the middle of nowhere.'

'It doesn't make much sense, I guess. What you've got to understand is there are about a million hills in Korea. Each one's been given a number and each one has been taken or lost at some time. Many have gone back and forth several times.'

'No one seems to be any closer to winning the war.'

'The hills are good observation points, but most are just territory markers.'

'Markers.'

'You know much about lions or wolves, Danny?'

'Not really native to Australia, are they? I can tell you a lot more about kangaroos and wallabies.'

'Lions and wolves mark their territory by pissing on anything they see. I guess they have an individual scent or something. If another animal comes along and sniffs the scent he knows he's gonna have a fight on his hands if he don't vamoose.'

'Sounds pretty gross to me. I'm not sure our blokes will appreciate being compared to lion's piss either,' Danny said.

'Maybe, but it's the same deal. We post guys to mark our territory. Trouble is there ain't enough to go around that's why they're spread so thin and have to rely on artillery and air support.'

'It doesn't seem like a very good plan to me.'

'Damn right it ain't. There's no aim – first rule of warfare is to have an aim and we don't have one. I mean we can't just march into Manchuria and then on down to Beijing and tell Chairman Mao to stop being such a pain in the ass. It was different in the last war. All we had to do was kill enough Nips and Krauts until they surrendered. These Slopes are different. They ain't gonna surrender no matter how hard we hit 'em.'

'It's not so much about Korea as us against the Reds.'

'Now you're getting it, kid. The Cold War's lurking in the background while we scrap it out here. At least it stops some zealot pushing a red button and setting off a nuclear bomb. It'll be bombers like that B-47 or missiles that'll do the job.'

'Some people might think it's a good idea.'

'General MacArthur was all for it. I reckon that's why President Truman sacked him.'

'It just seemed like a waste of all those lives for absolutely nothing.'

'Mao probably told his generals there's an armistice coming up. There've been peace talks on and off just about since this whole mess started, but they don't come to anything. Nor will they while Joe Stalin has a say in the matter.'

'Why do peace talks make a difference? Surely if negotiations are going on, there's no point in fighting. Why risk getting killed if there might be a cease-fire tomorrow?'

'That's the rub you see. If – and it's a great big if – there is an armistice, then whoever holds the most territory has the most negotiating chips which might define where the cease-fire line is going to be.'

'So there's nothing worse than peace talks.'

'Absolutely. Now you're getting the picture. Peace talks always cause trouble.'

Danny just shook his head.

'Makes you wonder how we can possibly lose with hardware like that bomber.'

'I'm sure the Russians will have something to match it before long.'

'On the strength of that, I think I'll trade this *Coke* for a beer. You want another one, Major?'

'Sure, thanks.'

Chapter 16 — Search and Rescue

Long Li returned later that evening in a particularly sombre mood for a man normally cheerful and optimistic. He joined Danny and Vic Armstrong in the mess tent, but only drank tea. Danny asked him how his trip downtown had gone, but Long Li merely shrugged and said it was *okay.*

'Don't you like Korean food then?' Danny insisted.

'It's not that. The place is just so damned poor. This war has sucked the country dry. There's not much to go round. The biggest growth industry appears to be whoring.'

Danny had no answer to that.

'For all the billions being spent defending Korea, it's not helping the locals.'

'Better than the Commies, I guess?'

'You're right there,' Armstrong said. 'Y'know there's a bunch of pansy college kids back stateside sprouting, "Better Red than dead" — what a load of crap. If it was up to me I'd kick their faggot asses into next week and ship 'em all off to the army. That'd knock the *mommy's boy* outta them.'

No one felt like celebrating their victory anymore, so Danny turned in with a C S Forester *Captain Hornblower* novel. The officer's club had a surprisingly good selection of books, although it included some 19th century classics that Danny found heavy going. He also discovered a witty fantasy by an English professor called J R R Tolkien that he'd rather enjoyed. Danny was able to finish several by New Year's Eve. He'd had little opportunity to read as a boy and found he rather liked being immersed in a well-written yarn.

Whirlybird Central celebrated New Year in as much style as they could muster. Armstrong's equipment master-sergeant somehow produced a pallet load of beer. The weather was still bitterly cold as a winter storm swept in from Siberia, effectively bringing the war to a standstill. Danny could only wonder how the poor sods up on Hill 303 were faring. At least no one would be shooting at them. The storm raged for a week, but abated for Danny's birthday.

8th January 1953 dawned clear and calm. Everyone at *Whirlybird Central* congratulated him while Long Li produced a cake with candles. As all crews were on standby, they celebrated in the briefing tent by demolishing the cake and washing it down with hot cocoa. It was a milestone for Danny in that he could now vote and legally drink in a pub because he was a serviceman while civilians had to wait until they turned twenty-one.

The strains of *Happy Birthday* and *For He's a Jolly Good Fellow* had barely died when a stranger entered the tent. He wore a leather flying jacket over his RAAF uniform. His most striking feature was an eight-inch handlebar moustache.

'I'm looking for Pilot Officer McAlister,' the stranger announced abruptly.

'That's me, sir,' Danny replied knowing instinctively that this bloke was a 'sir'.

'Wing Commander Hubble, CO 77 Squadron,' the stranger said without bothering to extend a handshake.

Yep, when in doubt throw some 'sirs' about.

'I understand you were in command of the FAC chopper guiding my blokes a couple of weeks ago.'

'Yes sir, if you mean Hill 303,' Danny replied uncertainly.

'Precisely. Is there somewhere we can talk?' Hubble asked.

'Use my office,' Major Armstrong offered.

Office was something of an over-statement. Armstrong occupied a corner of the briefing tent where his administration clerk kept *Whirlybird Central's* records and endless paperwork up to date. Hubble nodded to Armstrong as he sat at the major's desk. Danny stood as smartly to attention as he could, considering he had no drill training or knowledge of military etiquette. They were still hazy concepts. Danny also wondered whether he had somehow done something wrong without knowing it.

'Pull up a chair, McAlister,' Hubble said.

'Am I in trouble?' Danny asked as he sat. He'd taken an instant dislike to Hubble and the feeling appeared to be mutual.

'Why would you think that?' Hubble asked.

Struth, I hate it when they answer a question with a question — all I wanted was a 'yes' or 'no'.

'Nothing, sir. I just thought we should get straight to it if I was.'

Danny thought he saw Hubble give a hint of a smile for a micro-second, but he couldn't be sure. It was probably more like a sneer.

'Let me just say that when I discovered there was a stray RAAF *boggy* running around Korea with no visible command structure, I thought I'd better come and find out what you were up to.'

'I'm attached to Major Armstrong's marine chopper unit, sir.'

'Attached from where precisely?'

Danny pondered the point. It was a grey area now he came to think about it.

'I have a contract working for CAT.'

'So you're one of Chennault's mercenaries, eh? What're you doing in a RAAF uniform?'

'Colonel Serong recruited me into the RAAF active reserve, sir. He arranged for me to be attached to Major Armstrong's command.'

'Did he just? I wonder how that army spook gets to hire untrained pilots for the RAAF. What exactly does Colonel Serong want you to do?'

'Evaluate rotary-wing ops, sir.'

'You seem a bit young.'

'That's what I told Colonel Serong and General Chennault.'

'And what have you revealed so far?'

'I only conducted routine support ops during training with Major Armstrong. My first combat sorties were resupplying Hill 303 and pointing your jets in the right direction. That's about the strength of my rotary-wing combat experience, sir. It's early days, but choppers — the H0-3 at least — are handy and versatile, but vulnerable to enemy fire and have serious weight and range limitations. I'm hoping I will have a fuller report for Colonel Serong and General Chennault with more experience.'

'I'm not sure I like the idea of a loose cannon rolling around the countryside, doing whatever he pleases, McAlister. So I think we'll take you under 77 Squadron's wing.'

'Won't I be needed here now the weather has cleared?'

'I'm not used to having my orders questioned, young man. You will report to my HQ at Kimpo at zero-nine-hundred tomorrow. Is that clear?'

'Yes, sir. I don't think Major Armstrong will be too happy though.'

'Leave Major Armstrong to me. I outrank him and you are an Australian servicemen after all.'

'I have a civilian CAT crewman, sir.'

'Bring him with you.'

'May I ask what I am to do, sir?'

'What you're told, like all my other *boggies*.'

'Yes, sir.'

'Good,' Hubble said.

He stood and exchanged a few words with Vic Armstrong. The major shrugged and saluted. Hubble returned the salute and left the command tent without another glance towards Danny.

'Looks like you've got a new boss, Danny,' Armstrong remarked when the Wing Commander was gone.

'He doesn't seem very friendly,' Danny replied unhappily.

'I hear he gets results. I guess he doesn't think the war's a popularity contest.'

The following morning Danny said goodbye to Vic Armstrong and the marine pilots. He and Long Li packed their gear and flew the short distance from *Whirlybird Central* to Kimpo. Danny was assigned a camp bed at the officer's quarters while Long Li was given a berth in the Sergeant's mess. Danny knew there was nothing he could do about the accommodation arrangements now he was officially in the military system. Once again Long Li was sanguine and found his quarters adequate.

Apart from the more senior flight commanders, 77 Squadron pilots were a cheerful group of officers and NCOs who were not much older than Danny. Some had seen action in WWII, while for others Korea was their first taste of action.

They welcomed him as one of their own although he wasn't an elite Meteor pilot. It didn't take Danny long to discover why he was so popular. He was to be the squadron's SAR unit.

Wing Commander Hubble had pounced on the opportunity to have a helicopter at hand to retrieve any downed pilots, but for Danny it was a blow. He didn't mind the idea of rescuing airmen, but they didn't need rescuing very often. Meanwhile he was stuck at Kimpo twiddling his thumbs while waiting for something to do. He felt under-utilised and wrote a memo to Colonel Serong implying that his and CAT's asset was being wasted on the ground at Kimpo.

At least he was finally able to complete his FAA licence exams which CAT had arranged for him to sit by correspondence. That was unusual, but CAT's CIA connections had obviously pulled some strings in the background.

In fact it seemed to Danny that Wing Commander Hubble used the chopper as his personal taxi-service. If he felt like popping across to Seoul or any other military HQs, he called on Danny to chauffeur him back and forth, often keeping him waiting for hours in the bitter cold. Long Li wasn't essential on these trips, but when he was unaccompanied by an aide, Hubble insisted he come along simply to open and close the chopper door for him. Throughout these flights, the wing commander remained aloof, always addressing Danny by his surname.

Fortunately he was able to fly to *Whirlybird* Central regularly because no 77 Squadron mechanics were qualified to service the

Sikorsky. On one such flight Danny asked Major Armstrong to forward the message to wherever Colonel Serong might be. Strictly speaking Danny was undercutting the accepted chain-of-command, but he felt he'd been hijacked by Hubble who wasn't really his boss.

Danny heard nothing for the next couple of months while he idled away in 77 Squadron's command centre. The weather improved although it was still hideously cold through January and February. The thaw began at the beginning of March, but it was still a long way from when the first apple blossoms were to appear.

Then pandemonium erupted.

Two Meteors were flying a photo-reconnaissance mission along the Yalu River. There had been a resumption of Chinese troop movements from the north. Intelligence suggested large numbers of men and equipment were crossing the river using portable pontoon-bridges. 77 Squadron had been assigned the job of obtaining photographic proof.

The two-jet Meteor flight was taking photographs at low level when they were bounced by half-a-dozen Migs.

The squadron command centre radio burst into frantic calls for help. Both Meteor pilots transmitted *Mayday* calls. One plane was hit in the port engine which burst into flames. The pilot managed to shut down the engine and limp southwards at tree-top level.

The other Meteor was being chased westwards by the Migs. Approaching the coast the plane was sprayed with cannon shells. The Meteor was in desperate shape. The pilot reported he was only able to maintain limited power on one engine while the other had seized after bullets tore into its compressor and turbines. The Meteor looked doomed, just as a flight of F-86 Sabres were vectored to the area. They took the Migs on in a spiteful dog-fight that saw one Russian plane spiral to the ground in a deadly fireball.

While the swept-wing fighters battled up and down Mig Alley, the crippled Meteor came under heavy ground fire and was forced out to sea beyond enemy weapons' range. The pilot then turned south parallel to the coast, attempting to limp back to Kimpo. Danny and Long Li didn't wait for orders. They dashed for their chopper and were airborne within minutes. It was a race against time. Danny's plan was to reach the stricken jet, or at least get as close as possible. Seoul radar was tracking the Meteor and vectored Danny its last known position, about ten miles out in the Yellow Sea.

The Meteor pilot then reported he was having problems controlling his jet. All the engine instruments were haywire and he was worried his remaining engine was about to explode. Reluctantly he turned his plane towards land even though North Korean and Chinese forces still lurked along the coastline. He felt he'd rather be over land than the freezing yellow Sea if he was forced to bail out.

Danny finally made radio contact with the stricken aircraft's pilot who sounded remarkably calm considering his plane was about to disintegrate around him. The Meteor was still two miles 'feet wet' — over water. Then Danny saw a speck ahead that quicky developed into a recognisable aircraft shape. Smoke trailed from the plane's one operative engine. The Meteor certainly wasn't making spectacular progress. It seemed to Danny it was hardly faster than his chopper which had a maximum speed less than one hundred knots.

'I'll follow you in,' Danny reassured the pilot when only a couple of miles separated both aircraft.

'Roger that, my instruments are off the clock,' the pilot said. Although he sounded relieved, there was now a hint of agitation in his tone. His urbane casualness had been replaced by growing concern as his plane became less controllable by the second.

There was worse trouble to come. Danny sensed a flash from the shoreline. Two white trails streaked towards the Meteor. Danny knew exactly what they were.

'Bail out,' he urged the Meteor pilot. 'Two incoming rockets at your nine o'clock.'

One thing you can say about knuckleheads is they're trained to make quick decisions. The Meteor pilot was well aware that his plane was in no condition to evade a missile attack. He jettisoned his cockpit canopy and pulled the ejector handle. His seat blasted clear of the plane just as the first rocket struck. The second rocket exploded a second later, blasting the jet to a shower of metallic confetti that tumbled downwards, splashing into the sea and disappearing instantly.

Danny saw the pilot shoot away from the airborne fireball, but couldn't tell if he was harmed by the explosion. The pilot's seat arched to its zenith then dropped sharply. A parachute drogue released and was dragged into the airstream, followed by the main chute that separated the pilot from his seat. The main chute deployed, gently descending to earth, but drifting dangerously close to the coast. The pilot splashed into the sea about half a mile from a narrow beach between the water line and a small cliff face. His bright yellow *Mae West* filled with air, holding his head above the surface.

Danny knew he'd have to be quick. Spring was still three weeks away and the sea remained ice cold. The pilot would be lucky to last ten minutes before he froze to death.

'Arm the winch,' he instructed Long Li.

'Already done — standing by.'

Danny flew so low that the chopper's main rotor sprayed seawater onto the windshield. He was forced to climb a few feet to keep a clear view of the downed pilot who'd managed to let off a hand-held smoke flare to guide Danny towards him.

'He's alive, Long Li.'

Danny was now going to attempt one of the more difficult helicopter manoeuvres for the first time. Up until then fast motor launches were used to rescue aircrews from the sea. Helicopter pilots operated in uncharted territory most of the time. Hovering itself was not particularly tricky once you mastered the skill. You normally had some reference point such as a tree or other ground feature to focus on and maintain position. The amorphous ocean swell provided no means of orientation, so a hovering chopper could drift in any direction without the pilot being aware of the fact.

Danny recalled Vic Armstrong's tips on the subject:

- Assess the wind and fly very slowly into wind.
- Assess the swell and don't let its motion confuse you.
- Assess the wave direction, which may not be the same as the sea swell.
- Let the winch drag along the water surface keeping it stable and giving the survivor the best chance of grabbing the halter.

So Danny lined up about a hundred yards from the pilot and crept toward him. He knew he would lose sight of the pilot under the cockpit floor when he came closer. After that Danny would have to rely on Long Li who manned the electric winch mounted above the chopper's door.

'Right two feet, Danny ... Steady ... ten yards to go ... left one foot ... further ... steady ... yes ... hold that course ... five yards to go ...four ...three ... two ... one ... shit, he's missed it.'

'Going around again.'

Vic Armstrong had told Danny that to try and back up was futile. He'd just wobble all over the sky in ever increasing oscillations. The quickest option was to go round for another go. Danny lined up on the airman, knowing that if he didn't make it this time, he might as well not bother. The poor bloke would be dead from hypothermia.

'Oh, shit,' Long Li said once more.

'What?'

'Looks like a Red patrol boat is coming out to meet us.'

Sure enough Danny saw a great sinister shape surging towards them. Its mountainous bow-wave suggested it was making twenty knots or more.

'We won't make it in time,' Long Li warned.

'I'm not leaving that poor bugger to freeze to death or spend the rest of the war in a Commie POW camp.'

They had reached the pilot who, although weakened by the numbing cold, was well trained. He grabbed the halter and knew how to secure it under his arm-pits.

'He's on,' Long Li said, activating the winch switch. 'I'm bringing him up now.'

Just then a tendril of .50-cal machinegun shells laced towards them in a neat line of spray as they hit the sea. Tracer rounds slashed the waterline where the downed pilot had been only seconds ago. The bullets streaked past just below his feet that now dangled only inches above the surface.

'Time to go, Danny,' Long Li urged. 'Now!'

Danny needed no further encouragement as another burst of tracers snaked towards the chopper.

With the airman dangling on twenty feet of winch line, Danny pivoted the chopper on its axis. He tilted the cyclic pitch forward, forcing the chopper's nose forward and accelerating into translational lift. The extra weight slung below the chopper now acted as a pendulum. The downed airman started to swing in ever increasing arcs, dragging the chopper from side to side. Danny knew he must slow down before the oscillations became uncontrollable.

He had to get the airman aboard anyway. With the added chill-factor of the slipstream, he'd die in no time. When Danny decelerated and brought the chopper to a hover, the winch steadied and Long Li retracted the last few feet.

As Long Li helped the Meteor pilot struggle aboard, the Korean gunboat was almost upon them again. As the pilot collapsed gasping and shivering on the cabin floor, two rounds smashed through the windscreen spraying reinforced Perspex throughout the cockpit.

Danny was unhurt, but didn't wait to check on Long Li or their passenger. He pushed the cyclic forward, hoisted the collective pitch lever to its limit and accelerated south. He only reduced power when he heard the maximum airspeed warning sound. At this stage he was far enough away from the gunboat to relax.

The Meteor pilot was alive, but in bad shape. The cold and shock were at a point where he could easily succumb. Long Li shrouded him with thermal blankets that were part of their SAR equipment.

By then they were beyond enemy territory and weapons range. Soon they approached UN occupied territory, although it was often difficult to determine exactly where that was at times. The pilot was shaking uncontrollably. He didn't speak, but nodded his thanks or perhaps it was just uncontrollable shivering. So Danny headed for the nearest MASH, which hadn't been relocated since the Hill 303 incident.

Chapter 17 — The Customer is Always Right

The Sikorsky flew well enough at first, but shortly Danny sensed a slight vibration through the flight controls. Danny was unaware that a stream of small arms rounds had penetrated the tail boom. The lead missiles rattled around the tail cavity without initially doing any appreciative damage. As the vibration increased, Danny suspected that the tail rotor drive shaft was damaged.

Long Li soon became aware of the tremor.

'You reckon we'll make it, Danny?' he asked.

'Got to. That bloke needs medical attention.'

After a few minutes the vibration seemed to stabilize into a constant buzz so Danny pressed on. He tried to radio his intended fight path, but discovered another shot had smashed the transceiver. As a result, when he approached the MASH helipad no one was waiting for him which proved to be very fortunate indeed.

Landing and take-off were the most stressful phases of flight on both engine and airframe. As the chopper reached the pad, Danny flared the aircraft, raising the nose to bring it to a hover. As the tail dipped, several rounds that were loose inside the tail-boom tumbled aft and lodged solidly into the tail rotor gearing. The effect was instantaneous and catastrophic. The gears shuddered to a grinding halt, snapping the drive shaft and sending the tail-rotor spinning away. It smashed into a nearby tree, shattering into shards of lethal metal along with wooden splinters that splattered into the dust just short of the MASH tents.

With no tail-rotor to stabilise the chopper, it spun sharply on the main rotor shaft axis. Danny had no choice but to flatten the collective pitch lever and reduce the engine torque to prevent the plane spinning further. That of course killed all lift from the main rotor blades and the chopper dropped to earth. The undercarriage absorbed most of the impact force, but the wheels were wrenched from the fuselage. The chopper bounced about six feet back into the air before crashing down.

Danny kept his head and cut the engine fuel supply. The motor stopped instantly and the rotors wound down. Luckily the rotor hub stayed intact without shedding the blades which could have done untold injury and damage.

The chopper then settled, slumping forlornly at a precarious angle. Danny and Long Li hauled the Meteor pilot through the door and scrambled away just seconds before fuel from the ruptured tank seeped onto the glowing engine exhaust pipe.

The remaining fuel exploded with a whoosh rather than a bang as the chopper was down to its reserves, containing the fireball to a small, but furious blaze.

Danny, Long Li and the pilot slumped down, gasping for breath.

'That'll warm you up, mate,' Danny said to the pilot who grinned for the first time. 'Sorry I can't offer you a smoke.'

'Danny, do you ever land a plane normally?' Long Li asked with a grin.

Their arrival of course didn't go unnoticed. A medical team rushed to the helipad accompanied by a squad of ROK soldiers equipped with fire extinguishers. The troops set about dousing the fire while the medics examined what they saw as the survivors of a fiery crash.

A triage doctor declared Danny and Long Li fit while the pilot would be fine after a warm bath, dry clothes and a gallon of hot coffee.

The same careworn nurse Danny had met previously was with the triage team. Danny grinned and she returned his smile.

'Sorry I trashed your helipad,' he said.

'These guys will have it cleared up in no time,' she replied. 'That's not the first chopper wreck we've seen here.'

Danny thought she was pretty, but it was a case of *ships-passing-in-the-night.* Ignoring the fact that she was at least ten years his senior, the MASH was a busy place and she was needed elsewhere. Danny and Long Li's immediate problem was what to do next.

They marched to the orderly room, found a clerk with a radio phone and contacted *Whirlybird Central.* Danny didn't feel much like talking to Wing Commander Hubble who'd have no use for him now he'd lost the chopper anyway. Vic Armstrong was sure to be more understanding. He wasn't around, but his EXO merely said, 'These things happen', and sent a chopper over to pick up Danny and Long Li.

When they arrived at *Whirlybird Central,* the marine aircrews greeted Danny and Long Li warmly. Danny was at something of a loss. He no longer had a chopper to fly and wasn't actually authorised to fly the American aircraft. Armstrong was only expected to be away for a day or two and had left his executive officer, a cheerful captain, commanding the helo-flight. The EXO said Danny and Long Li were welcome to stay at *Whirlybird Central* until the major returned. He was sure they'd work something out then.

Unfortunately Wing Commander Hubble got there first.

The following morning Hubble arrived at the marine camp. His Jeep screeched to a halt in front of the operations tent where Danny and Long Li were sharing a coffee and idle conversation with the marine aviators. Hubble barged in, brushing the tent flap back dramatically.

'McAlister, what the bloody hell have you been up too? Where's my SAR chopper?'

'I've been saving one of your knuckleheads,' Danny replied before he thought about it. Hubble was really pissing him off.

'Watch your tongue, McAlister. Who authorised the flight?'

'No one. I took off as soon as I heard your pilot was in trouble.'

'You don't just race off without authorisation,' Hubble said.

'Your bloke would be dead if I'd waited. It was touch-and-go as it was, but *we* got him safely to the MASH.'

'Yes, they contacted me. My pilot is recovering well, but what's this rumour I hear about the chopper being damaged.'

'No rumour, sir and I'd say "damaged" is a bit of an understatement.'

'What the hell do you mean?'

'I reckon it's a write-off.'

Hubble's face turned purple and Danny was sure he noticed the wing commander's moustache tips bristle upwards.

'Of all the incompetent, brainless, reckless idiots I've met, you must take the cake, McAlister. You've lost 77 Squadron's only SAR chopper. You moron!'

'With all due respect, sir,' Danny said in a tone that suggested no due respect whatsoever. 'I'm the moron who saved your downed jet pilot. He'd be dead or a POW if it wasn't for Long Li and me. It wasn't your chopper anyway and I'm not in your bloody precious 77 Squadron.'

'How dare you back-chat me. You're on a charge and believe me I can make you sorry for your insolence.'

'What is wrong with you? Do you put your wretched chain-of-command ahead of your pilots' safety?'

Danny was in a rage. There were no 'sirs' now.

'That's it. You're under arrest. I will not be questioned by an upstart *boggy*.'

'Now hold your horses, John,' a familiar voice warned as Colonel Ted Serong and Major Vic Armstrong entered the ops tent. They were accompanied by two lean, severe looking men in US Army fatigues. They both wore captain's twin bar emblems pinned to their collars, but showed no regimental insignia. One was a Caucasian while the other was a Negro, which was unusual, because integration was still a novel concept for the American military.

'You keep out of this, Ted,' Hubble insisted. 'This is between McAlister and *me*.'

So Hubble and Serong knew each other although there appeared to be no love lost between them.

'Sorry, I can't do that, John,' Serong replied evenly. 'I recruited Danny. He's under my command even if he *is* a RAAF officer. These two gents want a word with him as well.'

Serong indicated the brace of mysterious captains

There was a stand-off while Serong and Hubble glared at one another. A wing commander was an equivalent rank to a lieutenant colonel and certainly senior to a captain. Although, from what Danny could make out, that didn't appear to bother the two strangers who gave the impression they didn't take orders from anyone.

'I'll be making a full report to Brigadier Winton. You haven't heard the last of this, McAlister,' he raged and stormed out.

'What the heck did I do to him?' Danny asked rhetorically after Hubble was gone. 'We saved his flaming pilot yesterday. A "Thank you, Danny and Long Li" would have been nice.'

'Don't worry about John Hubble, Danny,' Serong assured him. 'He's a little fish in a big pond. I can catch anything he throws at you, and as I said, these two gentlemen would like to have a word. They have been following your progress with interest.'

It appeared to Danny that Ted Serong had unusual clout for a mere lieutenant colonel and was on abnormally intimate terms with the American spooks. But then Serong was a fanatical anti-Communist who was about to spend considerable time in Burma assisting the military there to stem the insidious 'Red Tide'.

'I haven't done much yet,' Danny replied. 'I spent nearly two months ferrying Wing Commander Hubble around.'

'Don't run yourself down, kid,' the black captain spoke in a growl. 'We know how you handled yourself during the attack on the Commonwealth line and yesterday took guts, brains and initiative. That's what we're looking for, you see.'

'Allow me to introduce Captain Black and Captain White,' Serong said, indicating the two men appropriately.

Danny smiled as he shook the soldiers' hands in turn and introduced Long Li.

'Meaning no disrespect, sirs,' Danny said. 'But I'm certainly not going to mix you up.'

'We are *customers* and like to keep our identities off the record,' Captain Black explained.

So they were CIA spooks which explained the lack of regimental identification.

Once again they took advantage of Vic Armstrong's 'office'. Armstrong excused himself, saying he'd organise coffee for his visitors. It seemed the marine pilot didn't want to know what the CIA was up to.

'I received your initial report, Danny,' Serong explained.

'I have more to add after yesterday, sir. I have a detailed draft assessment back at Kimpo.'

'I'll arrange to have it picked up with your gear. Yours too, Long Li.'

'We're not going back to 77 Squadron then?' Long Li asked.

'No, you're going to work for Captain White and Captain Black.'

'You are a civilian, Mr Sim,' Captain Black addressed Long Li courteously. 'You and Danny have made a good team, so we'd like you to volunteer, but there is no obligation.'

'I'll stay with Danny,' Long Li said with a smile. 'I don't know what he'd do without me to get him out of trouble.'

'You don't know what they want yet,' Danny protested.

'I'll stay,' Long Li insisted.

It was what friends did, wasn't it?

'What if *I* don't agree?' Danny said.

'You don't have that luxury I'm afraid, Danny,' Serong replied urbanely. 'You're still on the active reserve list and have to follow orders. I've got to dash off now, so I'll leave you in the capable hands of Captain Black and Captain White.'

He shook hands with Danny and Long Li and left just as the coffee arrived.

'Gentlemen,' Captain White announced, 'what we are about to discuss is top-secret. It goes no further. We are bound by our US National Security Legislation and you are both subject to the Commonwealth Official Secrets Act. Is that quite clear?'

'Yessir.'

Both Danny and Long Li nodded.

'Good,' White continued. 'What do you know about covert ops?'

'They're secret?' Danny suggested.

'Precisely. You may not know, but this war has taken a significant turn and it is our job to see if we can capitalise on that situation.'

The captains went on to explain that two important events had occurred that would potentially affect the outcome and even bring the conflict to an end. The first was the death of Russian dictator, Joseph Stalin, who'd taken a hard line on the conflict. The Soviet Union supplied the North Koreans with military hardware and MIG pilots on the condition the North Koreans prosecuted the war in earnest. The Presidium of the Central Committee was thrown into turmoil in the vacuum left by Stalin.

Nikita Khrushchev was one rising star in the political upheaval. Although he'd certainly got his hands dirty in the many 1930s purges when thousands upon thousands of 'political dissidents' were summarily executed, Khrushchev was considered a moderate compared with the former Russian leader. Khrushchev had seen action at Stalingrad and the Battle of Kursk and possibly saw Korea as an unnecessary drain on Soviet resources.

The other notable change was that General Dwight D Eisenhower had recently taken up residence in the White House. Eisenhower's competent performance as Allied Commander-in-Chief during Operation Overlord and the successful defeat of the Nazis in North Europe was well known to everyone in Korea. Now as president, if anyone could sort this out, then it would be 'Ike'.

'So you think there might be a cease-fire soon?' Danny asked.

'No guarantees, Danny,' Captain Black replied, 'but it seems more likely now.'

'So what does this have to do with Long Li and me? We're not exactly high-flying peace negotiators.'

'We've been interrogating a lot of prisoners who give conflicting reports. We have some ROK volunteers who are prepared to do some sneaking around behind enemy lines to see what they can discover about the general mood of the Commies.'

'And you need transportation, I assume,' Long Li said.

'Precisely Mr Sim — you don't mind if we call you Long Li, do you?'

Danny noticed that neither CIA captain offered his first name.

'Please do. When do we start?' Long Li grinned.

'ASAP,' Captain Black said.

'Uh, Captain,' Danny said uncomfortably. 'Aren't you forgetting we no longer have any transport?'

'Not at all. I'm surprised you didn't hear our arrival,' White said, waving Major Armstrong to join them.

'Vic, would you mind showing these guys their new equipment while we finish our coffee.'

'Sure thing,' Armstrong said and guided Danny and Long Li outside. 'You're gonna love this,' he added with a grin.

'I thought you were trying to make yourself scarce, but you are in on this whole thing, aren't you?' Danny challenged.

'Guilty I'm afraid,' Armstrong replied, pointing to the flight-line where his H0-3s were parked in line. 'But look what we've got for you to make up for it.'

Another machine stood at the end of the tidy row of choppers that was massive by comparison. It was a Sikorsky S-55 Chickasaw utility helicopter. It carried a load of up to twelve troops or six casevacs which made it a far more useful tool than the H0-3s. Its gleaming metal fuselage carried no identifying markings or military insignia.

'That's your new toy, gents,' Armstrong beamed, 'and I've got a week to teach you how to fly it.'

Chapter 18 — Covert Ops

Danny found flying the Chickasaw helicopter was quite an unexpected pleasure. The aircraft was far more stable and the cockpit similar to the height he was used to in the *Gooney-Bird*. Having learnt the unique skill of chopper piloting, the conversion to a larger plane proved simple enough. The fact that Wing Commander Hubble wasn't breathing down his neck was also a great relief.

Almost immediately after his conversion training, Captains Black and White showed up to claim their pound of flesh.

The battle lines between the UN and Communist forces were still by no means clear. Although the allies had pushed right up to the Chinese border, those northerly positions had proven untenable and were now occupied by the Communists once more. In 1950 UN forces had even taken Pyongyang, the North Korean capital, but now it was back in Red hands surrounded by a number of POW camps.

Black and White's informants had discovered that one of their spooks had been captured and now languished in one of the Suan camps awaiting transfer to Pak's Palace for interrogation. They were formulating an audacious plan to spring him.

'You're kidding,' Danny said in disbelief. 'Even I know you can't just march into a Commie POW camp. What are you planning – fly the chopper over the wire and hoist the poor bugger out?'

'We did consider that,' Black replied blandly, 'but there're too many variables. A stray bullet into your whirlybird would be a disaster with all our eggs in one basket.'

'So ..?'

The two CIA spooks explained their plan, which involved a full allied commando battalion co-ordinated with some heavy duty air and naval support. Danny's jaw just about touched the floor when he heard the entire plan although Long Li remained impassive. He was rather keen on the part where the CIA planned to mount a .50-cal machine gun at the door of the S-55.

'Isn't it going to be risky?' Danny asked and received a well deserved pained look from Long Li and the CIA captains.

'School teachers say there is no such thing as a damn-fool question, but you've just proved them wrong, Danny,' White admonished. 'This is war. *Everything* is risky.'

Danny was going to mention the fact that he had originally signed up to be a transport co-pilot flying milk runs from Japan to secure bases in South Korea. But he knew that would sound pretty weak, so he shut up. Like so many things in his young life, they just seemed to spiral out of control.

'Okay, what's this chap's name?' he asked with a resigned sigh.

'Lieutenant Green,' Captain White replied.

'Yes, of course it is.'

'But, isn't this risky in another way?' Long Li said, eyeing the CIA men suspiciously. 'I've heard scuttlebutt that there's a big POW swap planned this month.'

'Nothing is certain yet except that Lieutenant Green won't be among those exchanged. He's a South Korean national who's built up a complex spy network. Right now we hope the Reds think he's just another ROK prisoner. If he's transferred to Pak's Palace we'll never get him out. '

'Won't it threaten the exchange?' Long Li asked.

'That's hard to tell, the Commies are so volatile,' White said. 'They see any form of conciliation as weakness. They are obsessed with propaganda however blatant. North Koreans have been isolated to the extent that they believe anything the government tells 'em. You gotta remember none of them have travelled more than a couple of miles from home. It's easy to pull the wool over their eyes. So we keep pushing 'em to show we're tough customers.'

The four men went on to study the exact location of the Suan camp. The extreme chopper range bothered Danny, but Captain Black told him not to worry. He wouldn't be flying all the way.

'I believe you and Long Li are good sailors, Danny,' White beamed. 'That's going to come in handy. You get airborne at zero-six hundred tomorrow.'

'Where are we going?' Danny asked

'Need to know basis for the time being,' White grinned. 'Don't worry, we'll show you the way. We're coming with you.'

Both captains seemed very cheerful about the prospect of facing imminent danger.

*

Sure enough, the CIA captains were waiting beside the S-55 when Danny arrived half-an-hour before take-off. They were dressed in combat fatigues and insulated jackets. Additionally they carried fully loaded backpacks containing plastic explosives and were armed with assault rifles, automatic pistols, ammunition bandoliers, bayonets, and as many hand-grenades as they could carry.

They'd also loaded four extra ammo-boxes aboard. The machinegun was bolted onto a bracket that required the chopper door to be permanently pinned open. Another four boxes of the high-calibre ammunition lay on the chopper floor. During his preflight inspection Danny noticed a quick-release bracket had been attached to the lower fuselage between the main wheels.

'Blimey, there's no room to move in there,' Danny commented as he clambered into the pilot's seat. 'It's going to be damn cold with the door open.'

'We'll live. We're not going far,' Captain Black assured him.

They headed straight out over the Yellow Sea for ten miles where the *USS Rochester* awaited them. The cruiser not only bristled with nearly ninety guns of various calibres, but had a helipad constructed aft to support its four H0-3 choppers. Apparently Vic Armstrong had failed to mention to the CIA spooks that Danny had never landed on a moving warship, which posed its own gamut of technical difficulties. Even at that early stage of marine helicopter operations, the ocean was littered with choppers that had come to grief while approaching rocking decks.

Fortunately the sea was relatively calm, but the naval controller explained that Danny should approach from abeam the starboard bow because superstructure and radio masts obstructed the ship's stern.

Because of the cruiser's forward speed, Danny was committed to a steady cross wind and would actually touch down while flying sideways to keep up with the moving helipad. It was best not to think about the aerodynamics of the situation. Danny simply concentrated on his landing spot. It was rather like flying in close formation. If he just kept focused on one spot and held it steady, he'd be fine.

It wasn't the most elegant touchdown Danny had ever made – firm, but safe. It was then he understood what the tie-down point on the chopper's belly was for. A team of sailors raced under the main rotor lugging heavy cables. They hooked the cables to the chopper to prevent any further movement. A crew chief then ran his finger across his throat, indicating it was safe for Danny to cut the motor.

'There you go. Piece of cake,' Captain Black said, patting Danny shoulder.

They met the cruiser's captain and EXO during the briefing that followed. The skipper explained it was *Rochester*'s last mission in Korea and they'd be steaming for Long Beach by the end of the week.

The plan was a complex collaboration between all three arms of the service. Just prior to dawn, Danny was to take off under cover of a naval bombardment. Simultaneously B-26 medium bombers would raid anything surrounding the Suan camp that intelligence claimed vaguely qualified as a military target. A sabre-jet squadron would escort the bombers to see off any Migs that might get in the way. Ground forces also planned diversionary action in the south.

Meanwhile Captains Black and White would rendezvous with their ground agents and blow the POW camp wire where Lieutenant Green would be waiting. That was of course if he'd managed to bribe enough people inside the camp, hadn't been discovered and received the breakout message correctly – if at all. In fact, there were any number of variables that could cause disaster. There was no doubt that the CIA agents were extremely brave men, if a little crazy in Danny's opinion.

The food on board was excellent by military standards, so Danny and Long Li tucked into a mega-breakfast although they were puzzled why Americans poured maple syrup over everything. It was okay for pancakes, but bacon and eggs..?

Danny spent the remainder of the day ensuring the S-55 was fully refuelled. He hoped he'd have ample fuel endurance to return to the *Rochester*, but you never knew. Also a full fuel-load could prove to be a two-edged sword as Danny was about to discover. Together with Long Li and the CIA men, he pored over charts and memorised radio frequencies, although either Captain Black or White would take over communications with ground stations.

They liked their secrecy – it was a CIA 'need-to-know' thing.

After some hours Danny was sure he'd remember every minute detail of the LZ, which was vital because they would be landing in darkness.

No sweat, Westland Lysanders had done the same in tiny mud paddocks in France during WWII. Sure they were effective STOL aircraft, but they couldn't hover.

The LZ was a small space between a screen of bamboo and an apple orchard surrounded by rice paddies. It was hoped the bamboo would hide the S-55 from camp guards and also shield Lieutenant Green as he made his getaway.

The EXO gave Danny and Long Li a guided tour around the ship, which was impressive, although the CIA officers showed no inclination to join them. After supper Danny and Long Li were assigned bunks close to the wardroom. Danny found sleep difficult although Long Li was snoring in seconds.

Danny must have dropped off because the next thing he knew was a sailor shaking him awake and offering a cup of steaming coffee. Long Li was already awake and sipping his drink.

'EXO's compliments, sir,' the sailor reported. 'You're due at your chopper in five.'

It was all go from then on.

Once on deck, Danny saw *the Rochester* was cruising slowly, so take-off wouldn't be difficult. As he started the S-55 engine, Black and White clambered aboard. Once again Danny admired their grit. A two-man team plunging deep into enemy territory took pure guts, especially as they knew what to expect if they were captured.

He estimated a thirty minute flight to the LZ which, at sea level, put *USS Rochester* just on the edge of North Korean radar range. That meant the S-55 would be picked up almost immediately even though Danny flew just above the waves. He'd have to gain altitude after ten minutes or hit terrain once he crossed the coast. That was of course unless the radar operators weren't distracted, which is exactly what happened next.

The Rochester's twelve five-inch and nine eight-inch guns opened up. Shells roared five miles into the atmosphere and crumped down somewhere in the distance. As Danny crossed the coast he climbed to two thousand feet which he knew would clear any obstacles en route.

Pyongyang didn't erupt into view with a blaze of illumination like a modern city. There were few street lights at the best of times and wartime deprivation had forced the city into an involuntary blackout. Danny's destination was to the south east of the city so *Rochester's* guns pounded incendiary shells into known military bases in the area and to the north. Orientating himself by the glowing hot spots, Danny was able to track along the correct course. He also utilised *Rochester's* radio beacon although it would soon drop out of range and he was too low to pick up beacons from UN airfields to the south.

However the dedicated CIA officers knew the locations and frequencies of North Korean beacons from which Danny could triangulate his exact position.

As the S-55 reached the city limits a mass of explosions splattered several miles to the north. The B-26s had found their targets. The air raids and shelling were to last for the entire operation's duration. The intensity of the bombardment should throw even the most hardened troops into despair. Even if they survived direct obliteration from a blast, ear drums would burst and internal organs be crushed by the shockwaves.

Although the military had chosen its targets with care, there would be considerable civilian collateral damage. Fortunately Danny had no time to consider that aspect of the action. At the same time the commando battalion was already making its diversionary strike in the south, drawing Communist units away from the POW camps.

Once Danny had left his final radio fix, it required precise timing to reach the LZ. A minute out he switched on his landing light. This was a powerful beam that shone from the chopper's nose. Danny descended the S-55 until he spotted trees and rooftops using the light as an aid.

Hopefully the rotor-blade and engine noise was drowned by the thundering shells and bombs. Danny picked up the bamboo screen which stretched ahead for over half a mile. He located the clearing wedged between the orchard and bamboo.

Blimey it's small! It seemed bigger from the maps and recon photos.

Danny brought the chopper to a hover a few feet above the tree line. Long Li guided him down, taking care to ensure the tail rotor cleared any vegetation. The trees might look soft from the air, but a tail-rotor strike could be fatal. As he eased the chopper onto the LZ, Danny saw that there were maybe twenty yards of clearance ahead and fifty to his left. He stayed as close as possible to the orchard side for protection. If anyone emerged from the bamboo it put the maximum distance between them and the chopper.

The wheels had barely touched the soft grassy surface when Captains Black and White grabbed their plastic explosive packs, leapt out and disappeared into the bamboo. They'd instructed Danny to keep the engine running. *Of course he was going to keep the engine running. What did they think he was – a bloody idiot?* Meanwhile Long Li checked the .50-cal ammo belts were in place and cocked the gun's firing mechanism. They both kept a sharp eye open for enemy troops or anyone who strayed into the wrong place at the wrong time.

Artillery flashes popped up everywhere like a gigantic fireworks display. Not only were bombs exploding, but North Korean retaliatory artillery and ack-ack opened up to make the bomber crews' lives miserable. Then several explosions blasted so close by that the chopper was rocked by a series of shock-waves. Danny guessed the POW camp wire had just been blown.

Still the CIA captains were away for a frustratingly long time. Danny noticed the shadows fading as dawn approached.

Then men broke through the bamboo and raced towards the chopper. Danny expected to see just three men – Captain White, Captain Black and Lieutenant Green – but there were close to twenty of them. Some looked fit, but others were being helped by their comrades.

Captains Black and White brought up the rear. Danny saw muzzle flashes from their assault rifles as they calmly squeezed off economic three-shot bursts. The CIA officers didn't rush, even when North Korean soldiers burst from the bamboo.

'Cover them, Long Li!' Danny yelled.

Long Li swivelled the .50-cal and jammed his thumbs onto the push-triggers, raking the bamboo with deadly accuracy. Bamboo shredded into lethal splinters that impaled anyone close by. The .50-cal slugs were huge and a hit simply blew a man's torso to scarlet mush and bone chips. The initial burst stopped the pursuing troops, but others pushed forward from behind only to meet another burst of sizzling lead.

As the escapees reached the chopper, Danny lost sight of them when they clambered on board. Half a dozen of the men were Korean freedom-fighters and they simply ran past the chopper and disappeared into the orchard. It still left fifteen POWs plus the CIA agents, Danny and Long Li. To make matters worse the fuel tanks were almost full.

Even in the emaciated state of some of the POWs, the chopper was critically over-weight. The engine power was insufficient to even hover, so they'd never clear the trees of the LZ. Long Li continued to give covering fire, aiming at any troops or muzzle-flashes he saw at the bamboo's edge.

All the time Captains Black and White calmly backed towards the chopper, firing to keep any enemy heads down. When they reached the chopper the POW survivors were crammed into the cabin, while Long Li literally hung out of the door.

'We'll never get airborne!' Danny yelled.

'Who're you gonna leave behind?' Captain Black asked without emotion.

'You're kidding?'

'Nope. We came for Lieutenant Green — we've got him. These guys came along because they heard about it. They have to take their chances.'

Danny saw that all the men on board were either American or UN servicemen except one very battered looking Korean who must be Lieutenant Green. They'd never evade the Communist troops and who knew what reprisals they'd receive when they were recaptured. Danny noted that neither Captain White nor Captain Black offered to stay behind. That was understandable as they probably were a prime source of top-secret intelligence that Colonel Pak would just love to wheedle out of them at Pak's Palace.

'We don't leave anyone behind!'

'Then let's get out of here and stop belly-aching.'

'Chuck out all the extra ammo. Only keep enough for covering fire.'

'The commies will get them,' White protested.

'I don't care.' Danny said through gritted teeth. 'Long Li, toss out anything you can. We've gotta reduce our weight.'

Bullets now flashed past the chopper as more North Koreans lined the bamboo and Long Li was having greater difficulty covering them all, especially those to the rear. He had to avoid shooting through the tail-rotor. The CIA captains kept up a steady fire as the survivors heaved the spare ammo cases overboard.

Then Black and White jumped to the ground, pulled their grenades, tossing them as far as they could.

'Long Li, tell 'em not to hit the bloody main rotor,' Danny yelled.

The spooks were old hands and knew what they were doing. Usually soldiers lobbed grenades with an over-arm bowler's action, but the CIA men threw with a side-arm, baseball-pitcher's style to keep the bombs and throwers' arms clear of the rotor-blades. They climbed back on board when they ran out of grenades. Danny kept lifting the collective pitch lever, but found the rotor RPM dropped as he reached maximum power and the chopper failed to leave the ground.

Okay Danny, you did it with the ammo resupply on Hill 303. Same deal.

Except for the tree line of course. *Whirlybird Central's* runway provided a comfortably long take-off run with no obstacles in the flight path.

Well, here goes.

He eased the cyclic control forward while raising the collective lever until he sensed the engine could provide no more power. It was imperative that he maintain the main-rotor RPM. If the blade-drag increased to a point where the rotor slowed the chopper would simply drop to earth.

The forward tilting main-rotor pushed the chopper forward. It inched ahead with agonising slowness. The fuselage rattled violently as it trundled over the rough grass surface. The tree line surged forward before the extra forward speed sucked airflow under blades. The chopper hopped, landed, bounced and hopped again then became airborne which would have been fine, but there was no way that the S-55 would clear the trees.

Danny sucked up more collective pitch. The chopper lifted for a second before the rotor low-speed warning light flashed. Danny lowered the collective pitch lever fractionally and the RPM returned to normal, but the trees were still smack in front of their take-off path. To make matters worse, the emboldened North Koreans surged from their bamboo shelter and started firing their rifles. The chopper was taking hits.

Danny continued to pump the collective pitch, and with one last surge of power the S-55 achieved sufficient speed for full translational lift to be effective. The chopper flashed over the tree line, scraping small branches and foliage as it went with a hail of Communist lead trailing in its wake.

Once clear of the orchard, Danny dived the chopper so it skipped over several miles of rice paddy fields until he felt they were clear of enemy gunfire. He thought the best option was to return to the *Rochester* rather than try to pick his way south over hostile territory.

By the time they reached the cruiser the captain was steering out of northern waters where the Reds might be tempted to lob a few rockets in their direction. Danny had to follow the warship for some miles until the S-55 had burnt off enough fuel to allow a safe landing.

Once the chopper was secure the POWs were whisked away for medical treatment and a square meal. The entire sortie had taken just over an hour, yet Danny and Long Li felt exhausted. The CIA captains showed no sign of either emotional or physical stress.

Captain White pulled a pack of *Lucky Strike* from his breast pocket and offered one to his companion. They both grinned as they lit up. Danny got the impression they'd enjoyed the whole thing.

Part 3 — French Indochina (Vietnam)

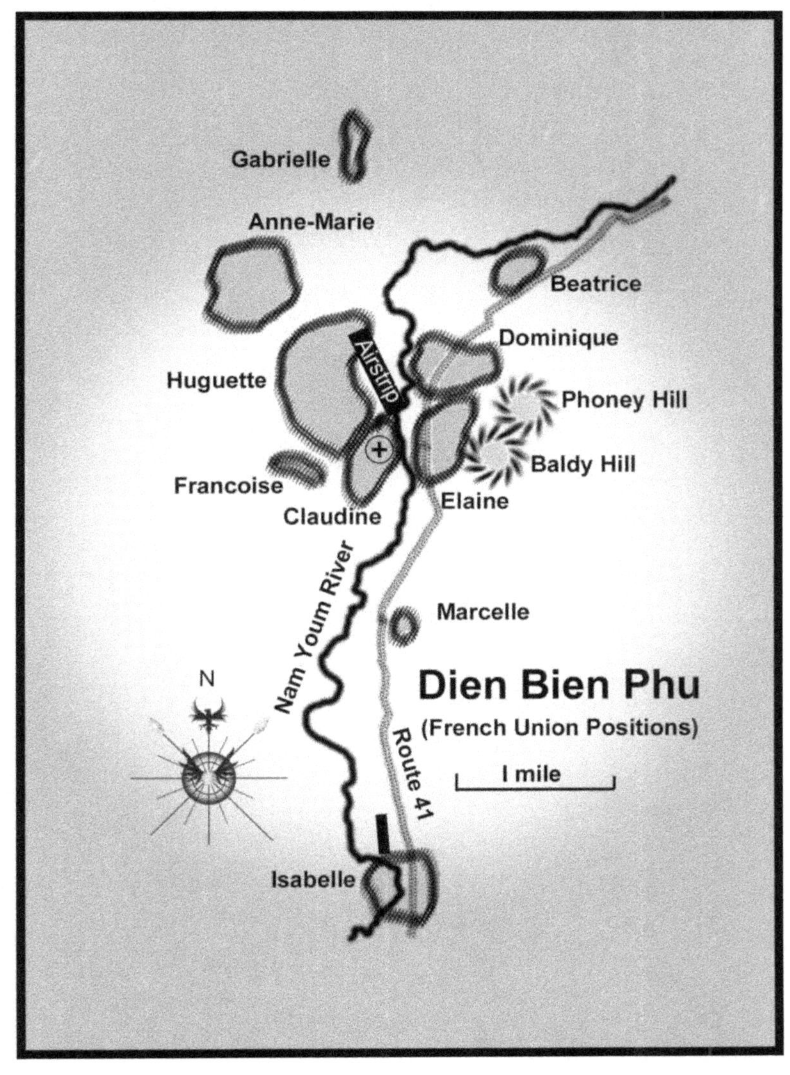

Chapter 19 — Cease Fire

Danny, Long Li and the CIA captains remained on board *Rochester* until the cruiser sailed within range of friendly territory. After determining that none of the bullet holes would stop the S-55 flying, Danny flew the four of them back to *Whirlybird Central.* Lieutenant Green had bucked up considerably and came along too for a thorough debriefing. The other POWs stayed in the ship sick-bay. The naval medical officer considered it the safest place for them to recover until they could disembark once *Rochester* reached Japan.

During the next weeks there was a remarkable change in climate as spring unfolded. Most spectacular were the orchard blossoms and a welcome return to milder temperatures. Unfortunately spring was accompanied by torrential rain that turned any non-sealed surface into a quagmire.

Danny and Long Li carried out several other missions for the CIA when Captains Black and White usually got into hot water. On one memorable occasion they radioed for help after being caught in a tall bamboo forest surrounded by a North Korean infantry company.

Danny called in an air strike. A flight of 77 Squadron Meteors came to the rescue. The jets were led by none other than Danny's nemesis, Wing Commander John Hubble. But give the man his due, he was a professional aviator and did a fine job keeping the enemy heads down while Danny hovered over the CIA men, as napalm ignited the bamboo.

There was no room to land, so Long Li lowered the winch to hoist the spooks up. The chopper was masked by smoke and twenty-foot high bamboo, so the enemy troops were unable to get a clear sighting. White was hoisted into the chopper first while Black kept the Reds at bay by blazing randomly into the forest to confuse them. Once aboard White laid down suppression fire while Long Li lowered the winch once more. They flew away with Captain Black dangling twenty feet below the chopper while still firing into the bamboo.

Danny flew for ten miles before finally hovering to hoist Captain Black into the chopper cabin.

As the year progressed, the temperature rose steadily until by early July it was unbearably hot. Armistice talks dragged on in Geneva while fighting continued to a grinding stalemate in Korea. It was the same old story, soldiers died while politicians and diplomats talked.

Danny and Long Li found themselves flying casevac missions for 2RAR troops who held a lonely outpost called Green Finger. It was located among a labyrinth of trenches north-west of Seoul in an area called The Hook where Aussie and Chinese troops slugged it out WWI style.

Under cover of early morning darkness on 26th July 1953, the Chinese made a consolidated attack, but were driven back with heavy casualties – some claimed over two thousand! The following day Danny flew to Seoul, carrying the bodies of three young Australians who'd been killed during the night. Kevin Cooper, Ron McCoy and Leon Dawes, all aged between nineteen and twenty-one, were the last Australians to die in Korea. As Danny and Long Li grimly flew away from The Hook, the Armistice was signed.

It was time for Danny and Long Li to leave the S-55 they'd come to love. They were flown back to Hong Kong by Monty and Earthquake McGoon after a hearty reunion. Danny and Long Li were met at Kai-tak Airport by Bob Rousselot who told them they had a meeting with General Chennault and Colonel Serong straight away.

CAT had leased a suite at the Miramar Hotel on Nathan Road as its planning station and temporary HQ. The *customer* was paranoid about security and had the rooms regularly scanned for bugs. Earthquake and Monty were unimpressed by the Miramar, choosing to stay at the Sunlight Palace instead. They knew it well and they were close to Gingle's Cafe which was of course Earthquake's favourite watering hole.

Rousselot ushered Danny and Long Li into a large, well furnished room where Serong and Chennault sat in lounge chairs sipping tea. A thick file lay on the coffee table between them. Both men rose and greeted Danny and Long Li warmly.

'Pull up a chair,' Serong said, pouring tea for everyone.

Once they were settled, predictably the colonel got straight down to business.

'This file pretty much covers what you two have been up to for the last six months. It's from the CIA, Commonwealth Brigade

HQ and Marine Corps point of view of course ... oh and a colourful annex from Wing Commander Hubble.'

'I'm sunk then,' Danny sighed.

'Well no, actually. He didn't care for your attitude as a RAAF officer, but he speaks very highly of your operational skills — both of you.'

'It's a glowing report all round,' Chennault added. 'I'm proud of the job you did. It reflects very well on CAT.'

'What we really want to know is what *you* two made of helo-ops.'

Danny and Long Li had come prepared. Both men had lengthy reports of their own. They simply recorded the sorties they'd done in Korea which pretty well spoke for itself.

'It's all there, General,' Danny said. 'The main points are weight limitation, airborne vulnerability, low airspeed problems, range, manoeuvrability pitfalls, especially high rates of sink, altitude restrictions and defence.'

Chennault arched his eye-brows.

'Do you have any positive feedback?'

'Hell yes, sir. I can see massive potential – say with large formations that can lift whole companies – even battalions. Maybe with chopper escorts as dedicated gun platforms. I like to call them gunships. These choppers could lay down suppression fire before putting troops into the field and cover hot extractions. If we could replace reciprocating engines with turbo-jets, I reckon that'll take care of much of the power problems. It might be a good idea to make provision for a co-pilot.'

'Surely a chopper was simple enough to be flown by a single pilot?' Serong said with a puzzled frown.

'Not if he gets shot,' Danny said. 'There's no back-up then. We copped plenty of bullets. Long Li and I were just lucky.'

They went on to discuss matters for the next couple of hours. The outcome was that General Chennault decided that choppers weren't essentially suitable for CAT's roles, but Ted Serong was extremely interested. He paid special attention to the notion of mass chopper troop movements and gunships in a jungle environment. Ultimately the meeting wound up with both Chennault and Serong satisfied that Danny and Long Li had earned their pay. The general then gave both men a month's furlough and told Danny he would begin command training on the C-47 when he returned, with a checkout date before the end of the year.

Chennault also asked Long Li if he wished to consider pilot training. Long Li refused, saying he was happy as a loadmaster and, in a rare display of immodesty, considered he was doing a pretty good job of it too.

'Fine,' Chennault said, appreciating a straight answer to a straight question. 'Where would you like to take your vacation? You can always hitch a ride on one of our scheduled services.'

CAT did actually run an RPT network just like any other airline.

'I'd like to go down to Singapore,' Long Li said. 'The war's long ago. It might be time to go back and maybe catch up with anyone who's left.'

'I think I'll stay in Hong Kong, sir. I have some unfinished business that needs taking care of.'

'Fine. Enjoy your break and we'll see you back ready for work in a month.'

They shook hands all round and Rousselot escorted them to the hotel foyer.

'Good work,' the chief pilot said in one of his rare moments of intimacy. 'You can pick up your travel documents and tickets at the airport, Long Li. Let me know if you change your mind and want to go anywhere, Danny.'

He smiled and left.

'There's some mail for you at the reception desk,' Rousselot said over his shoulder almost as an afterthought.

Among the letters were several from George bearing New Guinea stamps and another with a Singaporean stamp. Danny wrote to his father regularly although replies had always somehow come through the CAT network. Danny wasn't sure whether the CIA had something to do with that and thought it was better not to ask. There was also a small well-padded package with British stamps and addressed in neat very familiar hand-writing.

He opened an official envelope from Colonel Serong informing him that he was released from active duty, but could be recalled from the reserve list whenever the government felt like it. There was also a pleasingly plump bank statement showing that Danny's pay from CAT and the Australian Government had been paid regularly and was up-to-date.

He unwrapped the parcel. It was the first correspondence he'd had from Angela since leaving New Guinea. The package contained a letter and a Queen Elizabeth II Coronation mug dated 2nd June 1953. The mug was handsomely decorated with Union Jacks, the Royal coat-of-arms and a portrait of the beautiful new twenty-five year old monarch and empress. Danny grinned. Angela was such a Pom, but he'd drink his morning coffee from the mug anyway. Whatever his opinion of Queen and Empire,

Danny would treasure the mug because Angela had thought of him when she'd bought it.

He unfolded the letter:

Dear Danny

(You'll notice we've come down a notch from, 'My Darling Danny')

It is so long since I have written. I am so sorry, but study has rather taken over my whole life. University is going well and I passed every exam with flying colours.

Atta girl, Ange, no false modesty from you I see.

I have a simply amazing tutor and mentor who has taken me under his wing and is coaching me personally. He is such a wonderful teacher and dear friend.

Yeah, I just bet he is, Ange.

His name is Doctor Jacques Chevaliers.

Oh no, not another ruddy frog!

I've heard from your father that you are now in Korea. Oh Danny, please be careful. We hear such terrible stories of what is happening to our boys out there.

You got that right, Ange, but it's all over now.

Anyway I have some fabulous news. I'm coming back to the Orient at the end of the summer holidays. Jacques...

Jacques, not Dr Chevaliers?

... is specialising in tropical disease research and he's asked me to join him on a field trip to Indochina. We'll travel to remote villages where these ailments are rife.

It is an awesome opportunity and Jacques thinks we can make a difference. He is such a wonderful, dedicated human being.

He's a ruddy idiot, that's what he is, Ange. Doesn't he know there's a bloody war raging in those 'remote villages'? The Viet Minh are beating the pants off the French Union forces.

We will be so close to where you're flying. I do hope we will be able to get together and catch up on old times. That would be so wonderful - I know you'll just adore Jacques.

Pig's arse, I'll 'adore' snotty-nosed Jacques. I'd like to meet him just to tell him what an idiot he is and give him a swift kick in the pants.

I shall write again when my
itinerary is finalised. Until then:
Love from
Angela X X
p.s. I hope you like this gift and
will think of me when you have a
cuppa.

Danny folded the letter and put in his pocket. He'd reply when he calmed down and try to talk Angela out of her madness. Mind you, he'd never talked her out of anything before. He left George's letters unopened. He'd read them later. His father was an entertaining correspondent and Danny would enjoy his tropical anecdotes over a cold beer during the cocktail hour.

The final letter was in a hand that was vaguely familiar, but Danny couldn't place it. He opened the envelope revealing a short note from Zhang Wei Peng asking Danny to meet him as soon as he could. As it turned out Danny didn't have to bother because Peng and his wife Daiyu were waiting at Gingle's Cafe.

Earthquake had sent a taxi to pick up their friends. It was time for another reunion to celebrate Earthquake's return from Korea. Actually Earthquake didn't need an excuse to celebrate. He was constantly in party-mode.

Peng looked cheerful enough until he sighted Danny and then his mood became decidedly sombre. Danny greeted Peng and Daiyu cordially, noticing that Jiao and James Weo were nowhere to be seen. He was pretty sure they hadn't gone to New Guinea yet, because he'd heard nothing about it. Danny was about to ask where they were when Earthquake thrust a beer glass into his hand.

'We must talk,' Peng said before Earthquake could divert him.

'Sure we have some catching up to do,' Danny agreed.

Earthquake stood behind Peng shaking his head and looking unusually grim. Danny gave him a *what?* look.

Peng drew Danny aside while Long Li joined the others. They drew up chairs to a corner table.

'What's troubling you, Peng? Aren't you pleased to see us back all in one piece?' Danny asked. He felt he'd progressed beyond the Mr Zhang stage.

'That indeed gives me the greatest of pleasure, I assure you, Danny, but I must tell you that I am ashamed of what I have to report. Jiao has brought shame upon me and my family and her ancestors.'

'Surely not, she's a fine girl. Any father would be proud to have her as a daughter.'

'She is no longer my daughter!'

Struth, I don't like the way this is heading.

'Okay, Peng. What's she done?'

'She has left Hong Kong.'

Crikey, I didn't see that coming.

'You'd better tell me what happened,' Danny said after pausing long enough to digest the news.

'She and James Weo spent much time together. She tried to help him with his residency application. They filled in the forms, visited lawyers and attended interviews together. They made good progress with UK status, but the Australian Consulate was not so obliging.'

'Hit the *White Australia Policy* brick wall I guess.'

'Yes. It seems becoming a British subject is proving to present few difficulties, but although that makes white people eligible for Australian citizenship, it does not apply to other ethnic groups.'

'Well, that's not so bad. I mean James Weo will become a British subject and won't have to go back to the Commies.'

'Yes. He has gone to live in London.'

'Good luck to him then.'

'He has taken Jiao with him. They married in secret and have eloped.'

It was the same old story. Jiao and James Weo had grown closer in adversity as they struggled to prevent James being deported to mainland China. Danny was away and absence doesn't necessarily make the heart grow fonder – especially if there is a handsome, willing substitute right there at hand.

Danny was quick to realise he was off the hook. Much as he liked Jiao and there was no denying she was a beauty, he didn't want to marry her. Nevertheless something told him not to be too happy about it. Peng was already in the depth of despair and Danny had no intention of rubbing his nose in his own misery.

'I have no way that I can atone for my daughter's infamy,' Peng said, rather dramatically in Danny's opinion, but he knew how fanatical Chinese people were about the whole face-saving concept. Jiao and James Weo were among the first trickle of colonial immigrants to move to Britain as its empire imploded. That trickle was soon to become a flood.

'Look,' Danny said. 'Maybe they'll make a go of it and do well in England. I know it will be hard on all of us, but shouldn't we give them a chance if they're happy together.'

'You are too generous. I do not think happiness comes into the equation,' Peng said. 'I gave you my word and now I have broken it. There is no greater shame than that.'

'Hang on, Peng. You haven't broken your word. You didn't know Jiao and James Weo were going to fall in love.'

'I'm not talking of love either.'

'Surely you love Daiyu?'

'Our marriage was arranged by our families, but yes, we came to love each other.'

Then Daiyu joined them. She too looked solemn, but not as distressed as Peng. She carried an object about half the size of a house-brick. It was wrapped in layers of coloured paper and tied with ribbon.

'We offer you this in recompense,' she said, smiling thinly and proffering the gift.

Danny was surprised how heavy it was when he took it. He untied the ribbon and unfolded the paper, revealing a golden dragon statuette. The icon was meticulously crafted and quite striking although in a fiery, aggressive sort of way.

'It is solid gold,' Daiyu said. 'We know it will not repair what is done, but we hope you will accept this gift.'

Danny noticed that Daiyu didn't speak of shame, but rather mild disappointment and inconvenience.

Danny was speechless for a moment, but eventually accepted the gift.

'Thank you,' he said. It was all he could think to say, and indeed was all he needed to say.

The atmosphere lightened considerable after that with Peng assuring Danny if he ever needed a favour, he need only to ask.

'I might just take you up on that someday,' Danny said, returning to the festivities.

With nothing to keep him in Hong Kong, Danny flew back to New Guinea to spend a couple of week's quality time with his dad. Ted Serong once again had smoothed things with the PNG authorities and no one mentioned the Crazy Al incident. Dave had bought out *Alabama Aviation* and seemed to be making a go of it. He said that if Danny was ever looking for employment when he finished globe-trotting, *Alabama Aviation* could always use good pilots.

After a fortnight surfing, snorkelling and fishing, Danny wasn't sure whether he wanted to return to South-East Asia or not. In the end he left the coronation mug and dragon statuette with his dad for safekeeping and caught a flight to Hong Kong. It was right in the middle of typhoon season, but other than some turbulence en route he arrived safely at Kai-tak Airport.

So Danny swapped his RAAF uniform for CAT livery and went back to work. He immediately started command training with Monty who ran Danny through his paces ensuring he hadn't picked up any bad habits. After a month Monty was satisfied so General Chennault and Bob Rousselot congratulated Danny and assigned him a C-47 of his own. His co-pilot was a young Chinese national called Ng Huang who didn't know anything about aviation, but whose family was well connected with Chiang Kai-shek. Long Li requested to be Danny's loadmaster and Bob Rousselot saw no reason to refuse him.

Just as Danny was enjoying his initial flights as a captain, the French Government embarked on one of the most ill-conceived, badly planned, incompetently executed and unbelievably woefully supported military enterprises of all time.

On 20th November 1953 during an airborne operation codenamed *Castor,* battalion after battalion of French regular infantry, legionnaires and French Colonial units including Moroccans, Vietnamese, Algerians and West Africans parachuted from dozens of C-47s. Their target was a series of villages spanning the Nam-Youm River in north-western Tonkin close to Viet Minh supply routes. A WWII Japanese airstrip lay close to the river. About fifteen thousand people lived within a few square miles. That number would double with the influx of French Union troops.

The area was to become known as Dien Bien Phu.

Chapter 20 — Paris of the Orient

Viet Minh units were already in the valley so fighting around Dien Bin Phu began almost immediately. The Grand plan for Operation *Castor* was formulated by the newly appointed C-in-C for Indochina, Lieutenant General Henri Eugène Navarre who assigned Major General René Cogny to oversee the task. Navarre based himself in Saigon, taking control of military operations throughout Vietnam, while Cogny was stationed in Hanoi closer to the action at Dien Bien Phu. Colonel Christian de Castries was appointed military commander on the ground at Dien Bien Phu.

The problem was that the generals had differing opinions on how to do the job, so Colonel Castries received a lot of mixed messages. Navarre believed a massive troop build-up at Dien Bien Phu would draw the Viet Minh forces into an open pitched battle that favoured the French Union tactics. Cogny, on the other hand, felt his battalions should strike out from Dien Bien Phu, taking the fight to the enemy. The two generals disagreed vigorously on their strategies of choice.

At first it seemed that General Navarre might have been right. General Võ Nguyên Giáp who commanded Viet Minh forces in Tonkin was indeed massing his army corps in the north and intelligence reports indicated thousands of troops were heading for the Nam-Youm River Valley. Though only sporadic fighting had occurred so far, the French Union forces started out badly. A Thai auxiliary battalion occupying Lai Chau, thirty miles north of Dien Bien Phu, was overrun by several Viet Minh regiments. The Thai column was forced to fight a retreating action back to Dien Bien Phu. Only a handful made it.

But how did Danny fit into the big picture?

Once French Union troops had landed at Dien Bien Phu they were essentially cut off other than by an air bridge. Route 6 connecting the base to Hanoi and Route 41 that ran to French strongholds in Laos were little more than tracks. They were impassable in the wet season and always prone to Viet Minh ambush. Fortunately the airstrip at Dien Bien Phu had been covered with pierced steel plates known as *PSP*, so the runway could support C-47 planes. Unfortunately the French Air Force had neither sufficient planes nor trained pilots to keep the base resupplied so CAT signed a contract to help them out.

CAT had done this before while Danny was flying his S-55 in Korea. Several CAT pilots, including Monty, Earthquake and Felix Smith had learnt to fly giant Fairchild C-119, 'flying boxcar' planes at Clark AFB in the Philippines. These aircraft carried a load of ten thousand pounds and because of their high twin-boom tail and rear opening cargo door, they were ideal for air-dropping heavy equipment and large numbers of paratroopers on a single pass. The previous contract had lasted only a few weeks, but now those qualified pilots returned to fly the C-119.

Although its payload was just over half of the C-119 and cruise speed fifty knots slower, the lion's share of sorties were still handled by the indefatigable *Gooney-Birds*, known in Vietnam as Dakotas. Ten thousand C-47s had been built so there were simply more of them around than other aircraft types. Due to prior commitments CAT operations were not due to start until March, but as Danny, Monty and Earthquake were available, Bob Rousselot sent them ahead to evaluate the task and prepare charts and SOPs for the later aircrews. So in December 1953, Danny flew north-east to Bach Mai airport on the outskirts of Hanoi.

If he had any doubts, a monthly three-thousand dollar paycheque resolved them.

Danny landed at Saigon's Tan Son Nut airport on Christmas Eve. It was the most pleasant time of year in the middle of the dry season when the temperature was coolest. A CAT representative met the C-47. He explained they were waiting for the arrival of medical supplies to be airlifted to Hanoi and then on to Dien Bien Phu. As it looked as if the shipment wouldn't arrive that day, the CAT agent drove the crew to the Continental Hotel on the Rue Catinat.

Although the French Government was happy to see CAT, they weren't prepared to put civilian aircrew up at the Majestic or the Grand where senior French Union officers, bureaucrats and diplomatic staff stayed. The rates at the Continental were about half those of the other two hotels so its guests consisted of foreign journalists and minor clerical officials. Nevertheless Saigon's expatriate community loved the atmosphere at the Continental, which was always a hot bed of intrigue and gossip.

Danny and Long Li headed for the bar, but co-pilot Ng Huang declined. He wasn't a great socialiser. In fact he didn't appear to be interested in anything very much. The bar was full of Christmas revellers. Danny waded through the crowd and tobacco smog to order drinks. They decided to take one of the street tables that were surrounded by more agreeable air.

There were two spare chairs left at a table occupied by a fifty-year-old European and a pair of giggling young women dressed immaculately in tight-fitting tunics and slacks.

'*Pardon, monsieur, pouvons-nous nous asseoir?*' Danny asked. He'd been studying French ever since he'd been told he was coming to Vietnam. He knew he hadn't a ghost of a chance of mastering Vietnamese, even if he could discover which dialect to work on. He actually found he had quite a talent for picking up the language by associating English words with French. *Maison* was like mansion so he connected it with house: *fille* with filly: *rue* with route: and so on. Earthquake suggested if he couldn't think of a word, then just speak in English with a French accent.

'Oh please do, dear boy,' the man said with what Danny discerned as a very plummy English inflection. 'I do enjoy the company of strangers, and you certainly sound like one.'

'Guilty. Australian and my friend is Singaporean although we call New Guinea home. I'm Danny McAlister and this is Sim Long Li.'

'How interesting. I'm delighted to meet you, gentlemen,' the Englishman greeted. 'These two young ladies are just leaving because I can no longer afford to keep them in champagne at these extortionate prices. Unless of course you wish to assume the financial burden.'

Danny and Long Li shook their heads so the Englishman shooed the girls away. They pouted, but realising they'd exploited their opportunity to its fullest and were unlikely to make any further progress, flounced away to brighter prospects.

'My name is Greene — Graham Greene.'

'You sound like a Pom to me,' Danny said. 'You're a long way from home.'

'So are you for that matter. I'm a war correspondent for the *Times* and *Le Figaro* reporting on Indochina. I've been here for a few years now watching this country slowly bleed to death.'

Greene refilled his pipe, lit up and ordered another round of drinks while Danny and Long Li admired the beautifully elegant Vietnamese girls walking past. Some were perched gracefully on the pillion seats of motor scooters that were replacing bicycles as a favoured mode of transport in the city.

'Exquisite creatures, are they not?' Greene commented. 'They so complement this beautiful city. It's such a perfect blend of east and west. Saigon is called *The Paris of the Orient*, you know?'

'Is that so? You'll certainly get no argument from me about the girls,' Danny replied.

'What do you mean when you said this country is slowly bleeding to death?' Long Li asked.

'Listen carefully. What do you hear above the traffic noise and the food stall hawkers?'

Sure enough when they concentrated, both Danny and Long Li heard the distant popping of what could only be explosives. Once in a while there was a bright flash although there were no thunderstorms anywhere around.

'Fireworks celebrating Christmas?' Danny suggested. He knew Asian people loved pyrotechnics and, although the population was predominantly Buddhist, many Vietnamese were staunch Roman Catholics so Christmas was of great significance to them.

'Not fireworks, Danny,' Long Li observed. 'Gunfire and grenades maybe.'

'Well deduced, Mr Sim,' Greene said. 'The Viet Minh have infiltrated every corner of Indochina. Right now that will be French Union forces ferreting out a bunch of insurgents who are terrorising someone who has annoyed them. Not a day goes by without an outbreak of violence somewhere or another.'

'They won't come here though?' Danny said.

'Don't count on it, young man,' Greene replied. 'Do you see that shopfront across the Rue Catinat – the one boarded up? That was a popular cafe with Foreign Legion officers until the Minh tossed a Molotov cocktail along with a few hand grenades through the front door. Two legionnaires and a waiter were killed. The owner is too fearful to make repairs and reopen.'

'It seems to me the UN made a big mistake letting the French come back,' Long Li said. 'After all they abandoned the country to the Japs without putting up a fight.'

'I agree,' Greene said, but then he would. He'd dabbled with Communism prior to WWII, but he'd outgrown the concept. He was now a sceptic although he remained a Christian. 'You know the Americans didn't want to allow the French back, but some fancy talking and double-dealing by Charles de Gaulle persuaded the Europeans to side with him. I think Uncle Ho is too chummy with the Reds for America's liking these days anyway.'

'Uncle Ho' was of course Ho Chi Minh who was running a very successful independence campaign for Indochina in general and Vietnam in particular.

'I wouldn't have thought the Americans have got anything to do with what goes on here,' Danny said.

'I wouldn't bet on it. CIA and MI6 agents are crawling all over the place.'

They spent a convivial evening with Graham Greene who was an excellent conversationalist and knowledgeable traveller. They ordered a variety of Vietnamese and French style dishes for supper, eating more than necessary, but it was all so delicious. Greene mentioned he was writing a novel about life in Vietnam based on much of what he'd seen.

'I don't know if it will sell,' Greene lamented. 'Secret agents might be here, but I don't think the western public is interested in a Southeast Asian backwater much.'

'What're you going to call it and I'll look out for it?' Danny said. 'I like adventure novels. I loved the *Hornblower* series and Hammond Innes' novels. I'm reading a brand new story called *Casino Royale* by Ian Fleming. It's about a spy called James Bond!'

'Admirable selection,' Greene agreed. 'I haven't thought of a title for my story yet. One of my protagonists is an American. They usually come across as boisterous and rowdy. Maybe I'll call it *The Quiet American*. Who knows?'

Danny and Long Li sat up late with Graham Greene sipping drinks and talking, ever aware of the background explosions and gunshots, although what part was Christmas cheer or insurgent bloodshed remained unclear. Mindful of an early start for Hanoi, Danny and Long Li finally turned in, leaving Graham Greene to further ponder the heartbreak gathering throughout Indochina.

As it turned out they could have stayed up all night. The following morning they arrived to find the medical stores still hadn't turned up and didn't for several days. Apparently that kind of inefficiency was common. The French dispatchers merely shrugged, saying Danny and his crew should return to their hotel and he'd contact them when the cargo arrived.

Frustrating as the situation was, that was no particular chore as they took the time to idly explore Saigon's sights and night-life. Although the outward city bustle seemed normal there was always the shadowy hint that the Viet Minh were lurking close by ready to strike if they got the chance. So they went everywhere armed.

But the city was a delight from its elegant street cafes, bars, boisterous clubs and fashionable restaurants. Orange robed monks roamed the streets with their begging bowls. Everyone was so respectful towards the monks who did pretty well. It seemed such a waste of time to Danny's who thought they'd do better by getting a day job. The beautiful young women continued to catch Danny's eye, but he knew they were taboo other than the ubiquitous bar girls. Long Li warned him to steer clear of them as they were expensive and medically risky. Danny was smart enough to accede to Long Li's wisdom.

The supplies arrived in late evening five days after Christmas. It was too late to take-off that night, so early on 31st December Danny, Long Li and Ng Huang were driven back to Tan San Nut. They were met by a moon-faced lieutenant nurse from the French Air Force. She introduced herself as Geneviève de Galard. From the little English she spoke and Danny's rudimentary French she told Danny she was looking for a lift back to Hanoi after accompanying wounded troops from one of the many amorphous battlefields of Vietnam.

The nine hundred mile flight to Hanoi took just over five hours. It proceeded uneventfully other than occasional Bearcat fighter and B-26 bomber formations crossing their path to spread festive cheer among unfortunate Viet Minh positions. Danny was surprised when he passed a flight of three ponderous pre-WWII Junkers JU-52 tri-motor planes lumbering through the sky at eighty knots. Geneviève de Galard explained the French air force was so strapped for equipment they'd kept the vintage transports in service well beyond their use-by date.

As they approached Hanoi's Bach Mai airport the C-47 shuddered as flack suddenly exploded around its wingtips.

'What the blazes is going on,' Danny radioed the Hanoi controller, who dismissed the ack-ack as merely routine and cleared the C-47 to land.

Despite vast concentrations of French Union forces, the Viet Minh still confidently operated all over the Red River Delta between Hanoi and Haiphong Harbour. Danny turned to see Lieutenant Galard was calmly reading a magazine, oblivious to the gunfire around her.

After landing, Danny was marshalled to a small tarmac area designated for CAT. Elsewhere French Air Force planes were surrounded by a human ants' nest of activity. Aircraft were being loaded with ammunition, trucks, medical supplies reinforcements and even bulldozers and tanks. The bustle was a seething mass of men and equipment. How anyone made head or tail of it was a mystery to Danny.

To Danny's surprise, Lieutenant Galard bade them *adieu* and boarded one of the Dakotas bound for Dien Bien Phu.

Maybe she'd slept for much of the flight from Saigon, but didn't the woman need to take a break sometime? It was New Year's Eve after all.

The Hotel Metropole was considered the premier location in Hanoi, but once again the CAT crews were accommodated in a more modest establishment a few doors away. They'd had a long day, but that didn't stop Danny and Long Li wanting to investigate the renowned establishment and celebrate the arrival of 1954. As Earthquake and Monty were already in town they all suited up and went to look for themselves. Once again Ng Huang remained behind. It was almost as if he was afraid to venture into Hanoi's tree-lined boulevards or he simply didn't know how to have a good time.

Had they been in France on the evening of New Year's Eve, the chances are everything would have been shut. The French were great ones for closing their trading and hospitality establishments for long lunches, weekends, half-days, religious festivals or if they just felt like it. Fortunately Indochina didn't appear to suffer from that Gallic languidness.

Indeed Ng Huang may have had a point. Saigon tolerated its insurgent outbreaks with business as usual with an untamed festive air that reminded Danny of Wild West movie scenes with bicycles and motor-scooters. Hanoi seemed more cautious. Maybe because Viet Minh activity was most prevalent in the north, everyone took extra care.

A greater military presence was evident with heavily armed police and Foreign Legion patrols randomly checking the credentials of Hanoi citizens. The four CAT crewmen had to present their papers before they were admitted beyond the Metropole lobby. The concierge was hesitant at first, but Earthquake's steady glare and a couple of ten piaster notes greasing his palm persuaded him to admit them.

French officers, diplomats, government officials, their wives and mistresses filled the ball room where a swing band was belting out Glen Miller and Tommy Dorsey hits. The crowd was having a whale of a time and right smack in the middle of the festivity, dressed in a shimmering satin gown, complimented by substantial bling and turning every male head in the room, stood Angela Holyman.

Chapter 21 – Angela

Danny simply stared. She was absolutely stunning. Always a beautiful girl, she had developed into a sensational young woman. As she glided across the dance floor, she only had eyes for the tall, urbane man who guided her in his arms. He looked in his mid-thirties with a slickness that was just too perfect right down to his tuxedo and pencil-thin moustache. He reminded Danny of Errol Flynn in an oily sort of way.

Well Danny was having none of it. He marched across the room although how he hoped to compete with Angela's sophisticated, worldly partner was uncertain.

'*Pardon, monsieur,*' Danny said, '*C'est ma danse, je crois ...*'

The Frenchman turned and glared at Danny, while Angela stared wide-eyed. At that moment the band stopped playing as the compere announced the arrival of 1954. Suddenly the crowd was counting down from thirty. As midnight struck the band began the familiar refrain to Auld Lang Syne and the crowd burst into song.

It seemed Robert Burns' iconic melody was well known beyond Hibernian borders.

'Danny!' Angela squealed, flinging her arms around him. 'What a wonderful surprise.'

Her words were nearly drowned out and then everyone on the dance floor crossed arms and joined hands to complete the traditional circular dance. It was some time before Danny and Angela had time to catch up.

While the New Year dancers were occupied, Earthquake and Monty had hijacked a table, several bottles of claret and had already ordered beer chasers.

'Monty and Long Li are here,' Danny said. 'Come and say hello.'

Of course Angela was keen to be reunited with the people with whom she'd shared so many dangerous adventures, but she looked uncertainly at her partner.

'This is Jacques,' she said taking his hand.

'I thought he might be,' Danny replied. 'Bring him along if you like.'

'Jacques is my beau now,' she announced smugly although the Frenchman looked slightly uncomfortable with that particular title. Only Angela would use a word like 'beau' anyway. It merely made Danny feel even more like knocking Jacques' block off.

Angela greeted Long Li warmly and Monty with her usual reservation. What she made of Earthquake was uncertain. She introduced Dr Jacques Chevalier.

Danny shook his hand stiffly although the others had no such former prejudices against the man. What Angela and Jacques' precise relationship entailed was also ambiguous. When Angela described him as 'her beau', did that mean a torrid, physical love-affair or merely a girlish crush? It was always so hard to tell with Angela.

Give him his due, Jacques ordered champagne all round although Danny stuck to a beer out of sheer bloody-mindedness.

True to form, Angela bubbled on, telling them what an *awesome* time she was having at university and what *amazing* people she was working with and how *sublime* her Jacques was – how clever, gifted, handsome and any other superlative she could think of. And to top it off, how lucky they were to be flying out to Dien Bien Phu later that morning. What a wonderful opportunity to experience a field hospital under actual combat conditions.

'You're ... '

It was followed by 'stark raving bonkers', 'crazy', 'nuts', or 'barmy' depending whether you heard Danny, Monty, Earthquake or Long Li because they all spoke at once.

'Angela,' Monty said with genuine concern, 'it's ...'

'Don't tell me it's no place for a girl,' Angela snapped.

'I wasn't going to. It's no place for anyone who doesn't absolutely need to be there.'

'Nonsense,' Jacques intervened. He was hoping to avoid actual danger while scoring combat brownie-points that would impress folk back home. 'The Viet Min *Bo Doi* are few and their main force is a hundred miles away.'

'Don't believe your own propaganda, Doc,' Earthquake growled. 'We're still coming back to Hanoi with bullet holes in our planes.'

'I thought you came here to study tropical diseases?' Danny said.

'That can wait,' Dr Chevalier shrugged. 'We may not get another opportunity to experience wartime medicine.'

'Most people would think *not* experiencing war was a good thing,' Long Li suggested, but Chevalier just stared at him blankly.

'Well I'm going and this time you can't stop me,' Angela smirked, remembering the time she'd sneaked aboard a dingy tied behind Danny's yacht when he sailed into action. On that occasion Angela caused all sorts of complications before the fight was over. She had a point though. Angela was still under twenty-one, but only her parents really had any authority to tell her what to do.

'Anyway I have Jacques as my chaperone,' she said triumphantly.

'I thought you said he was your boyfriend,' Monty observed with a sly grin. 'He can't be both. The two roles aren't compatible.'

'Mr Montgomery, your mind is still permanently in the gutter, I see,' she replied primly, saying no more on the subject while Chevalier eyed her with sly inscrutability.

But there was no dissuading her. Indeed the CAT aircrew had to turn in because they too were due to fly to Dien Bien Phu in a few hours. The night sorties would return by dawn. The planes would be quickly loaded and refuelled before flying back to the stronghold. Although the main CAT contingent was yet to arrive, Danny, Monty and Earthquake still flew regular sorties along with the French Air Force.

Danny was to fly in a formation of Dakotas and once again he had to learn on the job. Monty and Earthquake explained the drill as best they could. The two months proved to be the most hectic in Danny's life so he had little time to ponder on Angela and her Frenchman. Even his birthday passed with no more than a toast from Monty and Earthquake.

The faster C-119s flew ahead to airdrop their loads before the C-47s arrived over Dien Bien Phu airstrip know as *Torri-Rouge* –

Red-Earth. The flight time was just over an hour and routine other than some confusion between French ATC whose controllers were reluctant to speak in English and the American pilots who generally knew little French. Danny followed the gist of it and joined a holding pattern south of the airfield. The Daks flew at different levels in a holding 'stack'. Each plane was assigned an initial altitude and gradually descended as the planes ahead made their approaches and landed.

As it came closer to his approach time, Danny realised that ack-ack shells were exploding randomly among the planes. He was also able to spy out the lay of the land. At 1260 yards, *Torri-Rouge's* runway was a comfortable length for C-47s to take off and land, but Danny wasn't happy about what else he saw.

Dien Bien Phu was the HQ for Operational Group North-West known as GONO. It wasn't a continual base, but a series of 'impregnable' strong-points clustered around the airstrip. Each of these fortified positions bristled with barbwire, machinegun posts, 105mm artillery emplacements and mine fields not to mention units of French Union troops that included a number of Foreign Legion battalions.

Each strong-point was named after a soldier's girlfriend. Dominique, Elaine, Claudine and Huguette formed the centre while two mini fortresses, Beatrice and Anne-Marie were situated alarmingly apart to the north. A mile further away was Gabrielle, but worse still in Danny's opinion was Isabelle lying three full miles due south of the central camp. Its isolation was so acute that it had its own airstrip. One other minute redoubt, Françoise, buffered the western flank of Huguette and Claudine while a final lonely outpost called Marcelle was sited along route 41 half-way between the main base and Isabelle.

What Danny really dreaded was the fact that GONO lay in a valley surrounded by hills that rose only five or six miles away. To make matters worse, General Giáp had deployed 105mm artillery batteries along the ridgelines. These guns were protected in caves dug along the hillside and hidden by jungle, making them tricky targets to knock out. Throughout the day they lobbed shells onto the base causing most of the French Union casualties. Just like Korea, it was all about flaming hills again and Angela somewhere down there in the middle.

As Danny made his approach a flight of Bearcat fighters strafed the suspected enemy gun positions then dropped napalm clusters along the ridgelines for good measure. Once he landed Danny immediately taxied the Dak to the aircraft pens at the southern end of the strip that was at least partially screened from the Viet Minh artillery spotters by revetments and the structure of Claudine and Huguette's bastion.

A flight of Bearcat fighters, S-55 choppers and Morane Cricket spotter planes were permanently based at Dien Bien Phu. They too were parked in the same protected area. These aircraft were used for instant response sorties while the B-26 bombers and C-119 box-cars made the hour-long flight from Hanoi to reach their targets. Tunnels honeycombed underground where aircrews and maintenance teams were billeted.

The central hospital was located at Claudine, close to the aircraft pens and a relatively short distance for medical orderlies to carry the supplies and bring out the wounded. The hospital had been excavated into a massive underground chamber with wards, operating theatre, X-ray room all joined by tunnels and trenches. Here forty-year-old Major Dr Paul Grauwin ran the field hospital and senior medical student Angela Holyman had decided – in the blink of an eye – to stay and help him. At that stage the hospital was able to cope with the number of wounded especially as the Daks could airlift up to twenty stretcher patients at a time.

Casevac was to become Danny's major job and he wasn't always going have the luxury of sheltering under the cover of Claudine and Huguette's ramparts. But at this stage there was an air of optimism around the camp brought on by its sheer mightiness and immense troop build-up. General Navarre had spent Christmas Eve at GONO while General Cogny was a regular visitor.

Angela was in attendance as several stretchers were loaded aboard Danny's plane. Meanwhile Jacques was somewhere in the dugout ingratiating himself with Major Grauwin. The stretcher cases were serious but not critical and would ultimately return to Dien Bien Phu after surgery in Hanoi or Saigon. Most of them puffed cigarettes as they were carried to the plane.

Angela was already dressed in army fatigues and combat boots. She worked with the nursing staff and it appeared Jacques had taught her sufficient French to get by.

'Oh Danny, this is such an adventure,' she gushed when she saw him.

'It's not an adventure, Ange,' he insisted. 'It's flaming lunacy. There's a war going on and you're slap in the middle of it.'

'Nonsense. All the men here say the forts are impregnable.'

'Nowhere is impregnable if the enemy is determined enough.'

'According to Jacques there are only a handful of Communist rabble out there. They'll never get in here.'

'What the hell does bloody Jacques know about it? This war's been going on since 1946 — eight ruddy years — and I don't see the Viet Minh giving in yet.'

'Don't be so negative. I'm needed here so *here* I'll stay,' she snapped. 'There is nothing you can do about it.'

'Oh yeah?'

He hoisted her over his shoulder and, much to the amusement of the Algerian soldiers loading the wounded, marched her to his plane. She kicked and screamed, but Danny was strong and determined. He wrapped a tie-down strap around her arms and cranked it tight before attaching it to a restraining ring on the C-47 floor. Undoubtedly she'd struggle free, but he figured he'd be airborne by then.

'Long Li, see that she stays put,' Danny bellowed as he strode to the flight deck.

She sulked all the way back to Hanoi. After they'd landed and cleared the casevac stretchers she stormed towards him and slapped his face as hard as she could.

'I hate you, you pompous bully. You're not a gentleman like Jacques.'

She then rushed away and promptly boarded the next C-47 flight back to Dien Bien Phu. The Algerian and Vietnamese loaders weren't prepared to challenge her while the crew simply accepted whatever was assigned to their plane.

After that, time sort of got away from Danny, Angela and just about everyone else. Over the next two months the military situation changed so insidiously that it was too late to rectify when the defence of Dien Bien Phu spiralled into crisis. General Giáp was certainly marshalling forces as General Navarre had hoped, but five divisions with another in reserve? Who'd have thought the Viet Minh could muster an army of that size? Not only did General Giáp command a massive infantry force, but it was supported by serious artillery – not just a couple of field howitzers.

With Chinese help, Giáp's army included two artillery battalions as well as mortar, rocket, heavy machinegun and anti-aircraft units. What made this arms build-up so impressive was that each piece of equipment was dismantled and manhandled from the Chinese border along mountainous jungle trails to be reassembled at Dien Bien Phu. Every shell had to be carried too. Ultimately over two hundred and fifty heavy gun emplacements overlooked the Nam-Youm River Valley. If anyone still thought the Viet Minh was just a bunch of rag-tag guerrillas, they were in for a nasty shock.

Throughout January, February and early March Viet Minh engineers dug a cobweb of trenches that inched towards the French Union defences. French patrols struck out from the main base and inflicted serious casualties on the *Bo Doi*, but sustained serious losses in return. Even with intense air support, attempts to clear the high ground around GONO met with very little success.

What Danny and Angela noticed was the steady build-up of casualties. Initially Danny flew only one or two stretcher-cases on the return flights to Bach Mai, but as the weeks passed this number grew to around half-a-dozen and often he'd take a full load of twenty stretcher-cases on a single flight. Angela also noted that, along with Major Grauwin and his medical team, her workload steadily increased.

Earlier Grauwin had suggested it might be time for Angela to return to Hanoi, but she refused and now he'd come to rely on her to a point where he rather hoped she'd stay. Jacques Chevalier worked competently if not spectacularly, but grew more nervous by the day. He took great pains to stress that he was a researcher not a surgeon after all.

The weather had remained fine, but the wet season was due in April and who knew what would happen to the air-bridge then.

In early March Danny was inbound to *Torri-Rouge* as usual when an ack-ack barrage burst all around his C-47. As the plane bucked through the shock-waves, Ng Huang screamed and buried his head in his hands. There was nothing Danny or Long Li could do to bring him to his senses. He was in such a blind funk, he ceased to be a functioning crew member, not that he'd been much use at the best of times.

'We've got a hail of flak here,' Danny informed the ground controller. 'Where's our air support? We need suppression fire on the high ground — west and east!'

The controller mumbled something that Danny couldn't make out.

'Where the hell are the Bearcats?' Danny demanded.

'They are despatched. B-26s are above,' the controller finally replied apathetically. He was under fire as well. The Viet Minh artillery spotters often looked for radio aerials as targets.

Danny saw two Bearcats rolling along *Torri-Rouge* strip and streaking airborne, each carrying a 500 pound underbelly bomb load.

The French bombers had decided to fly high and fast to avoid ground fire. This might have been safer for the bomber crews, but led to dismally less accurate bombing. In truth this was not entirely the French pilots' fault. Most of the B-26 crews consisted of transport pilots with little or no bomber training.

If the B-26s had indeed completed a run over the ridgeline, Danny saw no evidence of them hitting their target. Finally as he manoeuvred to line up on the runway, the Bearcats dived towards the high ground flanking GONO, but pulled away when they ran into heavy flak.

'Great,' Danny muttered. 'Just great!'

Needless to say Danny was in a foul mood when he landed. French Union 105mm howitzers steadily cracked away from the main camp trying to gouge out the offending Viet Minh guns from their hidden emplacements. Danny hauled his co-pilot from his seat, shoving him into the cabin.

'You stay off my flight-deck until you're prepared to do your job. Right now I'm better off without you.'

As the plane was unloaded, Danny relieved himself behind a sandbag revetment. It didn't help his mood when he returned to a line of stretcher-cases ready for evacuation attended by a medical team under Angela's supervision. She looked strained, mud-spattered and dog-tired. She smiled at him weakly and silently mouthed 'no' when she saw his pleading eyes. Danny understood there was nothing he could do to persuade her to fly back to Hanoi with him.

Chapter 22 – Beatrice

By the beginning of March Danny, Monty — with a little help from Earthquake, who wasn't a particularly studious type — had completed all the instrument let down procedures and operating instructions for flights in and out of *Torri-Rouge*. As it turned out a dozen C-119 crews arrived, but Danny was still the only C-47 pilot. He'd unofficially sacked Ng Huang, choosing to fly without a co-pilot rather than with a useless one. Monty and Earthquake voiced their concern, but Danny insisted he'd manage. If Bob Rousselot found out, he could bloody-well send Danny a competent replacement.

CAT's schedule was a gruelling two or three round trips to *Torri-Rouge* per day. Some of the pilots boasted they'd flown more hours during the Berlin airlift, but no one was shooting at them then.

Each time Danny landed at *Torri-Rouge* he hoped he'd see Angela again. Sometimes she was with the casevac patients and sometimes she wasn't, but he looked for her every time. What was becoming increasingly obvious was that his time available on the ground was growing less by the day. Viet Minh artillery was slowly intensifying and increasing its accuracy. Most crews didn't even stop their engines while their planes were being loaded and unloaded. Danny flew two and occasionally three sorties a day in and out of *Torri-Rouge.*

Angela's presence did not go unnoticed. Even in a muddy khaki combat uniform she was a looker. One person who was to take particular interest in Mademoiselle Holyman's arrival was Foreign Legionnaire, Sergeant Aleron Duval, erstwhile vicious pirate of the South Seas. Angela and Danny had scrapped with Duval before when he'd gone by the name 'Frenchy'. Now that hardly seemed necessary at Dien Bien Phu where he was surrounded by Frenchman, so he preferred the sound of *Le Boucanier* — The Pirate. But Danny and Angela would always know him as 'Frenchy'.

Frenchy's field promotion to sergeant reflected the parlous situation the Legion found itself in. Several years previously, with shrewd insight, he saw the French presence in Indochina as ludicrous and decided to get while the going was good. He'd have got away with it too, but he caused so much trouble around New Guinea he was finally caught and shipped back to the Legion. He received twelve cane strokes and was promptly returned to the ranks. He helped defend Na San the previous year and the Legion forgave his past sins.

Na San stronghold was less than fifty miles away and it seemed to Frenchy that was a mini dry-run for Dien Bien Phu. On that occasion French Union forces held the Viet Minh a bay, but only by the skin of their teeth.

Attrition and veteran legionnaires returning to France or North Africa after their Indochina tours had decimated the ranks of battle-hardened ex-WWII vets. Many of those men had been ex-SS storm-troopers who'd found anonymity and a safe haven in the Legion. Most were prime suspects for the Nuremburg war crimes tribunal. They may not have been particularly pleasant human beings, but that's not who you wanted beside you when facing a huge well-organised enemy. In Frenchy's opinion, the meaner and tougher his comrades, the better he felt about it.

He led many sorties from Beatrice against the encroaching *Bo Doi* which had all resulted in spiteful, scrappy fights that left both sides bloodied. Although the French Union forces generally got the upper hand in those contests, they failed to consolidate their victories simply because there were too few soldiers available. The Viet Minh always returned when the French withdrew. The *Bo Doi* numbers seemed limitless.

By the second week of March, the legionnaires' forays into enemy territory had all but ceased. The raw recruits of 3rd Battalion, 13th Half-Brigade defending strong-point Beatrice now waited for the massed attack they knew was imminent. Frenchy spent much of his time patrolling the defence line, encouraging the nervous young men he now commanded. He may have been a thoroughly villainous scoundrel, but Frenchy Duval was no coward. Now there was no way of sneaking out of this tight spot, he faced the danger with courage and determination.

What troubled him were the series of small hills close to Beatrice that the Viet Minh now controlled. The positions made good observation and mortar posts. Still Frenchy drew some comfort from the rows of barbwire infested with minefields surrounding all Dien Bien Phu strong-points.

'Don't worry,' he encouraged a squad of young legionnaires who were sharing a smoke. 'No one's going to cross that lot, eh? And if they try we'll show em.'

He patted the machinegun barrel aimed into the killing ground beyond the barbwire barricade. He'd seen the tenacity of the *Bo Doi* before and didn't believe his own words for a minute.

The French expected an attack to the point where Colonel Castries actually predicted it with unnerving accuracy.

'They'll come tomorrow night,' he calmly told his officers at a staff meeting on Friday 12th March.

At five o'clock the next evening Viet Minh artillery and mortars launched a bombardment. The *Bo Doi* 105 mm gunners could keep up three rounds a minute steadily all day. That meant that with ten guns zeroing into Beatrice a shell exploded every two seconds. A mixture of ordnance slammed into the outpost. HE shells blasted great gouts of mud skywards while the shuddering shockwaves left men stunned senseless. Anti-personnel rounds released fragments that scythed through limbs and torsos with murderous indiscriminate finality.

After one-and-a-half hours of mind-numbing bombardment, Beatrice's command centre was struck by a direct hit. The half-brigade CO Major Paul Pégot was killed instantly along with all his HQ staff. A single HE shell had wiped out the base's chain of command in a flash. Each company, platoon or squad was now on its own just as General Giáp ordered Major General Le Trong Tan's 312th Infantry Division to unleash his horde and advance on Beatrice.

Around seven-thirty — Frenchy really had lost track of accurate time — the bombardment ceased. An eerie silence followed for minutes. It was almost as if the legionnaires were suddenly enclosed in a vacuum. Their senses were distorted with every man suffering from blurred vision, varying degrees of deafness and a thumping headache. As his head cleared, Frenchy heard a cacophony of whistles, gongs, drums, bells and bugles. He'd heard it before at Na San and that filled him with dread.

Frenchy fired a parachute flare into the darkness. As the pyrotechnic plopped alight and drifted downwards, Frenchy was dismayed at what he saw in its shadowy glow. The ground ahead to the northeast was simply a seething throng of *Bo Doi.* Thousands of drab-grey uniforms surged towards the Beatrice redoubt. Each soldier wore the familiar dome-shaped helmet that bobbed like a gigantic undulating field of human tortoises. As they reached the barbwire, the front ranks threw their bodies across the coils allowing their comrades to scramble over their backs.

Periodic eruptions of dirt, rock, pulverised flesh and bone exploded when an unfortunate soldier detonated a mine.

There was no general order to open fire, each French Union unit acted individually. They braced for action from the protection of their trenches reinforced with rattan sacks that had become treacherously slippery after being soaked by nightly rainfall.

'Fire!' Frenchy yelled.

All the riflemen and two machine gunners opened up, raking the barbwire where Viet Minh bodies now piled several deep. Some lay still while others writhed, hopelessly trapped below layers of human carnage. They struggled and screamed under the weight of those above while barbwire tore into their flesh under a hail of hot lead.

Frenchy was now a company commander as all the commissioned officers were either dead or incapacitated. Mind you, the company he commanded had been reduced to the size of little more than a platoon. At last count his unit strength was fifty, but that changed by the minute. Sure there were losses, but dazed and confused men joined him from other companies so badly mauled by artillery fire that they'd ceased to exist as individual units.

Despite the horror along the barbwire the *Bo Doi* inched forward. The 312th Division was ten-thousand strong and the reserves kept pouring in.

'Hold the bastards. Steady! Steady,' Frenchy roared emptying his pistol into the overcrowded mass ahead.

The Viet Minh not only slowly advanced, but poured streams of a withering return fire into Beatrice's fortifications. Bullets smacked into the rattan bags filled with gravel dug from the trenches. The rattan splattered apart blasting the Legionnaires with grit and stones that acted like tiny shrapnel fragments.

Frenchy still had a radio at his disposal although he'd lost two operators within an hour.

'Get me Colonel Piroth at Huguette,' he ordered.

Colonel Charles Piroth was Dien Bien Phu's one-armed artillery commander. Frenchy had no time for 'yes sirs'.

'We need a barrage north-east of Beatrice.'

'How far ahead?' Piroth's voice cracked uncertainly through the static.

'Ten metres!'

'*Mon Dieu*, I cannot guarantee not to hit your position.'

'It cannot be any worse than it is now. The Reds are only metres away. Lay down everything you've got!'

Within seconds HE shells pounded into the barbwire, but the *Bo Doi* were already clambering over the rattan bags. Viet Minh dropped into the trenches firing at anything that moved. Frenchy slammed another clip into his pistol and blasted into enemy troops who were forced to stay in single file along the narrow trench. Other *Bo Doi* rushed along the trench rim pouring deadly fire into the Legionnaires trapped in the dugouts.

Frenchy saw more shadows clearing the barbwire killing ground. He flung two grenades into the Viet Minh, but didn't wait to see the results. The enemy was so tightly pressed he knew he'd done some damage.

'Time to move out, *mes enfants! Allez! Vite!*'

Frenchy was battered by the shockwaves as more artillery thundered into the front line. It was too little too late however. The Viet Minh now had cleared paths through the barbwire and minefields so the next wave of *Bo Doi* reached Beatrice's bastion with only light casualties. They shot or bayoneted anyone who didn't immediately surrender. Some legionnaires, trapped by the crush of their dead and dying comrades, were left with no option but to lay down their rifles and give up the fight.

Frenchy wasn't one of them. He and his last surviving men wound their way back through the trenches with *Bo Doi* baying for blood only yards behind. Frenchy lobbed another grenade into the path of the oncoming Viet Minh ripping the first soldier to shreds. Fortunately for those following, the trench was so narrow the leading victim shielded them.

Once he reached the centre of the compound, Frenchy was joined by rag-tag elements of the half-brigade. Shattered men trudged back from the forward defences. All told the same story. Despite horrendous losses, the Viet Minh stormed forward and swamped the defenders by sheer weight of numbers.

Frenchy regrouped the survivors. Only ten of his original company now stood beside him. They gathered any spare ammunition they found. There was plenty to be found by raiding the corpses that littered the base. Frenchy ordered any wounded who could no longer hold a rifle to make their way to the rear. Stretcher cases would just have to be left where they lay.

Frenchy now had a solid core of men in the ravaged central redoubt where Major Pégot and his staff had been killed. The HQ looked like a pit cluttered with the chaotic debris left after the Viet Minh barrage. Frenchy ordered the men to pile the rattan bags at the rim and position themselves behind the barrier. The *Bo Doi* had paused to regroup, but the respite only lasted minutes. Suddenly they charged into the HQ area. Viet Minh poured from the trench exits and over the top until they reached the centre of Beatrice.

'Fire!' Frenchy bellowed.

A savage volley cut the leading ranks of Viet Minh to pieces, but others leapt over the bodies only to die in the face of such concentrated fire-power. Despite the legionnaires' bitter resistance, the Viet Minh numbers once again overwhelmed their position. *Bo Doi* crushed towards the legionnaires' barricade. The first enemy leapt over the rattan bags, firing into the French Union troops.

Men crashed into each other, fighting hand-to-hand with rifle butts, bayonets, knives or just their bare hands. Legionnaires and *Bo Doi* battled with equal ferocity. Men screamed and cursed and died in an amorphous swamp of carnage.

Once again Frenchy was forced to withdraw his troops. He lobbed two more grenades into the charging Viet Minh causing their advance to falter momentarily allowing those remaining legionnaires to retreat, firing their rifles from the hip.

So inch-by-inch, redoubt-by-redoubt, struggle-by-struggle, death-by-death, the legionnaires slowly withdrew to Beatrice's southern perimeter. By midnight the post was no longer tenable.

Although individual clashes could be heard all over Beatrice, they were usually brief and viciously resolved.

Beatrice had been over-run and Frenchy's problems were getting worse.

About a dozen men now surrounded him as they raced down the embankment away from Beatrice. Viet Minh followed, but were hampered by the barbwire and minefields. The legionnaires made sure they'd familiarised themselves with the safe paths that cut through the killing zone.

However, not all of General Tan's 312th division had stormed Beatrice. Some units were circling around the flanks to cut off any retreating French Union troops. A company of Viet Minh infantry now blocked Route 41 leading to Dominique nearly two thousand yards away.

Frenchy hustled his men into scrubland on the left side of the road. It was almost impossible to move through the undergrowth in darkness. Branches stabbed into men's faces and snagged their uniforms. Some tripped while others became detached from the main group, stumbling away totally lost to be caught or killed by the enemy.

By dawn Frenchy and six men reached the barricade at Dominique where they were challenged by nervous Algerian riflemen who were in a mood to shoot first and ask questions later. One man was wounded when the Algerians opened fire. Luckily their commander, Captain Jean Garandeau, recognised Gallic expletives when he heard them, positively identifying Frenchy as 'friendly'.

Garandeau greeted Frenchy with trepidation.

'Is it true, sergeant ... we heard rumours over the radio?' he stammered, as if loathe to use words like 'over-run' or 'destroyed'.

'Beatrice is no more, captain,' Frenchy rasped as he gulped a water canteen dry. 'Gone – obliterated.'

'An entire half-brigade?'

'*Oui monsieur,* we're all that's left as far as I know. And that's the core of the matter, *n'est-ce pas?'* Frenchy sneered. 'We talk about "half-brigades" and "battalions" while the Reds talk in terms of divisions and armies. We're trying to hold back the tide with a child's sea-side bucket.'

All the Beatrice survivors were wounded. Frenchy had two glancing bullet wounds that bled freely. Garandeau requested a tank from Huguette. When it finally arrived, the men piled aboard then ran the gauntlet with Viet Minh artillery as the tank crossed the airstrip to the central camp.

Frenchy sat with his men in triage overseen by senior medical student Angela Holyman. Their eyes met as she assessed his wound.

'You ..?' she whispered, wide eyed.

'*Bonjour, mademoiselle Angela,'* he grinned as he lit a cigarette. 'I heard a rumour that une *fillet très jolie* was at Huguette. *Mais quelle surprise agréable.'*

Chapter 23 — Gabrielle

'I should just let these cuts go septic,' Angela muttered as she injected a local anaesthetic to numb Frenchy's wounds before she probed for metal fragments and spent lead still lodged in his flesh. Essentially his wounds were minor if properly treated, but the risk of infection was ever-present in the muddy squalor that was developing in the over-crowded human maelstrom that Dien Bien Phu had become.

She removed the shrapnel and bathed the wounds with antiseptic before binding them.

'Try to keep this clean,' Angela admonished. 'Come back tomorrow and someone will replace the dressing and check for infection. Remember your worst enemy is filth — try to keep the affected area clean.'

'I thought the *Bo Doi* were our worst enemy and is there somewhere clean in this toilet-bowl?' Frenchy grinned and even Angela smiled in reply.

Dien Bien Phu had been described as a bowl almost as soon as the French Union forces occupied it during Operation Castor. That had soon developed into 'toilet-bowl' as the full implications of the base's vulnerability became apparent. Everyone who parachuted into Dien Bien Phu quickly learnt the danger they faced, but General Navarre stubbornly clung to the theory that the base should be held and its defences would stand against anything the Viet Minh threw at it. General Giáp was just a trumped-up provincial school teacher after all.

'What will you do now?' Angela asked. 'I understand your unit has been destroyed.'

Frenchy shrugged.

'I will be attached to another battalion. It is not like I have anywhere else to go.'

'Unluckily you aren't hurt badly enough for Danny to casevac you out.'

'He is here?'

'He's flying one of the Dakota evacuation planes.'

'There seems no way that boy can keep out of trouble.'

'He wants me to leave the base,' Angela said.

'That is good advice,' Frenchy replied with what Angela thought was genuine concern. 'You should take it while you can.'

'Why do you care?'

'Other than the *Bo Doi*, you two are the most worthy enemies I have faced. I admire your spirit.'

'It's a soldier thing, I suppose.'

'*Oui,* it is a soldier thing. I suppose I hate the Viet Minh, but I admire them as enemies. And now I must go back to being a soldier.'

Frenchy was reassigned to Huguette's defences. He slept until afternoon then scrounged around to re-equip his personal weapons before taking up his new position covering the airstrip. He took command of a mortar crew whose job was to protect the casevac planes by spotting enemy positions and making sure they kept their heads down until the planes took off or taxied clear to the aircraft pens. Many of the C-47s had Red-Cross symbols painted on their tails, but the Viet Minh made no allowance for that. Frenchy didn't particularly know much about mortars, but the crew's sergeant had been killed by an indiscriminate piece of wayward shrapnel and sergeants were in short supply. His job was mainly target spotting anyway while the crew did all the technical work.

Angela often accompanied the wounded to the planes even though artillery shells, mortars and machineguns fired at targets on the airfield. As the day passed into late afternoon, rain showers hampered the C-47 landings. B-26s continued high-level bombing raids on targets surrounding Dien Bien Phu, but after two spotter planes were shot down, no one bothered to check whether the raids were successful or not.

Six CAT C-119s airdropped supplies of guns, ammunition and barbwire. The American crews flew lower than the inexperienced French Air Force pilots and achieved greater accuracy although some loads still landed on Viet Minh held territory. CAT planes were taking more hits than anyone else. The CAT pilots complained about the poor quality of bomber and fighter support, but received little sympathy from Colonel Jean-Louis Nicot who was in charge of transport operations between Hanoi and *Torri-Rouge*.

Danny landed at about 4 pm while Frenchy laid down covering fire onto two hills to the east of strong-point Elaine. The hills were called *Baldy* and *Phoney*. They were so close to the GONO perimeter, they became favourite spots for the *Bo Doi* to lob mortars onto the base.

Danny parked the Dak and scrambled from the cockpit to help Long Li load the stretchers. Angela met them with a smile.

'You'll never guess who I ran into this morning,' she said cheerfully as if she was talking about an old school chum. 'Frenchy Duval. He's a legionnaire sergeant now.'

'All the more reason to hop on the plane and come back to Hanoi with me,' Danny said without any hope of persuading her. 'You know Beatrice was abandoned last night, don't you?'

'Yes,' she replied defiantly as if it didn't matter.

'It's starting to look like a house of cards to me, Angela,' Danny growled.

'All the more reason for me to stay.'

'How's Jacques handling things?'

'Okay,' she replied uncertainly.

In fact Dr Jacques Chevalier wasn't handling things well at all. He'd planned to stay at GONO for the least time possible, have his photograph taken with Colonel Castries, Lieutenant Colonel Pierre Langlais, Major Grauwin and any other senior officers he could find before taking the first plane back to Hanoi. He planned to write of his 'war experience' and be published in a fashionable Parisienne magazine. He also wanted to impress Angela even though she was half his age. He'd achieved the photo-shoot component of his scheme, but the stupid girl was obsessed with her sense of duty. She insisted on staying when they should both be tucked up in bed at the Metropole Hotel engaged in champagne-enhanced carnal ecstasy. If she wanted to be his *petite amie* it was high time she started acting like it.

The Dakota was quickly loaded, but mortar bombs were landing uncomfortably close by so Danny started the engines and took off without delay. It was his last sortie for the day. It was just as well. The Viet Minh now turned their attention to the airstrip and aircraft pens, hammering them for hours with everything they had. By evening all the GONO support aircraft – Bearcats, S-55 choppers and Morane 500 Cricket observation aircraft were damaged to some extent. Many were totally destroyed. The runway length was drastically reduced due to *PSP* damage. GONO's on-site air force had been eliminated in one afternoon.

As night fell, Frenchy remained at his mortar station surveying the burning wreckage and aircraft carcasses strewn from one end of the airstrip to another. The shell of a C-46 cargo plane lay prominently beside the runway right in the airfield centre as a tragic icon symbolising aviation's demise at Dien Bien Phu.

He ate cold canned stew and drank coffee brewed by his newly assigned crew. The distant crump of artillery explosions continued from the direction of Gabrielle, but with a sudden more urgent intensity. Immediately radio chatter cluttered the airwaves. Gabrielle was manned by the 5th Battalion 7th Algerian Regiment supported by the 2nd Foreign Legion Mortar Company. The rattle of small arms started up and drifted in from Gabrielle as a constant popping while explosions flashed along the horizon.

As he watched Gabrielle suffering the same fate as Beatrice the night before, Frenchy became aware that someone crouched beside him.

'I've come to check your dressing,' Angela whispered.

'*Merci beaucoup, mademoiselle Angela,*' Frenchy said with a grin. 'I am honoured to get special treatment.'

'Just helping an old acquaintance,' she replied mischievously, adding 'Oh my God,' when she saw the devastation along the runway. Many of the wrecks still glowed as they smouldered in oblivion. Angela had been totally occupied in the underground hospital during the shelling.

'I heard and felt the shells of course,' she said, 'but I had no idea where they were landing. No planes will be able to use the strip now.'

'If we can clear the wreckage at the end of the strip, I think Daks will still have a chance, but everything else is finished. The air force will not replace those lost planes.'

'Why not?'

'They have nothing to replace them with.'

'That'll mean Danny will come back.'

'Unless he sees sense,' Frenchy said,' but he will return while you are here if he possibly can.'

'What makes you so sure?'

'*Il vous aime,* – he loves you, *n'est-ce pas?* You can see that, *non?*'

She lowered her eyes and blushed a little, knowing full well that she loved him whatever their differences. But was he like a brother, a friend or more? And what about Jacques? It was so complicated.

'What's going on out there?' she asked noticing the distant mottled eruptions. 'That's towards Gabrielle isn't it?'

'*Oui mademoiselle,* they are being pounded like we were last night.'

She finished re-dressing his wounds and declared that he was healing satisfactorily.

'I think you should try and sleep tonight, Angela,' Frenchy said with surprising kindness. 'I believe you will be needed more than ever tomorrow morning.'

'I'll try, but although I'm exhausted most of the time, it's hard,' she replied and turned to leave.

'Thank you,' Frenchy said.

She smiled thinly.

'Old enemies, new friends perhaps?' he suggested.

'You were so brutal to us. I used to forgive more readily, but I'm finding that harder to do these days. We'll see.'

'That is all I ask,' Frenchy said sincerely. 'I think you will need brutal men at your side before this fight is done.'

She nodded and returned to the hospital.

That night Gabrielle fell under the *Bo Doi* onslaught. Once again the strong-point command centre suffered a direct hit from enemy artillery. Base commander Major Roland de Mecquenem and his replacement, Major Kah, were both seriously wounded, effectively eliminating Gabrielle's command structure.

The following day Colonel Castries ordered a counter attack employing one of the base's M-24 tanks. After stiff resistance from the Viet Minh and heavy French Union losses, the assault faltered before grinding to a halt at the foot of Gabrielle's defences. With no immediate air support to prise the Viet Minh out, the strong-point was doomed. Fifteen hundred French Union troops were killed, wounded, captured or posted as missing, in Gabrielle's collapse and the subsequent counter attack.

Of course those casualties poured into Major Grauwin's surgery which quickly resembled bedlam. Angela was assigned to triage duty, attending a never ending stream of wounded men. Some were silently in shock, while others moaned or screamed in agony. Angela and her team of medical orderlies applied dressings, injected morphine and selected those casualties requiring immediate surgery. There were plenty of them – far more than Claudine's base hospital was designed to cope with. Soon stretchers formed a line stretching out from the hospital entrance.

Now no one was under any illusions that GONO was in big trouble. Not only did the Viet Minh control the high ground surrounding the strong-points, they now occupied two fortified positions close to the main base and no amount of artillery or air strikes from Hanoi could budge them.

General Le Trung Tan installed his own spotters at Beatrice and Gabrielle so the Viet Minh bombardment grew even more accurate. As the day wore on, more survivors straggled in from the beleaguered strong-points, but they were pitifully few. Angela was relieved in a way, because there were fewer wounded to deal with. Major Grauwin's teams were now just keeping pace with the backlog.

Of course it means those poor boys trapped out there are either dead or prisoners, she reflected sadly.

It was nightfall before the last patient passed through triage. Angela, who'd been on duty since dawn, had also worked through half the previous night. It was only when Major Grauwin ordered her to bed that she finally grabbed a few hours rest. But first she needed some fresh air. The medical staff quarters were right next to the casualty wards and Angela just wanted a few minutes away from the horror and misery of suffering men.

As she stood by the barbwire overlooking the aircraft pens lightning flashes blended with artillery explosions. The rumble of shell blasts mingled with thunder to a point where Angela couldn't tell the difference.

Oh Danny, I should have listened to you. How I'd love to be arguing the toss with you somewhere — anywhere but here in this hell. But how can I leave these stricken men now. Some aren't any older than us, Danny.

'*Pardon, mademoiselle,*' a voice spoke quietly. Angela spun around with a start. A friendly faced man stood beside her. He'd approached so quietly, she was completely unaware of his presence until he spoke.

'Forgive me,' he said. 'I didn't mean to frighten you, but do you think it wise to stand out here? Look at our smart fellows. They keep their heads down and stay in the trenches or under cover.'

The man beside her was about forty years old. Although there was nothing particularly remarkable about him, even in the night's dimness it was impossible not to notice his left arm was missing. Angela had never met the man before, but she recognised him as Colonel Charles Piroth, GONO's artillery commander. He'd lost his arm when his unit was caught in a Viet Minh ambush near Saigon back in 1946.

Pulling a pack from his uniform jacket pocket, he single-handedly fumbled for a cigarette. He offered one to Angela and, although she didn't smoke, she accepted it anyway. She took his lighter and lit both cigarettes, gagging when she drew her first lungful of smoke. After that she just held the cigarette. Smoking was supposed to be sophisticated and adult, but she didn't think she'd make a habit of it. Mind you she'd said that about alcohol, but now enjoyed a glass of wine from time to time. She recalled that Danny, for all his vices, hadn't succumbed to tobacco's addiction either.

'Do you mind if I stay here with you a while, mademoiselle?' Colonel Piroth said in a rather resigned, dispirited tone.

'It will be my pleasure, colonel,' she replied sincerely. He appeared to be such a pleasant man although his face looked wracked with pain and self-doubt.

They stood in silence for a few minutes while Colonel Piroth dragged on his cigarette.

'I couldn't help them, you know. I'm sorry,' Piroth said softly, almost in a whisper as if talking to himself.

'Help who, colonel?'

'Our men at Beatrice and Gabrielle. There were just so many targets and I had so few guns. I tried to meet all the demands, but my crews were overwhelmed. If only I had more howitzers and gunners to man them. I should have demanded more heavy guns when I had the chance. We were just spread too thin.'

That was true. General Tan had ordered many smaller *Bo Doi* diversionary attacks before concentrating on Beatrice and Gabrielle in turn. The wily Viet Minh general knew other GONO strong-point commanders would demand artillery support to the detriment of Beatrice and Gabrielle's defences.

'I'm sure you did all you could, colonel. No one could have done more.'

'Thank you,' he said even more vaguely. His mind seemed to be drifting. 'If you don't mind me saying, you are a very beautiful woman, mademoiselle.'

'Not at all, colonel,' Angela replied with a smile. 'No girl should mind if a gentleman calls her beautiful.'

'I remember the beautiful girls of Paris and Saigon walking or cycling past the cafes. Is it wrong to admire beautiful girls, mademoiselle? Is it sinful?'

'Not if you mean them no harm.'

'Oh no, it made me happy that God created such lovely creatures and I was privileged to witness their beauty. I shall miss that.'

'I can see nothing wrong in appreciating beauty. I think we all do that. I'm sure those girls would be charmed to know you admired them so. You are a Frenchman after all. I think it is expected of you. I'm sure you'll be back in Saigon enjoying the ladies before long,' Angela said with a smile.

'Thank you, mademoiselle, but I don't think that will be the case,' Piroth said as he finished his cigarette and stubbed the butt into the muddy ground. 'It has been my great pleasure to speak with you.'

'Come and chat any time, colonel. It's nice to talk to someone who isn't wounded,' she said then realised that Colonel Piroth had endured life with only one arm for eight years.

'I'm sorry,' she stammered, 'that was thoughtless of me.'

'Not at all, *ma chère*,' Piroth said softly. '*Au revoir.*'

As he walked away Angela was left with an unsettling impression that he was so forlorn and guilt-ridden, his heart was in the depths of despair and there was nothing she could do to cheer him up.

Angela's assessment was correct. Colonel Piroth walked slowly to his command bunker and retired to his quarters. Sitting on his cot, he drew a grenade from his pocket and pulled the pin with his teeth as he held the weapon to his chest. Four seconds later his chest was blown to mush.

Chapter 24 — Trapped

GONO might have its troubles, but all of Tonkin was seething with unrest and the airports around Hanoi did not escape the Viet Minh's attention. When Danny returned to Bach Mai Airport after three harrowing sorties to *Torri-Rouge* he taxied his plane to the usual parking bay. The casevac patients were transferred to ambulances and driven away with the Air Force nurse who'd accompanied them. Danny had nothing but admiration for these women who calmly went about their duty while bullets zinged right past them in a world of tumultuous hell.

Danny's Dak had received half-a-dozen skin punctures from small arms fire, but the duty mechanic assured him there was nothing serious and he'd have the plane ready sometime after midnight.

Danny and Long Li grabbed something to eat from the French Air Force mess and fell asleep on a couple of battered lounge-chairs in the CAT crew-room. Monty and Earthquake landed shortly afterwards. After the growling C-119s' engines clattered to a stop, Earthquake inspected one of the tail booms on his plane. It was significantly damaged with one rudder surface completely shot away. Monty's plane was in better shape having sustained only minor shrapnel damage.

'Dammit, it was a bitch to get back here,' Earthquake declared. 'We nearly didn't make it.'

The CAT crew-room was equipped with a shower, bunks and lockers where aircrew kept their navigation bags and extra clothes when it simply wasn't worth the time to return to their hotel in town. Earthquake also kept a stash of Tennessee whiskey that never seemed to dwindle even though he shared the booze generously and certainly didn't skimp when it came to his own consumption.

He was in a glum mood and wanted company so he woke Danny and Long Li, handing them each a mug of sour-mash. Earthquake had only been stateside once since WWII. He didn't seem to fit in there anymore, preferring to call Asia home. Having endured China, Korea and now Vietnam, he'd been flying in war zones for over ten years with hardly a break. The stress was starting to take its toll.

Monty returned from the mess-hall with a boxful of baguettes, cold meat and tomatoes that he shared around. Monty complained that he'd kill for a decent cheeseburger, but made short work of a baguette *avec le jambon, le fromage n cru et la tomate.*

'GONO's in deep shit,' Monty opined. 'You know how they lost Beatrice and Gabrielle in forty-eight hours. Now the Reds have blasted the crap out of *Torri-Rouge.*'

'It's still Dakotable,' Danny reminded him wearily. 'Crickets and Beavers can obviously get in too.'

'Yeah, but for how much longer and what bloody use are Crickets and Beavers?'

Around midnight the CAT pilots were awakened by popping gunfire close to their quarters. Earthquake woke in a flash, but the others weren't far behind. They grabbed the variety of weapons they carried on their flight-decks. Danny was now armed with two 1911 Colt .45 automatic pistols. They were tough, reliable and he had no trouble obtaining spare ammo – not that he'd actually fired them much. They also packed a slightly bigger punch than the similar Browning 9 mm issued to French Union forces.

Mayhem raged outside the crew-room door. Tracer rounds zipped past, ricocheting off anything solid or thudding into softer targets. Air Force guards rushed helter-skelter, blazing away at anything that moved. Only Earthquake's bellowing saved the CAT pilots from becoming targets as well.

'What the hells' going on,' he roared at the nearest nervous looking sentry.

'*Bo Doi* commandos, monsieur. They 'ave breeched the wire!'

As if to confirm the fact, a rocket streaked towards the aircraft flight line, erupting into a fireball when it smacked into one of the C-47s.

'Cheeky bastards,' Earthquake muttered. 'C'mon let's flush 'em out.'

Danny, Monty and Long Li followed the big American to the nearest point along the perimeter wire. One group of ADGs was baled up behind pallet loads of cargo while firing at a group of shadowy figures lying flat just within the wire. They'd cut a narrow path just wide enough for men to fit in single file.

Another rocket flashed away in the direction of the guards who dived for cover effectively stopping their fusillade into the raiders.

From other more distant uproars, Danny sensed that the group they were approaching was only one of several. It was a squad-sized knot of men that hadn't noticed they were in danger of being outflanked. The four CAT men opened up from almost point-blank range. The Viet Minh commandos' bodies bucked then lay still as bullets ripped into them.

The French Union guards recovered and regrouped, driving the other commando teams back through the airfield perimeter, leaving twenty dead in their wake. Normally the Viet Minh carried their casualties away, but the French retaliatory fire was too intense. Several planes were damaged including the C-47 and a Bearcat that were totally destroyed.

While the ADGs cleaned up the mess, Danny and his companions returned to the crew-room where Earthquake's liquor supply awaited. It had been such a short, sharp fight that they were all still pumping adrenalin and a shot of booze was just what they needed to steady their nerves.

'Don't these buggers ever give up?' Danny wondered aloud.

'Why should they?' Long Li replied. 'They're fighting for their freedom.'

'Communism doesn't sound much like freedom to me.'

'Half the *Bo Doi* probably don't even know what communism is,' Long Li said. 'They just want to get rid of the French, especially General Giáp. He spent over a year in prison while his father, wife, sister and sister-in-law were all killed as insurgents by the French. That would have to make a man bitter.'

'Well, look at you, Mr Historian,' Danny quipped.

'I talk to people in the streets when I get time off,' Long Li replied. 'They tell me stuff and it helps me learn the language. I pay attention and that helps me to fit in.'

Danny was coming to realise that Vietnam was not nearly as simple as Korea. Long Li explained that the country had pretty much been at war for a thousand years. Mostly the trouble-makers were Chinese, but then the French came along to grab what little was left of the world that hadn't already been snapped up by other European super-powers. The Vietnamese didn't always get along with each other either and were continually hacking it out in gory internal squabbles.

The following day, Danny was airborne at first light. His plane carried medical supplies, plasma and blood. Long Li was the only crewman although they were accompanied by an Air Force nurse to tend the casevac patients returning to Hanoi. Danny was shocked when he saw how the base had changed. Most noticeable were the charred aircraft wrecks littering *Torri-Rouge.* French Union engineers had used bulldozers to clear most of the wreckage from the runway, but the *PSP* surface was so badly torn up that the effective length had now been reduced by over a third.

Flak from positions on the high ground was thick, forcing Danny to hold clear of the base until B-26 bombers dropped a barrage that temporarily reduced the Viet Minh guns. Instant Bearcat response raids were now out of the question.

During a lull Danny seized his opportunity and dived for the runway. It wasn't the prettiest landing he'd ever made, but he pulled up before the strip turned into a tangled mess of jagged steel that would puncture the landing gear tyres instantly. Colonel Nicot had ordered that all transport and casevac planes turn around with their engines running. This was fraught with danger in the crowded chaos surrounding the planes while harassed dispatchers unloaded supplies and loaded stretcher-cases. More than one inattentive victim was shredded into a scarlet spray by an idling propeller.

Initially Danny defied the transport commander's decree, judging it the lesser of two evils to shut down the motors, avoiding prop damage if they struck anyone while he was parked. That didn't last long. As the Viet Minh trenches inched closer to the central GOMO stronghold, their artillery spotting gradually improved. By the third week in March, Dakotas simply landed, unloaded and loaded at the strip end before turning around and taking off in the opposite direction.

To his utter chagrin, Danny only glimpsed Angela occasionally from the cockpit. She waved when she saw him, but hastily returned to help evacuate the casualties. Towards the end of the month the *Bo Doi* were snapping at Anne-Marie and Dominique's heels. Despite reinforcements parachuting into the valley, the French Union forces seemed incapable of stemming the inexorable crawling advance. Manned by disheartened Vietnamese and North African colonial troops, Anne-Marie crumbled into fragments without much of a fight, leaving only a quarter of its original area in French hands.

Air drops of both men and matériel were becoming increasingly hazardous. A quarter of the resupply loads fell directly to the enemy, while too many paratroops dropped wide of their DZs only to be shot as they floated to earth or captured after they landed. Two airborne battalions and two airborne medical teams parachuted into Dien Bien Phu between 14-17 March. Major 'Bruno' Bigeard who commanded one of these airborne brigades was to become involved in an intrigue that fundamentally changed GONO's command dynamic.

On 24th March Lieutenant Colonel Langlais and Major Bigeard persuaded other senior officers to mount a military coup. Colonel Castries was sidelined and although he kept nominal command of the base, the operational tasks were henceforth directly under Colonel Langlais' control. Langlais wanted to go on the offensive, taking the fight to the Viet Minh and recovering lost territory, dubbing the strategy 'offensive defence'.

As for Danny and Angela, it simply meant more wounded to cope with. Despite the arrival of two new airborne medical teams, the main hospital was still swamped with casualties.

By late March Danny and Long Li were pretty much only working, eating or sleeping, but one night they decided to have supper at the Metropole. While Danny moped over a pre-dinner beer he was approached by an elegant woman in her early forties.

'Hello,' she greeted, extending her hand. 'Danny McAlister, I presume? I'm ...'

'Mrs Holyman,' Danny said. There was absolutely no doubt this lady was Angela's mother.

'Indeed,' she replied.

'Please, sit down. Would you like a drink? This is my friend — and Angela's — Long Li.'

'It's so nice to finally meet you both. Angela talks about you all the time. I'll have a gin-and-tonic, please.'

Danny caught a waiter's eye and ordered Mrs Holyman's drink and another two beers.

'I certainly see where Angela gets her looks,' Danny said then wondered if he was being impertinent, but Mrs Holyman accepted the compliment with a gracious smile.

'I suppose you know why I'm here,' Mrs Holyman said. 'Angela's father and I only discovered what our daughter was up to a week ago so I flew here as soon as I could. Gordon will arrive tomorrow.'

'What do you plan to do?'

'Go and fetch our girl, of course. I always thought her relationship with that French fellow was inappropriate. Gordon and I intend to put a stop to this nonsense right away. It's time Angela took responsibility for her actions and knuckled down to her studies again.'

'You'll get no argument from us,' Danny assured her. 'Long Li and I fly casevacs out of *Torri-Rouge* nearly every day. We've been trying to persuade her to leave Dien Bien Phu since she and Jacques Chevalier first went there.'

'Then I will come with you on your next mission,' Mrs Holyman declared resolutely.

'Sorry, I can't allow that,' Danny insisted. 'It's far too dangerous. We cop bullets all the time.'

'You must. All Gordon and I want is our baby back.'

'I'll throw you off the plane, if you try board,' Long Li said brutally, but that's what was needed right then.

Mrs Holyman gazed at him and then burst into tears.

'I left Angela and Gordon once,' she sobbed. 'When they returned to England I realised how much I loved them and had missed them so desperately. I can't let that happen again.'

Mrs Holyman had indeed yearned for London's high-life when her husband was a missionary doctor in New Guinea. She'd returned to England, but the family was reunited some months later when Dr Holyman took up a country practice in Dorset.

'Look, Mrs Holyman,' Danny said softly, offering her a napkin to dab away her tears. 'You sit tight here in Hanoi and I promise you Long Li and I will do everything we can to persuade Angela to fly back with us tomorrow.'

So, at dawn on 27th March, Danny took off from Bach Mai once more bound for *Torri-Rouge*. He passed an outbound Dak piloted by Captain Bourgereau, carrying nineteen casualties he'd airlifted under cover of darkness. Danny's load was medical supplies as usual. On this occasion Lieutenant Geneviève de Galard was aboard to care for the wounded on the return flight.

When they flew over Dien Bien Phu the sky lit up with flak. It was the heaviest Danny had ever encountered. One Dakota was hit at ten thousand feet. There was nothing Danny could do but watch the flaming debris tumble to earth. He saw no parachutes open. Another Dak was hit so badly it couldn't remain airborne although the pilot managed to wrestle his plane to the ground, before crash-landing at the Isabelle's auxiliary airstrip. The crew escaped with minor injuries, but the plane was stuck on the ground with no chance of repair.

Danny fared little better. An ack-ack shell slammed into his starboard engine, but fortunately failed to detonate. The engine shredded to metal splinters while the prop separated from its drive-shaft, pulling the gearbox after it before whirling away and finally smashing into the jungle, scything vegetation to shreds. The plane almost flipped onto its back with a violent jolt before Danny gained control.

There was nothing for it but to limp back to Bach Mai and hope the wing's main spar stayed intact. It was an agonising two hour flight and when Danny finally arrived at Hanoi his problems weren't over. The starboard landing gear was completely immobilised by damage from the distorted engine cowl. Danny touched down on the port main-wheel. As the plane decelerated the tail dropped and the right wing tip settled onto the runway edge. When it touched, metal ground against concrete as the Dak was dragged sideways before veering off the strip.

Danny cut the fuel supply valves and switched off all battery power to reduce any fire risk. Fire trucks roared towards them as they clambered down from the cargo door that was now several feet higher than normal because of the Dak's unusual angle.

'Thank you, *messieurs*,' Geneviève said graciously as he and Long Li helped her to the ground. 'You are a splendid pilot, Danny.'

'Sorry I couldn't get into *Torri-Rouge*.'

'I will try again,' Geneviève said confidently. 'Major Blanchet is scheduled to make a flight tonight. I shall accompany him.'

'Meanwhile I'll have to find a new plane,' Danny grinned.

Finding a new plane wasn't as hard as it might have seemed. The French Air Force had nearly a hundred Dakotas at its disposal, but barely enough crews to fly three-quarters of them. Colonel Nicot was only too pleased to assign Danny another plane. After the day's serious losses Nicot decided to reduce daylight sorties and step up night operations. Danny had done several night sorties and, provided the weather remained reasonable, found being guided by only a couple of beacon lights was okay once you got used to it.

The hazards of a night approach into the black-hole of *Torri-Rouge* were more than compensated for by the lack of flak. On these occasions Danny switched off all the Daks navigation lights and anti-collision beacons and only activated his landing lights at the last moment. So far he'd avoided any enemy damage during night flights.

Danny then had to deal with Angela's distraught mother who was inconsolable, even when her husband arrived during the day. Gordon Holyman greeted Danny and Long Li warmly. He was very fond of the two men who'd helped his daughter out of so many scrapes before. Once again Danny promised he'd do all he could to bring Angela out on his next flight.

Just after 2 am Major Maurice Blanchard took off for his first night landing at Dien Bien Phu with Lieutenant Geneviève Galard on board. Danny was airborne two hours later. The flight to *Torri-Rouge* was uneventful. Although there were scattered rainclouds en route, weather conditions at GONO proved no problem.

Major Blanchard landed safely, but snagged his tail-wheel on coils of barbwire at the strip end as he turned his plane. At first it seemed as if the plane could be freed without difficulty, so the wounded were loaded on board anyway. Unfortunately enemy gunfire disabled one of the Dak's engines and it was left stranded on the runway.

Major Guérin, the senior air-traffic controller instructed Danny to return to Hanoi until the Dakota was either fixed or cleared the runway. Danny replied that he had sufficient fuel to hold until dawn and then assess whether he could land and pick up Blanchard's casevacs. Medical teams laid the wounded along the airstrip just in time. At daybreak the crippled Dak became an irresistible target for Viet Minh gunners, who started to pound it with everything they had. Now the stretcher-cases were in serious danger of becoming collateral damage.

Danny saw that he could just manage to land and stop his plane before the strip-end where Blanchard's Dak was quickly being reduced to scrap metal. After landing, Danny turned his plane and taxied to the runway end furthest from the stricken Dak.

The medical teams quickly gathered the stretchers, loaded them onto flatbed trucks and jeeps or carried them down the runway to where Danny was waiting. To his utmost relief he saw Angela was leading the medics. She carried her grip with the white laundry pole sticking from the flap. Major Grauwin had finally decided that as she was a civilian non-combatant, it was high time for her to leave the base. Jacques Chevalier was also waiting for a ride to Hanoi.

As soon as the wounded were aboard, Danny called Angela into the co-pilot's seat.

'Thank heavens you've finally seen sense. Your Mum and Dad are waiting for you in Hanoi,' he sighed.

She smiled, but he could see she harboured mixed feelings about leaving GONO. She also knew she was going to cop a right ear-bashing from her parents for sure.

'Where's Lieutenant Galard?' Danny asked.

'She said Jacques was a civilian and should take her place. She'll take the next plane out.'

'Jeeze Ange, we could have squeezed her in — *he's* just a waste of space.'

She glared at him this time.

'All set,' Long Li called from the rear. 'You two can chat later, let's get going.'

Danny pushed the throttles and mixture controls to full power as the Dak lurched forward.

Please make it over that wreck at the end of the strip.

He'd barely accelerated the plane to twenty-five knots when a mortar shell landed in the centre of the right wing, blowing it into oblivion. A house-size blaze enveloped the fuselage as the wing fuel tank erupted in flames. Although the left wing hadn't yet produced enough lift for the plane to take off, it was enough to flip it onto its side.

The Dak scraped along the *PSP* surface, grinding as the aluminium fuselage was ripped open. The plane surged ahead of the fireball then shuddered to a halt. The smell of AVGAS filled the cabin. Even in his disorientated state Danny knew to cut the fuel and battery power.

'Are you okay, Ange?' he yelled.

'Yes,' she replied a little uncertainly.

'Come and give me a hand,' Long Li called. 'It's a shambles back here.'

Danny and Angela scrambled aft into a chaotic scene from hell. The stretchers had tumbled in all directions and now lay in a jumble along the fuselage side that had become the plane's floor. Men lay groaning and screaming in panic. Those strong enough tried to struggle clear, but often trampled on their comrades. Field dressings and plasma bags had scattered amongst the struggling men. Some remained still and probably beyond help.

Danny reached the rear. He hoisted Long Li onto his shoulders, so the crewman was tall enough to open the door. Long Li then clambered outside, balancing precariously on the slippery, curved fuselage. Danny then lifted Angela after him. A second later Jacques Chevalier shoved Danny aside and started piling debris into a heap high enough for him to stand on and reach the door.

'Good idea,' Danny cried, thinking the Frenchman was finally of some use. Chevalier turned and glared for a second before hauling himself through the door and bolting for safety.

'I'll try and get these blokes up to you,' he said. 'It'll take both of you to lift them clear.'

It took longer than he expected to lift the dead-weight of a semi-conscious man high enough for Long Li and Angela to grab him. Then Danny had to push upwards so the wounded men almost tumbled out of the door down onto the *PSP*. Matters didn't improve when Chevalier's debris platform collapsed, but legionaries were racing to the rescue.

Just as help arrived Danny turned in horror. Fuel was pouring through cracks in the fuselage wall from the ruptured wing tank. It only took a drop to splash onto the hot engine exhaust pipe to start a trail of fire that snaked into the cabin. Suddenly the whole plane was shrouded in flames and oil-ridden smoke. Angela and Long Li instinctively jumped clear — there was nothing else they could do. Danny couldn't recall how he'd managed it, but he leapt upwards, grabbed the door frame and hauled himself outside. In one fluid, if not graceful movement, he flung himself to the ground.

Helping hands grabbed him and guided him away at sprint. He was aware of Angela and Long Li being led to safety by the medics. Even amid the chatter of machinegun fire from Frenchy's mortar pit, Danny heard Angela was wailing about the wounded still on board, but the heat was overwhelming and it was unlikely there was anything that could be done for them. Just as more Viet Minh guns opened up the Dak exploded and that unlikeliness became a certainty.

Torri-Rouge was now totally blocked. The previous night Captain Bourgereau's Dak had been the last plane to take-off from Dien Bien Phu.

Chapter 25 — Para Patrol

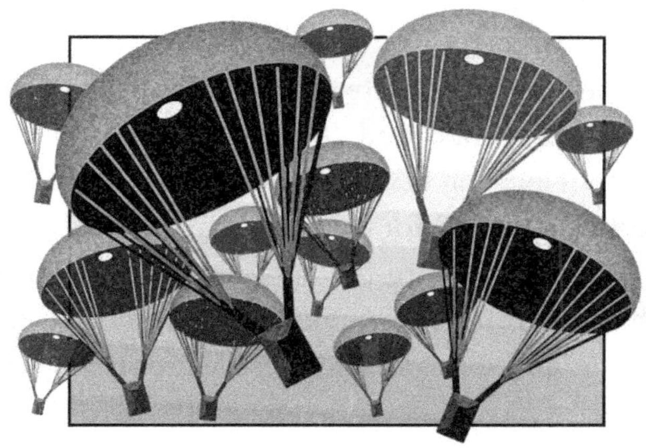

While Angela was able to return to her original quarters and find room for Geneviève, Danny and Long Li had to find somewhere to stay. Later that day a recovery team found Angela's backpack that had remarkably survived the fire. The legionnaires were mildly puzzled that she valued a metre-long white pole, but had not time to ask about its significance.

Equally surprising was where Danny and Long Li found a home. From his gunnery position beside *Torri-Rouge,* Frenchy Duval had witnessed the entire disaster. Indeed his mortar team had laid down intense covering fire onto Viet Minh positions that enabled Danny and the others to reach safety – well, relative safety. Nowhere at GONO was safe anymore. Frenchy left his post and went to meet Dien Bien Phu's newest residents.

'Welcome to dreamland,' Frenchy greeted with largesse.

'Crikey, this is a turn up for the books,' Danny declared.

He was ambivalent about Frenchy's offer of hospitality, but accepted although he certainly wasn't going to shake his arch-enemy's hand. Frenchy merely shrugged, introduced them to his team and showed them where they could bunk down. The mortar crew had constructed cots from wooden crates and covered their position with curved corrugated metal sheets.

'Sorry, it is not the Metropole and it will not stop a one-o-five direct hit,' Frenchy conceded, 'but it keeps most of the rain off.'

He delegated one of his men to escort Danny and Long Li to the quartermaster's HQ for extra clothing and canteen and hygiene supplies. Danny still wore his automatic pistols and carried spare clips in his shoulder-strap pouches. Long Li had no difficulty finding a rifle and extra magazines. More importantly, they were each supplied with a steel GI helmet.

'So what will you two do for amusement during your stay in paradise?' Frenchy asked when they returned.

The answer was obvious immediately. Danny and Long Li became stretcher-bearers. There were plenty of customers.

That very day firebrand Major Bigeard launched an attack on enemy artillery positions to the west of Dien Bien Phu. His men from Foreign Legion and Colonial battalions successfully cleared the lower slopes, killed a few hundred Viet Minh while capturing a significant weapons cache along with a dozen *Bo Doi*. Unfortunately there weren't sufficient French Union troops to hold the captured positions and they were forced to withdraw after losing twenty men and returning with nearly a hundred wounded.

And so began a month-long nightmare for Danny and everyone else trapped in Dien Bien Phu's 'toilet-bowl'. On April-Fool's Day the monsoon arrived in a deluge that turned Dien Bien Phu into a muddy hell-hole. Angela had returned to triage in her underground hospital bunker. Danny met her whenever he could, but it was usually when he and Long Li carried a shattered soldier from some part of GONO. Water sloshed through the tunnels until the medical teams worked in knee-high goo.

General Giáp's strategy remained constant. His engineers continued their burrowing crawl towards GONO's strong-points. Attack followed attack and counter-attack while aerial bombardments pounded the surrounding hills. However the Viet Minh gunners had learnt to cease fire when the bombers approached. With no muzzle flashes to aim for the French Air Force simply dropped their ordnance and hoped for the best. Occasionally they were off-target and French Union positions copped a pounding.

By mid-April Danny's and Long Li's world was a blur. They based themselves at GONO HQ where staff officers directed them to where casualties were reported. If Lieutenant Colonel Langlais was surprised at the sudden arrival of an Australian and a Singaporean, he gave no indication. His chisel-face expression rarely changed. A cigarette stub was permanently wedged between his lips.

It was an agonisingly slow process because they could only carry one stretcher-case between them. They often raced through a hail of bullets and exploding mortars or struggled along the maze of trenches, losing their way on many occasions.

When they returned to triage it was always the same story. Stretchers were lined up in the open exposing the injured troops to blistering sun and regular tropical downpours. The men needed shelter or they'd die more from the elements than bullet wounds. Angela was in despair until Danny saw a solution.

Dien Bien Phu and the surrounding country were littered with hundreds — probably thousands — of abandoned parachutes. These were left by reinforcements who'd been airdropped into the toilet-bowl or discarded after recovery teams had risked Viet Minh mortars and machinegun fire to retrieve cargo dropped from transport planes.

'What a wonderful idea, Danny,' she gushed, flinging her arms around him although neither of them were at their intimate best. But spotting the chutes and retrieving them were two different things altogether.

'We need men to gather those chutes,' Angela said to a legionnaire who'd just helped a wounded comrade to the hospital.

The trooper looked at her blankly.

'The parachutes, we need to make them into shelters for the wounded.'

Angela knew he understood. Her French had become quite fluent and wasn't 'parachute' a Gallic word anyway?

'Get some men and gather as many parachutes as you can,' Angela ordered as only Angela could. The legionnaire still stood his ground.

'These men need shelter!'

If she'd thought about it she would have understood the legionnaire's reluctance. Those chutes that had dropped safely into the compound had already been gathered and used by the soldiers as shelter or bedding. The remaining chutes that hadn't already been salvaged by the Viet Minh lay in exposed areas vulnerable to *Bo Doi* snipers and machine-gunners. Angela decided she needed something to urge the legionnaires and she thought she knew exactly the man to do the urging. Leaving Geneviève in charge of triage, she headed for the airstrip with Danny and Long Li in tow.

She found Frenchy Duval dozing in his mortar pit, seemingly oblivious of the frequent explosions around him. Half of his men were keeping up a steady rate of fire whenever they sighted a target while the others organised more mortar shells from the arms depot. They didn't need him to tell them how to suck eggs. Although fighting was continual somewhere around the perimeter, most large-scale attacks came after dark so Frenchy's team rotated their rest breaks throughout daylight.

'Frenchy, I need you!' she yelled shaking him awake.

'Ah, I have that effect on girls,' he leered. 'But where do we find somewhere private?'

'Not for that, you idiot,' Angela retorted. 'You have to persuade some men to gather parachutes to shelter the wounded. We don't have room underground.'

'It seems a good way to get shot to me.'

'Men will die if we don't. Danny and Long Li have volunteered.'

'More likely men *will* die if we do.'

'Danny and Long Li will go with you.'

Frenchy sighed as he heaved himself to his feet, gathered his rifle and pistol and clipped hand grenades to his uniform straps. It was the first Danny and Long Li had heard about volunteering, but that was probably a given since Angela was bossing everyone around and it was Danny's idea in the first place.

'You will leave me in peace if I get your precious parachutes, *oui?*'

'*Oui.*'

He shrugged and went to round up a squad, including a flame-thrower operator. The area surrounding the airstrip was actually a good choice as most of the airdrops were aimed somewhere along its length, even though they weren't always successful. Retrieving parachutes was a lot easier said than done. For one thing they were deceptively large and cumbersome especially the massive forty-eight foot diameter G-5 cargo chutes. Even when packed they formed a huge bundle. Some were rain soaked which made them even harder to manage.

It didn't take Danny and Frenchy long to work out they needed a truck – but a truck was a tempting target for any vigilant Viet Minh rocket team.

'We'll have to wait until dark,' Danny suggested.

'That is when the *Bo Doi* come out to play,' Frenchy said.

It was true. The Viet Minh sent company-sized patrols probing for soft spots and hopefully killing or capturing a few more French Union troops while they were at it.

'What about an air strike?'

'I can't see Colonel Langlais approving that for a few abandoned parachutes,' Long Li said dismally.

Ultimately they made a compromise. By late afternoon the sun was at their backs. Frenchy radioed the remaining Vietnamese and Colonial troops who still held on grimly to Elaine. They agreed to cover the parachute patrol and warn Frenchy of any enemy advance.

So the truck rattled out of the aircraft pens, over a Bailey bridge crossing the Nam-Youm River. They skirted the east riverbank that looked to be where the best picking could be found. One of Frenchy's crew drove while Danny and Long Li jumped out and gathered any parachutes they passed. Frenchy and his squad, including the flame-thrower, stood ready to ward off any *Bo Doi*. Their path quickly took them away from the airstrip as they followed a trail of parachutes lying on the ground or draped languidly over low vegetation. Like a paper-chase they randomly followed where most chutes lay.

Two months ago this area was thickly wooded around a village called Muong Thanh, but now the landscape was just bare and pock-marked with artillery craters. They reached a wooden bridge and turned left along a road that led to Route 41. Four of Elaine's isolated strong-points now surrounded them and could provide covering fire. But this track led them perilously close to hills *Baldy* and *Phoney* controlled by *Bo Doi*. It was nerve-wracking work. Danny felt totally helpless with his arms full of bulging nylon canopies and tangled shroud-lines. Having Frenchy riding shotgun gave some comfort. Danny was well aware just how ruthless he could be.

After an hour the truck was bulging and it was time to retreat. Just at that moment the radio crackled. Major Bréchignac, Elaine's commander, warned them a large force was spilling out of the closest trench and advancing. It was time to go. Brechignac's troops blazed away with enfilading fire as the Viet Minh tried to sneak between the five strong-points that now comprised Elaine.

The *Bo Doi* must have sensed something was up, or their spotters on *Baldy* and *Phoney* had picked up the truck's movement. A line of enemy troops charged into view. There were at least two platoons in the van and Danny had a bad feeling more *Bo Doi* were bringing up the rear. Danny and Long Li stuffed the last parachutes into the truck. Long Li grabbed his rifle and raced to join Frenchy's squad. Danny swapped one of his pistols for the driver's rifle and followed Long Li to take his place in line.

Frenchy's men took cover behind scrub and in bomb craters while Frenchy radioed for support from his mortar pit. Danny had to hand it to Frenchy. He might be an amoral totally evil bastard, but when it came to disciplined soldiering, he was sublime. The enemy was only a couple of hundred yards away when mortars burst into their ranks. At the same time Frenchy's squad opened fire with controlled, well aimed shooting.

Long Li remained his inscrutable self as he squeezed off one calculated shot after another. He rarely missed an enemy target. Danny tried to remain cool and aim accurately. *Bo Doi* fell, yet more replaced those who'd been shot. There was no end of them. Frenchy calmly redirected his mortars. Seconds later a group of *Bo Doi* were thrown upwards as a shell exploded among them. A couple were killed, but several others lay screaming with hideous injuries including severed limbs.

The Viet Minh regrouped, charging forward at a sprint, yelling gruesomely. Frenchy's men kept their heads. When the enemy was barely a hundred yards away, Frenchy nodded to the flame-thrower operator. Danny had to admire that man, who probably had one of the most hazardous jobs in a war which provided an endless choice of dangerous tasks. Anyone carrying a tank on his back containing a mixture of petrol, propellant and ignition medium was running a risk with so many stray bullets flying around.

Frenchy waited until the first *Bo Doi* were within fifty yards.

'*Vite! Les éclairer. Brûlez les salauds.*'

A jet of flames streaked towards the approaching troops, blazing a trail along the way. Undergrowth flared while thick oily smoke obliterated what little visibility remained. Frenchy didn't wait to see what the damage was, he ordered a retreat and his men needed no encouragement. They raced for the truck. Four men managed to squeeze into the giant nylon cushion at the back. Danny, Long Li and one other trooper shoved into the cab beside the driver, while Frenchy and his remaining two men stood on the running board, clinging on for all they were worth while firing a few parting shots at the Viet Minh who emerged through the smoke and fire screen.

More mortars and support fire from Elaine poured onto the Viet Minh who saw that the opportunity was lost and withdrew.

Danny and Long Li spent the next week constructing shelters for the men who now lay in their hundreds around Claudine's hospital. They salvaged timber and wrecked radio aerials for tent-posts and used the parachute shroud-lines as guy-ropes. Once the canopies were erected, Danny and Long Li lugged sandbags to build a protection wall. Even when the structure was complete they then had to continually repair damage caused by Viet Minh artillery and mortars.

Angela bustled among the wounded, but she and Danny were too busy to say much. The night after the parachute raid, she turned up at Frenchy's mortar pit with two back packs. They contained jars of Vinogel. After ammunition the jellified wine was the most popular substance airdropped into Dien Bien Phu.

'I brought this for you and your team,' she said. 'You should be able to make a few bottlefuls. *Merci beaucoup, messieurs.*'

She thanked each soldier in turn.

I've also brought something for you and Long Li,' she said to Danny, giving them each a Red-Cross armband.

'I want you to wear these all the time you're outside,' she instructed as only Angela could when she was in bossy-mode. 'The armbands may stop the Viet Minh shooting you.'

Danny thought he'd better not mention that Red-Cross symbols painted on his plane hadn't deterred the Viet Minh from shooting. It was a kind thought and he promised to do what he was told.

She could only stay a few minutes but accepted a mug of diluted Vinogel which Frenchy described as *Pinard* – very ordinary cheap wine. Maybe so, but none of the mortar crew complained.

'How's Jacques getting along?' Danny said trying not to sneer.

Apparently that hadn't gone well at all. She'd had a blazing row with her 'beau'.

'He blamed me for being stuck here.'

'That's hardly your fault. He could have got on a plane any time if he felt uncomfortable.'

'He wanted me to go with him.'

'So did I, but that doesn't mean I hold you responsible.'

'He said he only wanted me around because I'm young and pretty.'

'No argument there,' Danny smiled.

'When I asked him about "us", he told me there was no "us". He wasn't interested in foolish love-struck teenagers. He used me unforgivably, Danny,' she lamented as tears welled in the corner of her eyes.

Used you or wanted to use you? Danny wondered, aware of the significant difference, but Angela said no more on what was obviously a painful subject.

'Where is he now? I'll go and punch his lights out for you,' Danny said, meaning every word.

'He left the bunker today. I don't know where he went.'

'I have a pretty fair guess,' Frenchy said, but didn't elaborate.

Chapter 26 — Rats and Angels

April dragged on with perilous monotony. Many French Union troops were so numbed by constant shelling they barely flinched when artillery and mortars exploded close by. Rain continued to swamp GONO while the Viet Minh cleared one defensive position after another. Frenchy's mortar was replaced by a quad .50-cal crew. Mortars were needed elsewhere around the perimeter while the new weapon had been brought in from the ever shrinking Dominique. It was a mighty weapon consisting of four fifty-calibre machine guns mounted on a steel shield. With all guns blazing at once it was capable of truly awesome destruction that could cut advancing infantry to ribbons.

Danny and Long Li were fighting a losing battle trying to shore up damaged sandbags and replace parachute canopies ripped to shreds by shrapnel and bullets. Angela's position was no better. Men were so overcrowded in the underground squalor that had once been a hospital, they lay two to a bunk and many were simply left lying on the floor in their own filth. The wards reeked of stale sweat, vomit, urine and excrement. Even after a mess was cleared up, nothing could remove the cloying, almost overpowering, stench of human decay.

Antiseptics were running low and wounds either became septic or infested with maggots. Having your flesh crawling with distasteful maggots was actually the lesser of two evils. Apparently they only devoured putrid tissue thus cleaning the damaged area by default.

Many minor tragedies struck among the overall major tragedy that was Dien Bien Phu. Angela had selected several men to be relocated outside, assigning Danny and Long Li to carry them. As a torrential thunderstorm raged above, lightning strikes put out several radio masts while water cascaded into the trenches.

Danny and Long Li waded through water now as high as the lower bunks. They pulled half-drowned men from the water and hauled them through the tunnel entrance. As he passed the OR, Danny noticed Major Grauwin working calmly. He never raised his voice or became agitated, he simply stayed focused. Perhaps that was his way of dealing with the chaos around him. Danny felt he had never admired a single human being more.

The ground around GONO was now so saturated that water seeped through the tunnel, eroding mud and gouging rivulets into the walls. Danny, Long Li and the medics tried to get pumps into action, but they weren't powerful enough to stem the rising water level. Arc lights flickered and often blew when water short-circuited the electrical supply. Occasionally a generator would fail and plunge sections of the hospital into absolute, terrifying blackness. Dr Grauwin simply had to stop, freezing on the spot until either electric lighting was restored or someone could fire up a kerosene lamp. Sometimes he'd look only to see there was no point in continuing. His patient had died because of a blown fuse.

Water was also creeping up within the sandbag ramparts protecting the outside patients. Danny breached several walls, dragging the sandbags aside to allow the torrent to surge away down Claudine's ramparts towards the Nam-Youm River. All the time a thunderous drumming rain poured onto Dien Bien Phu. The parachute canopies sagged under the weight of water, often collapsing and drenching the already soaked men below. Danny spent hours tipping water out of the bulging nylon canopies. The trouble was they refilled in minutes, making it an ongoing and thankless task.

When the rained eased and he felt he had the situation under control, Danny returned underground. He was greeted by Angela's scream.

'There are men trapped in there,' she wailed, pointing down the tunnel to the wards.

Danny sloshed past the OR and X-ray unit to the furthest end of the ward. There Long Li was trying to free patients who'd been buried by a mud slide. There was little room to get a grip on limbs that protruded from the quagmire. Arms and legs just slipped out of Danny and Long Li's grasp. All round the tunnel was filled with the cries of desperate terrified men. Dr Grauwin worked on. He knew his team was doing all they could. Better to concentrate on the life he might save on the operating table than be distracted with something beyond his control.

Danny and Long Li dragged two men clear, but the others suffocated before they could be saved. Danny knew they'd have to dig another shaft to accommodate a pump, but there was no way he could start work until the rain stopped and there was daylight to work by.

It was a manpower problem all round. In the first two weeks of April the hospital admitted dozens of casualties, performing operations on nearly half of them every day. Even with new medical teams airlifted into Dien Bien Phu, the workload was unbearable.

'If only we had more nurses,' Geneviève lamented. 'We need to care for the wounded men's basic needs. It is not pretty work, but it is basic nursing. General Cogny won't authorise more female personnel into GONO now. None are parachute trained anyway.'

Indeed some reinforcements especially support and technical specialists were making their first drop into Dien Bien Phu.

'We need more men with strong backs to help repair the shelters and carry casualties from the aid posts,' Danny agreed. 'We can't keep this up. Everyone is exhausted and right now we're no good to man or beast.'

They were having breakfast in Frenchy's quad .50-cal pit before another day's torment. As the Viet Minh stranglehold tightened around GONO the area was growing smaller, but increasing rain and casualties made the job of moving them to safety even more arduous.

'You are not looking in the right place, *mon ami*,' Frenchy suggested.

Danny reflected that he no longer objected to being called 'my friend' by Frenchy. The feeling may not have been reciprocated, but Frenchy wasn't his enemy any more.

'What do you mean?'

'Put the rats and Ouled Nail to work. They are both idle right now.'

Then Frenchy explained what he had in mind.

'If we can get 'em, can you train them, Geneviève?' Danny asked.

'*Certainement, mon cher.* You must take Angela, she is very persuasive.'

'Yeah, like a sledgehammer.'

They found Angela in triage as usual. She was reluctant to leave, but a new medical team had just parachuted successfully into Claudine and taken over, assisted by Geneviève. Danny, Long Li and Angela headed for the river bank where a remarkable community had established itself.

The population dwelt in tunnels, dugouts and caves sited between Huguette, Claudine and what remained of Dominique and Elaine, thus making it the most protected area of Dien Bien Phu. That was not to say it was particularly safe, but the best of a bad lot.

There were two distinct groups haunting that riverbank labyrinth. The first was made up of internal deserters who now numbered probably in their thousands. These men came from all units, but were primarily Moroccan, Algerian, Vietnamese Colonial troops and Thai militia. The term 'internal deserters' was used because these particular men had chosen not to either slip through the Viet Minh lines or lay down their arms and surrender. What they had done was simply stop fighting.

And in some ways they might well have been justified. Incessant propaganda blurb blasted through loud hailers from the Viet Minh extolling communist virtues versus imperial enslavement and degradation. All the colonial troops had been born into French imperialism. They knew nothing else, so they didn't have much to make a comparison with. What the communists neglected to mention was that life under Red domination wasn't going to be a barrel of laughs either.

What the Thai and colonial troops did see was that they were at the thin end of the wedge and they weren't prepared to sacrifice their lives for a piece of muddy Tonkin real-estate. Colonels Castries and Langlais accepted the situation pragmatically. They merely ordered all the deserters' weapons to be confiscated, leaving the miscreants to fend for themselves. What was he going to do – shoot them all? GONO didn't have enough bullets for the enemy let alone waste them on deserters. They became known as *the Rats of Nam-Youm.*

How they survived was unknown. Whether they ate stolen airdropped supplies, scavenged at night by raiding unguarded stores, rifled through the effects of dead soldiers, ate rats or each other remained uncertain. Colonel Langlais did utilise the Rats as porters, trench diggers and any other menial tasks he could think of – and there were plenty in the squalid swamp GONO had become.

The trio dashed helter-skelter across Claudine to the river. Several individual battles raged on either side. Danny thought the experience surreal, hoping the Red-Cross armbands would protect them. As they reached the warren of tunnels and dugouts, many of the Rats, including Jacques Chevalier, made themselves scarce, but others were merely curious at the arrival of three strangers.

Angela gasped when she spotted her former mentor, but he skulked away, disappearing into one of the tunnels. Angela didn't try to follow him and Danny couldn't tell whether she was heartbroken, disappointed or just plain angry. But they hadn't come to the Rats' lair to patch up broken relationships.

With Angela and Long Li's help Danny was able to conscript twenty of the Thai Militia to help repair the covered area at Claudine and act as stretcher bearers. Danny was surprised how little coaxing they needed. Most of the men were happy to work, especially as it meant extra rations. It appeared that their sense of duty included helping comrades in trouble. They simply didn't want to fight anymore.

The other group of people who'd billeted themselves close to the Rats were the women of *Bordels Mobile de Champagne*. Also known as a BMC, this mobile brothel had been established immediately after Operation Castor. The girls were one of the first resupply items flown into *Torri-Rouge*. Although front-line brothels were not a unique concept, the French military embraced the idea with admirable fervour. BMCs helped war-weary soldiers to at least enjoy some home comforts.

GONO's BMC was staffed by eighteen girls, half of whom were Vietnamese prostitutes while the others came from Northern Africa. The Algerian girls were Ouled Nail, a Berber tribe where females were trained as courtesans from an early age. They plied their trade until they'd secured sufficient wealth for a handsome dowry before settling down as wives and mothers.

The Vietnamese girls were street walkers from Saigon who'd no idea what they were getting themselves into. They'd been enticed to Dien Bien Phu by promises of steady business and profits beyond their dreams. That might have been the case to begin with, but as the soldiers' desire waned with the escalating battle, the girls were in dire straits. What little trade they did now was for food, protection or shelter.

That concept struck a raw nerve within Angela's sometimes puritanic idealism, but her brand of muscular Christianity had taken a severe beating ever since she'd arrived in Tonkin. She was also pleasantly surprised by her new recruits.

Geneviève put the girls to work in the hospital. Unexpectedly she found they all knuckled down and did their best to keep the hospital clean as well as caring for the wounded troops. Conditions improved quickly as the girls cleared the filth from the wards, set up a laundry service to clean the casualties' clothing and recycle bandages which, like everything else, were now in short supply. They appropriated Angela's white pole, using it for its original purpose once more.

'Okay,' Angela conceded reluctantly, 'but I want it back.'

The puzzled Ouled Nail girl nodded uncertainly. Why anyone would hold any attachment to a laundry stick was beyond her. The Berber girls valued more tangible, valuable artefacts, notably gold and silver discs worn as headdresses and necklaces. They brought the precious metal medallions as part of their wedding dowry. A prosperous Ouled Nail nubile was much in demand and could pick and choose her marriage partner with every intention of training her own daughters to follow in her footsteps.

As the wet season developed the weather that had been tolerable by day grew ever more overcast and punctuated by frequent rainstorms. Daylight airdrops were dramatically reduced while night resupply runs were constantly inaccurate. Increasing amounts of matériel dropped straight into enemy hands. Entire sticks of paratroopers never made it to Dien Bien Phu and simply disappeared.

Regular nightly downpours meant the hospital's new workforce had arrived in the nick of time. Having established sleeping quarters and rations for their 'Rats and Angels' as Angela dubbed them, Danny and Long Li returned to the quad machinegun position to find that Frenchy was no longer in command of the unit and had vanished.

One of the Algerian gunners was now in charge. Danny noticed the new chevrons on his arm indicating he'd been promote to a sergeant.

'Where's the boss?' Danny asked.

'Gone to the western defences,' the new sergeant replied. 'Everyone is promoted.'

Danny and Long Li stared at him.

The sergeant explained that a mass promotion had been authorised by General Navarre and General Cogny. Colonel Castries was now a brigadier general, while Langlais was promoted to full colonel, Major 'Bruno' Bigeard a lieutenant colonel and so on all the way down the line. Frenchy Duval had been caught up in the net and was now a lieutenant. He'd been assigned to command a company formed from the remnants of other units. His men were from all branches of the GONO's forces — legionnaires, Algerian, Vietnamese, Moroccan colonial troops and even Thai Militia with some fight left in them.

Danny was surprised that he felt a certain amount of regret that Frenchy was no longer with them in the bunker. They never saw Frenchy Duval in Dien Bien Phu again.

'You know, I'll miss the evil bugger,' Danny confided to Long Li.

'Funny the way that is,' Long Li reflected. 'Maybe it's just that we have something in common.'

'Or that the Viet Minh are so tough, Frenchy seems like a pussy-cat by comparison.'

'I don't think anyone who's fought him thinks he's a pussy-cat.'

'It's a funny old world though.'

'What do you mean?'

'Well when they set up GONO there were over fifteen thousand men here and Castries was just a colonel. Now that his force has been reduced by probably a third they make him a general. He doesn't do anything anymore either. Everyone knows Colonel Langlais has taken command — make *him* the general if you're going to promote anyone. "Go figure" as Earthquake and Monty would say.'

'Hitler promoted all his staff officers just before committing suicide with the Russians banging at his door.'

'I didn't need to know that.'

'You should read more.'

'What about James Bond books?'

'That doesn't count.'

'Whatever. Look, I reckon we'd be better off bunking down at the hospital to make sure there's no backsliding among those Thai boys.'

'Sure, let's get our kit.'

Chapter 27 — Earthquake's Last Ride

By the end of April GONO's garrison had shrunk to less than half its original size. Isabelle was cut off by a full Viet Minh division to the south and the outer strong-points were reduced to isolated pockets of resistance. Huguette was now in seven fragments individually held by companies made up of the surviving remnants of entire battalions. Some new strong-points had been renamed. Françoise, Lily, Junon, Epervier and Opéra were born but not expected to live more than a few days. *Bo Doi* infiltrated every French Union position. Sometimes they were driven away, but sometimes they over-ran the defenders who were totally exhausted and fighting like robots.

Most of the ammunition, fuel and food depots had been destroyed and could not be adequately replaced – not by a long chalk.

France and their High Command had abandoned the men on the ground so they fought for their comrades and personal sense of honour. A cloud of lethargy hung over the garrison. Talk of American intervention had withered as did a rescue attempt from the south. Lieutenant Colonel Yves Godard's column hacked its way towards Dien Bien Phu, but met stiff resistance, grinding the advance to a halt. What good could a single battalion do anyway?

Amid this mood of despair Danny was surprised when he was summoned to Colonel Langlais' Claudine HQ bunker sited close to the hospital. Danny was unaware that the garrison commander even knew he existed. Lieutenant Colonel Bigeard and Langlais' chief-of-staff newly promoted Lieutenant Colonel Hubert de Seguin-Pazzis were also in the command bunker. Two other officers stood in the background. One was Colonel Guy Vaillant, who'd replaced Colonel Piroth as artillery commander. The other officer was Captain Yves Hevouët from GONO's tank squadron. Despite being wounded and wearing plaster casts on both arms, he still commanded his unit.

Blimey, the gang's all here!

They represented the very peak of the command echelon and they wanted to see Danny. Still with a cigarette firmly jammed between his lips, the chiselled-jawed colonel greeted Danny civilly enough before introducing his staff officers, and then got straight down to business.

'General Castries extends his apologies, but he is indisposed. You should not be here at all, I understand,' Langlais said sympathetically.

'No, sir. Wrong place at the wrong time, I guess.'

'I believe you are a civilian contractor.'

'Yessir. I fly for CAT, although I am a pilot-officer – a lieutenant – in the Royal Australian Air Force Reserve. I served in Korea.'

Although Danny was technically no longer a serving RAAF officer having been released from the active reserve, he saw no harm in letting Colonel Langlais know about his war record.

'Yes, I was told that. We do check up on stray personnel wandering around our compound, you know. I have no idea what the Viet Minh will make of it though,' Langlais said. 'I also hear that you and your two companions have been of great service to GONO.'

'Just keeping ourselves busy while we're in town, colonel.'

That seemed to amuse the senior officers.

'There is a mission taking off from Hanoi as we speak. Your American colleagues are piloting the planes.'

'I've seen them overhead often enough, colonel. They nearly dropped a load of concertina barbwire on my head last week. That stuff sure does bounce and you'd be a goner if it hit you.'

'*Oui, oui*, but enough of that. Sometimes instructions are mixed up during the drops.'

Danny was well aware of the confusion between French ground controllers and American aircrew. He'd misunderstood communications on many occasions even though he had a reasonable mastery of the language. Other CAT crews were by no means fluent and often mistook map co-ordinates, subsequently dropping their cargo off target. What was new?

'This cargo must land accurately,' Langlais insisted. 'You will report to Major Guérin and liaise with the American crews. This must be an accurate drop, there can be no mistakes or I do believe the Legion will mutiny.'

Danny stared at him in disbelief. If the Legion mutinied, that would be the end of GONO in an instant. Bigeard and Seguin-Pazzis looked mildly amused, which was unexpected because neither man had much to smile about.

'I'm sorry, sir. I don't understand.'

'You will,' Langlais replied with even the hint of a smile. 'Now off you go — *allez vite*. The aircraft will be here in an hour.'

He left the HQ bunker accompanied by Vaillant and Hevouët who both had their own radio operators in tow. Colonel Bigeard decided to tag along too.

'We will call on Isabelle for artillery support if needed,' Vaillant explained.

As the only Air Force staff officer surrounded by army men, Major Jacques Guérin was perhaps the most harassed man in a garrison full of harassed men. He was in charge of airborne support and he was blamed for all the aerial short-comings. Colonel Langlais had once quipped he should booby-trap resupply cargo, because it only fell into enemy hands anyway.

When Danny reached his command post he saw that Guérin was a sick man. The strain of three months' incessant demands had taken its toll. Having once been the Bearcat fighter leader, he'd seen the entire GONO air component annihilated, *Torri-Rouge* destroyed, many bombing and resupply operations in tatters and dozens of aircraft shot down.

'It's scandalous,' the major declared when Danny reported.

'What is, sir?'

'All this flap for a bunch of drunken legionnaires. Do they think I have nothing better to do with my time?'

Danny had no idea what he was talking about, but had learnt not to query senior officers when they asked rhetorical questions.

'You will take over the transport frequency, monsieur,' Guérin instructed, handing Danny the telephone mike for one of his radio sets. You must guide the planes and make sure there are no mistakes.'

'Do they have fighter escorts?'

'*Oui,* we have co-ordinated them and a B-26 raid on the hills as well. I will communicate with strike squadrons on another frequency.'

'Are they ready?'

'They are on station now, waiting for the transport planes.'

He was delighted to recognise Monty and Earthquake's voices when the CAT planes came within radio range.

'Hey man,' Monty declared. 'It's great to hear from you, buddy. We had no idea what happened to you.'

'Long story, Monty, but it'll have to wait.'

'Roger that. Where do you want this stuff?'

'We need it at the Claudine HQ. Best run-in is from the south. Enemy positions are right up to the *Torri-Rouge*. Call me ten-mile-initial heading three-six-zero. I'll fire a smoke marker. Break right immediately after the drop and exit on the reciprocal track. '

Monty acknowledged.

'Earthquake, this is Danny, over.'

'Go ahead, pal.'

'Come in on Monty's wing-tip. Stick to him like glue and drop on my mark.'

'Wilco. You hang in there, kid. We'll ram this load right down your throat.'

'Thanks, guys,' Danny replied, turning to Major Guérin. 'Send your bombers in now, sir.'

Danny knew he must see what the position was for himself. He tapped the radio operator on the shoulder, indicating for him to carry the set outside. The operator didn't look particularly happy about it, but followed when Major Guérin glared at him. The artillery and tank commanders were already positioned at the best vantage points although it exposed them to enemy shelling.

'Hey Danny — over,' Monty's voice crackled through the radio.

'Go ahead.'

'One minute to initial approach fix.'

'Roger, starting suppression fire now.'

Danny turned to the communication centre entrance.

'Send in your fighters, Major — now!'

Guérin nodded and reached for his radio handset.

'Put everything you've got on the hills now, Colonel,' Danny said to Vaillant before addressing the tank commander. 'Captain Hevouët, have your tanks facing south and at Isabelle. Fire a low trajectory along Route forty-one between the bases. Keep the bastards' heads down. Colonel Bigeard, lay down mortar fire around *Torri-Rouge* to cover the planes' getaway.'

Most of Danny's orders were in a mixture of rudimentary French, punctuated with English and a lot of pointing and gesticulation, but everyone got the message. Surprisingly Danny felt quite at ease issuing instructions to senior officers.

Six Bearcats streaked overhead at treetop height — although all the trees had been blown to shreds at GONO. Each plane dropped napalm canisters. From such a low level they couldn't miss and the terrain north of Dien Bien Phu was engulfed in flaming jelly. Danny saw the bomber and artillery barrages erupting all along the hillside flanking the valley while tank shells cleared the roadway between Isabella and Claudine.

'Running in now, buddy,' Monty said. 'Three minutes out.'

Danny pulled the smoke flare's ring-release and tossed the incendiary a few yards away. A billowing cloud drifted skywards.

'Smoke thrown,' Danny reported.

'I see green smoke,' Monty replied.

'Green confirmed. Put your load right onto it. Follow route 41 straight to us.'

Monty and Earthquake dived to three hundred feet above the jungle.

'Looks like artillery fire is marking the way,' Monty commented.

Minutes later the two lumbering C-119s roared into view. Earthquake had dropped back into line-astern formation to narrow the spread of parachutes. It meant he was flying in Monty's wake, but what was a little turbulence compared with being buffeted by flak for two months.

The planes rushed overhead, peeled away to the right and were gone in what seemed a heartbeat leaving fifty canisters drifting to earth. Every single parachute landed within Claudine's defences. Viet Minh ack-ack opened up again and both Monty and Earthquakes planes were hit by shrapnel but made it safely back to Hanoi.

'See ya, buddy,' Monty called as the planes disappeared. 'Give my love to Ange.'

The Viet Minh barrage resumed its desultory routine after the airdrop, yet Legionnaires risked the bombardment to retrieve the canisters.

'What's in those containers,' Danny asked, 'Ammo?'

'*Non, non, monsieur*' Colonel Bigeard replied. 'Vinogel.'

'Vinogel! You mean we used up tons of ammo and risked God knows how many planes for a cargo of piss?'

'You do know what today is, *n'est-ce pas?*'

'It's Friday, I think.'

'*Non, c'est* Camerone Day!'

'Well, that's okay then.'

'You do not know of Camerone Day?' Bigeard looked genuinely surprised and a little hurt.

'No, sir.'

It turned out that back in 1863 when Legion regiments were stationed in Mexico, an incident occurred in an otherwise unnoticed village on the road between Vera Cruz and Mexico City. A sixty-four man company of international bad-boys led by veteran tough guy, Captain Jean Danjou volunteered to escort a mule-train carrying ammunition and around three million francs for the headquarters payroll. Unfortunately the convoy was ambushed by over two thousand Mexican guerrillas. Danjou and his company held off the attackers at Camerone while the convoy escaped. All but three of Danjou's company perished, but Camerone Day has been revered and celebrated as a tribute to their courage and honour by the Foreign Legion ever since.

That night Danny, Long Li and Angela were invited to the nearest Legion dugout where the occupants were well under the influence of the airdrop cargo. Despite continued shelling and torrential rain, the legionnaires were celebrating with gusto. Geneviève de Galard was summoned and pronounced an honorary member of the Foreign Legion. Everyone toasted Danny and Long Li for the fine fellows they were, while more than a few eyes scanned Angela with interest.

'Am I the only one who sees the irony of this?' Danny asked Angela.

'You mean they're celebrating a last stand when they face exactly the same fate?'

'*Justement, ma chère,*' Danny said, kissing her to a chorus of whistles and cat-calls from the legionnaires. This time she kissed him back and really meant it.

'I've been such an idiot,' she whispered. 'I should have stayed safe in Hanoi with you.'

'I'd still have flown casevacs and probably been in the same boat, but yes, I'd like you to be safely back in Hanoi too.'

Then it was back to work, wounded soldiers weren't going to wait for anyone.

The following day, the legionnaires awoke with sore heads only to be greeted by a barrage of bugle-calls, gong-banging and tuneless singing. The Viet Minh were celebrating May Day with a lot of noise and rice wine. It was an opportune moment for a respite. *Bo Doi* morale was at rock-bottom and why wouldn't it be? They'd been fighting not just for the three months around Dien Bien Phu, but for the previous nine years. Until now they had never sustained such chronically heavy casualties.

Desertions and reluctance to fight were rife to the point where General Giáp threatened to shoot anyone accused of 'rightist leanings'. Indeed several of his commanders had been dismissed for lack of results.

But the end was in sight with GONO simply going through the motions. The defenders were just too weary to fight on. No help was coming and Colonel Godard's relief column was still thirty miles away and was too small to make any difference. The Viet Minh made inroads into the garrison everyday during the first week of May. Their trenches now butted up against the defensive barbwire. They'd planted a huge mine at the edge of Elaine that blew through the barbwire, opening a pathway in.

French Union forces mounted small counter-attacks and reinforcements were still airdropped, but they were too few and virtually on a suicide mission.

Generals Navarre and Cogny sent urgent messages from their secure Saigon and Hanoi HQs, insisting that Castries must fight to the last man. How easy that is to say when you're not going to be the last man. The generals expressly forbade anyone to raise a white flag. Some of the colonial units flagrantly disobeyed and were quietly marched away by their captors.

On 7th May, the last day of the siege, Danny manned Major Guérin's ATC radio to guide Earthquake on course for Isabelle to drop an artillery piece that might help Colonel Lelande's isolated strong-point make a breakout. There were two C-119 Boxcars involved and the first plane flew low enough to successfully drop its cargo although receiving some flak damage.

Approaching Isabelle, Earthquake's plane was struck in one engine and its tail. Struggling at the controls, Earthquake barely managed to keep his plane upright, but eased it southwards to a small airfield fifty miles away in Laos. They nearly made it too, but the C-119 clipped a hilltop tree just short of the runway. The plane cart-wheeled once before it slammed into the ground in a fireball. Earthquake, his co-pilot and crewman were killed although a Thai Militia officer on board survived, only to be captured by the Viet Minh.

That afternoon Colonel Castries ordered all military equipment to be destroyed and declared that those units who wished to could lay down their arms that evening, provided in a twisted sense of Gallic pride, they did not raise a white flag.

As dusk fell an eerie silence pervaded throughout Dien Bien Phu. The stillness was so peculiar that Danny left his post in the hospital dugout to try and understand the situation. As he emerged from the tunnel adit he saw endless columns of *Bo Doi* calmly marching towards GONO HQ.

They filed from the undergrowth across the Nam-Youm River bridges, along the runway negotiating twisted wrecked planes. They clambered up ramparts and cut their way through rows of concertina barbwire. They came down from *Phoney* and *Baldy*, rounding up the remnants of the eastern strong-points. Occasionally gunfire broke out when they met pockets of resistance that preferred to fight to the end.

One such scuffle broke out by the wooden bridge just to the east of the hospital and only yards from where Danny stood. A Viet Minh mortar crew decided to end the struggle right there by lobbing a salvo into the defiant French Union troops.

One shell fell wide, exploding in front of Danny. The blast hurled him backwards, with a force that ripped the breath from his lungs. Splattered with mud and lacerated by debris, He tumbled into the hospital tunnel. The last thing he heard was Angela's scream before his world went black and silent.

*

Monty sat at the bar in Hotel Metropole's main lounge. He'd lost count of the drinks he'd poured down his throat, but nothing could deaden the pain and downright sadness he felt. Other miserable CAT pilots sat around him although they didn't talk much. They were joined by Dr and Mrs Holyman.

'Here's to ya, Danny,' he said raising his glass unsteadily. 'You were a good kid and I'm gonna miss ya. Here's to ya too, Earthquake. You dopey bastard for getting killed on the last day. And Ange, I wonder what has become of you. You may have been a pain-in-the-ass, but you sure were a gorgeous one.'

Mrs Holyman burst into tears.

Epilogue – Merimbula Airport

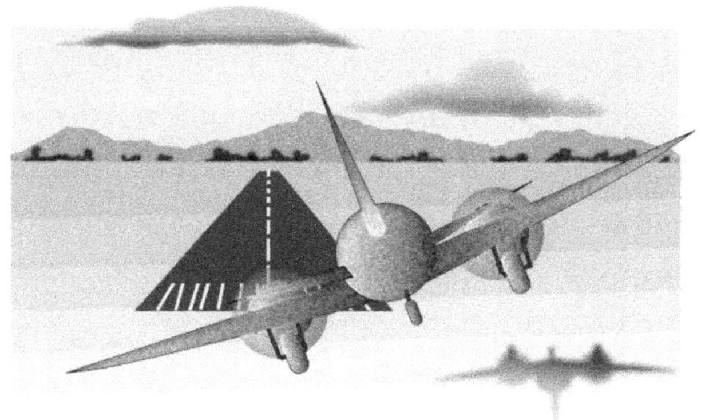

'I know the bomb didn't kill you, Grandpa,' I said rather unnecessarily, 'but how the blazes did you get out of that mess?'

We were eating lunch in the *Port Coffee Shop* at Merimbula Airport waiting for Angela to arrive. She was due shortly on the next REX flight. Grandpa had finished his story on the drive from his place.

'You know it was probably that blast that saved my life in the end.'

'How did that work?'

'The explosion broke one of my legs and peppered me with grit and other rubbish. There was plenty of blood around, although the wounds were superficial. Angela cleaned out my cuts as best she could and set my leg, using her silly damned white stick as a splint. It was all that was available.'

'But what did the Viet Minh do?'

It turned out that the Red-Cross arm bands did actually prove useful. The *Bo Doi* left the medics to it, but herded other French Union troops away. Ten thousand men were marched off to POW camps on the Chinese border. Large numbers of Viet Minh withdrew as well, making sure they were interspersed with the POWs to deter French air attacks.

The POWs were held for four months until exchanges could be negotiated, but less than half survived. It wasn't so much cruelty that caused the unprecedented attrition, simply indifference. The Viet Minh had little enough for their own sustenance, so they were hardly prepared to waste food and medicine on their former oppressors.

'The men left at Dien Bien Phu fared much better,' Grandpa said. 'Luckily I was one of them. Major Grauwin spent the next week tippy-toeing around the Viet Minh commanders. They wanted the Frenchmen to sign confessions condemning their action at Dien Bien Phu. Those who refused were packed off to POW camps.'

'Did you sign?'

'I was so pumped up with morphine, the whole week was a blur, but Angela signed for me. I think she, Geneviève and Dr Grauwin signed dozens of them. No one took them seriously anyway. Who did the Commies think they were kidding?'

During the following week resupply planes were permitted into *Torri-Rouge* and then the first casevac flights took off for Hanoi. Angela ensured Danny was on one of those early flights out. Major Grauwin put her on the same flight, knowing that the discovery of a British subject at the garrison would only cause unnecessary complications. Surprisingly Angela didn't object. She was happy to accompany Danny. It took over a month for all the wounded and medical staff, including Geneviève de Galard and Major Grauwin, to be evacuated.

'When we reached Hanoi,' Grandpa reflected with obvious regret, 'Angela's parents were waiting with British consulate officials and a couple of MI-6 agents. Despite her protests, she was whisked home on the next flight out of Vietnam. She only had time to say goodbye and retrieve her laundry pole that was now stained with my blood. I think she wanted to hit the MI-6 blokes with it.'

'Bummer, not much of a souvenir, is it? And just when you could have got together too.'

'I was still pretty crook, but Colonel Serong was also waiting. I was flown to Singapore to recover and then back to New Guinea. I was as big an embarrassment to the Australian Government as Angela was to the Poms. It was nice to be with my dad again, but, I think I was bit of a wreck for a while. Losing Angela once more left a big hole in my heart, I can tell you.'

That seemed such a softy-thing for Grandpa to say, but I think I understood.

'At least that moron Jacques Chevalier got his come-uppance.'

'Well — yes and no.'

I looked at him blankly.

It seemed Jacques had emerged from the Nam-Youm River rats' nest, announcing he was a doctor once more. Major Grauwin wasn't particularly pleased to see him so he assigned the born-again medico to tend the POWs. Before he knew it, Jacques was marching away with the others to the Chinese's border. Whether he was of use or not, no one seemed to know. However, as a doctor, he received officers' privileges especially as he willingly attended the Communist 're-education programmes'.

He was repatriated with the survivors, wrote several magazine articles and a book about his exploits. He was feted in some social circles, married an heiress and became a very wealthy man.

'There's no justice,' I muttered.

'It didn't work out so well in the end,' Grandpa grinned. 'Apparently he wasn't much of a driver and killed himself in his missus' Ferrari when it went over a cliff on one of those twisty roads around Monte Carlo.'

There was a certain amount a satisfaction in that piece of information.

'Jiao and James Weo did all right in the end too,' Grandpa added as an afterthought. 'They started a martial arts school in London and made a go of it. Eventually they went back to Hong Kong when things seemed to have settled down. The last I heard they were stunt consultants for Jackie Chan movies. I'm pleased it worked out for them. It worked out for Peng's two sons as well.'

'How's that?'

'Remember they were conscripted into the People's Volunteer Army?'

'Yes.'

'They were both captured and interned in a POW camp near Pusan. One of the biggest stumbling blocks facing the Korean armistice negotiations was the exchange of prisoners. The Commies wanted all their POWs back, which was fine by the UN except many of them didn't want to return including the Zhang boys. In the end the UN sort of let anyone who wanted to escape. It took months, but finally they contacted their father who arranged for them to be repatriated to Hong Kong. A good result all round, wouldn't you say?'

I nodded in agreement.

'So Angela went back to study at Guys while I returned to fly for CAT on their RPT routes. Neither the British nor Australian Governments wanted to be embarrassed by having their citizens mixed up in a war where they had no business to be. So we were both gagged with dire threats of long prison sentences if we said a word about being at Dien Bien Phu. Monty and I stayed with CAT for a while. You know General Chennault insisted on paying for the time I was on the ground at GONO.'

'So he bloody-well should have. You earned it.'

'Ted Serong said I deserved a medal and put me up for a gong for my work in Korea, but I think John Hubble squashed the recommendation out of spite. Mind you, we did some interesting stuff back at CAT, especially when Captain White and Captain Black showed up.'

'Another story?

Grandpa nodded.

'You know who I feel sorry for?' Grandpa asked.

'Everyone involved I should think.'

'The BMC girls.'

'How come?'

'Well the Ouled Nail girls were sent home okay, but the Vietnamese girls were packed off to re-indoctrination camps. No one knows what became of them. None of the girls received any recognition for their contribution. I can tell you many lives would have been lost if it hadn't been for their dedicated hard work.'

But there was one most important person Grandpa hadn't mentioned and I was almost too frightened to ask.

'Long Li ..?' I ventured tentatively.

'Yes, Long Li. What a great bloke he was, wasn't he?'

I didn't like the sound of 'was', but then I remember what a resilient chap he was.

'You know I didn't have a clue what happened to him for three years. I thought he'd been captured or killed. I dunno which would have been worse.'

But Long Li was a hard man to pin down. He'd dodged the Japanese for years during WWII and was at home in the jungle. After he saw Angela and Danny safely aboard the casevac plane, Long Li realised that his Red-Cross arm band might have reached its limits and his luck could be running out. Maybe the *Bo Doi* mistook him for a Thai Militiaman and left him to tend the wounded. But soon they started rounding up all Indochinese and marching them off to re-education camps, it was time to make himself scarce. Now that the Viet Minh allowed other medical teams to fly in, he felt Dien Bien Phu could look after itself without him.

Sneaking into the jungle at night wasn't particularly difficult for Long Li. *Bo Doi* patrols were thick on the ground, especially to the south and east of the garrison where they were mopping up any French Union fugitives trying to slip through their lines to Hanoi. So Long Li headed west.

He swapped his clothes for the uniform he found on a dead *Bo Doi* who'd been overlooked. Although the Viet Minh did their best to retrieve all their casualties, there were still bodies lying in the jungle in a very unpleasant condition.

Long Li washed the uniform in a stream and melted into the forest as only he could. He headed for Thailand and freedom. How he dodged and fooled Viet Minh units he came across was something he never talked about, but his Canungra training came in handy. Apparently tigers, rogue elephants, poisonous snakes and insects were more of a problem than enemy troops, but Long Li had never been a quitter.

Three years later a handsome, well-appointed junk sailed into the Bismarck Sea. The forty-foot vessel moored at *Kagotaun* Pier. The first thing the skipper did was head for George McAlister's pub, order a cold beer and introduce his Thai wife and baby daughter. Long Li was home.

His adventuring days were over and Long Li settled down to raise a large family. His CAT wages had mounted up significantly while he was gone. He used the money to finance a comfortable house at the edge of town.

'That only leaves Frenchy Duval,' I said. 'Was he killed at Dien Bien Phu?'

'You have to remember that Frenchy was a survivor and about four thousand French Union troops did eventually get home ...'

But that was all Danny managed to say.

'REX Flight ZL 133 is now approaching the terminal,' a girl with a pleasant voice broadcasted over the airport PA.

We downed our coffees and walked to the arrival gate. I could tell Grandpa was nervous. I really don't know what he expected. I didn't know what *I* expected. Grandpa anxiously scanned the line of passengers filing into the terminal.

'What if she doesn't recognise me?' Grandpa stammered.

And then we saw her.

She may have been in her seventies, but Angela was still a strikingly beautiful woman. Although I'd never seen her, I immediately knew who she was. She was dressed in a smart, tailored suit, fashionably high-heels and just enough bling to complement her outfit. Her hair was flecked with silver, but elegantly cut without a single errant wisp. This could be no one else but Angela.

When she saw Danny, her eyes truly light up. She smiled which only made her even lovelier.

'Oh, Danny – darling,' Angela almost whispered, flinging her arms around him and squeezing tight.

Darling, that's a good sign ☺

'Hello, Zach,' she said, turning to me.

She squeezed my hand and kissed me lightly on the cheek. It was nice that she didn't say something trite like, *'you must be Zach'*.

'I'm very pleased to meet you,' I replied, putting on my best manners.

'No laundry pole, I see,' Danny said and seemed disappointed about it.

'It's in my check-in baggage,' Angela winked. 'The airline said it was too dangerous as carry-on.'

'They have a point,' Danny said, staring into her eyes.

'Come here, Danny,' Angela murmured huskily. 'There is something I have been dying to do for ages.'

She embraced him once more and kissed him passionately. The kiss lingered and there was no sign that it would end soon.

'I'll go and get your bags then, Angela,' I said although no one was listening.

The End

(For Now)

Appendix

Troop numbers vary, especially during a battle when losses occur, but for anyone unfamiliar with military units, here is a rough guide.

Squad	the smallest unit approximately 10 soldiers led by and NCO
Platoon	A number of squads commanded by a lieutenant
Company	A number of platoons commanded by a captain or a major
Battalion	A number of companies commanded by a major or lieutenant colonel
Regiment	A number of battalions commanded by a lieutenant colonel or full colonel
Brigade	A number of regiments commanded by a brigadier or colonel
Division	A number of brigades commanded by a major general
Corps	A number of divisions commanded by a lieutenant general
Army	A number of corps commanded by a general or field marshal

You'll notice that a major general is a junior rank to a lieutenant general, yet a major is senior to a lieutenant. That is because a major general used to be known as a sergeant-major general.

About the Author

Richard Marman was born in Swindon, UK. His father was a RAF pilot who had served with distinction during WWII. The family moved from base to base after the war, including four years in Germany. They immigrated to Fremantle in 1962. Richard attended six primary and three secondary schools, so he is familiar with the 'new kid on the block' status.

After school, Richard joined the Royal Australian Air Force and trained as a pilot. He served for nine years, including a tour in Vietnam and a significant time flying in New Guinea. In 1975 Richard left the RAAF to fly with Ansett Airlines until the company closed in 2001 at which time he was a Boeing 767 captain. Afterwards he trained Singapore Airlines pilots on Lear Jets until 2006.

Leaving aviation behind, Richard completed a Diploma of Visual Arts at Tewantin TAFE and a Bachelor of Arts at the University of the Sunshine Coast, majoring in creative writing and design.

He lives on Queensland's Sunshine Coast with his wife Judy. They have twin daughters who live interstate.

For more information visit www.richardmarman.com

McAlister's Line

Available in eBook and paperback from most online bookstores
or via Abela Publishing and www.richardmarman.com

In praise of *The McAlister Line*

2012 Australian CYA Writing Competition Judges:

'...Masterfully handled and quite eloquent...Wonderful.'
'I like this book [McAlister's Way] ... it covers issues that need to be addressed.'
Amazon.com reviews:

 'Waiting for the sequel.'

'This is a great and interesting novel written in an easy-to-read way. Loved all the characters and settings as well as the action-packed events. Really enjoyed reading it.'

'McAlister's Spark is a fast-paced, action-riddled amazing read you will struggle to put down.'

'A great action read for teenagers and great graphics ... a great literary effort... '

'...a decent read [McAlister's trail] and a fun romp across the Southwest.' Sandy Whiting for Western writers of America's Roundup Magazine.

A Tale of Two Turtles

Set in the Pacific Ocean and Australia's Great Barrier Reef; follow the thrilling story of Wave, a young female green turtle, from her birth on a tropical night through her perilous adventures with boyfriend, Web. Together they face many natural and man-made dangers including sharks, storms and pollution. Each page is colourfully illustrated with a text to delight and amuse children and adults alike.

'Beautiful, colourful pictures that made me smile. Lovely story that is entertaining and fun to read. Really enjoyed this book'. Amazon.com

Whale's Tale

The second Wave and Web adventure sees the couple dodge hungry tiger sharks and meet Davo, a juvenile humpback whale on his way north to warm, tropical waters for the southern winter.

Davo describes his hazardous journey dodging great white sharks, killer whales and worst of all – whale hunters. The book is brilliantly illustrated with colourful images that are not only humorous, but also challenge the need and justification for whaling in the 21st Century.

As with the prequel, *A Tale of Two Turtles*, Richard Marman's narration is fast and amusing, making enjoyable and thought-provoking reading for children and adults alike.

Also Available in eBook and paperback online

The Wealth

Approaching his sixteenth birthday, Henry is thrust into a perilous quest when his village chief's wife is abducted.

Joined by three companions and his pet wolf, he vows to track down the mysterious kidnappers. With no magic or special skills they can only rely on their courage, determination, wits and friendship to survive in a cruel realm that makes no concessions for youth or innocence.

Danger mounts with each challenge until ultimately they face a seemingly unconquerable foe at the gates of a hostile, alien city.

Dragon Stalkers

A mighty dragon called Brimstone is terrorising the quiet village of Oak Tree. Prince Roger and his sister Princess Crystal set out to hunt the fiery beast.

They are ably assisted or hindered — as the case may be — by an evil knight, a mysterious good-guy, the local sheriff, loyal men-at-arms, forest brigands, ogres, trolls and Oak Tree's villagers with a bunch of attitude.

There are thrills, spills, romance and heaps of rollicking fun to be had by all.

www.ingramcontent.com/pod-product-compliance
Lightning Source LLC
Chambersburg PA
CBHW070743190726
48292CB00002B/400